THE ART OF GETTING WRECKED

To Gerhard Botha

THE ART OF GETTING WRECKED

A MAN, A QUEST, AND A CARIBBEAN ADVENTURE

Peter Roren

© 2019 Peter Roren

Herstellung und Verlag: BoD – Books on Demand, Norderstedt 2019

ISBN 9783750423442

Table of Contents

1. A Genealogical Dive 7
2. The Explorer 17
3. The Dice Man 27
4. The Ark 35
5. The Ocean 57
6. The Reef 79
7. The Sinking 91
8. Archimedes' principle 101
9. The Moneychangers 117
10. The Art of Passing it On 125
11. Big Blunders 139
12. The Broken Mast 147
13. The Slave Ship 169
14. The Last Resort 199
15. Ensenada Pargo and Jungle Exploring 205
16. The Revolution 219
17. The Rogue Wave 233
18. The Crankshaft 247
19. The Island of Bequia 253
20. The Move Ashore 281
21. The Fixman 297
22. The Reverse Combustion Engine 307
23. The Butterfly Effect 313
24. The Long River 317
25. The Hidden Treasure 339
26. The Memories 343
27. Tribute to a Mate 351
28. Tribute to a Ship 357
29. Thanks 361
Map of Venezuela 363
Map of the Grenadines 364

1. A Genealogical Dive

Where do I start?

Maybe at the beginning. Beginnings are important. I often think how great Jehovah is- he who created birth and death, and put death at the end of life, not at the beginning.

So, let me begin with the beginning.

Who am I?

My name is Peter Roren.

For the full picture I'll have to go back in time and do a genealogical dive into the past.

There are two sides to me, my mother's and my father's.

My great-great grandfather, on my father's side, Henrik Øhlenschlager, or something like this, was a travelling German troubadour and court jester who, for some unknown reason, made his way northwards and settled down in Bergen on the west coast of Norway. I know very little about him other than that he was quite a flamboyant guy and extremely popular with the high society ladies in the city between the seven mountains. He changed lovers, plans, and interests as often as he changed his underwear. His last venture in his turbulent and unsettled life was to turn a herring cannery into a distillery in order to produce a potent and lethal spirit made out of a mixture of nettles and the hollow stems of dandelion. He changed his name from Øhlenschlager to something more Norse, Røyrvin (meaning tube-wine). He died of a massive overdose of his own wine when he was in the prime of his life, only 35 years old. Where family background is concerned, not really much to brag about there.

Henrik's only son, my great-grandfather Roald on my father's side, was chairman of the Sons of Norway Temperance Movement. He found his father's death quite an embarrassment, sold the distillery business, and changed his surname from Røyrvin to Røren. He had his father's restlessness, flamboyancy, and way around the ladies. Extensive gambling put him in serious debt, and he found no other way out of penury than to leave his family and emigrate to the US of A to search for gold. On the 4th of July 1825 he joined the first group of 52 emigrants to cross the Atlantic on the 54-foot sailing vessel *Restaurationen*. The passage took three months with multiple storms and mishaps. On sailing into New York harbour my exhausted great-grandfather vowed that he would never set foot on a deck again. He had burned his homeland bridge.

Records at the Old New York Hospital on Broadway show that a Mr. Roald Roren was admitted with musket shot wounds in his butt on 14th of February, 1826, after he had been involved in a street battle between Irish immigrants and federal troops. The fact that he was shot in the butt indicates that he probably had been running away. Who knows? What we do know is that a postcard dated May 1st, 1826, arrived in Norway a year later, sent from a town called Dahlonega in Georgia. According to my great Aunt Bertha my great-grandfather was a man of few words. The postcard simply read:

"My dearest Bertha. In America to find gold.
Roald"

He had come to Cherokee country to find gold. We don't know much more about my great-grandfather's presumably colourful life on the other side of the Atlantic other than according to his gold rush friends he sent many extremely short telegrams back to Norway. Samuel Morse had just invented the electrical telegraph system, and it cost a small fortune to send this modern miracle message across the vast ocean. However, it was a complete waste of money. Only the telegraph operator read all his messages as the transmission wire ended over the other side of a hill east of the telegraph station. Roald never got a reply from his family and friends back in the Land of the Midnight Sun because they never heard a word from him in the first place. Even if the telegraph operator hadn't been a scammer it wouldn't have worked because the laying of the transatlantic telegraph cable had yet to be completed! The only news that came out of the New World was that postcard from Dahlonega.

My grandfather Wilhelm, again on my father's side, retired just past puberty, married the rich widow of a timber merchant, and lived the same intense and hedonistic life as his dad. He was spontaneous and impatient and had the same appetite for women as his male forbearers, and his escapades and interests went in all directions.

Sailing, stamp collection, tennis, chess, music, art, you name it- he could even dance the Argentine tango. He introduced me to the art of sailing and hedonistic philosophy, taught me about the bees and the birds and the Meaning of Life. Grandfather Wilhelm had Norway's most extensive stamp collection, he wrote chess strategies for Oslo's largest newspaper, and he modelled for various famous artists, amongst them Edward Munch. In a church in Oslo there's a four-meter-tall fresco altarpiece of my grandfather robed as Jesus Christ.

His dream of becoming a world-famous concert pianist never came to be. Every Sunday morning his neighbours would close their windows when he dragged the piano out onto his balcony, and with Beethoven turning in his grave, Wilhelm would hammer out *Für Elise*, over and over again.

Apart from writing chess quizzes and shooting squirrels he never did a day's proper work in his entire life. His definition of a meaningful life was getting laid as often as possible in between fun and games. His patient wife Agnes, perhaps due to the fact that she was getting laid among all the other women, did not complain. However, she did not share his views and interests. She was a tolerant and forgiving woman in many ways and managed to keep her promiscuous husband happy and the farm and family running without his involvement.

And finally, there's my own father, Haakon, who desperately wanted to be a sailor. He was too young to sign on for crew and go to sea, so he sneaked aboard a ship bound for the Far East. He was discovered halfway across the North Sea hiding in a lifeboat and was set ashore in London where he found work in a Chinese laundry and finally ended up as a bartender at the legendary Brown's Hotel. The laundry gave him a soap-allergy and the bar multiple hangovers.

Haakon had a pining for the sea and returned to Norway to study navigation and become a sea captain. After several years in the merchant navy, ploughing the oceans of the world, he got a pining for the fjords and returned to Oslo just as Hitler's troops invaded. He joined the police force but did not get on very well with the new Nazi Chief of Police. He was interned and tortured at the Grini concentration camp, but managed to dig his way out, escaping over the mountains to Sweden. The Swedes were neutral during WWII, but not neutral enough. He was arrested by the Swedish police and sent back to Norway by train. The deal between the Swedish government and the German occupiers in Norway was for the Swedish border guards to arrest and return illegal immigrants, but only if they were criminals. However, the Nazi view was of course that political prisoners were nothing but criminals. Fortunately, my father's accompanying guard was more neutral than the Swedish Hitler-friendly government, and he looked the other way when his prisoner had to relieve himself as the train stopped at a signal light near Gothenburg. My father once again became a stowaway. He slipped unseen on board a freighter bound for Scotland, where he joined up with the Royal Norwegian Navy in exile.

In South Queensferry near Edinburgh in 1942, in between his Atlantic convoy duties, he and his shipmates would turn the town upside down and build up courage to do another voyage to Murmansk, from which they most likely would never return or survive. There was a film set in South Queensferry where the government made propaganda films. There he met my mother who once worked as a hairdresser for Bette Davis. My mother had been married before, to an RAF pilot and had a child with him, my half-sister Giselle. When Wing Commander Rose Phillips was shot down and killed over Germany, my mother-to-be spent a week in grief, pulled herself together and immediately married another young RAF pilot, who also was shot down and killed. The War Office actually encouraged young girls to marry young airman as soon as they were called up, due to the fact that they thought fighting men fought better when there was a young wife waiting for them at home.

Mother had had enough of airmen getting shot out of the sky. Why not go for a sailor instead?

My father won my mother's heart with a pair of nylon stockings he bought for a small fortune on the black market. When the hairdresser told the captain that she was pregnant (with me) he once more "jumped ship" and "enlisted" with Bette Davis instead. Come to think of it, I could have been the son of an American screen idol.

My mother got so mad at him that she threatened to report him to the Admiral of the fleet and to charge my father with weakness and cowardice in the line of duty. Two days later my parents, the hairdresser and the captain, were married. Eight months or so later I came prematurely into the world with a loud bang; I was born the night the Luftwaffe bombed Liverpool- June 27th 1943. I entered this senseless world at war, screaming in an ambulance full of wounded children who were picked up on the way to the hospital from bombed out buildings.

In the hospital in Ainsdale outside Liverpool I was hastily first baptized, then washed and then a doctor cut out a piece of my private part because my Jewish grandmother was in charge. She was always in charge. That's what Jewish mothers do for a living- be in charge.

Anyway, the sirens also started their howling in Ainsdale, and we all managed to get to the shelter in time. The hospital building didn't survive. Neither did the town hall and registrar office. That's why I have no birth certificate. I am born a circumcised Brit with no birth certificate, but I have evidence to show for the circumcised bit, a paper document that is.

Torpedoed in the arctic waters of the Barents Sea and north Atlantic together with his horrific experiences in the German concentration camp took the spark of life out of the otherwise lively Haakon. Easily frustrated and full of anger and hatred he'd growl at anyone living outside his own bubble world. He hated Germans of course, the Swedes for turning him in, Italians because they ate garlic, and he threw in for good measure Arabs and blacks and the Sami (indigenous) people of northern Norway. He hated the Arabs because, in the Suez Canal, some badass towelhead (his word) Arab sneaked on board and nicked his underwear off the clothesline; blacks because they were black and he really didn't know why he hated the Sami, he just did. He didn't have a dog, so he would beat the living daylight out of me for my slightest "mishaps." Being a war hero, he quickly advanced to the rank of Rear

Admiral. Only 50 years old, with Norway being a part of NATO, he was, against his will, bestowed with a German lieutenant as a personal secretary. When the hand-picked and quiet spoken young lad made the grave mistake of clicking his heels together on his first day on the job, my father lost it completely and attacked him, sending him to the hospital for three months with a broken jaw and arm and the removal of his front teeth. The incident hit the headlines and the Navy gave him another medal, another stripe, and a healthy pension. He was so gung-ho on warfare and fighting fascism that he left for Spain to join forces against General Franco, but he arrived too late. He'd got it all wrong. Franco was still a fascist, still alive but the Spanish civil war was long over. He liked Spain. And General Franco was kind of all right since he let the immigrant ex-pats keep their pensions in full.

He finally settled down on the outskirts of Benidorm growing oranges and strolling the beaches taking photos of bikini-designs with his Kodak Instamatic. After my mother died, the hairdresser from Scotland who had held out with him for unbelievably many decades, it didn't really surprise me a bit when he remarried at the ripe age of 82. His new wife was 55; the old Viking dog had still a bit of the old Røren spark and spunk left in him.

That was my father's side of the family.

My mother's side is a totally different cup of English tea. My great-great grandfather spent his entire life stacking stones on top of each other. That's all he did, honestly, and that's about all I know about him. He moved from farmhouse to farmhouse stacking stones in long rows. His stone walls stretched for hundreds of miles across the Scottish Highlands.

His son, my great-grandfather Angus, was a wee bit smarter than his dad and went in a different direction, literally. Downwards. One could make more money digging up the black gold buried deep down under his father's stone walls. He was only twelve years old when he did his first trip into the mine. I've been told that before he was recycled he'd done the trip down 21,600 times! The mine closed around the time when he was old enough to decide for himself what to do with the rest of his life. And what did Angus do? He moved to Wales where he continued to take the elevator up and down the mine shaft until he died of chronic obstructive pulmonary disease, due to all the black dust that got stuck in his lungs.

The only highlights in his entire life were the three days his three boys were born. There were also four girls, but they weren't worth a farthing in those days. Those were the days when the mining company paid him 10 guineas if he promised to send his boys down the mine. Which he did, and they all ended up underground too young of age, literally underground. However, there was one exception- my grandfather- David Waddell, the youngest of the three boys..

He was only thirteen years old when he, dressed in his dad's oversized tweed suit and struggling along with a cardboard suitcase, was sent off to an uncle in Carlisle to be educated. Sewn into the lining of his underpants were 30 guineas. He was trained and educated as a filing clerk and spent nearly the rest of his life shuffling documents in the Foreign Office in London. The only day out of the ordinary was the day he angrily slammed the filing cabinet shut with both hands, clipping the tips off each forefinger. One Sunday afternoon in Hyde Park, he apparently saved a young ballet dancer, Minnie Rombach, from drowning in the Serpentine Lake. Minnie had fallen off a skiff and could not swim. She turned out to be the daughter of a Jewish jeweller, and also my grandmother. They were married shortly after the lake incident.

David was a devout Catholic and could not swim either. Fortunately, he was tall enough for his feet to reach the bottom of the lake. The only highlights in his mundane career were, similar to his father, the days when his seven children were born. That's what I've been told anyway. I'm not so sure. He had been known at times to have said that they were a blessing. I'm not so sure if he thanked the Catholic faith for the size of his family, or blamed it.

There actually was another highlight, though he didn't see it that way. Grandfather David and his family were transferred to the British Embassy in Tokyo where he continued shuffling and filing his never-ending piles of documents. On the first of September 1923, a massive earthquake struck Japan- the most powerful earthquake in living memory, 8.9 on the Richter scale, leaving 30,000 people dead. Tokyo, Kobe, and most of Yokohama was levelled to the ground; Kobe resembled Hiroshima after the bomb.

Minnie and her seven children, who lived on the outskirts of Kobe, survived the quake thanks to a cat. When Grandma saw the cat carrying all her kittens out of the house, she knew what was coming and ordered the servants to carry out the huge oak table in the living room and place it in the garden. She and her seven children, the maid, the gardener, the cook and the cat with her kittens fit safely under the table, and all hell broke loose. The entire building came down like a house of cards. They all survived, except David who was at work; he possibly lay dead under enormous amounts of rubble. He was pronounced missing and most likely deceased. They never found his body.

Japan's cities were ablaze and in turmoil. Even in the countryside there were riots, chaos, and anarchy. To add to the mayhem, there was a lot of hostility towards Westerners. It took a week for my grandmother, her children, and the house staff to reach the British consulate in Kyoto on the west coast. An amazing story- I have submitted the screen-rights to Oliver Stone and Steven Spielberg. The directors apparently didn't get very excited about it as I never heard back from either one. In any case, the family reached the consulate and were shipped to Shanghai on an American warship.

Walking down the gangway with her children in Shanghai, Grandma Minnie met a surviving employee from the embassy in Kobe. He was happy to see that the entire family had survived the disaster.

"Not my David," she answered. "He is still buried under the collapsed embassy."

"But that's impossible- he just walked down the gangway five minutes ago. I'm sure it was him. I even noticed that the tips of both his forefingers were missing."

It's pretty obvious that there are enormous discrepancies between the men on my father's side and the men on my mother's side.

If the story about David's survival is true, and that he took the opportunity to "jump ship" so to speak, we have here a major deviation in my line of genealogical inheritance.

Going back to my father's side, you have four (or maybe more) men with a great appetite for life, guys who could never fit in to what in those days was seen as customary, acceptable, and normal. These guys were restless and adventurous dreamers who lived out each day as if it were their last.

On the other hand, on my mother's side were four generations of men living in a sort of treadmill boredom, living each day as if it was a battle for their survival.

Which of these genes do I carry? If both, which are the dominant genes and how would they determine my destiny? Should I live each day as a challenge and from there on experience victory- or should I clock myself in and out of a factory where my only good memory was the day I won 5 pounds in the lottery or the time when dad came home from a voyage to the USA with a bag of pink jelly-powder? The finished bright red wobbling jelly was solemnly carried from the kitchen as if it were the crown jewels. On its way it slipped off its tray. My parents, my sister, and I tried to grab it, causing it to disintegrate as it fell from hand to hand into a bucket of clothes pegs. We all sat together for hours on the kitchen floor, laughing our heads off while scraping jelly of the pegs. This is about my only good and happy childhood memory of family togetherness.

Family photo 1943. My father Haakon, me, my mother Lily and my half-sister Giselle.

Whenever I was down and low after that incident, my big sister would say, "Remember the jelly in the clothes pegs," and the tears would stop flowing.

Was Grandfather David the odd man out, the first to break the tedious heritage line? Even if I would happen to slip into tediousness, there might be a way out.

Had he really survived the quake? Is there anything in the rumours that he built himself a small yacht and sailed away in secrecy? Could there be something in the story about a Scot with only six complete fingers who had been shipwrecked off Tahiti?

If he did do a runner, was it really an achievement, something to brag about- leaving his wife and kids stranded in Shanghai?

Due to the fact that his remains were never found, my Grandmother never received her widow's pension from the British Government. Until all her kids had grown up and left the nest she stayed in Shanghai, bringing up her children, living in a two-room apartment, and working as a geisha in a Japanese teahouse and a dancer in a Shanghai nightclub.

I was only nine years old when I first heard about Grandpa David's possible vanishing act. Could he really be out there somewhere? Maybe living as a hermit on a desert island or a king in some faraway island paradise- or maybe roaming the seven seas as a pirate?

I gradually got more and more convinced that it was all true, and out there somewhere he was waiting for me. Maybe on Tahiti?

I suddenly had the future lined up. I had a plan. I would someday in the not so distant future build my own ship and sail away to find him.

It became more and more an obsession, and I finally came to a conclusion which side of my family my genes derived from. I knew the path to follow. If I was wrong, with Grandfather David in mind, there was still hope.

2. The Explorer

I was named after Peter Pan, the boy who never grew up, and I still do my best to live up to it. My earliest recollection was the Blitz on the great city of London. Not really a recollection, more a sub-conscious reminiscence of the traumatic experience of having to seek shelter in the London Underground when Werner von Braun's bombs fell from the sky. I know the reminiscence is encoded in my hippocampus because I have felt extremely uncomfortable on the few occasions I've been underground in London. (In this case *underground* refers to the tubular, underground railway system and not into hiding or on a secret operation.) I prefer to sit upstairs in the front seat of a big London double-decker bus. I also feel nauseated and a slight touch of terror when I see documentaries with wailing sirens and frightened people running for shelter.

As a military family we were constantly on the move. For a brief period, we lived in Liverpool, very near Penny Lane. With my nanny drowning in pink gin in a nearby pub, I would spend most of the day in a children's playground called Strawberry Fields. Does this ring a bell? I have discovered that John Lennon might have been there at the same time. Just think of it- if my family had stayed in Liverpool, I probably could have become a Beatle! I called John once to find out if he could remember me, but it must have been a wrong number; he didn't answer the phone.

I was only six years old when I first read Robert Louis Stevenson's Treasure Island. It took a long time to get through that story, reading it page by page at a snail's pace. I couldn't help myself from drifting into a fantasy world of swashbuckling pirates, and I became more and more the little boy who encountered dangers and countless adventures to find my missing grandfather. From then on, I was fascinated by stories of pirates and the heroes of the seven seas.

There was no end to my imagination. This happens when kids are lonely.

I didn't have any friends my own age, probably because I was always hanging out with my older half-sister Giselle.

I received the nickname "Sissy," which didn't help me much to fit in with boys of my age. I had other friends, but they were always only a part of my vivid imagination. The nearest friends I had to a living being, or someone who really existed, were the Kings and Queens of Southport.

Southport is a seaside resort on the west coast of England, some twenty miles north of Liverpool. Like every other seaside resort in England the town had a pier, a long wooden structure on stilts which stretched far out to sea. At the end of the pier lay *Pleasure Land* where I would find pleasure in interesting machines, like the mystical Indian fortune-teller in a glass case who was able to predict my future. When I pushed a farthing into the slot I would hear strange music and then the fortune teller's chin would start moving up and down and a little card would pop out.

I was told that I would soon be going on a long journey.

Most intriguing of all was a machine called *What the Butler Saw*. Inside, a roll of black and white photographic cards would spin around very fast and for a penny you could peek through a keyhole and watch a grinning, fat lady remove her clothing all the way down to her underwear. It was the live movement of flashing pictures in this early cinematographic miracle that caught my eye, not so much the smiling lady in her lacy underwear, and then of course there was the illegality of it all- the challenge of peeping through a key under a notice saying:

FOR ADULTS, ONLY ONE PENNY. (Or was it "FOR ADULTS ONLY, ONE PENNY"?)

What attracted me most, and what made me venture out on the pier so often, were my friends. There were gas powered lamps on green painted metal posts all the way along the pier. On every lamp-post was a royal crest with the name of an English King or Queen. All the Kings and Queens of England were represented, starting with the earliest by the beach and ending with King George VI, right next to *What the Butler Saw*.

On the top of each lamp-post a seagull perched. They all had names, and King George was my best friend. I would spend hours chatting with King George. He didn't have much to say in return, but that didn't matter, he listened patiently. He was my best friend. I would tell him about Jim Hawkins, Billy Bones, and Long John Silver, about Robinson Crusoe and his friend Friday. I would tell him about the great explorers Cook and Magellan, and I candidly disclosed to him my plan to sail away to find my Grandpa and maybe a hidden treasure or two.

Although King George didn't say much, he would occasionally nod and agree and always wanted to know more about my future voyages. And he was always there for me. One day I made him a promise. When I was ready to sail away, I would take him with me. I was convinced he would appreciate coming along for the ride, because he couldn't fly across the ocean by himself. If he could, he would have gone long ago.

I had confided in two grown-ups whom I felt I could trust: "Uncle" Bill, the old man who made candy floss that was the same colour as his pink face, and who always had time to listen; and Charley Jones, the one-legged man who left his other leg on the beach in Normandy. Charley owned and ran the Punch and Judy show, a puppet-show where Mr. Punch was continuously beating his wife Judy on the head with a stick. There was a policeman involved also and all he did was to beat the shit out of Mr. Punch. It was, in fact, quite a disgusting show of violent entertainment for children. Maybe this was what caused my emerging pacifism.

Charley took a liking to me because while all the kids would sit watching the show in front of the stage, I would be behind the scene, peeking through a hole in the tarp to see how the puppets worked. When the puppet-show manager saw what I was doing, he did not chase me away but instead asked if I would like to come inside to give him a hand on Saturdays and Sundays when there was no school. Both Uncle Bill and Charley said my ideas on nautical adventures were great but they kept telling me that it was more important to go to school. They finally convinced me that I should get an education of sorts and learn math to be able to navigate and geography to be able to know where to go before setting off on such an adventurous undertaking.

When my father discovered my relationship with these two uneducated but understanding men I received a two-month curfew. Education was more important than anything else. He said I wouldn't grow if I was to spend the rest of my life spinning candy floss and messing around with puppets. Growth was necessary if I was to be a sea captain and be able to see beyond the horizon. He had a strange way of saying things, my dad. Surely it wouldn't be an issue if I was a bit on the short side. It would be just a matter of climbing up the mast. Such nonsense only intensified my belief that, with two exceptions, all grown-ups were either potential liars or just plain stupid.

My parents would often go out at night partying, celebrating the end of the Great War. Every time I asked them where they were going, they would answer, "Out to see a man about a dog." I never got to see that dog. I just became even more convinced that all grown-ups were compulsive liars.

Then came that terrible day when everybody was running frantically around shouting, "The King is dead, King George is dead!"

I was miles away from the sea but ran all the way to the pier not believing a word what everybody was screaming about. It was all a big lie. There he was, my best friend, very much alive and perched on his lamp-post. I decided there and then never to believe any grown-up person anymore, and I told King George the sixth to meet me the following day by the lake at noon. It was time to go.

The sky was overcast and dull grey, giving off a light drizzle. There was no wind. Hardly a day to go sailing, but the planning and preparations had been going on for such a long time. It was now or never. I had to hurry. It wouldn't take long before they would start missing me at school and would start organizing a posse to hunt me down.

For several months I had been secretly building a ship. This was to be the day, the moment of truth, the day on which I was to cast off. The ship was built to carry me and King George across the ocean, far away from my dad, from schools, teachers, homework, washing up, house-arrest, and all that had made life no more than the an ultimate misery.

I would cross the seven seas and experience fantastic adventures. Adventures like the ones I had read about in the Hornblower books. It took an hour by bicycle to get from my house to the "sea." A rolled-up sail was fastened to the back of my bike. The sail was made from three cotton sacks sewn together by my big sister. She had promised not to tell anyone about the voyage.

It just could not be helped that the captain's uniform looked suspiciously like an English Primary School uniform turned inside-out. However, the moth-eaten black coat with brass buttons helped make me appear more nautical. It was a present from Charlie Jones. It was barely long enough to cover my bare, frozen knees. I didn't care about my freezing knees; I was on my way to warmer climates. Around my waist I carried a wide leather belt with a sword made out of marine plywood.

On my way I passed many small "seas" but my destination was a sea so huge that you could hardly see the other side. *When I get to the other side of the ocean, wondrous things will happen*, I thought. I was puzzled by that fact that it seemed as if every "sea," or more accurately, every pond of standing polluted water, contained a partly submerged, rusty, broken bedstead head. Such an obstruction would surely be a hazard to navigation.

Little did I know that such an obstacle would soon change my life.

KEEP OUT- TRESPASSERS WILL BE PROSECUTED read the sign as I turned off the main road down a narrow path. I wondered what "prosecuted" meant. Could it be a fate worse than keel-hauling, the plank, or even the cat o' nine tails? I hid the bicycle under some bushes. The grass all around was as tall as me. The path twisted and turned down to the water's edge with other paths continuously branching off to nowhere, probably made on purpose to throw robbers and customs officers off track. And there she lay, totally inconspicuous amid the high grass.

She bore the name HMS EXPLORER, written on her bow in big dramatic letters. She was a full-rigger, twelve feet long- eighteen if you counted the bowsprit. Her decks were made of solid oak and possibly a part of a garage door because you could read "NO PARKI" on it. Her decks were flawlessly secured with hemp rope to three empty oil-drums. Two of the drums were missing the filler cap, but that was not a problem as the holes were above the waterline and on her port side. I expected the heaviest seas to come from starboard, from the direction of the gas-works. At that moment in time I had no idea of the fatal consequences such filler cap holes would cause in the very distant future, on the other side of the world.

A low railing surrounded the deck and she had a little deck-house aft. The deck house was a bit too small to seek cover in case of a storm. However, it contained some pretty important nautical equipment that would come in handy on such a long voyage. It was obvious what was front and back, or more precisely, bow and stern on this magnificent ship. There was a long bowsprit protruding from a hole in the forward oil-drum. It took a whole day to make that hole!

In addition to the deck-house there was one more important item on board- a cannon. The EXPLORER was definitely no warship, but you never knew what dangers lay ahead out there on the seven seas. I had no gun-powder or shot. I would just have to improvise. That is not very difficult when you're only six years old. The great thing about the cannon was that it could also be used as a telescope. It didn't take long to raise the mast, but the forestay was too short so I had to lengthen it with my belt. It didn't really matter as I had lost my sword somewhere along the road. It wouldn't matter if my pants dropped either. Good thing I had the cannon!

The sail was attached to a yard- previously a broomstick. The shrouds and stays ran down from the masthead to the railing. King George had not arrived, but I could wait no longer as a sudden breeze set in from the northwest. A length of galvanized wire, serving as a mooring line, was cast off and the sail billowed. The EXPLORER was finally under way. A brass band played *Britannia Rule the Waves* and the crowds cheered and shouted in unison, "BON VOYAGE!"

I did not look back. My head was held high and my eyes were fixed eagerly on the horizon ahead. If I had turned around and looked back, I would have noticed that I had left my rudder behind. Never mind. Heyerdahl on the Kon-Tiki didn't steer, he just let the winds and currents take him across the ocean and eventually he arrived at his destination.

I had better check the chart. The rain had made a huge ink smudge but I could still figure out my overall surroundings. On my port side I had China, to starboard India, behind was England of course- where the wind came from- and somewhere up ahead lay Norway, a land where the sun shone at night and trolls were as big as houses with trees growing up their noses and who lived under stone bridges where they kept their *hulder* wives imprisoned. (A *hulder* was a seductive forest creature found in Scandinavian folklore.) At least that was what my father had told me. Just another pack of lies of course. If it were true that the sun shone at night, it should get pretty nice and warm there? A good reason to keep on that course.

It was time to have something to eat so that I would not succumb to scurvy. The ship's provisions consisted of biscuits and a bar of Cadbury's milk chocolate. The biscuits had disappeared; probably there had been rats on board. Dead ahead lay an uncharted hazard to navigation- a half-submerged rusty bedstead head. I was on collision course with this peril and had no steering! My starboard shroud got tangled up with the rusty contraption, resulting in her Majesty's Ship veering broadside to the wind and heeling slightly to starboard. Water rushed through the holes that were by now underwater and the EXPLORER sank slowly and gracefully into the mud, with only her mast above the water.

Only the swallows high above were witness to the tragic maiden voyage and the muddy, depressed young captain wading ashore. There was going to be some keel-hauling executed by the Commander in Chief when he arrived home.

That's how my childhood passed. Dreams of sailing the seven seas, finding hidden treasures, and later, during puberty, topless beautiful, smiling Tahiti women wading out through the surf to greet me and lay wreaths of flowers round my neck.

I actually saw very little of my parents. Father was out at sea most of the time and my mother was always on the move working on various film sets. My older half-sister became my "mother" and baby-sitter and we became very close. My baby-sitter would always take me with her on her evenings out on the town. That's how I learned to dance, how to mix a pink gin, a horses neck, and a shandy; how to kiss a girl without drooling, what to expect the day I became a teenager, and how to win the hearts of girls. At ten years old I knew practically everything there was to know about the birds and bees.

When I was not attending school, Giselle would take me with her- everywhere- and when my mother found out that I was spending a lot of time at dance halls and sitting outside pubs she got really mad. She wasn't much into corporal punishment. She left that to my father. Every time I did something wrong she would yell, あなたのお父さんが 家に帰ってくるまで待つだけ"- Japanese for *Just wait till your dad comes home*.

He did not come home very often so the amount of corporal punishment from his side accumulated over time in accordance with my so-called bad behaviour. If I tried to defend myself she would shout "黙れyacamash," which was Japanese for *shut-the-fuck-up*. That's about all I know in that language.

The only solution was to send me off to a boarding school in Bristol, a bastion of cruelty. My only contact was with my closest friend and ally, my sister Giselle, with the help of Her Majesty's Postal Service. I wrote her horrific accounts of the torture and torment I was going through.

I made a bet of fives marbles and a lollipop with my classmates that I would dare to climb over the wall that separated the girls from the boys, kiss a girl on her lips and climb back again within twenty seconds. This unfortunately did not go unnoticed by the school's headmaster. After morning prayers, I received ten lashes in front of one hundred fellow students. It didn't really matter- I had won the bet. What did matter were the tears streaming down my face- very embarrassing to say the least. Since then, I have had a problem kissing girls.

Then there was the incident of the revolving doors. I would take a flying start and do a five-time merry-go-round hanging on to the bar on the door. Unfortunately, my Latin teacher got caught in the maelstrom with a pile of books in her arms. Another ten lashes. Since then I have had a problem passing through revolving doors. How's that for an education!

At the time my sister was 17 years old, but could have passed for 27 if she put on a lot of make-up and the appropriate dress, nylon stockings, and high heels. She came to the boarding school pretending to be my mother and released me from hell to heaven. Together we moved in secrecy to the seaside resort of Torquay where she enlisted me in a Rudolf Steiner school. While there I learned to think for myself, social survival skills, and my favourite subject, astronomy. For nine months we lived happily together in Torquay with me attending the Steiner school until the day when mum and dad asked the headmaster of the boarding school in Bristol where the hell their son was, and the shit really did hit the fan.

At this time my father had a case of post-traumatic stress disorder due to his convoy duty during the war. He lost command of his ship and was given an office job. That didn't help his nightmares and antagonism at all. It just made them worse.

Against my mother's will, we moved to Norway. Giselle enlisted in The London Art Academy and stayed behind. That didn't help me either, having to lose my life's confidant and caring support.

3. The Dice Man

I was ten years young and living in a strange country where nobody understood a word of what I was saying. It wasn't easy for a young English-speaking lad to fit in, especially wearing a blazer, striped tie, and short pants. Not being able to speak the language, I was seen as a *tyskerunge*, the son of a German occupying soldier. The enemy. Nobody spoke English in Norway at that time. I knew a few Japanese swear words which didn't help much.

The educational system didn't know how to deal with foreign kids, so their only resort was to put me in a school for children with learning difficulties and arrange a "specially designed" pedagogical curriculum. They seated me in the back of the classroom to translate a book of my choice from Norwegian to English. It would have worked better the other way around. The book of my choice was naturally Robert Louis Stevenson's *Treasure Island*.

It took me half a year to translate that book- a long time as I constantly drifted away into the story and only came back to reality when I got a broadside from the teacher's desk. The new language came on fast, not due to my translation, but from learning it on the street. The bullying from my peers decreased when I managed to tell them that the reason for me being "speechless" was due to the fact that I'd been shipwrecked and had lived alone on a desert island for a long time, and that I had been discovered and saved by a captain of a warship, a captain who had adopted me and was now my father.

I must have been very convincing when I pretended to have an anxiety attack and asked the headmaster to summon my father. I knew he was at work and would arrive in full naval uniform. My tormentors were really impressed. The bullying decreased somewhat, but not entirely.

The day we as a family were to move from the south all the way up to the world's northernmost town I invited all my bullying "friends" to a party on board my father's ship which would be docked off the town hall.

My greatest childhood revenge took place as I was comfortably on my way north on a train. I heard later that fifty kids arrived on the dock only to find a rusty old barge with a note taped to her hull. SWEET REVENGE IS MINE. STOP BULLYING THOSE WHO ARE DIFFERENT. GONE SAILING WITH MY FATHER. ENJOY YOURSELVES AND F*** YOU ALL- PETER LONGSTOCKING.

Pippi Longstocking is a fictional character in a series of children's books by Swedish author Astrid Lindgren. Nine-year-old Pippi is unconventional, assertive, and has superhuman strength. Her father is a pirate somewhere in the South Pacific.

Kirkenes was a depressing and desolate town, so far north that night lasted from October until March. However, it actually turned out to be true that the sun shone at night, although only during the summer months. Apart from the polar foxes that raided our garbage bin, there was not much in the way of excitement, and the only good news to brighten up my dark, barren, and arctic world was that my sister Giselle was coming from England to visit us and to enrol at the University in Oslo. On her passage across the North Sea she met a man who she found "interesting." They dated a couple of times in Oslo before taking a trip up north to us.

I didn't like the guy for some reason, and he didn't like me because his girlfriend spent too much time with me.

After only one week we said goodbye, and she and her friend returned to Oslo. She soon found out that there was something "wrong" with him. After several arguments, where he turned quite violent, she broke up with him. Soon after that we got the bad news.

He had pleaded with her and asked if they could meet on a deserted beach outside Oslo. He wanted to say he was sorry and start over again. Apparently, according to the court reports, she put up quite a fight before he ended her life, stabbing her fifteen times with a carving knife.

Murders were rare in Norway in those days. It was headline news for a long time. The glamorous English student so tragically taken away by a psychopath.

In order to protect me, I was not told the truth. The big lie was that the most important person in my life had gone to Australia and would not be coming back for a long time and that my parents would be going with her, but would soon return. I was sent away to a distant relative, my Uncle Hans, far away up a hundred-mile-long fjord, where there was no radio and miles away from newspapers and people. Four months into my stay I heard my uncle arguing with my parents on the telephone. When it was over my uncle said, "Let's go fishing, Peter boy."

He told me that it was all a big lie. Giselle would never come back. He gently told me what had happened. I still haven't got over it. I never will. I get tears in my eyes just writing about it.

My dear sister's murderer got life imprisonment, which in Norway is only 25 years. He is out and about now, if he's still alive. He can only pray his path does not cross mine.

Mother found relief in God and I denounced the same god that had let this happen. We moved back south to Oslo and I felt relief the last day I had to go with my parents to say prayers by her gravestone.

With Giselle taken away in such a way, my mother became overprotective and for the first time in her life started to spend time with me. She was a great fan of Puccini and of course *Madame Butterfly*. I got to enjoy opera and decided to go for a career on stage. After high-school and several appalling amateur stage performances with the English Dramatic Society in Oslo, I sent in my application for Drama School, but my father wanted otherwise, and he enlisted me, against my will, to be educated as a naval officer and to sail in his wake. Basically, my dad "volunteered me" into the navy- to choose a career I had no interest in whatsoever. I only went along with it due to the maritime connection.

The relationship between my father and me gradually went from bad to unmanageable. Hoping it would somehow help to break the ice he gave me a pair of speed skates for Christmas. These are skates with long blades and the whole idea is to cover a certain distance many times round a rink in the shortest possible time. He wanted me to become a reincarnation of the world's fastest skater, even though this Norwegian Olympian champion was still alive at the time. Father often used that word- reincarnation. I believe he thought the word meant improved. Anyway, I found it totally absurd and meaningless running around the circumference of the ice-rink without experiencing anything else other than getting dizzy and out of breath. However, what did seem interesting was a group of young boys and girls dancing on ice to music, out in the centre of the rink.

I sold my much-detested speed-skates and bought a pair of white ice-dance skates with short blades and rounded points and, if I may brag a little, got to get quite good at it until one day my father came to see how fast I could do the 10,000 meters. He was not impressed by the fact that I could spin around myself ten times in three seconds instead of twenty spins around the rink in twenty minutes. Such behaviour on ice was for "fairies" (gay boys) and girls. My ice-dance skates ended up in the garbage-bin and that was the end of that career.

A precipitating factor during my adolescence that propelled me into politics developed due to a busty and beautiful young lady who was a leading member of the Communist Youth Party. She had red hair and her influence led to a relatively strong political consciousness. And not least- a growing confrontation with my father- a war hero who had almost died for the Fatherland. His son was now a disgusting communist!

He strongly believed that the navy would take care of that. But marching in step with a bunch of other guys, all dressed the same, was as meaningless to me as speed skating. I also had great difficulty in taking orders without asking questions. Due to bad eyesight, I was transferred from deck-officer training to engineering. At least there was something meaningful in knowing how to fix diesel engines and electrical stuff. Such knowledge might come in handy one day.

After two interesting years in the classroom and a miserable year mostly underwater inside a leaking submarine, I still had three years to go before the end of my "signing up" period. I had had enough and handed in my uniform, side-arm, and resignation. My only good experience in the navy was a 10-

month stint on board the Royal Yacht. In spite of my engineering training, I was posted on board the yacht as King Olav the Fifth's personal assistant. I was the guy who made sure his shoes and medals were shining and that there were always cigarettes and an Agatha Christie novel on his bed-side table. We had something in common, the King and I. Both our mothers were English, both our fathers were named Haakon and we both enjoyed sailing. When I told His Majesty the story about my friend King George the seagull, he laughed his head off and took a liking to me, and we became friends. The King and I.

Being on good terms with royalty did not make desertion any easier. One just cannot do things like that- spontaneously walk away. Such an action was defined as desertion; I would have been shot if we had been at war. The main reason for my "resignation" wasn't so much pacifistic or political- it had more to do with opposition to my father.

I was tried and convicted to spend a month in prison and a year in a detention centre. I had no feeling of being a convict at all as I was in good company. The special open detention centre had housed some very high-profile conscientious objectors: Trygve Lie, the first General Secretary of the United Nations, and Einar Gerhardsen, a great politician who later became Prime Minister of Norway. A clever lawyer managed to get me out after only 8 weeks on the grounds that I was underage at the time I was forced by my father to sign the 6-year contract. I felt sure I was born under a lucky star.

This was too much for the vice-admiral. During the following 20 years he would not see me or talk to me.

However, my training did come in handy. I was employed by the Department of Physics at Oslo University, building equipment for an experimental particle generator and saving every penny I earned to buy a boat. Then all went wrong after I made a wrong connection on Norway's first transistor. I "fried" it, a transistor which today is worth 2 cents and in those days was worth 1000 dollars!

Suddenly my life and future turned upside-down. My girlfriend Berit, whom I had trustingly hung out with since college, was pregnant with my child. We got married and I became a father at the immature age of 20. Parents on both sides were demanding an abortion. My son, who I wanted to name Dennis, was born on the day Kennedy was shot. My father wanted to name him Haakon, after himself. After a long argument, I threw in the towel- thinking it might improve our relationship. It didn't.

The job at the Physics Department was badly paid and boring. We had no home, no savings, and a baby who slept in a drawer in my mother-in-law's commode.

I found a well-paying job working for a technical publishing house. It was well paid because there was a lot of overtime and there was a lot of overtime spent with the editorial staff going out on the town after overtime at the office.

As I mentioned, I was too young and immature to have a family. The wife was not happy being stuck at home with a baby born prematurely and very often sick. She didn't like being alone during the evenings and week-ends, and my testosterone was boiling like crazy. After only three years of married life, baby number two, a girl, arrived into my confused world and, to be quite frank, promiscuous lifestyle.

I was 24 years old with two children. Our marriage was falling apart. I was "running around" when things abruptly changed.

I came across a novel written by the American psychiatrist Luke Reinhart called *The Dice Man*. Few novels actually change your life. This one did. It told the story of a psychiatrist who began making life-altering decisions based on the casting of dice. Feeling bored and unfulfilled, he started making decisions based on rolling his dice. It worked this way- when it came to making a decision, which normally happened umpteen times a day, you set up different options and let the dice decide which way to go.

I started to roll the dice and was instructed to leave my family. Divorced, I quit my job and went for a long, very long, aimless journey. I walked for 60 days around the coast of Norway looking for a boat, rolling the dice at every crossroad.

I still had not figured out where I was going, in which camp my contrary genes lay. Was destiny just chance, or was there something deeper involved?

I found no answer other than it had to do with chance. So, I let the dice decide under the motto "Who am I to question the dice?" When chance resulted in something weird or bad, I felt no guilt, no remorse, because it wasn't me who'd made the decision.

I eventually found a boat which the dice told me to buy. Sailing it back to where I started from, it sprang a leak and sank under way. Nothing really dramatic. It just gave up due to old age.

Then came the guilt due to abandoning my kids. So, the dice told me to build a house next door to their mother's house. For the rest of their childhood my kids moved freely between two homes. When they got pissed off with me, they moved in with their mother, and vice versa. A great arrangement, at least they thought so.

The same guilt led me to start working with kids, running a youth club. The Oslo Municipality's Youth Department was so happy with my work they sent me off to school, and within three years re-educated me to a Child Behavioural Therapist with a degree in child psychology. During my studies I lived on an abandoned farm, basically to try and find out if I could live alone and be independent. I couldn't. Three years without female company wasn't my cup of tea.

After my studies I was employed in various institutions around Norway, including a year in a children's hospital in Spain. I finally ended up working on the streets of Oslo saving young, underage prostitute boys and girls. We were a team of three social workers- Gert, Mariann, and me. It was hard and depressing work- mostly at night. After work, early in the morning, we would go to a 24/7 café for a snack and a drink. After many years of scraping kids off the street who thought they could fly out of high-rise buildings, and after we had knocked down several beers, my colleague Gert started questioning what the hell we were doing. Were we really made for this? What were our dreams? Was it time for a change? I let the dice roll again. Two sixes meant make a serious big change and follow your dreams.

Gert's dream was to become a writer; he had already published some poetry. I wanted to build a boat and circumnavigate the world. I had already "lost" three other rotten hulks and the only sensible option now was to build a new one. Gert knew a bit about carpentry, I had some experience having built a little wooden cabin for myself.

The next day we handed in our resignations and established a two-employee construction company specializing in refurbishing old wooden homes. Our goal was to work until we had accumulated enough funds for Gert to survive for three years writing novels and for me to be able to build my dream ship. After two years we thought it best to call it quits as the tax authorities were lurking around the corner. We took our company into liquidation and we had our final board meeting on the island of Madeira. We "invested" 10% of our earnings into blackjack at the Funchal Casino and lost it all within 3 hours. We thought we had worked out a system, but it didn't work, of course. Anyway, it was fun and the drinks were free.

Today Gert Nygårdshaug is one of Norway's most acclaimed authors with 35 published novels.

In July 1984 I quit throwing the dice and smoking cigarettes. It was time to launch my dream- to sail around the world.

I never made it around the world. I was shipwrecked before I even got halfway.

Here's the story.

4. The Ark

The Oslo fjord in Southern Norway is not a particular dangerous place to go sailing. In spite of this it probably has more wrecks per square nautical mile than the Bermuda triangle. There are three reasons for this: Norway has the highest percentage of pleasure craft per capita in the world. Most of the population live on and around the Oslo fjord because it's too freezing cold, dark, and miserable up in northern Norway. Because everybody wants to live by this fjord and park their boats in a nearby marina, marina costs are sky high, forcing people to moor their boats offshore where they get trapped in the ice during the winter.

Most of these small vessels are made of wood. The frozen sea freezes up in the underwater joints between the hull's boards. When the ice starts to move in the spring, it rips out the caulking between the boards, and the vessels end up in Davy Jones' locker. A fair number of these unfortunate losses belonged to me. After the sad incident on that English pond, it was just one boat after the other. I was obsessed with the notion of sailing around the world, and I would go to extreme lengths to try and achieve that goal.

The first disaster was named *Monday Monday*, a fiberglass catamaran (hence the double name). She was named after a popular 1966 hit by the *Mamas & the Papas*. She sank four nautical miles south of the Færder lighthouse at the entrance of the Oslo fjord due to a fire in one of her two engine rooms. Nothing dramatic, and there were no salty tears. It happened in good weather. I had a pleasant sail back to port in my 7 foot sailing dinghy, *Tuesday*.

Tuesday's Child was named after the nursery rhyme, "Tuesday's child is full of grace." She was a tired old 40-foot fishing boat with a one cylinder Petter diesel. The name was a contradiction in terms- she wasn't at all graceful. I acquired her for about the equivalent of a hundred pounds after selling my old Czechoslovakian CZ motorbike, which had also seen better days. It was a bad investment. I purchased her literally off the shelf, still on land with her hull newly painted. I should have checked underneath that paint. She sank as soon as she hit the water.

Tuesday's Child

My next nautical disaster was a 45 foot fishing boat called *Odin*. I renamed her *Onsdag,* the day of the week named after the Nordic god Odin, the god of wisdom, poetry, death, divination, and magic. She was a present from my dear Uncle Hans. This magical one sank alongside a dock when the 5 foot tall single-cylinder engine ran wild, ripped itself off its mounts, and sent its 400 pound flywheel clean through the boat's belly. If the engine bed had not been so rotten the *Onsdag* probably would have survived many more engine start-ups. My uncle had written clear instructions on how to start the engine. However, like most eager and impatient men, I seldom read instructions when I'm about to embark on an exciting task. I'm only human.

A desperate attempt to hoist her up only resulted in her breaking into two parts.

Tor was a fishing-boat I found on the back page of a local newspaper. What a coincidence, *Tor* might become *Torsdag* (Thursday).

The *Torsdag*, pictured advertised for sale "as good as new"

I did a quick inspection together with Finn, the previous owner. It was a swift examination because he had a train to catch, or so he said. Only a minute after the paperwork was completed, I was the proud owner of a smart looking vessel that could be rigged as a sailing ketch. I was down in the engine room shouting up to Finn asking how to start the engine. There was no reply. Finn had disappeared. I have never seen him since. A helpful harbourmaster came on board to show me how to start the engine. After the previous mishap with *Onsdag*, it seemed like a good idea. He didn't actually *come* on board- he *jumped* on board- from the dock, and went right through the deck. A closer look at the deck unveiled tiny dandelions seedlings growing between the planking. The motor-vessel *Tor* became COS-condemned on the spot. The harbour master took pity on me and bought me a pint of beer. *Tor* ended up as a dive-site.

The *Tor* incident was so pathetic that I can hardly bear to write more about it. I did a lot of thinking, assessing my possible options for getting around the world on my own keel and accord. I was also running out of days of the week.

All my dubious previous purchases floundered on the same inevitable stumbling block- money, or rather the lack of it. I was a low-paid government employee with two kids, a house with a garden, and two post-boxes in order to make room for all the bills. The only pleasure crafts I could afford to acquire were rotten, derelict, and abandoned fishing boats. I had the tendency to put pleasure before maintenance, and their rotten skeletons were strewn all along the bottom of the Oslo fjord.

An old boat is like an astronomical black hole- you throw in a lot of money and energy and nothing comes out of it. I finally came to my senses and understood that if I was to accomplish anything credible, there were only two options. Either to buy a new one, or build one. The first option was scrapped within a few minutes after visiting my bank manager.

"A second mortgage to buy a boat to sail around the world! You must be out of your mind, my boy." My bank manager was like any other "bankster," not very cooperative or supportive.

"Forget it, and don't ever call me *my boy* again, you old fart. I'll find a way," I replied. I walked out, crossed the street, and entered the public library where I spent the next four weeks reading every book on DIY boat-building.

I learned that boats can be constructed from a wide range of materials, from papyrus reeds to high-tech composite materials. Ferro-cement- concrete with reinforced steel- seemed a good idea, and it was cheap. However, after several fact-finding missions to various building sites and after speaking with several disillusioned amateur shipwrights, cement wasn't an attractive option any more. I visited an optimistic amateur boat-builder and previous potato farmer high up in the mountains, and I was finally convinced. Ten years before meeting him he'd become fed up with potato farming. All his life he'd dreamt of cultivating breadfruit in Tahiti after reading *The Mutiny on the Bounty*. He'd been working on his ferro-cement project for ten years, had gone through 500 feet of chicken-mesh, 2000 pounds of rebar, and two broken marriages, and he was still only half-way finished.

I was to discover that the Norwegian countryside was scattered with barns containing half-completed concrete dreams. I didn't have time to mess around with such time-consuming research. There had to be a better and faster way.

Wood became the final solution. Norway is full of Norwegian wood, which is why the Beatles wrote a song about it. The Norwegian wood that I could afford was unfortunately not to be found in the lumber yards of downtown Oslo- I nearly had a heart-attack when I received a quote from the cheapest lumber yard, a quote equal to the cost of sending a whole football team to a luxury resort in Tahiti for a month.

It was a shot before my bow, and I seriously contemplated instead of buying a load of timber to check out the nearest travel agency to go for a one-way trip to Tahiti.

After some serious considering of my options, I decided that I might be able to afford the wood option by actually buying the wood "on root" as they say, purchasing living, growing trees with roots, bark, and branches.

After weeks of running around and trying to persuade forest owners to part with a few meagre pine-trees I hit the jackpot. This forest owner was so fascinated by my project it resulted in a very good deal. Fifteen pine trees were happily growing far up a mountain valley. There were no roads or railway lines to the site, and I had to personally cut down the trees and organize transportation.

No big deal. This is how it was done:

Three good friends who were to become future crewmembers helped out. Not much of a problem with a powerful chainsaw, a paraffin heated snow tent and warm sleeping bags. The hard work was dragging all the heavy logs over deep snow onto an iced-up river without the help of a horse.

When the ice melted in the spring, the logs were transported free of charge down the river ending up at a sawmill. I paid the old retired manager and owner of the ancient sawmill with my car and a bottle of the finest Scotch whiskey, and voila- within a day or two I was the proud owner of a huge pile of the best milled yellow pine south of the arctic circle.

In the beginning there was wood

The sawmill was ancient and had not been in operation since the Second World War. The waterwheel had been replaced with an electrical motor. The rusty machines were driven by a network of overhead pulleys and leather belts. All the machines I needed were there. The owner of the forest and the old mill was present when I blew the dust off the machines and flipped the switch on the old electric motor.

Mr. Pedersen must have been of the same age as his mill, looking just as tired and worn down. With missing finger-tips on both hands, he made me think of my missing grandfather. As the electric motor whirred up, I saw a slight smile on his lips. I wondered if the smile had anything to do with his old mill working again or if he was contemplating if this city boy was sane or making a fool of himself.

I was well prepared. I had brought along an eager crew of engineering students who had serious plans to do some sailing with me in the future.

Mr. Pedersen was also invited to embark- but he was quite happy with taking over my battered Citroen 2CV along with a bottle of Johnny Walker Black Label.

Now why would anyone in their right mind want to spend years in the prime of their life and lots of money building a wooden boat, then years more sailing around looking for something, though they really didn't know what they were looking for? I had no idea at the time. Thor Heyerdahl had built the *Kon Tiki* to cross the Pacific and had proved that somebody else might have done the same journey a thousand or so years ago. God told Noah to build the ark because a big flood would occur at any moment. Not the Almighty, but an inner voice told me to build an ark and sail away from a life that would never be complete without something exceptional. I had no idea what that exceptional could be. All I knew was that I was in need of something more than what the average and traditional way of living would provide. A challenge? Somewhere in my psyche there was lurking a need for a greater challenge than what my boring house-and-garden life and 9 to 5 social work job could offer.

My homeland was in a state of political, environmental, and cultural decline. I wanted to escape from it all. I had been standing on the barricades too long, and I felt that I had done my share of the battle. I was depressed, fed up with my work scraping kids off the streets, kids that were abused, homeless, and drugged to the eyeballs. I was tired of the hatred and the xenophobia against immigrants and other minorities. I was disgusted with how the government had and was still treating the indigenous Sami people in the north. I was exhausted by constant new authoritarian and dictatorial regulations telling us that that it was a criminal offence to parachute off a mountaintop, or not to wear a seat belt, not to walk against a red light, but to accept the draft while encouraging us to join an international organisation that wanted to nuke our Russian neighbours, and so on and so on.

There wasn't really much to hold me back. The cold, dark, and depressing Arctic winter certainly didn't.

Then there were the dreams- dreams of crossing tranquil oceans on gentle trade winds. Finding my own tropical island paradise, with maybe a hidden treasure or two; living with nature, with no money problems and not having to get up *every* morning to catch the 6:55 to the office. To discover an island paradise without nuclear fallout, smog, or CO_2 pollution, mercury in the drinking water, subway flu, and everything else that makes you sick and short-lived.

A place where there were no annual income tax declaration forms to fill out, visiting census takers who wanted to know how many toilets you had in your house or how many times you'd been married, and if you refused to answer you'd be hauled before a magistrate.

There had to be somewhere on this planet that would suit an aging anarchist like me. That somewhere could well be simply to live in my own micro-cosmic world, fifty feet long and seventeen feet wide. Then move around and explore and maybe, just maybe find my Shangri La.

All this made sense, so much sense that all possible obstacles seemed insignificant. What of the complicating factors like money to keep things moving? No problem. Build an ark large enough to accommodate enough people to sail with me enabling me to cover the running and maintenance costs. Gone were the days of having to shanghai criminals and lowlifes from bars and brothels, having to pay and feed them until they jumped off at their next port of call.

So how do you build a wooden boat to manage storms and tribulations and carry a crew of 13? You start with a kit for a tiny skiff. If you can manage that project and can operate electrical power tools, then you can build something larger as your next project. Something big and strong enough to bring you safely across a large body of water.

Navigation? No big deal. GPS had not been invented at the time, but there were lot of books on basic navigation using a sextant, precise clock, and tables. After only a few hours of practice, it was just as easy to find a tiny rock or your position in the middle of Oslo fjord as it was to find a pub in Dublin, and may I add you can sit and smoke as much as you want on that rock!

I found the book *The Gougeon Brothers on Boat Construction,* using West System epoxy. It included building and assembly instructions on how you put together a fifty-foot long, 30 tonne replica of an 1887 Colin Archer sailing rescue vessel. Here's how:

First you pay a visit to the Maritime Museum in Oslo and purchase the complete line drawings for as much as you would have to pay for a half pint of lager.

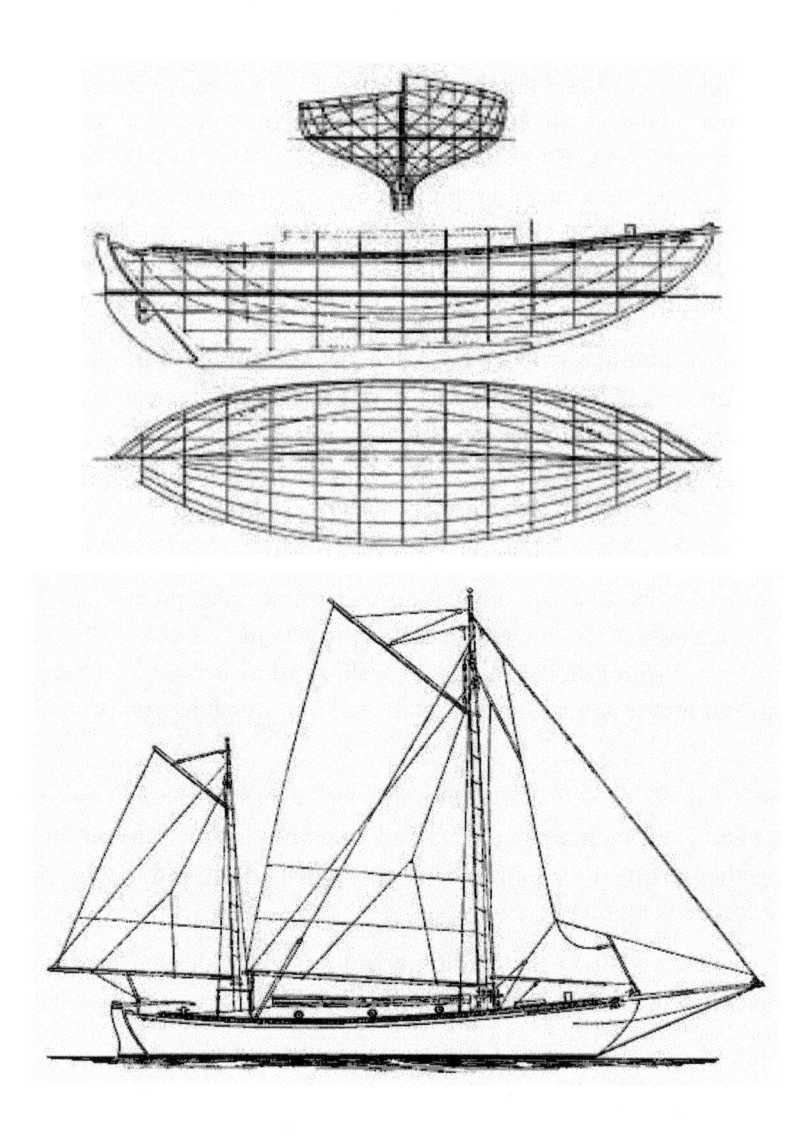

Then you remove a few apple trees in your garden to make room to build.

Erect a big tent out of two-by-fours and reinforced plastic tarpaulin. Inside this tent you laminate a keel in the shape of an upside-down "T" and attach 44 laminated frames to it.

Laminated keel and frames

Plywood deck ready for planking and caulking in the apple orchard

The frames are shaped by slicing the wood into thin strips so that you can bend them. Glue them together when they are bent and attach them to the keel. Within a very short time you have the skeleton of a ship.

When the skeleton is completed you start "planking her up." This is the easy part. You initially feed the wood through a machine at an old derelict sawmill and it comes out the other end of the machine as a two-by-two-inch square strip with a concave topside and convex bottom side. Then you simply glue and nail the strips one above the other. It's just like laying bricks. As the strips are so thin, they bend easily to follow the longitude curving of the hull. The concave and convex profile allows you to follow the curvature of the frames. This method is known as "strip planking." When complete, you lay on three layers of epoxy, on both sides, to stop any movement or expansion of the wood.

Then you lay on a deck and attach a heavy keel and you have your dream boat completed within two years, one month and six days. Engine instalment, interior, masts, and rigging take place after launching.

There were of course a few minor inconveniences and problems during her construction, such as when a hurricane-force winter storm threatened to "sink" the whole project. A long night was spent battling the elements. The irony of the incident was that it didn't occur off Cape Horn, but in a house and garden neighbourhood in the suburbs of Oslo. The plastic tarp, shredded to pieces, was later recovered three blocks down the street. On its windy passage it had demolished my neighbour's plastic deer and a miniature Dutch windmill. The good news was that it had also ripped away my neighbour's miniature fountain that had kept me awake all night.

The neighbours were not very happy or supportive in spite of the fact that I had forewarned them all that I was going to build a boat in my garden. I guess they expected a little sailing dinghy, not a reduced version of the *Titanic*. First of all the pretty blonde on the port side of my property could not lie on her porch in her bikini during the short summer months as the massive hull put her, the porch, her plastic deer and miniature windmill in the shade.

I offered her a place on my sunny deck- very appropriate, I thought. That didn't work so well. I told her she looked great in that bikini. That didn't work so well for her husband.

My project attracted many interested and inquisitive passing-by men. During the summer months, this resulted in my bikini-clad neighbour becoming the centre of attention instead of the boat, and her husband threatened to light a fire under her (the yacht's) keel. In desperation, my non-supporting neighbours ganged up on me by sending letters of complaint to the Housing Planning Committee, the Police, and The Ministry of Environment.

The neighbours on my starboard beam nearly had a heart attack when I told them I would have to lift the ark over their house to get it out of the garden and onto the main road. They threatened to blow up my dream with dynamite. What really got them worried were people who would pass by and come up with "funny" comments like, "How the hell are you going to get this ark out of the garden and down to the sea? Waiting for the big flood, are you? You'll never get it out of there!"

There also were quite a few people who kept on coming up with all kinds of "advice." Old experienced boat-builders would tell me that the glue would dissolve in water and that the boat would fall apart. They wouldn't listen when I tried to explain that today's epoxy glue wasn't what old-fashioned glue used to be- a boiled-up mixture of fish-skin and sawdust.

There was indeed so much "advice" on the right way to do things- warnings on what would never work, and that I would never be able to finish such a huge undertaking on my own. It just made me more dedicated to the task and only more determined not to give up. Eventually I began to understand that it wasn't so much the boat in the garden that upset my neighbours. It had to do with the fact that I was different from them. I did not conform to the neighbourhood's house and garden standards.

I had no miniature plastic windmills, miniature trickling fountains, plastic deer, elves, or gnomes in my garden. A perfectly manicured lawn bordered with pretty flowers did not exist. I didn't even have curtains in the windows of my house. If the lady in number 27 stood on a chair on her balcony, she could see straight into my bathroom shower cabinet! These people had the same attitude towards me as they had towards the gypsies camped up by the playing field or the friendly family from Pakistan in number 24.

These were not the most daunting obstacles to overcome. The one that caused the biggest stumbling block was the keel. A sailing vessel must have a heavy keel, or it will topple over with the slightest breath of air.

Here's how to build a keel in the least complicated way.

You construct a wooden box of plywood, shaped like a canoe. Then you fill it with heavy scrap metal such as engine flywheels, engine blocks, and five hundred lead wine bottle top covers (that was a lot of wine to consume, but the project did last for a period three years). When all this is positioned neatly inside the box, you call in a mobile cement delivery vehicle which arrives and pumps the box full of concrete. When the mixture hardens, the plywood is ripped off and the result is a nine-ton keel with twenty-two threaded bolts sticking out the top. These bolts are used to attach the heavy concrete keel onto the wooden keel. This is it in theory. Unfortunately, things don't always work as planned.

It took a whole month to build that keel, with all the attachment bolts carefully spaced out to fit exactly up into the corresponding holes in the wooden keel. Due to the five degrees slope of the garden, the whole contraption had to be mounted horizontally on various low wooden supports. Unfortunately, the lower support gave way to the heavy load of steel, lead, and liquid cement. Conforming to the rules of gravity, it slid backwards off the supports and the whole design went crashing to the ground. The pressure inside the box was too great and the sides fell apart up causing a tsunami of liquid concrete to flow out over the garden!

How do you get rid of a slab of hardened concrete the size of half a tennis court, complete with four tonnes of scrap-iron and lead wine bottle-tops? You run down to the nearest school and bring back fifty kids. With their help you convert the still liquid slab into five hundred lumps, light enough to pick up and throw into a container.

When the separation of cement was completed, the garden looked as if a hoard of elephants with diarrhoea had just passed through. My pride and joy's first keel was now buried in a landfill just outside Oslo. The kids had a great time and were awarded with Pepsi, chocolate cake, and a video cassette movie showing of *Mutiny on the Bounty*.

I was so depressed after this incident that I decided to drop the whole boatbuilding project and fly away to some distant remote tropical island. I was fortunate to find a great introductory deal to an atoll in the middle of the Indian Ocean. I was surprised to meet a Norwegian lady on the island who was married to a local. Her husband was also building a boat. He happened to be the king of the island state. Another king in my book. This king and I also had something in common, and we became good friends. When my two weeks' vacation was up, I promised my new friends that I would be back one day on my own keel. A keel soon in the making. I flew back home full of buoyancy, energy, and optimism.

The second keel was designed in a more intricate and sophisticated way- completed with a steel casing with welded stays and supports, and from then on everything worked out rather well.

Finally, it was time to cast off from the apple garden. A massive crane arrived to build another massive crane to lift her over my neighbour's house. The operation gathered quite a crowd, which of course included my anxious neighbours. Their lawyers were also present, contra to my neighbours, hoping that something might go wrong.

The ark was transported on a long trailer through the city of Oslo at night. Crews from the power and phone company had to cut and reconnect interfering power and phone lines. A special tram had to be called out to lift the overhead power cables. Seven police cars with flashing blue lights made up the rest of the most unusual procession ever to pass through the city. On the motorway the convoy suddenly came to an abrupt standstill. An overhead slanting footbridge proved to be too low to pass under. The police had to block off the main traffic flow in the opposite direction for several miles so that we could cross over to the other lane and get clearance under the higher side of the bridge. We all moved along at an appropriately slow pace. Slow enough for me to keep up the rear of the procession on my bicycle.

After another year of work at a seaside marina, she was finally ready to be launched. It took two cranes to lift her into the sea, accompanied by a rock and roll band playing *Ode to Joy* as a bottle of the best champagne was smashed against her bows to signify a new chapter in the *Fredag Project*. The name of my vessel meant *Friday* in Norwegian. Of course. It just had to be; after *Monday Monday, Tuesday, Wednesday,* and *Thursday.* Friday was also Robinson Crusoe's best friend. The word "*Fred*" means peace and "*dag*" means day.

Christening celebration

It took two mobile cranes to lift her thirty tonnes

51

Boatbuilders on cloud nine. Daughter and godmother in white dress

"Peace day's" keel was laid on Friday the 13th. She was launched on a Friday the 13th and she left port on her maiden voyage on a Friday. Many superstitious people would say the choice of day was not a good idea. If I had known at that time what the future was to bring, I would probably have called her something else, and sailed upon a different day.

The old battered car, TV, and lawn mower (all my belongings that would not fit into my tiny nautical world) were auctioned off. The newly acquired second-hand car covered the cost of charts for sailing around the world from Oslo to Oslo, a circumnavigation divided into six legs, each a year in length and with a crew of twelve on board at all times. I could have built a smaller boat for a tenth of the cost and sailed off with more funding, but who wants to sail alone, furthermore the "large" option seemed a better investment. Anyhow, finding a crew was no problem at all. I had young adventurers from all over Scandinavia fighting to come on board in various ports all over the world.

The first crew member, my neighbour Mariann, was to be my first mate, partner, and companion for many years to come. This happened to be the lady in number 29, not the bikini lady in number 27!

During the initial construction period I was getting very frustrated with the conditions I was working under. The epoxy glue wouldn't set in the low winter temperatures. I had to erect smaller tents with gas heaters within the big tent over every part to be glued. The winter storms would thrash the big tent and as all the frames were held in place and connected to the surrounding tent structure, the unstable skeleton framework would be constantly moving, making it extremely difficult to take exact measurements. This uncontrollable problem, combined with having to work in arctic conditions where everything I touched was sticky and hardly being able to breathe due to the fumes, made me scream constant obscenities.

My next-door neighbour Mariann either got fed up listening to all this foul language or felt sorry for me, or maybe a combination of both, so she jumped over the fence and asked if I needed a hand. As both of mine were nearly falling off, I told her that she was more than welcome to pitch in. From then on she became a regular working visitor on the site.

A shipwright in the making.

Now we were two.

Shipwright definition- a person who builds and launches wooden vessels

One day she was sitting high up in the apple tree, staring out at sea and eating a banana with a distant look in her eyes. She called me over, asked me to climb up beside her and said she had something on her mind.

"I want to come with you around the world," she said.

Suddenly it wasn't Peter's Ark anymore; it was Peter and Mariann's Ark. My girlfriend and Mariann's husband did not approve.

Thus started a long relationship between two people who were in many ways very different and often poles apart, but who had something in common, a desire to conquer whatever challenge might arrive, a love for sailing and travel. Our differences became an asset as we fulfilled each other by launching our dream. As a team we felt we could move mountains. We could never have gone through our future trials and tribulations on our own, without each other.

First test-run on the Oslo Fjord

5. The Ocean

It was a calm, grey Friday afternoon in July 1984. The *Fredag* and her first crew were ready to set sail on the circumnavigation's first leg to the Canary Islands, three years after the keel was laid out in my back garden. We were all hung over after the Grand Farewell Party the night before. We had rented the restaurant at the Nautical Museum in Oslo. Everybody of importance was there, friends and family, helpers and future crew members, even the king of an Indian Ocean island state. Like everyone else who had played an important part in the project, he was invited. To our great surprise, he came and it was kind of special to call out and announce His Majesty's arrival.

A huge crowd of well-wishers and curious spectators were on the dock to wave goodbye. Even the Lord Mayor of Oslo had found time to come down, give a little speech and hand over a pointless crystal vase with the Oslo city emblem etched on it. Just what we needed- an unstable vase to put pretty flowers in while we rolled and pitched over the ocean waves. The state TV and radio reporters were there covering the occasion and asking silly questions.

"Where are you going?"

"From Oslo to Oslo via Cape Horn," we replied.

"When will you be back?"

"In about six years from now!" we yelled as the big clock on the town hall in Oslo struck 12 bells. The original Colin Archer coastguard vessel gave us a salute with her two-inch cannon and the crowd applauded loudly, adding to the fanfare. We let go, in both senses of the word; we let go our mooring lines and headed courageously out towards our New World.

Casting off for the long voyage

As a sudden gust of wind cleared away the smoke from the cannon, I gave my first command to set all five sails. A flotilla of yachts escorted us out of the harbour. I did not look back; my eyes were on a lighthouse on the Dyna Fyr rocks up ahead. Translated, it means "The Bedcover Lighthouse," and it reminded me of the bedstead incident on my first childhood voyage.

One by one our escorts fell back and we were alone, gently gliding down the fjord. All was very peaceful and quiet, with everybody deep in thought. Someone switched on the radio. We listened to the local news announcing our departure with recorded interviews and ending the commentary with my favourite music; the Spartacus overture from the Onedin Line television series. The perfect symphony in six movements for the start of a very long voyage around the world in six legs.

The wind subsided, but we were are still moving, drifting sideways with the current. Heading south in the right direction out towards the open ocean. As the sun set, we anchored off a tiny island, only five miles down the Oslo fjord, actually only five miles from our final destination but with about 30,000 miles to go- the long way around the world! We hung out on the island for a week in order to get a long well-deserved rest. No rush! We had all the time in the world!

It is a given fact that the wind nearly always comes from the direction you want to go. That's why so many mariners prefer motorized vessels. It was a pleasant surprise when, with one day's exception, the wind always came from behind and blew us for thousands of miles along the European continent down, literally downhill, along the west coast of Africa and across the Atlantic.

Although the wind and good fortune was with us all the way, there were some teething problems to begin with. I discovered that my so far floating, horizontal and stable residence was not straightforward and easy to live in when Mother Nature started tossing it around. To walk from one end of the saloon to the other in bad weather, without holding on to something, turned out to be nearly impossible. Gravity seemed to work in mysterious ways. As on board the space shuttle, objects were constantly on the move, the difference being that on our nautical shuttle things were flying, not floating around. During a spell of nasty weather on crossing the Bay of Biscay all the books on the port bookshelf took off simultaneously- except one. I have twelve witnesses who can verify and validate that the above-mentioned solitary book was Erica Jong's *Fear of Flying*.

Right from the start, with an offshore gale along the lee coast of Denmark, I started to wonder what it would be like rounding the dreaded Cape Horn. Here the sea was calm, but the wind was certainly not. With all five sails set we heeled so far over that the port rail was under water. We were flying along at a speed of ten knots, extremely fast for an old-fashioned forty-tonne gaff-rigged ketch. I heard glass breaking down below, the woodwork creaked, and the rigging groaned under the stress and power of the wind. Would our homemade vessel be able to stand up to Roaring Forties? Not to worry. The Horn was far away in both miles and months. When the time came, we'd be prepared.

The *Fredag* stood her first test. We had done a good job. But what about her crew- would they stand up to problems that were bound to arrive?

We were lying dockside on the tiny Danish island of Anholt. The battery had to be charged. For both nostalgic and cost saving reasons all our lighting ran on paraffin (kerosene) with the exception of a tiny electric bulb in the head (bathroom). The female crew were literally pissed off with males not being able to shoot straight. Even our navigation lights were old-fashioned, brass paraffin lanterns. However, we needed battery power to start the engine and operate the VHF radio. Our "entertainment centre" consisted of a mouth organ, a Walkman tape player that kept ruining our tapes, and an old-fashioned mechanical wind-up gramophone with about fifty baculite discs that were called 78s, due to the fact that the recorded discs revolved 78 times a minute.

The electrical generator that charged our power source, a single car battery, was connected to the engine with a belt and pulley. The belt was a bit slack. I had the problem noted on my list of endless things to deal with. Until I got around to it, I would get the slipping belt moving by putting a little pressure on it with a screwdriver with the engine running.

I was sound asleep in my cabin and didn't hear the beeper telling us that battery power was getting low. My trusty mate Mariann never had a problem dealing with "male" issues. Instead of waking up the captain she did what she had seen me do on several occasions. Unfortunately, she managed to get her index finger between the belt and pulley, with half of her finger ending up in the bilge below the engine. We managed to locate and retrieve the oily, mangled body-part and called for help on the radio.

We expected a wailing siren from an ambulance, not the chop-chop of a helicopter.

With her finger in her mouth, because I had read somewhere that that was the right thing to do, we landed on a hospital roof in Copenhagen. It was not a clean cut so it was not possible to sew it back on. She was offered a plastic prosthesis but declined. With a plastic finger the point of a prosthesis was literary pointless. As usual, Mariann would always take a humorous approach to any disaster. Children would later scream with fearful delight when she pushed the short stump of her finger up her nose to scratch the back of her eye. Later, a shark nearly took her whole arm, but that's another story.

The next time we were put to the test was when we nearly lost it in the English Channel- and I'm not talking about body parts or the boat.

We were on the verge of losing our minds.

The narrow strait between England and France is one of the world's most busy and dangerous waterways. Getting in line with the other vessels, small and large, would normally not be a problem. Radar stations along the coast are all connected to the coast guard station near Dover. Traffic controllers keep watch and guide the traffic in the same way as air traffic controllers do. Furthermore, most vessels have their own radar, enabling them to judge distances to shore and other vessels.

We didn't have such a device. I had the choice between buying a cheap, second-hand radar or an antique gramophone. I just *had* to have the gramophone, including a stack of 1920 hits and a little box of pick-up needles which had to be changed on a regular basis. Situated in the middle of the Channel in thick fog, I wished I had gone for the radar instead. The fog came out of the blue, literally. I could not see our bowsprit from the cockpit, fifty feet away. Sailing in thick fog is like driving a car blindfolded, with the exception that with a sailing vessel one cannot stop and park somewhere safely out of the way.

The electronic LORAN positioning system, a device the size of a suitcase and costing a small fortune, had just been invented. It was a clever bit of technology, but it would only work around the British Isles, and as I had planned to sail around the world, and certainly not the straits of Dover on a foggy day, I didn't see the point of buying one. However, I did have a really fancy sextant, but with the sun hanging high above the fog and not visible, our only navigation instrument stayed in its velvet-lined cedar box. My only way to find out where we were was to use what is called DR navigation- dead reckoning. This is basically guesswork based on observed speed and direction. If you don't reckon right, you're dead. The system worked if you were crossing a calm lake on a calm day, in addition to being in a calm state of mind. It wasn't easy when you had current and wind on your beam, sending you off course. Furthermore, I always had trouble with the math when I wasn't in a calm state of mind. Our best chance of survival was to make a lot of noise with our mechanical crank-driven fog horn, hooting out every ten seconds and receiving loud and deep booming acknowledgement from the ships around us. There was no point trying to figure out where other vessels were located. We were basically totally blind- sitting ducks slowly moving along and hoping for the best.

A gigantic rusty, moving wall appeared out of nowhere, moving so close to us that the top of our mainmast nearly touched the tanker as we rolled in its bow wave. We could hear the rumbling of her engine deep in her bowels. Her engine's cooling water was spewed out through a hole in her side and over our deck. Then, as sudden as the moving wall had arrived, it disappeared silently into the thick fog, leaving behind a stinking wake of diesel and a strong whiff of curry, I could read her name on her stern before she disappeared: *Final Bell* of Calcutta. That was just about the final bell for us.

It took about 15 seconds before I started getting the shakes. Fear was starting to get a grip on me so I began calling for help on the radio. A very calm coast guard traffic controller told me to relax and to do a full circle turnaround.

Sheer madness I thought; like doing a double u-turn on the M1 motorway during rush hour.

I stopped hyperventilating when I was told that we were visible due to our double u-turn and that we must maintain speed and steer a course of 275 degrees until told otherwise.

The fog eventually cleared and revealed a cozy and interesting little safe haven called Polperro. Relieved and grateful towards the traffic controller, we were safely moored to the quay behind the breakwater, next to a huge sign that read: NO YACHTS OR PLEASURE CRAFT ALLOWED.

The friendly harbourmaster said that as we had come all the way from Norway, and if we promised we would do no raping or pillaging, we could stay one day.

What he did not know at the time was that the *Fredag* had a 7 feet draught and that we had barely made it through the harbour gates on a spring tide. The next tide high enough for us to depart, would occur after 28 days.

We made many friends in Polperro over the following four weeks and we needed a break anyway after our scary channel passage. I also nearly made friends with my dad. The admiral and I hadn't talked for twenty years, ever since I walked out of detention for objecting to a naval career and not following in his wake. Someone had whispered in his ear that the *Fredag* was berthed in Polperro. He had reluctantly, with pressure from my mother, decided to make up with me. After all, he had an excuse. I was now a captain and in command of my own vessel. He arrived unexpectedly, in uniform, shook my hand, made a quick inspection of my ship and crew and said that I should get rid of that bloody ring in my ear and to get a haircut! Like the *Final Bell,* he was gone before I could open the champagne to celebrate my family reunion. After he left, I started having the same dream again, the one with the red telephone booth.

Ever since I was a little boy, I would have this surrealistic dream- more or less always the same one. It only differed in that there was a short continuation every time, so the dream got a bit longer with each episode, but it never reached a conclusion. I dreamt I was sailing up a river, searching for something or someone.

I feel sure I will find out later what it is I'm searching for. There are Indians on the river banks and they follow me as I navigate up the river. I end up in shallow waters. I get stuck in the mud. There's a peculiarly English red telephone booth on the shore. All the Indians have vanished except one. He is watching me. He shouts out a six-digit number. After entering the phone booth, I put some coins into the pay slot. As I am going to dial the number, hot chocolate pours out from the coin return. I never get an answer. Only gallons of hot chocolate. In the most recent dream, my father answered but was immediately cut off. I didn't get any hot chocolate this time.

I simply had to sail up the River Dart in Devon. I had this tremendous urge to sail up rivers, always on the lookout for red telephone booths.

I was determined to go up the Dart, in spite of all the warnings of treacherous tidal currents, sandbanks, and the fact that I had heard that sailing on the river was prohibited.

Some of the footage in TV-series about the Onedin Line, was shot on the River Dart, instead of the Amazon River. This was done in order to save costs, even though the river was a bit short of tropical vegetation, alligators, and small brown men with bowl-shaped haircuts and sticks through their noses.

With all sails set and the wind astern, we wound our way up the river at a good pace as there was hardly any current against us. We had to keep a good look-out, not for obstacles in the water but to be able to dodge overhanging branches.

With a little goodwill and imagination, I could imagine that the long logs lying in the riverside mud were threatening crocodiles having a mid-day nap. When the depth-sounder told us that the fun and joy-ride had come to an abrupt end, we dropped anchor before a low stone bridge. We were conveniently stuck in the mud and could no longer continue our mission into the "rainforest," which was more an open Devon landscape dotted with sheep, cattle, and funny-looking miniature ponies.

It was a convenient anchorage because there was a pub, *Nelson's Arms*, a pistol-shot away on our starboard beam. It didn't take long for my thirsty crew to spring into action and arrange an expedition shore. I ferried them to the quayside but remained on board to guard against any attacking natives.

An elderly person of authority, wearing Bermuda shorts, a Royal Yacht-Club blazer, and a naval cap with gold leaf on the brim suddenly appeared out of nowhere and climbed on board without asking for permission. He demanded eighty pounds for illegally sailing up a privately-owned river that belonged to his best friend, the Prince of Wales. He didn't believe a word about *my* royal connections. He remarked that he had been born at night, but it was not *last* night. However, when this dressed-up river-authority noticed the Norwegian flag, he gave me a detailed narrative on how he had personally blown up a lot of stuff and killed a bunch of Germans in Narvik in northern Norway during the war. After a few beers, some aquavit, pickled herring, and more aquavit we became best of friends, and the Prince of Wales lost out on eighty pounds, poor man.

The river was only half a meter deep when I decided to row ashore in the spare inflatable dinghy and join my crew at the pub. The quay wall had now grown another 17 feet taller since then. I tied the dinghy to the lowest rung on a rusty and slippery iron ladder.

The natives in the *Nelson's Arms* were friendly and nice people and showed no signs of animosity or cannibalism. They were intrigued that the Prince's guardian of the river had refrained from collecting the fee and had not charged us for breaking the law.

After a few pints and a pub lunch, we were told that we should get on board immediately as the tide was in and running back towards the sea again. This phenomenon is something that happens on a regular basis, often causing major problems.

The tide was up as high as it would get. I found the iron ladder, but the dinghy was gone. I summoned a passing police officer to let him know that someone had stolen my dinghy. He looked down the ladder and told me I should have used a longer mooring-line. Looking down, I could just see the dinghy through the murky water, tied on a short line, standing on edge and unsuccessfully trying to re-surface. Another lesson learned.

Then it was back to sea again under a tail wind and tidal current with the deck strewn with spiky chestnuts raining down as our topmast frequently raked the treetops. Another river adventure, but no red telephone booth dispensing hot chocolate.

After a brief stop at Falmouth to take on corned beef and brown ale, it was goodbye England and downhill across the Bay of Biscay to Santander on the north coast of Spain.

The Bay of Biscay, which is bounded by the west coast of France and the north coast of Spain, is known for its rough seas and violent storms, and much of this is thanks to its exposure to the Atlantic Ocean. We got away with a light gale, nothing scary, but one of my crew was so scared that he refused to come up from his cabin take his turn on the helm. In my book, that is defined as mutiny, penalised by a dozen lashes with the cat o'nine tails, a whip with nine knotted lashes. The nine cords or tails represent the nine lives of a cat and the whip also left marks like the scratches of a cat.

However, the mutineer had a choice, either the "cat" or get off my ship at the first port of call. He chose the latter.

We eventually had to take a break to modify the ship and make our home and means of transportation more suitable for the roller-coasting of steep open water. A great place to do such home improvement is somewhere calm, far up a river, moored to a bollard outside a winery.

We had met Joachim and his family in a tiny fishing port in northern Portugal. I mentioned to him my passion for river sailing and told him about our amazing sail up the river Dart in southern England- a river for the occasion pretending to be the Amazon with the aid of a few palms including a dozen stuffed crocodiles and a couple of dead Norwegian blue parrots nailed to overhanging branches.

My Portuguese friend said that he could pilot us up the Douro River to the city of Oporto. When he explained that this was where the famous Sandeman Winery was situated and there was free port wine, madeira, and sherry sampling from sunrise to sunset, it didn't take me long to make a decision on our next port of call.

"Let's go, man! What are we waiting for?"

I started getting second thoughts after reading the pilot guide.

"Navigation on the river is possible but is often hampered by rip-tides and occasional flooding over the lower sandbars at the mouth. The entrance permits only shallow-draft vessels (under 4 feet) to enter. Vessel with draft less than 4 feet- must enter with the utmost caution in high swells."

We "parked" in the Atlantic Ocean, off the mouth of the River Douro, or to phrase it in more nautical terms, we were hove to waiting for the right moment. *Hove to* means staying put with the jib backed and the tiller to leeward. The boat tries to point to windward but this is balanced by the force of wind and waves. A handy bit of free information for you if you ever go sailing and need to take a break.

According to Joachim, who claimed to have done this manoeuvre many times with his dad, when he was a little boy, there was nothing to it.

"Wait for a big wave and ride the surge over the sandbar. A piece of pie. Facilissimo!"

I found it strange that Joe, with his inadequate English, had used such a strange colloquial idiom as a piece of *pie*. I replied, "You mean a piece of cake?"

Huge Atlantic waves were rolling in and when they met the out-flowing river current, they towered up to twice their height, steep and angry. In between the wild and jagged waves there are maelstroms of swirling water with brown foam and river debris.

This did not look very good, not good at all.

A crowd had gathered on the breakwater. They were waving to us and shouting something, but they were too far away for us to understand what they were yelling. Even if we could hear, we wouldn't understand anyway since our Portuguese was- to be honest- extremely limited.

Joachim was looking intently out to sea, waiting for the big wave. I was just about to call the whole deal off when he screamed, "Go go go! Now!"

Taken somewhat by surprise, I gave the order to let go the sheets, and I slammed the engine into full ahead.

As the bow swung towards the river entrance the sails filled and the big wave lifted us up. With our forty tonnes we were surfing at a speed far exceeding her fastest ever.

"Keep as close as you can to the breakwater," shouted Joachim.

I could now see that the crowd were not giving us welcome gestures, they were actually waving us away. They were trying to warn us, trying to tell us to turn around and get the hell out of there.

"Don't worry about them!" shouted Joachim, "Portuguese people are like that. They get all excited about nothing!"

It was too late to turn back. We were over the sandbar and suddenly all was smooth and calm, and my heart started beating at a normal pace again.

And the Sandeman Port Wine? The music? The captivating city of Oporto with its many enchanting fado-bars? Wow. It was worth all the nerve-wrecking trouble of surfing over the sand-bar. The *Fredag* caused quite a stir where she lay tied up to the Sandeman winery. It had been more than a hundred years since a deep-keeled sailing vessel had come up the river fill their hold with a cargo of wine. Why not take on some cargo?

On returning down river with our precious shipment of wine several of the crew thought it safer to take the bus and meet up with us in Lisbon, further down the coast. If there ever is a next time for me to visit Oporto I think I'll also take the bus.

Taking on cargo in Portugal

What was it like crossing the Atlantic? Did you sail at night? How could so many people live together for such a long time in such a limited space?

People kept asking me these questions. Many seemed to visualize an Atlantic crossing as a steady battle fighting the elements, sails blowing out, crashing into whales, containers, freighters, and huge super-tankers, continuously throwing up and getting on each other's nerves, and worst of all- not knowing exactly where you were. But I actually found it quite boring.

As for fighting the elements, if you get your timing right and leave Africa at 10 am on the 10th of December, it will be downwind, smooth sailing, and cool running all the way to the Caribbean. As for blow outs, our only blow out was the pressure cooker because someone had tied down the release valve to make the bread "cook" faster.

The only crash was crashing into one's bunk after a long night's watch. Seasickness? It cured itself if you stopped talking and thinking about it. If you put the same question to some of my crew, you would get different answers. Upon arrival to the island of Grenada I asked my crew how they had experienced their Atlantic passage.

Some of them had thrived with the isolation and the feeling of being so far from civilisation. For them it was a micro world of tranquillity and serenity. I had been a bit worried that things would get out of hand with so many people cramped together in such a small area with no way of escape other than to climb the mast to the crow's nest.

With a crew of twelve, six of the punters were asleep at any given time. The other six were either reading, listening to music, preparing meals, scrubbing the deck, learning how to navigate with the help of the heavenly bodies, steering the vessel, or just cooling out. Not knowing where you were was not a problem. These days you can press the GPS button, but in the good old days, when navigation satellites were still on the drawing board, the issue was a bit more complex. But only a little more complicated. It would take me half an hour to teach an average IQ person, equipped with a sextant and a visible sun overhead, the art of finding out where you were- a little longer if dealing with the stars.

Here's the best method to find your *exact* position. You teach the whole crew the magical procedure by first standing with your legs apart, holding the sextant steady, adjusting the sun and the horizon to match up in the mirrors of the sextant before reading off the angle. With an accurate clock and some simple math, you have your latitude and longitude. The more accurate the clock, the more accurate your position. With a knowledgeable crew, you added up all the results and divided the result by the number of crew, and you would have the most accurate position you could imagine. Even if there was a slow learner among them, it wouldn't put you off more than a couple of miles. And what's a couple of miles in the big scheme? It's a piece of cake. Or pie.

Did some of the crew occasionally get on each other's nerves? Of course, but on the other hand, some very close friendships were established. Sometimes a bit too close where some couples were concerned- if you get my drift. I won't go into the details.

Here are some of the answers that were entered into the ship's log book by my crew. In addition to enter distance sailed and technical issues, I requested them to add personal details and experiences, entering these during the passage or upon reaching the other side.

Excerpts from the ship's logbook:

"…The days flew by too fast for me. This was the life, but I still couldn't wait to get back on land. And then there was Christmas. One I will never forget. A Christmas that was all blue and full of love and compassion and totally free of commercial garbage and financial worries." (Therese)

"…Time did not exist for me anymore. The ship's hourly bell regulated my life, a simple uncomplicated daily repetition. Everything was cool and easy and uncomplicated." (Arne)

"…No responsibilities other than keeping a good look-out to make sure that no harm would come to my fellow shipmates." (Lone)

"…Even though we pitched and rolled and I spewed my guts out, there was harmony and a sense of peacefulness inside me. Peace in my mind also. Even if I was half asleep all the time, I was more awake than ever. All very strange and new to me. Oh, and not to forget, the huge swordfish that leaped over the bow! Wow!" (Jurg)

"…It was all so much less dramatic than I expected. The days ran together. I enjoyed the nights most of all. Alone under the stars. Alone except for the company of playful dolphins and escorting whales. Fresh flying fish for breakfast and amazing sunsets." (Morten)

"... Thundering noiselessly through the night at full speed. That's what it sounded like. Listening to my favourite music on the Walkman. Having to hang on all the time and a feeling I was going somewhere, in many ways. Time, lots of time to think and reflect." (Ola)

"...Living close together, getting to know people very intimately. Being in synch with my surroundings and myself. A journey, from one continent to another. A journey, from one lifestyle to a different one." (Brita)

"...Total distance sailed 610 miles. A record 30 miles on my watch. Average speed 7.5 knots. The flag has a rip. Who's smoking cigarettes in the toilet?"

"...A huge swordfish leaped over the bow. Why are we always so tired and sleepy? Counted twenty-five shooting stars and made twenty-five wishes. One was that I wish you lot would stop snoring! Dogwatch- don't forget to wake up the cook at sunrise!"

"...Average speed 7 knots. We are moving along too fast and halfway to the other side already. Who has borrowed my electric shaver and did not put it back? Lots of flying fish in the bucket for the cook."

"...Lots of lightning, but no thunder? Saw a light on the horizon. I strongly suspect the captain is smoking in the toilet. Sorry about the bread, a sudden steep roller and the dough slipped overboard. Lots of happy sharks in our wake. Must be good bread."

"...Thank you whoever it was who put an orange under my pillow. Called up a Greek freighter on the radio. They confirmed our position. We are only 3 miles off! They said that American troops have invaded Granada! What have the Spanish done to deserve that? The Christmas gingerbread cakes are done."

"...Got a time-signal on the short-wave radio. Our GMT-clock is 3 seconds slow. Correction made. Boys, remember to lift up the ring on the crapper! The Christmas Eve menu is ready: Pickled flying fish in mustard sauce for starters. Canned-ham schnitzel with sauerkraut, sautéed potatoes for main course. Rice cream dessert with red fruit sauce, coffee, cakes, and liqueurs.

Our beloved Captain Bligh has lifted the alcohol ban during the Christmas dinner. Long live our Captain. The ban will be reinstated at midnight and will be in effect until we reach land! Thank God we're nearly there. Found a butterfly on the foredeck."

"…Tiny bird with yellow breast, hitch-hiked for one hour. Received Radio Barbados on FM radio. Will you guys stop singing so loud in the cockpit at 4 am. Please turn down the volume next time!"

"…Atlantic rollers at least 15 feet high. Don't look back! Lost my glasses overboard. Anyone got some spare specs, strength 2.3? It's been a hot night."

"…Saw a huge cruise ship, miles away, all lit up with people having fun on board. I would rather be here. Turn me over on my side when I snore. The speed-log got entangled with the fishing line. Frigate-bird tried unsuccessfully to land on the top of the mast. Killed 5 roaches today. Flying fish flew through the port hole into my bunk- not funny."

"... Land sighted 1607 GMT, Sail Rock off the island of Carriacou. I smell spices. I can imagine the sound of cold beer being poured into a glass. I have evidence that the smoker is the captain. Thanks for all the fish."

In West Africa an expert on the subject of calculation on estimated time of arrival showed me how to work out the Atlantic crossing time. I put all the factors into the equation and came up with a prediction of thirty days at sea. We were close to arrive at Grenada after only 15 days at sea, due to an unexpected strong blow from behind, all the way from West Africa's Cape Verde islands. It was clear that we would be celebrating Christmas on the Caribbean island of Grenada.

We had planned it so that we would spend and celebrate good old-fashioned Norwegian Christmas at sea. The ultimate blue to the alternative white Christmas.

We had to put on the brakes by reducing sail.

Just before sunset we had the only rain on the entire crossing. It was a short burst but long enough for us all to soap down and rid ourselves of layers of salt. We really looked good and smelled our best when we were ready for "the ringing-in ceremony."

Soaping down in a sudden squall

We lashed the tiller, and with only the storm jib set on the bow, let Fredag handle herself and went down below.

It took a lot of detailed planning and ingenious ideas to launch the festivities. The gimballed Christmas-tree with live candles, swaying in synch with the big Atlantic rollers, was quite an engineering miracle. To stop everything on the dining table from taking flight in the saloon, we criss-crossed the table with one-inch mooring lines to keep everything in place. We even had a Santa. When someone called out that we had a visitor, everybody rushed up on deck to see a fat and robed red Captain Santa climbing down the mainmast. By the time he was down below his entire foam beard was distributed along our wake.

Cool Santa with half his beard gone with the wind after climbing down the mast.

We all got presents, each gift donated from each member of the crew. The items had to be hand-made on board and were all thrown into Santa's sack. I got a cigarette holder, cut from the jaw-bone of a shark. One of the crew got a present from himself! Our youngest crewmember, only four years old, was thrilled with the load of presents from back up North. But the rest of the crew, receiving only one present, were just as thrilled with what they received.

We all became like children again, giggling and singing and fooling around and knocking down the wine and aquavit as if we hadn't seen any booze for ages. And we hadn't. All this took place while our ship ploughed through the night with a feisty gale behind her stern. Going on deck to smoke a big Havana cigar, I could see the distant lights from the hotels on Barbados. It looked like a row of distant Disneyland castles. I was very happy about the decision to spend this occasion at sea, snug on board our merry, surfing ship.

Notice criss-crossed rope to prevent our Christmas dinner from taking off

Passing close to the lee of the island of Grenada the following evening, I could smell the spices. The jungle was velvet black against the starry night sky. I could hear a distant Bob Marley and beating drums and if we listened carefully, we could hear the crickets and tree frogs in the background. With all our senses sharpened after days at sea, we really felt that we were in a new and alien world.

We were slipping down the lee coast, quietly and slowly towards our final destination, the careenage in the picturesque town of St. George's. Some locals were hanging out on the dock, following our approach with half-hearted interest.

Five feet from our final destination, I heard a muted thud and we came to a standstill. A tall Rastaman with dreadlocks, leaning against a lamppost, flicked the butt of his joint into the water and said, "Ders a stone der, mahn."

A Bequia Rasta-man

After three thousand miles we had softly run aground, slipping gently onto a stone, in a dead calm, only a few feet from the dock. Our next encounter with the sea-floor would not turn out to be so gentle.

6. The Reef

The sailing ketch *Fredag* had so far had a long journey. From Oslo, along the European continent, down the west coast of Africa, across the wide Atlantic with landfall on the Caribbean island of Grenada. The second leg of our circumnavigation was coming to an end for our Atlantic crew. It was time to change crew again so we headed north up the island chain with Puerto Rico as our destination. With a new group of adventurers on board, we set a course south, back to Grenada. The Horn was a ridiculously impractical choice of a route since there was a safe and manageable option by taking the short cut through the Panama Canal. But we were up for the challenge. That's just the way we were, my mate and I. Today I would have chosen differently. But then again, the story might not have been so interesting.

Our next running aground- after easing onto that stone in Grenada- would be a different and more serious incident altogether. Based on my accurate and extensive log-book records, noted down only a week after the ordeal, here's what I wrote:

"The boys are on deck tonight. Ready to go. They are waiting for the midnight eight bells to chime. This is when the anchor chain gets slowly rolled in and funnelled deep down into the boat's chain locker and the sails get set for a tropical night cruise.

"Below deck the Encyclopaedia of Insects was securely shelved, but the discussion continued in the cockpit. It's all about the unconquerable roaches. We read about how the pests had been around for 320 million years and of their amazing ability to survive almost anything, from pesticides to nuclear war. The discussion was muted so not to disturb the female crew sleeping below. They needed their sleep as they were scheduled for the early morning dog watch.

"Claus is a student of biology. He joined us in Martinique. He brought with him several scientific publications on cockroaches with detailed descriptions on how to get rid of these nasty creepy-crawlies. We know better. There is really no point in trying. We have lived with them for a long time. Nothing seems to work. The roaches are the ultimate survivors.

"Full warfare is the only solution to reduce the menacing roach population. Old fashioned combat gives the best results. Grab the nearest weapon you can find when one appears- a Norwegian cheese cutter, a shoe, or an edition of National Geographic- and whack it as you yell out loud, *Death to the roaches*! You don't get rid of them completely, but it works to keep the population under control. It also helps to let off steam- anger from having ended up with a large number of busted Norwegian cheese cutters. Even so, I prefer this solution to pesticides as we have domestic animals on board who are really not comfortable with roach poison.

"One can always solve the problem by sinking the boat," says Claus jokingly.

"Imagine a tropical midnight passage under a full moon along a Caribbean chain of islands. Sailing under a radiant tropical sun among emerald green islands is one thing, but sailing through the dark of night is quite another. Your senses are more alert and receptive. You can smell the spices and fragrance of exotic flowers drifting off the land. The surroundings and the heavens have different and deeper dimensions. Sometimes it feels as if you can take off and sail into the cosmos. You sense being alone and isolated, but not lonely. You're in closer proximity to the elements and the universe. At night the gentle trade-winds feel cool and refreshing on your body after a long day under the blazing sun. There is a greater demand for good seamanship and awareness. Another challenge. It's all about challenges these days.

"The last year has really moved in fast forward, though the vessel is heavy, old-fashioned, and slow. She is not a racer. We've got lots of time, but time passes no matter how slowly you sail.

"In and out of endless harbours and ports. Where were we yesterday? Saint something or other, wasn't it? It all starts to melt together- a Caribbean kaleidoscope of exotic experiences. However, to be honest, sometimes the encounters are not all colourful and exotic. Especially when entering into ports and anchorages in pitch darkness, bad weather, and strong currents. Add to that having wet spectacles, flyspecked charts, and thirteen guys looking over your shoulder who all seem to know better than you."

We had slowly moved south down the island chain with Grenada as our final Caribbean destination. The plan was to continue down along the east coast of South America in order to round Cape Horn. No Panama Canal for us. That would be cheating.

There was a full moon and the conditions were perfect. The new crew that embarked in Puerto Rico were the total opposite of my Atlantic crew of young novices without nautical experience. For this third demanding leg I had taken on a submariner, a couple of mountain climbers, a wilderness survivor, two regatta sailors, a fisherman, a scientist, a policeman, and a psychologist- an assembly of strong and eager experts in their field who worked well together as a team.

I was familiar with the area from a previous visit. We were in the magnificent Grenadines, with our anchor in the sand next to a palm tree on a tiny island appropriately named Palm Island.

The Grenadines are a chain of small islands that lie on a line between the larger islands of Saint Vincent and Grenada in the Lesser Antilles. The northern two-thirds of the chain, including 32 islands and cays, are part of the country of Saint Vincent and the Grenadines. Eight are inhabited.

The captain had by now finally mastered the art of navigation, or at least thought so. He sometimes believed he was the reincarnation of the famous navigator Magellan, a Portuguese explorer and navigator, who became the first European to navigate the Magellan straits in 1520 during his global circumnavigation. The strait became a short cut to eliminate passing around Cape Horn, where we were headed. After reading about the treacherous conditions around the Horn, I was considering taking this short cut as not cheating.

A little zigzagging between the reefs and islands would make the passage from Palm Island to Grenada unforgettable. It would also give us some good practice in preparation for navigating through the Magellan Straits. Captain

Bligh once said, *Those who do not have the nerve will gain no knowledge and skills- knowledge and skills to overcome the challenges ahead.* I was a great admirer of the old breadfruit Captain, and I felt proud when the crew referred to me as Captain Bligh, putting me in the same category as that old authoritarian salt. Yet it wasn't usually awe and admiration they felt when they mumbled under their breaths, *Aye-aye, Captain Bligh.*

From the log: "Eight bells. Time to cast off. Up on the foredeck Captain Bligh briefs the crew on the manoeuvring procedures. He's got the chart memorized, but not taking note of the small print at the bottom of the chart: *It is strongly recommended not to navigate these waters under bad visual conditions, at night, or with the sun in your eyes.*

"As if to emphasize this, the moon dodges behind a cloud. A sudden breeze whispers through the rigging. A sign of warning? An indication that all is not what it ought to be?

"The moon appears again and lights up the young enthusiastic and impatient faces of the first watch. All doubts and hesitation are gone with the breeze, so to speak.

"All hands, light the lanterns. Hoist the main and jib. Get moving, you lazy lot of ladies- if ye don't want to get a feel o' the cat! The crew perform their respective tasks with a smile, as they have done over the past four weeks, tip-toeing on deck so as not to disturb those sleeping below.

"It gets a little brighter as the white sails help to flood the deck with moonlight. All the halyards are neatly hung on their belaying pins- it's all very professional and seamanlike.

"Without the main engine running, bringing up the heavy anchor and rusty chain with the manual windlass is hard work. Slowly the yacht is pulled towards the beach. The bottom falls off steeply here and is not very suitable for anchoring, so the hook is buried in the sand under the palm trees."

Palm Island belongs to John Caldwell. He was the guy who wrote the amazing and entertaining *Desperate Voyage.* Stuck in Panama after the Second World War, with his wife Mary waiting for him in Australia, and with no experience with boats other than playing with one in his bathtub as a little boy, he set off single-handedly across the vast Pacific Ocean in a 29 foot sloop. No cruising sailors ever experience such unbelievable events as single-handers, and I have often wondered why.

In a storm John's little sloop did a head-over-heels (or stern-over-bow) *double* somersault. His narrative describes the incident in detail, including how he later ran out of food, ate his own shoes and drank *engine oil* to survive- come on give me a break!

His story was even more over the top than the yarn from old Tristan Jones, who claimed he poked out his left eye somewhere off Greenland. While fighting the helm in a storm with one hand, he shoved the hanging eyeball back in its socket and claimed afterwards that he could see better than ever before!

Nothing wrong with a good yarn, and John could get away with it because he was such a good storyteller. His sloop was eventually wrecked and he was washed onto a beach, more dead than alive, in the New Hebrides, not too far from his beloved in Australia. John once admitted to me that some of his spectacular yarns were a bit "inflated." His publisher didn't find his book exciting enough, so he threw in a chapter about catching a shark, then fighting for his life when he somehow landed it in his cockpit! He needed to sell *Desperate Voyage* to buy a new boat.

He made enough on his book to buy more than a new boat, he bought an entire island of five acres of mosquito infested swamp, then planted hundreds of coconut palms and built a small luxury resort so he could sell his book to his guests. Not a bad idea, eh?

It's easy and tempting for a storyteller to add a bit of flair to the narrative, but I was never a single-handed sailor. There were too many witnesses present when the faeces hit the fan. Therefore, everything written down here is accurately based on a v*ery* bona fide diary.

Along the beach, the crabs were lined up like soldiers. Their eyes were out on stilts, staring sceptically at us. The anchor crew gave me the signal that the anchor was hanging clear over the bottom. The jib was backed to catch what little was left of the light breeze in the lee of the island, and the bow swung majestically off and away from the beach. The crabs scuttled back down in their holes. The show was over- for them, but not for us.

The surface of the sea was like a mirror, reflecting the stars. They appeared to be not only above and around us, but under us too. It was magic. It's as though we were sailing straight into space.

To the west I could see the lights on Union Island. We were out of the lee of Palm Island. The ocean swell arrived suddenly, unexpectedly, and washed away the starry surface. The wind picked up and the rigging creaked and groaned as if it had developed arthritis after having been stationary for a few days. The vessel heeled, gathered momentum, and trailed a wide green phosphorescent wake.

I could see a white line on the horizon over the bow. It was the surf on the reef off Union Island. To the north was a faint red-flashing light. It was this flashing red guiding angel that would soon give me the bearing so that we could turn south to port on a safe course between the reefs and wrecks towards Grenada. The area had many of reefs and wrecked dreams, because *stupid navigators had not followed the warnings about sailing here at night!*

The crew on the aft deck were ordered to loosen the topping lift on the mainsail boom and to be ready to "fall off" from the wind. The red light was bang on the right bearing. All was going well and according to plan.

"Let go on the main sheet, fall off to port and get ready to jibe!" I said. It all sounded very nautical and grand. Nelson couldn't have done better. The tiller was hard over but my *Fredag* didn't respond! She just kept ploughing forward with a bone in her teeth at the speed of a locomotive running downhill.

This didn't look good, not good at all. The reason for not being able to turn was that the topping lift of the mizzen boom had been loosened instead of the one for the main, so the main boom would not swing out. With the force of the wind on the main with its boom and sail hauled tight, a long-keeled vessel has a real problem turning off the wind. Turning up the other way- to starboard into the wind- would have been no problem. All we had to do was loosen the correct topping lift. But with that done, the sheet for the mainsail became tangled and jammed in its three-wheel block and tackle.

The lookout in the bow yelled, "Buoy dead ahead!"

The boom would still not swing loose due to the jammed sheet, and we were thundering along in a straight line as if we were on a railroad track, rapidly approaching the raging reef. We had already passed our bearing to turn south and safely out to sea. We had to make a quick decision, or more correctly, I had to make a quick decision, while the crew frantically tried to undo the tangled mainsheet. The lookout yelled again that the buoy was only fifty meters ahead. The mainsheet had to be slashed, but the knife that was normally tied to the mizzenmast was missing! Someone had forgotten to put it back after using it to clean fish.

"The bread-knife from the galley, quick! Now!"

Precious seconds flew by before the sheet was cut. The boom swung out without the rope and tackle.

"We can't make it. We can't make it!" I could feel the panic in the lookout's voice.

I grabbed the helmsman by the arm and yanked him away from the tiller, which was silly- it would have been just as quick to relay the order so I could concentrate. But I felt I couldn't trust anyone anymore. I threw myself onto the heavy tiller; I could now clearly see the angry white surf on the reef.

I had three options, but there was no time to think. Starting the engine to go full astern would be like trying to stop a raging bull with a song. Steering hard to starboard into the wind to tack would be difficult without a mainsheet, which left turning hard to port now that the boom was loose, and saying a very quick prayer, hoping that there was deep water behind the buoy. I made my choice and turned hard to port.

The gybing boom knocked off the light on top of the buoy, showering the deck with broken glass. The 40-tonne *Fredag* responded, but so slowly. We were all holding our breaths. Prayers wouldn't help. We were in shallow water; the seas had grown enormous, partially blocking the wind. The shallow water also boosted the current and we were being pushed sideways, nearer and nearer the nasty jagged edge of the ocean.

The girls awoke with all the commotion and came on deck to find out what was happening. They couldn't believe what they were witnessing when confronted with the steep waves on our port side. For one brief moment it seemed we were going to make it when there was an almighty crash. The *Fredag* stopped in her tracks and those of the crew who were not holding on tumbled forward. We were hard aground! On the reef! All hell broke loose.

What now? Before I could think a huge swell picked us up and sent us crashing down onto the coral. Our home rolled over on her side. I could hear glass smashing below.

"No, no, no, this can't be happening! Damned bloody f******' reef!"

It took a moment before I realized what a serious situation we were in. It should never have happened, although the possibility that something like this could happen had always lurked in the back of my mind. We had been aground before, stuck on sandbanks and in mud many times, but never under conditions like this. To run aground onto mud in a protected harbour is no big deal for *Fredag* or for any other vessel for that matter, but this- this was unreal. This was a nightmare. It looked like the end of our wonderful dream.

It took some time before I regained my balance, in body and mind, and could come up with something sensible to try to get us out of this.

"Start the engine! Full throttle astern!"

The swell was high and the propeller intermittently churned the air instead of the sea. We hauled the sheets tight hoping to heel her over, reducing her draft, like it said in the book, but it didn't help. It was difficult to work and stand on the sloping deck with seas constantly cascading over us.

Soon the alarm went off in the engine room. The engine had overheated since the cooling water intake was out of the water! My first mate, Mariann, ripped open the doors, leapt down, and discovered the orange Peugeot diesel billowing blue smoke and scalding steam.

"The fire hose! Water! Quick for Christ's sake!"

The *Fredag* heeled over to an even steeper angle. It was hard to stand up. Floors and decks had become nearly vertical walls or bulkheads.

When Mariann unscrewed the reservoir cooling cap the vessel lurched again, and my mate fell over the burning orange monster. Boiling water shot out of the filler hole and cascaded over her.

This was not the first time the Peugeot had badly injured my first mate- she had severed her right index finger off the coast of Denmark. She hated that engine and the animosity worked both ways. She was immediately lifted up on deck, badly burned. Urgent first-aid advice came to mind.

Submerge the burns in water immediately! Lots of water! We had a whole ocean of it. A bright crewmember had a good idea and reacted quickly. He threw the inflatable dinghy overboard on our lee side. It filled with seawater in seconds and now couldn't be used as a life raft, but it had become a soothing chamber for burns. Mariann was carefully lowered into her semi-floating bathtub.

I soon understood that we could not re-float our yacht without assistance. Each swell rolling in just pushed us further and further onto the reef. To row out an anchor under such conditions was not possible; the dinghy had become a combination of ambulance and hospital bed. The sensible thing to do now was to proceed with distress procedures.

"All hands! Put on life-preservers, fire off distress flares."

Amazingly, all our flares worked. We put out a radio distress call:

"Mayday! Mayday! Mayday! Sailing vessel *Fredag* on the reef east of Union Island! Twelve persons on board, one person badly hurt! Need assistance immediately! Mayday! Mayday!"

Channel 16 on the VHF radio is the operational calling and emergency channel. In the Grenadines it was often clogged with illegal chit-chat, restaurant-bookings, and taxi communication. Now it was as silent as a cemetery. We repeated the call over and over. After half an hour, with our battery power in the red, we made contact with a station ashore. They passed on our message and very soon the radio was alive with chat and advice.

Everyone was talking at the same time creating total chaos. They all had good intentions and advice, but no one actually could come up with a solution. None of the big schooners in the harbour, moored safely behind the reef, dared to venture outside, because it said in the pilot guide: *one should not navigate in these waters at night!*

The coast guard vessel *George Macintosh* was contacted. It was in St. Vincent, 40 nautical miles to the north. It was carnival time and the coast guard crew had to be "located." It was old Murphy's Law again. If any more could go wrong, it would. We had to wait, be patient. Wish them a good carnival. Somebody turned on the tape deck with Bob Marley singing, "Everything's gonna be alright." It made me think of the band playing "Nearer My God to Thee" on the aft deck of the *Titanic*.

A tiny plastic tender with two very brave Frenchmen risked venturing out in the dark to see if they could help. Viva la France! They didn't want to get too near as there was a danger of getting smashed against us or thrown onto the reef, so they kept a safe distance. Two of my crew jumped into the inflatable and paddled out to them, sitting on top of the unfortunate burn victim and paddling against the wind and current in an inflatable full of water. We had to get our first mate to the hospital as soon as possible.

On their next venture my heroic crew managed to fasten a heavy nylon hawser to what was left of the buoy. We tightened up as best we could with the anchor windlass. This helped to put the brakes on being thrown further onto the reef.

Incredible. In spite of all the brutal treatment the yacht was still in one piece and not taking on water. Normally a traditionally built wooden vessel wouldn't last five minutes under such intense pounding. A prayer of thanks went out to the person who advised me to use modern building methods, a heavy concrete keel, and a strong laminated hull.

Just when things didn't look too bad, the news arrived from the aft storage.

"We've sprung a leak! All hands to the pumps!"

There was water over the floorboards in the main saloon. However, no need to panic yet. Our two powerful bilge-pumps seemed able to do the job. The exhaust outlet was no longer submerged as the *Fredag* was now heeled over at an angle of sixty degrees! The flange had been ripped off by the coral and the Atlantic was pouring into the yacht's bowels, where it shouldn't be- seawater should be kept outside the hull.

We stopped the water entering by nailing a cutting board over the hole. The board was covered with a plastic tablecloth to act as a seal. Another huge wave washed over us. The rudder broke. Four inches of laminated pine bolted together with one-inch steel bolts snapped into two as if it was made of plywood. Down below was a total disaster. The large heavy wooden saloon table that could seat 18 had broken loose and was jammed into the opening of the port bunk cabin. Contents of cupboards and books from the library were strewn everywhere.

We reefed down the sails, but it just made her more unsteady, so we set them again, hauling them tight to stop the rolling every time we were hit by a big wave. The radio had gone silent. We were told we could expect the coast guard in the morning. Maybe!

There was not much we could do but hang around and wait until sunrise for our saviours to arrive. We were all more or less in a state of shock. The crew were huddled together on the dry part of the slanting floor, asleep on the cabin floor.

I promised them a hard day tomorrow. I couldn't sleep. I lashed myself to the mizzenmast in the cockpit. Had the seas settled a little, or was it just my imagination? I looked down the companionway at the crew huddled together on the part of the saloon floor that was above water. Believe it or not, they were all fast asleep in their orange survival suits and life preservers, specially purchased for the icy waters and long haul around Cape Horn.

It was a long night. Every time a wave picked us up and slammed us down, it was like my own body and bones were being smashed onto the hard coral reef.

I could see the lights on Union Island where Mariann, standing on the beach, bandaged up like a mummy, was searching for a faint light out on the reef, anxious as hell, but optimistic- hoping that there would still be something left of her home when the sun rose.

I was desperately in need of a cigarette but there were no dry matches or lighters in this watery world. The worst part of waiting for assistance in circumstances like this was not being able to do anything. I therefore kept my sanity through the night by finding a way to light my cigarette. I finally managed this complex challenge with a spark from battery-connected wires and some petrol on a napkin.

Looking down the companionway I wondered how my crew were able to sleep. Why were they not up here keeping me company? Why was no one showing me any sympathy? What were they thinking and what would tomorrow bring?

7. The Sinking

The crew of the coast guard vessel looked unhappy and seriously hung-over. They were not exactly jubilant about being dragged away from their carnival celebrations. They were all dressed in spotless white uniforms which wasn't very sensible considering they messed around with dirty lines and rusty machinery. They didn't seem to have much energy left after two days of partying.

High and dry at sunrise

Their ship on the other hand had lots of power and energy. Although vomiting black exhaust fumes, there was the electrifying sound of horses- thousands of them- enough to pull us off the reef. It was quite a deafening team of horses. Did all Caribbean coast guard vessels have their exhaust mufflers dismantled and dumped overboard? Apparently the genius who came up with this brilliant idea believed this made them go faster, but the movement through the water wasn't the problem, it was getting organised and pulling the crew members out of the town's rum-shops that took time.

Anyway, they were finally here. They were somewhat surprised. They expected to arrive and find the reef decorated with broken timbers and a crew with broken expectations. Instead they encountered a fully intact vessel heeled over on her side, and an optimistic crew enjoying their breakfast on top of a slanting deck-house. They were amazed that such a huge yacht could be forced so far onto the reef.

The wind, waves, and current had subsided. A dazzling morning sun made the sea glitter and sparkle. In spite of the nightmare that I'd just recovered from, I took in the whole scene and could appreciate the beauty of the multi-coloured coral reef.

The *Fredag* was high and dry on her side with her starboard railing underwater. The damage was insignificant; a dented keel, broken rudder, a scratched hull and some broken wineglasses down below which someone had forgotten to stow away. Oh yes, and the smashed navigation light on the buoy- put it on my tab.

Beaming with optimism, we met up with the coast guard officers. My confidence dwindled a bit when I saw that the gunship had two captains. This was bad news. Any difficulty or problem that arose would be magnified 100% with two leaders in command.

There was one black and one white captain. The local black captain looked very distinguished, was extremely well-mannered, and looked like he'd been hauled out from behind a desk. The other was a bad-tempered Brit who was in what he'd call the Third World to train men to be first class coast guard officers. The hungover Englishman just wanted to get back into bed or back to England and I sensed that neither of them were happy about the other's presence.

I presented my plan to the two men. I wanted to wait for high tide, which was only a foot or so in the Caribbean, but every inch of higher tide would make a big difference. Our saviours didn't have time to wait for high water. Was it because carnival lasted only for three days? They wanted to get going at once.

The laminated hull had survived a whole night of serious beating. She should be able to handle a sleigh ride over the coral. Though one of the coast guard's main tasks is to protect the environment, they didn't seem noticeably geared towards environmentalism, and to be honest, all I could think of was to save my life's dream-project, home, and belongings. Under the circumstances, we cared little about the endangered coral.

The tow-line had to be set out at an angle from our bow, on the opposite side from where we were heeled over. We could have a major problem here. There was a risk that we could be pulled upright only to fall onto our other beam, damaging the hull. The two captains were made aware of this possibility, and we had agreed that if this should occur, we would call off the tow and inspect the hull for leaks before continuing into deep water. Even if we didn't topple over we would stop at the edge of the reef to make sure we weren't holed. During my years of messing around with small vessels I'd witnessed too many that were hauled off rocks only to end up in a watery grave.

The coast guard crew picked up the heavy nylon hawser we had running to the buoy. Forty tonnes is quite a heavy load, so we had tied and secured the hawser to the foot of the mast with extra lines to the bowsprit to spread the strain. Three hundred feet out at sea the men in white spoiled their spotless uniforms by handling the seaweed-covered hawser. Then they fired up their three thousand horses- the roar fractured the early morning stillness, and black smoke billowed from their stern. The three-inch nylon hawser audibly snapped as it tightened, forcing out shots of water. But we were not moving. Not an inch. It was like we were glued to the reef.

With a loud crack the hawser parted and came whipping back. We all ducked and were luckily spared serious injury. It wasn't our towline but their own rotten line which they had added to ours! We were all crouched on deck with our fingers crossed, except Sparky, our radio-operator. I joined him below to speak to the coast guard. They reconnected the broken hawser and resumed full power to their engines. The noise was so deafening that it was impossible to communicate over the radio, but we did move a bit, just a couple of inches before the line parted again.

The problem turned out to be a massive head of brain coral under the bow. Out came the long crowbar and sledgehammer. The environmentalists looked the other way. This was a matter of utmost importance and the continued existence of the most gallant yacht to sail the seven seas!

On the next attempt our bow broke loose, but the coast guard vessel veered off to port. The hawser was tied to their stern. If you, dear reader, happen to be an unfortunate boat owner and have ever tried to tow something or someone with a line attached to the back of your dinghy you might have experienced great difficulty in keeping on a straight course. This is the reason why the big towing-hook on a tugboat is positioned amidships. The coast guard vessel was not built for towing with a centre-hook positioned on a cleared aft deck. Their aft deck was cluttered with stupid stuff like guns and mine launchers that most likely didn't work, including a pretty flag and flagpole which the flying hawser had snapped off during their first attempt.

We were suddenly moving forward and we were moving fast! It felt like we were on a train that had jumped off the tracks. The *Fredag* raised to an upright position and then crashed onto her other beam with all her forty tonnes. Fortunately, nobody was hurt. All hands were hanging on for dear life as we lurched and groaned towards the reef's edge. I screamed over the radio, "STOP! STOP! STOP TOWING!"

No response! The coast guard couldn't hear us due to the deafening exhaust. Then the crunching sound of crushed coral against our hull and keel subsided, but it was too late; we had two large holes amidships on each side of a frame- both under the waterline.

At last we were afloat, but water gushed in with pieces of broken coral mixed with Norwegian pickled herring. The herring were dead, so it was no difference to them to be returned from whence them came. We tried to stop the flow by jamming pillows and mattresses into the holes. We soon saw that it was hopeless. It was like plugging a holed Hoover dam with a load of ping pong balls.

"We're going down, we're going down!" I screamed into the mike. "Head towards the beach!"

No answer. All I can hear was my own panic-stricken voice and the roar of the coast-guard's engines.

Heroic Sparky took over the radio communication- or the lack of it to be more exact- while the crew stayed on deck. We tried to get the coast guard's attention by waving and pointing towards the beach, and it seemed as if they now at last recognised the perilous situation we were in. They changed course and started on a long curve towards the narrow opening of the reef, leading to the calm and shallow lagoon behind.

Down below, water had reached Sparky's waist. Amazingly the radio was still working, even though the batteries were submerged, but our saviours were still not answering.

"We're going down! We're sinking!" I screamed, dragging Sparky away from the radio and up the companionway. The rest of the crew were now on the fore-deck which was still above water. The aft deck was awash. Trapped air in the forward cabins and the water pressure under the bow was keeping us afloat, as long as we were moving. This was like the final minutes of the *Titanic*'s demise, without the orchestra playing *Nearer my God to Thee*. The crew were desperately clinging to the forestay; a few had jumped overboard after seeing too many Hollywood productions about people sucked under by the sinking ship. We were all hoping or praying that *Fredag* would reach the beach before going down.

Just when it seemed that our prayers would be answered, the well-trained coast guarders decided to stop to shorten the towline before entering the lagoon. This was the moment that our damaged ship decided that enough was enough, and she started her descent down to Davy Jones locker, down eighteen fathoms into the deepest part of the channel between Palm and Union Island. The crew started swimming away when the water reached their waists. I wanted to be with her as long as possible, so I began climbing the ratlines.

Going down. The captain on his way up the ratlines, some of the crew in the sea and some ready to jump.

I had to climb quickly- the sea was snapping at my ankles- it was a race against the rising sea. I had this strange feeling that my yacht was standing still but the water was rising. I didn't experience the myth about life flashing before my eyes, but time was slowing down, and I was taking in all the little details of the rigging, thinking about the many hours of planning and work to create all the parts that made up this magnificent vessel.

I was right on top of everything, not in the real sense of the word, but up as far as I could climb, sitting astride the white masthead ball, when I had to let go, physically and emotionally. Looking down, the white top of the mainmast disappeared into the abyss with a cloud of rising bubbles. My dream had gone under. A conveyance to King Neptune. No exploding boilers, gurgling whirlpool or suction hole, no screaming sailors being eaten alive by sharks. It was just a very quiet, peaceful, and serene funeral.

Fishermen, tourists and yachties arrived in small tenders to the scene of the disaster. They picked up my traumatised crew and some odds and ends floating up from the deep, with a few exceptions. Nobody gave a damn about the struggling roaches who were frantically trying to board anything that floated, even onto the backs of their own family members.

Like a funeral procession, the small flotilla of tenders headed for the lagoon. All that was left on the surface was a thin film of oil, a tell-tale reminder of *Fredag*'s sad ending. There were a large number of people on the dock- caring spectators with outstretched hands help us up.

All I had left in my material world was what I was wearing- a wet T-shirt, a pair of marine blue underpants and a defeated look on my face. The crowd didn't say much. They didn't need to. They understood because they themselves were sailors. What could I say? I felt I had to be brave and show courage and not fall to the ground weeping.

"So that's the end of that chapter," I said with a forced smile, embracing my bandaged first mate.

I had my back towards the sea and couldn't see the miracle that was taking place behind me.

Clifton Harbour lagoon

"She's coming up again," Mariann whispered in my ear. "She's coming back!"

The *Fredag* has a long wide, heavy keel. Being a wooden ketch with a lot of buoyancy and nearly empty tanks, she ended her sleighride to the lagoon standing upright on the seabed. Perhaps because the coast guard had wanted to salvage their own hawser, our "saviours" had kept towing, through the opening in the reef and into shallow water, dragging our home along the bottom. And now, to everyone's surprise, a mast-top appeared- then a second smaller mast. It re-emerged like the phoenix, a mythical bird that rose from the ashes of its funeral pyre with renewed youth.

Without another word I dove in and swam out to give the mast a good hug. Floating on the surface and looking down, I could see her submerged deck through the clear water. It was like having an out-of-body experience- hovering above what I had always considered a part of myself.

The hotel manager kindly offered us free rooms for a few days. I was approached by a crew member from the coast-guard vessel with an invitation from the two captains to join them for a drink. I declined. I felt they were responsible for the sinking of my vessel. I wanted to raise hell, but decided against it- it couldn't alter the outcome; it would just create an awkward and embarrassing situation, for ultimately the fault was mine for running aground in the first place.

Mariann and I were surprised when half of our hand-picked strong and sturdy crew booked flights off the island, not interested in taking part in our salvage operation, leaving us to deal with our fate.

Island ex-pats, Uwe Gertsmann, a German engineer, and Patrick from Belgium were the first to offer assistance. Patrick was a professional diver and owned a dive-shop with a dozen scuba tanks and a compressor. My T-shirt was not even dry as we sat on the beach with a case of cold beer, drawing and making calculations in the sand. Now how did that old rule go that Archimedes came up with? Uwe knew the answer.

When the sun set with a green flash, a good omen, we had a plan and a strategy.

It was without question a sudden stop in our circumnavigation around the world, and yet it seemed that this wasn't necessarily the end of the line. Yes, I was gradually convinced that what happened was just the first chapter of a future adventure, with many more to come. Perhaps the beer helped.

Night comes quickly in the tropics, as if daylight suddenly gets switched off. I walked to the end of the dock in my newly donated clothes with a pack of dry cigarettes in my pocket that some kind and caring soul donated to a nicotine-starved, desperate shipwrecked captain. I smoked the whole pack. The first mate was asleep, knocked out by painkillers. I couldn't sleep this night either- all the self-criticism and regret didn't help.

I couldn't help thinking that maybe I should have stayed at home and watched the world go by on *National Geographic* or *Animal Planet*, stayed on my sofa reading travel books, maybe to embark on a massive liner for a Caribbean cruise. Just to have lived a normal life like everybody else.

I finally had to admit that there was no point going over and over what I should or shouldn't have done. In the end, I owed a lot to my partner and mate, Mariann, who kicked my ass (and would keep kicking it) to get out of my self-pitying mode and start thinking positively to get the salvage operation started.

8. Archimedes' Principle

Archimedes' principle states that the upward buoyant force that is exerted on a body immersed in a fluid, whether fully or partially submerged, is equal to the weight of the fluid that the body displaces and acts in the upward direction at the center of mass of the displaced fluid.

This principle applies to both floating and submerged bodies and to all fluids. When I first learned of this physical law, I had my own version.

"When you immerse your body in cold water, you leap up with a shriek!"

The *Fredag* was immersed in a fluid with only the top of her masts above the surface, and we needed buoyancy to bring her up. We had to figure out the volume of the seawater she displaced and replace this water with air. But how do you contain a large volume of air inside a sunken yacht?

I could not sleep trying to answer this question when I suddenly had the solution- ping pong balls! I recalled how Donald Duck's boat had sunk and how he'd brought it back to the surface by diving down and filling it up with ping pong balls!

Not much chance of finding a hundred thousand ping-pong balls on a tiny, remote Caribbean Island. But what you would surely find are lots of empty oil drums.

3.14 multiplied by the square radius of the drum multiplied by its height multiplied by 30 oil drums gives an upwards lift, or buoyancy of 30 tonnes. This nearly equalled the *Fredag's* displacement.

Eureka, we had a solution and a plan. There was light at the end of the tunnel. The nightmare was over. I could relax and sleep again.

When I woke up, the sun was high and so were my hopes and optimism. The tops of both masts were still there, as if to show that it was not all a dream. However, after more calculating we discovered that we needed more buoyancy. We had combed the nearest islands and had ended up with 22 empty oil-drums. Not enough.

A second intense search gave the following result: a five-hundred-gallon rubber water tank, two life-rafts, ten plastic jerry cans, a hundred plastic bottles and two ping pong balls.

To end up shipwrecked is quite a traumatic experience. This was the time to show solidarity and courage! Half of my crew were still with me. They had decided to stay with their submerged dream and take part in the salvage work, hoping to continue their voyage around South America at a later stage. And you know what? If the wrecking had to happen, the Caribbean was a jolly good place to do so. It would have been really bad news had the wrecking occurred in the icy and stormy waters around Cape Horn!

The first stage of the operation was for us all to take part in Patrick's intensive scuba diving course.

"If it hurts, come to the surface." Any PADI dive-instructor would not be impressed by such teachings, but we had to get moving as soon as possible. All our equipment and belongings were underwater, deteriorating by the minute.

My first dive inside the wreck was quite an unreal and bizarre event. The visibility was good but the mess was beyond description. A thick layer of oily, indescribable matter was "floating" overhead, trapped by the underside of the deck.

Fredag was a buoyant, wooden boat, so she stood upright with her heavy keel buried deep in the seabed.

Like a weightless astronaut, I hauled myself over to the navigation section. Equipped with a scuba tank and flippers, I just managed to squeeze in behind the chart table. A tiny colourful blue wrasse perched on my shoulder. Together we gazed at the photograph of my beloved ship on the bulkhead. The colours of *Fredag* under full canvas on her maiden voyage were already starting to dissolve. Beside it hung a picture of her designer, Mr. Colin Archer. His expression seemed sterner than ever. I apologized and my mouth filled with seawater.

The ship's heavy safe was the first item to be brought to the surface and transported to the beach. Its contents were still intact. Passports, ships documents and dollar bills were hung to dry on a line between two palm trees. Clothes-pegs were used to fasten the hundred-dollar bills. The gaffs, booms, and sails had now been transformed into a huge tent looking like something Lawrence of Arabia could have built. This is where we would sleep, eat, and store our belongings and other equipment brought up from the deep. Anything that had any weight, from the engine itself to the smallest teaspoon, had to be removed, with the exception of the heavy keel, of course. Anchors, chain, rigging, tools, pots and pans, all objects that could lessen the displacement were brought ashore, making our new "campsite" more homely and hospitable.

After this operation was concluded, we covered the hole in the hull with a rubber mat seal. Nailed in place with a sheet of plywood.

An average of six vessels a year end up on the reefs in the Grenadines. Remnants of small ships are scattered everywhere. The local population are used to seeing the unfortunate owners or renters taking off as soon as they have their insurance compensation verified. The insurance companies can't be bothered doing any salvage work, so the wrecks are left to the elements and to the robbers. Very soon there are very few remains.

The fact that we had not left the scene of disaster surprised the locals. When they learned about our plan to raise her, they seem baffled and claimed that it could not be done and that it would be a total waste of time.

It did not take long before they changed their minds. Encouraged by our optimism, they started to take part in the recovery operation. I had no objections; I needed all the help I could get.

A depth of twenty feet is not a major problem when scuba-diving. We were able to work underwater from sunrise to sunset without having to think about decompression. A one-hour lunch break was all we had time for.

Things were very soon looking much better. My depression had passed. All the self- criticism and blaming of the coast guard was finished. From then on we were entirely focused on one issue. Re-float her!

Working underwater was hard work. Falling asleep at night was not a problem. Every item salvaged brought new energy and it made me aware of the fact that being shipwrecked can also be an awakening and positive incident, offering even more challenges.

The experience of salvaging items that I had taken for granted and now had lost and found again was overwhelming. It didn't really matter that so much had been lost and destroyed. Some losses were greater than others. Photographs, colour-slides, manuscripts and twenty rolls of 8mm film were lost forever. Testimony of our adventures so far, all gone. However, memories are never lost and manuscripts can be recreated.

Worst of all our losses was the antique wind-up gramophone with the irreplaceable scratchy Glen Miller and Louis Armstrong 78's.

The library and the collection of music tapes were a total write-off. Brahms's Violin Concerto sounded like a dozen cats trapped in a spinning centrifuge. Most of the equipment stored on deck had floated off and had been carried away by the current and wind. Friendly local fishermen with wide smiles kept arriving with "presents" for the shipwrecked white sailors. Not one of them claimed salvage money or finder's fees.

More and more locals arrived at the scene- wreck plunderers I kept thinking.

I soon learned they were just offering help, dressed only in shorts and a diving mask. They seemed to come from nowhere, and they were able to hold their breath for an eternity. When underwater, it's difficult to say "Thanks mate," or ask, "Who are you?" Having a conversation just results in a lot of bubbles.

At the end of the working day, most of our helpers returned home and the others became unrecognizable to me in the dark.

"In the dark, all cats are black," goes a saying in Norway.

As a newcomer to the West Indies, I had a problem recognising and distinguishing black people from each other, even on land in broad daylight!

With our helpers wearing masks underwater, they were indistinguishable to me. This phenomena of not recognizing people due to skin colour sometimes worked both ways. Many years later I met a black man in a bar in Martinique who slapped me on the back and exclaimed, "Hey mahn, remember me?"

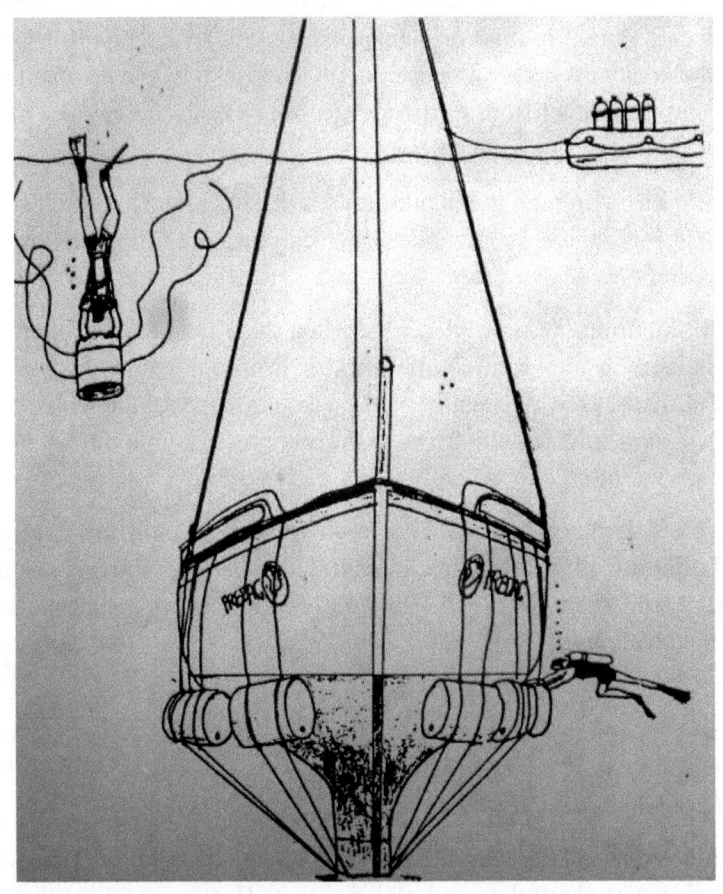

He told me that he had lived on Union Island when *Fredag* sank and that he was one of the guys who had worked by my side for a whole week, fastening oil drums and bringing down buoyancy.

Embarrassed, I pretended to recognize him. I really had no recollection of him at all. What was most remarkable about this encounter was that he had a photograph my yacht sinking, my crew in the water and me climbing up the ratlines on the mainmast (cover and page 96).

Here's the recipe for re-floating a sunken and long-keeled vessel.

Fill twenty-two oil drums with water- seawater- as there is so much of it around. Next, drop them to the bottom and fasten them along the waterline with a network of ropes. These ropes have to be passed *under* the keel. Most of the keel is buried in mud or hard-packed sand, so a scuba-diver on each side of the keel must dig a pit deep enough to crawl into and an opening must be dug under the keel from each side. Ropes to hold the net and drums in place are passed through this opening.

This work was extremely difficult due to stirred-up sand and mud resulting in bad visibility, and a strong underwater current kept filling the pit as soon as it was dug.

When all the drums were in place, we filled them (and all the other airbags and containers inside) with compressed air from our scuba tanks. We only had to fill them halfway because as the vessel ascended, the water pressure holding *Fredag* down would drop and the compressed air in the drums would expand, giving more buoyancy.

We were all working like maniacs, as hard as we could, from sunrise to sunset with only a half-hour lunch break. Hurricane season was just around the corner and there would be suitable conditions for tropical storm or hurricane development.

One of my crew had an ear infection. It was his job to fill the scuba tanks. As soon as an empty batch arrived at the dive-shop, a filled batch went out. The doctor had told Mariann to take it easy and rest as much as possible and to keep her bandaged burns away from salt water.

To tell Mariann to take it easy and rest when there is something of importance going on is an utterly useless undertaking, as ineffective as telling the captain that he must quit smoking.

She was in command of the beach camp. All that was brought ashore and was salvaged had to be sorted, repaired, and cleaned. Food had to be cooked and served. Cuts, bruises, and infections caused by extensive underwater work had to be treated. Entertainment, care, and empathy had to be handed out every evening. However, there was not much energy left in the crew after dinner to do anything else but climb into their hammock and sleep. We were too exhausted to even dream.

After two weeks of digging and mounting the drums we were ready for the ascent. The entire population of Clifton village was standing on the beach with their fingers crossed. The air was thick with anticipation and excitement. On my last dive into the wreck, I found a bottle of cheap Spanish champagne. I placed it on top of the Norwegian flag, tucked into a corner of the cockpit.

One by one we filled the drums with air from our scuba tanks. A long hose from the scuba tank was pushed through the filler-cap hole on the drum, a valve was opened and the air rushed into the drum forcing the water out through the same hole. We only filled the drums half full in order for the expanding air to escape when the vessel would start the ascent. This was basically it, in theory. The time had come to see if it really would work. It was our moment of truth.

I was sitting in the sand by the back end of the keel as the last drum was being filled. The bow suddenly started to rise, only a few inches but then fell back again. Theory is one thing, reality is another. I planted my feet firmly in the sand and grabbed hold of the bottom hinge of the rudder. Buoyancy and displacement must have been right on the point of balance. I lifted with all my might, or what was left of it.

The keel broke free! *Go baby, go!* I thought, still lifting.

"We have a lift-off!" King Neptune could not hold on to her any more. In a cloud of mud and sand she slowly started her ascent. It reminded me of a rocket lift-off from Cape Kennedy.

She started to rise very slowly to begin with, then faster as the air expanded, forcing the water out of the drums and giving more and more buoyancy.

This is unbelievable, I thought- *three cheers to Archimedes*!

I lay on my back, and I could see her hanging over me like a huge zeppelin airship, still rising.

For the people on land it looked like *Fredag* was heading for the heavens. With her bow first, she broke the surface. With the upgoing momentum, she shot high above her waterline, fell back, and rolled slowly from side to side like a huge, happy whale. It seemed as if she was trying to make up her mind if she really wanted to be back afloat. Then she gave off a gasp, some people said later that it sounded more like a fart, and then to our stunned surprise, she sank slowly to the bottom again.

"Houston, we have a problem."

Back to the drawing board.

The calculations were exact enough. What had gone wrong was due to the same problem I had with my first boat, *HMS Explorer*, over three decades before. Upon reaching the surface, the water had rushed back into the oil drum holes, resulting in negative buoyancy.

On the next attempt we had twenty-two swimmers on the surface with caps to plug the holes in the drums.

All was very quiet and the crowd held their breath when the sailing yacht *Fredag* broke the surface for the second time. Within ten seconds all the drums were watertight and German Uwe, our head of operations, gave the thumbs up. The silence was broken by a loud ovation from the crowd on the beach and hoots and bells from the surrounding yachts at anchor.

The flag was flying off the mizzen mast again. The deck got sprayed with champagne, tears flowed and there were fish in the cockpit for dinner, including a huge grouper trapped in the head.

Lines were brought on board, and she was gently towed towards the beach until her keel touched the sand. We wouldn't let her sink again!

An ancient, gasoline-driven pump that looked as if it had been hauled from a museum did the job of pumping the ocean back to where it came from. Slowly to begin with because waves kept washing over the deck and down the hatches.

Low in the water and pumping her out

With water finally barely over the saloon sole we could enter without having to breathe through a mouthpiece.

What a mess! Much of the provisioning done in Puerto Rico for the journey around South America had been destroyed. There had been a lot of food for a crew of twelve for ten months.

The water pressure had crushed about half of all the canned food, including cans of engine oil and paint. This mixture, blended with hundreds of pounds of flower, sugar, pasta, biscuits, and other assorted dry foods resembled a giant fermenting pizza floating in a fetid soup of multicoloured dreck, mixed with a year's supply of toilet paper. It looked suspiciously like the first stage of a sewage treatment plant- and that included the smell!

Smears of fire-engine-red Chinese lacquer defaced everything. Far into the future we would be struggling to remove this amazing paint. Long days of cleaning lay ahead. We were leaking like a colander so the bilge-pumps had to run continuously.

There were no haul-out facilities on the island and no lumber for us to repair the hull. Coconut palms are only suitable to swing a hammock from or offer shade at high noon while you are enjoying a cool pina-colada.

Once more we had to improvise. Without a drydock or slipway we would just have do the job of repairing the damage the old-fashioned way. We attached all our tackle from the mastheads to anchors out in the middle of the lagoon, and hauled her carefully over to expose the damaged hull.

Careening

We drilled small holes around the big ones and "stitched" a network of galvanised wire across the openings, added a few layers of chicken-mesh in-between and cast the entire makeshift repair in concrete covered with tar.

Our leak was reduced to about a gallon an hour. We could live with that, for a while.

My greatest concern was the engine. As soon as it was exposed to air, we filled the cylinders with oil and started to read that wonderful DIY book *How to Rebuild a Diesel Engine Without Knowing Anything About It*.

After I had taken the engine apart and put it back together without any parts left over, the crew were impressed. We held our breath in anticipation as I pressed the green start button.

She started! We simply could not believe our own eyes and ears. A bit unwillingly perhaps, accompanied by clouds of black fumes and some unusual strange noises. It ran like clockwork, but now sounded more like a second-hand Russian tractor, accompanied by occasional clanks and clatter.

The camp was dismantled and everything brought back on board with the exception of a number of items which we really did not really need for the voyage and had been set aside for a planned farewell party.

With a departure date on the horizon, we sat down with the remaining crew around the campfire for the last time to talk about the future. It was a strenuous and difficult meeting.

I had to admit that the *Fredag* was in no condition to continue on her planned circumnavigation. We had lost all our charts and navigational instruments. It would cost more than a second mortgage to replace all the lost and damaged equipment and do the necessary repairs to make her functional and seaworthy again.

By now most of the crew were exhausted by the hard work and upset that it would take a lot more time and effort to continue as planned. They just wanted to go home. We ended the meeting by agreeing to hold a big party first, then sail a hundred miles south to Venezuela to repair *Fredag*. Then we would decide on further action. It seemed a good plan. At least the party side of it made sense.

We had managed to salvage some of the provisions, including half a dozen cases of red wine from the Canary Islands and six bottles of Norwegian aquavit. The latter was actually supposed to be shipped around the world as a consignment for a financial supporter, but at the moment we were forced to make some alterations concerning the consignment.

Dear Sir,

I regret to inform you that your shipment of aquavit from Oslo to Oslo, to traverse the Equator twice en route, has been lost due the sailing ship Fredag hitting a reef and sinking in the Caribbean. Please accept my sincere regrets. If it is of any consolation, I will send you, free of charge, my future book that will describe the horrendous incident in detail.

Signed, PR (Captain)

Linje Aquavit is a potato-based spirit with a special blend of Norwegian herbs to be shipped in sherry casks around the world, twice crossing the equator. The constant change of temperature and the rolling of the ship speeds up the maturation and gives it its distinct flavour.

The owner of the *Sea View Restaurant and Bar*, which totally lacked a view of the sea, let us use his facilities rent-free for our farewell party. There were many names on the final list of invitations, and over a hundred guests for dinner. We served 70 pounds of chicken wings, which had been donated by the *Anchorage Hotel*, fresh cabbages and tomatoes from Janet Wall's garden- another gift- two sacks of potatoes that had survived being under salt water for two weeks, and our salvaged canned food that had been purchased in Puerto Rico for our trip around the Horn. Mariann made medals and diplomas for all those who participated in the salvage operation. Special prizes and honours were handed out. This is how we eventually parted with that stupid crystal vase, the farewell present from the Lord Mayor of Oslo.

The so-called "passed the equator" aquavit bottles (which never did cross the line) had lost their labels so we made new ones, renaming the consignment "Davy Jones' Aquavit," and we raffled them off. Everybody invited got a free raffle ticket. There were speeches, tears, more speeches, toasts, and dancing to calypso steel pan music long into the night.

Non-invited people started arriving, attracted by the loud music. They also had come to congratulate us and take part in the celebration of the most astonishing and inventive salvage operation ever undertaken on the island. For many years into the future, the population of Clifton village remembered the extraordinary salvage operation and the big *Fredag* bash.

I will always remember these two polar opposite images in my mind- the vision of the white masthead ball descending into the deep in a cloud of bubbles, and the raising of the flag after the ascent. They symbolised the ups and downs of life on the seven seas- lots of them!

It was quite a challenge raising the *Fredag,* and I have nothing against challenges. But this one? This one was a bit rough, but rewarding as well. It was also a test, a test to what was to come.

Here's one test that followed, immediately after the "sinking" and based on the ship's logbook.

"We have only a hundred nautical miles to go to the city of Cumana in Venezuela. Cumana has haul-out facilities for fishing-boats and a variety of good, cheap lumber. The repair to the hull and rudder is makeshift and we are not at all ship-shape. Our safety equipment is not up to acceptable standards. The VHF radio has departed the world of frequencies due to a long and salty immersion, the engine has developed perpetual hiccups, the running rigging is heavily amputated, the rudder is temporarily spliced with layers of plywood and some metal sheeting from a washing-machine, and the electric pumps have burned out so we have to hand-pump in shifts, 15 minutes every hour.

"A storm is brewing out east in the Atlantic, heading our way.

"A German sailor has kindly offered to accompany us by following in our wake with his own ketch, and to save our souls if something bad happens.

"The goodbyes on Union Island were hard to get through, especially saying farewell to Uwe Gertsmann. He was our Chief of Operations & Technical Support. Even though he had his own engineering business to deal with he stood by us every day for a whole month. We were now totally broke, so it was impossible for us to repay him with anything else than a hearty handshake. He understood and said, *No problem. Next time you see a similar situation with sailors in distress, pass it on. That's good enough for me. Pass it on!*"

I promised to pass it on. A year further into the future a situation occurred which enabled me to do so. I will come back to that one later. That's another story.

On August 15, 1985, as the pointed peaks of Union Island finally disappeared under the horizon, I made a note in the log that tropical storm Helene was on her way towards us, only 100 miles south-east of Grenada. I got the report as we were leaving, but decided to take the risk of heading out to sea as we would most likely will beat the storm by making landfall in Venezuela within 48 hours.

The barometer and radio were history, but there was obviously something going on. The sky far to the east was dark grey. We were beyond the point of no return when the wind picked up and the temperature dropped- a clear indication that a storm was brewing.

Our German friend was far behind us and a bit more to windward. I could see him reefing down, taking in all sails. Why would he? The wind was still fairly light.

The *Fredag* is a heavy and sturdy vessel, built to deal with heavy weather sailing, because she was originally designed as a rescue-vessel

I now understood her potentials and capabilities and that it would take more than a heavy gust for me to order a reef or two in the sails.

We could now see why our German friend reefed down. A squall was coming straight at us- it would hit him first. It was a white squall, a "twister of the sea." The German ketch was having problems. It heeled over so far that we can see her keel. He had not reefed down his mizzen. The mizzen mast snapped like a matchstick and the ketch disappeared in horizontal rain.

The wind reached such a force through our rigging that it sounded as though we were standing next to a jet during take-off. My first mate was screaming something I couldn't hear. Her mouth was moving, and her long hair stretched horizontally towards the bow. At least we had the wind from astern.

I could not stand unsupported. Once upon a time, when travelling by rail in France, I stuck my head out the compartment window for some stupid reason while the train was doing a hundred and fifty- inside a tunnel!

It felt like than now- hair-raising to say the least. I checked the wind speed indicator but the mast-top sensor was gone. I was not concerned about the wind and hull speed. I was hanging on for my dear life. Visibility was zero- white foam and horizontal rain lashed by back, and it hurt.

Someone down below screamed, "Oh my God, this is the end!"

The jib ripped to pieces. We had to turn into the wind to reef our other sails. This took extra time in a squall- you had to work with one arm and hang on with the other. Fortunately, I had six experienced crew members- strong hands on deck. With all sails reefed and a small staysail set up front, we swung around and resumed our heading south.

The wind was still powerful. We were safely on board, moving with a bit in our mouth. All was well, but I still worried about the chunk of concrete in the hull.

We were sitting in a bar on the island of Margarita sipping margaritas when our German friend arrived. He had actually thought we had gone down and spent several hours searching the area for wreckage.

The squall was part of an early wind spinoff from the tropical storm- an issue I would learn more about in the future.

We were lucky. We'd had the wind from astern with sufficient sea room ahead, miles of deep water with no reefs or jagged edges.

I promised myself never to be north of 12 degrees North in the Caribbean during hurricane season. We had made it to a safe harbour on the north coast of South America, with a few hundred dry dollar bills to buy wood, glue, and some good juicy steaks!

More margaritas first, then off to find a moneychanger.

9. The Moneychangers

Senor Cambio was the money changer above all the rest. His name was actually *Johnny Gambino,* but as the Spanish word cambio means *change* in English, it seemed more appropriate to call him *Señor Cambio.*

After I got to know him, he became *Chonny*. Here's the reason why.

Arriving back on board after I had done the rounds to clear in with immigration, customs, and the port captain, we were greeted on the bustling dock by the ever-present *Guardia National*, a small battalion of heavily armed soldiers. I held out my arms with open hands to show that I was unarmed and came in peace with greetings from the Arctic people far to the north, and that whatever they had heard about treacherous barbaric Viking behaviour was something of a myth.

They didn't understand a word of course and only seemed to be interested in the long-legged and blond female part of my Viking crew. A very short no-nonsense officer- their leader judging by the jingle-jangle on his uniform and cap- growled the very first word I ever learned in Spanish.

"Passaporte!"

He collected our twelve priceless documents and stuffed them in his pockets as if they were entry tickets to a local football match while the rest of his smart platoon stood neatly in line on the dock, keeping at least one eye on the lounging bikini-clad members of my crew.

I could then only do the obvious. I walked slowly down the line of warriors and carefully inspected each and every one of them. They seemed to be amused by this, but Lieutenant "Smart" was not, and that complicated matters a bit. I have since found out that Venezuelans really *do* have a good sense of humour, but army officers are like officers the world over. No sense of humour. Especially the short ones.

What they do like is to be pampered, so, after half a bottle of Aquavit and some tasty pickled herring, he pulled out his miniature army-standard-breast-pocket-photo-album and passed around photos of his beautiful wife for all to see, while his platoon was close to melting in the hot tropical sun.

This same hot sun, ice cold Aquavit, and our low-hinged boom hit him hard on his head as he stumbled up the companionway, and I was afraid things would start to go south again, but they didn't. He gave our flag a smart salute, commenting for the first time in perfect English that we had the Venezuelan courtesy flag upside down.

I apologized and said something about flying a courtesy flag upside down was an old Viking tradition- welcoming anyone on board to *drink* themselves upside down!

When we asked Lieutenant Smart where we could change our greenbacks, he told us that the bank exchange rate was 17 Bolivars to the US dollar, but that in a special, sleazy back-street bar, one could get 100 or more. That was illegal, of course, he said with a smile, performing a slashing gesture across his throat.

The reason for the extremely high black-market rate was a new government restriction on the importation of foreign goods. He said he would put us en contacto with an amigo of an amigo as his amigo's amigo needed hard cash to buy outboard engines, and that a certain Corporal Castro would be with us at one six zero hours local time, seguro.

Corporal Castro arrived in an old steaming jeep two minutes before the appointed hour. He really did look like old Fidel with his beret, camouflage fatigues, wild beard, and a huge Havana stuck out the corner of his mouth. My Danish friend, Captain Christian of the *Nana* and I jumped into the back of the jeep and we sped off.

We had a plan. Christian was to carry the cash as he could run the fastest, and I was to do the talking, as by then I had learned a few Spanish words. He was to hand over the dollars and I was to accept the foreign notes, but under no circumstances was he to deliver our US dollars before I had the wad of Bolivars pocketed. If we had to make a quick get-away we agreed we would split the dollars between us pronto and run like hell in different directions to confuse the enemy, hopefully raising the odds of saving half of our funds. If the exchange rate was not higher than a hundred to one, we would back out of the deal.

Castro put the pedal to the metal of the wheezing rickety old jeep, ignoring traffic lights and glancing contemptuously over his shoulder, as if checking to see whether we were being followed. It seemed that every time he turned around, we hit or managed to run over something. Daring to look back at one point I saw at least one dead dog and something that might have been a chicken in its former life.

We finally screeched to a halt in a remote uninhabited industrial area of town outside a small door. It was located in the middle of a larger metal sliding door of a huge neglected warehouse.

ERCURY, the sign by the door tried very hard to advertise, with an election poster pasted over the M. We were glad to get out of the jeep but Fidel made no move to accompany us, and as he roared away he shouted something that could have been, "You're on your own now, jerks. Good luck! You'll need it!"

Christian and I hastily went over our plan and then cautiously knocked on the door. That door reminded me of those low entrances the Vikings astutely built into their dwellings so that when an unwelcomed person entered, he would have to bow his head. This clever ploy made it easier for him to be decapitated!

We may just as well have knocked on a lost Egyptian tomb. No cheerful response or recorded friendly voice greeted us saying, *Welcome to the Illegal Mercury Exchange. At the tone, please give us the secret password.*

I tried banging on the door with my Swiss army knife to give it more weight, when a deafening crash made us leap from our skins. It was as if the god of the Black Market Cambio was answering, but then came the familiar sound of an electric buzzer. I pushed open the rusty door- its hinges creaked in agony.

It was dark inside, and the smell of death and decay engulfed us. We looked at each other, uttering the same words at the same time, "After you, mate."

The door closed behind us with a crash and a click, and the echo hung for several seconds. As my eyes became accustomed to the dark I discovered we were in a large, coffin-shaped hall with flattened cardboard boxes, a chewed-by-something Stephen King novel and some corroded engine parts strewn around the floor. At the far end stood a platform lit by a naked bulb hanging from the ceiling. We could have been in the Hall of Valhalla. It seemed as if the gods themselves were there, one sitting behind a desk and two more standing on either side, like Odin and his two raven messengers.

"Come in!" the order rolled down from the platform. We were already in, and I just wanted to get the hell out, but Christian pushed me towards the desk, and we warily moved nearer to the stage. I had a flashback of a similar walk, taken in a former life, up the aisle to get married. I had wanted to run away then, too!

The scene resembled one from a *Godfather* film. Don Corleone himself- big, fat and bald- sat behind a desk about the same size as a Toyota pickup, with two gorillas standing on either side. They were as bald as their boss, and they had the same deadpan expression on their faces.

"Come in." repeated the left gorilla.

Bravely staring into the Godfather's eyes, I spoke. "As far as I can see we *are* in, your honour, and we would like to have this matter settled as soon as possible. We have other important business…"

"What is your name?" demanded the Don. "Johnny," I lied. "And your friend's name?" "Uh, he's Johnny too."

There was a moment of serious thinking on the part of the Godfather, probably trying to figure out if these two morons could actually have identical names.

"And what, may I ask, is your name, sir?" I put to him before he could reach a conclusion.

"Chonny."

"And your bodyguards?"

"Chonny Tres and Chonny Quatro."

Well, so much for the formal introduction, I thought. The next question fell upon us. "How much you have?"

"Nine hundred and eighty, minus two per cent for bad lighting." I joked, hoping it would ease the tension a little.

"Me see."

I nodded to Christian and he put a neat stack on the edge of the desk. Shit! We had already broken Rule Number One. The left-hand gorilla picked up the stack and slowly counted it, licking his fingers after every tenth bill.

When he had finished, he selected two bills at random and held them up to the light, one after the other, scrutinizing them with one eye closed. Next he took out another two, held them up to his nose and sniffed.

He then did a second count and passed the whole lot over to the right-hand gorilla, while whispering something into the Godfather's ear. The right-hand gorilla repeated the procedure as the Godfather sat like a statue, staring out at some distant point well above our heads. The Godfather himself made a final identical inspection, and then put the wad back neatly on the edge of the desk. As he seemed satisfied, I asked, "And how many Bolivars for one dollar, my friend?"

"Seventy-one" he replied without hesitation. "No, we want one hundred, and we will throw in the rubber-band for free!"

Christian kicked me on the ankle and corrected: "He means one hundred and twenty-one."

"Seventy-one."

"One hundred and twenty-two." Christ, I was so nervous, I was bargaining uphill! "Seventy-one."

This was going nowhere. Determined not to break Rule Number Two, I looked at Christian and jerked my head backwards, the signal for *we're out of here*, and took back our wad of cash. I had my hand on the door-knob when a voice boomed, "One hundred, okay!"

We turned back.

The Godfather next pointed at the vacant spot on his desk. We both leaned over and looked very closely at the spot but did not discover anything wrong with the varnish. It took some time before I got the message. I was becoming more relaxed now, so I shook my head and beckoned him with two fingers to fork out his part of the deal.

He reached down to a side drawer in his desk, and I went all jelly and cold. *Jesus, this is where he brings out his piece*! This was it. But instead of a gun, he brought up five stacks of bills, each eight inches tall. He proceeded to stack them in front of him so high I could only see the top of his bald head, which resembled a full moon. I started counting, and eventually I was through with the first pile, bound with a rubber band. As the others were of the same height, I multiplied the amount by five.

Then I just could not resist. I pulled out two notes, held them up to the light and studied them- which was ridiculous as I had never seen a Venezuelan banknote and might just as well have been examining Afghan monopoly money. I finished off this piece of theater with the sniff test.

The three amigos behind the desk were still stony faced and pretended to be gazing out at that same distant spot. I beckoned to Christian to do a count, which he did in a similar fashion. It was when Christian reached the sniffing part that the left-hand gorilla started giggling. It spread to the right-hand man, but the giggles were abruptly stopped when the Godfather reached into the drawer on the other side of his desk. Oops! I knew it. *I knew it!* I visualised myself staring down the barrel of a 45 magnum!

Not to worry. It was only to bring forth three small dirty glasses and half a bottle of Black Label. His stern face suddenly broke into a million small wrinkles, and he began shaking all over, giggling, and soon he was roaring with laughter. So, we all joined in, and between his outbursts he gasped for breath, held his enormous stomach and proposed three toasts: one for his and everyone else's hero Simon Bolivar, whose face appears on every Venezuelan banknote; one for Ronald Reagan, who never got to have his portrait on a banknote though he tried his best, and one for all the "Chonnys" in the world.

The gorillas got no Black Label, so they stopped laughing.

Lieutenant Smart and Corporal Castro were waiting outside, cigars and jeep smoking away, and we piled ourselves and all the money into the back seat and yelled to him to put his foot down, *rapido!*

"And don't look back!"

10. The Art of Passing it On

The last of our "Cape Horn" crew flew home. It took us two days to knock out the reinforced concrete patch under the waterline. Bit by bit, we demolished our makeshift repair with the help of a powerful pneumatic drill, hammer, and chisel. Our home and means of transportation were almost a wreck, most of our equipment had to be disposed of and the engine was ready for the junkyard- where it had once come from. We just managed the bill from the shipyard for hauling out, a load of wood, three gallons of epoxy glue and a bucket of paint. The VAT was settled over a bottle of whisky in *Bar Stalingrad*, and the friendly yard manager made an exception to let us do the work ourselves.

After two days at the shipyard and with our home floating satisfactorily in the marina without a leak, we were delighted to discover that we had done a good job. The bilge was drier than happy hour at a rehab centre. We still had some wine left over from the Union Island party, but our safe was empty.

We decided only empty hearts and heads could hold us back, not an empty safe.

In spite of having no qualifications, I landed a job teaching English at the University of Cumana. They hired me so that their students could hear a "correct" English accent and pronunciation, spoken by a Norwegian.

A temporary work permit cost the same as a year of teaching and when, after five weeks, it was discovered that my students were speaking English with a heavy Norwegian accent, it was time to say goodbye. Another reason to quit was that I did not have a work permit and I was not really keen on spending time in a Venezuelan prison for working illegally. It seemed our best option was to return to the homeland.

My grandfather's pocket watch didn't even cover a flight to Miami. Would it be possible to hitch a lift all the way back to Norway?

After a series of rides on various dubious floating means of transportation, we reached the French island of Martinique where I exchanged my grandfather's pocket watch for two stand-by tickets with Air France to Paris.

I had a strange and uncomfortable feeling on the eight-hour flight across the Atlantic. A feeling that all my dreams had gone down the drain, having to return back to where I started out. Heading the wrong way through the jet stream at five hundred miles an hour, sardined into a narrow seat in the centre isle of a Boing 747 with no leg-room, not able to look out to see the sea, breathing canned oxygen mixed with the breath from nearly three hundred other passengers, not being able to smoke or drop a line to catch fish- this did not seem right. I survived with the memories of freedom on the open seas, fresh fish, warm trade-winds, sunshine, balmy nights in the cockpit, and moving along at a slow and natural pace.

November was certainly not a suitable time of the year for us two to hitch-hike through northern Europe. Our survival was only due to fact that we stumbled over a Salvation Army clothing outlet. In four layers of t-shirts and Air France blankets and sandals inside four pairs of cotton socks, a helpful trucker who picked us up said we reminded him of a movie about a couple of football players, victims of a plane crash who had crossed the Andes in South America dressed in layers and layers of their dead teammate's clothes.

We accomplished the last leg on board the overnight ferry from Kiel to Oslo. The captain accepted us as stowaways and let us spend the night in the cafeteria- if we promised not to tell anyone. When he realized that we were ship-wrecked mariners, he took pity on us and invited us for dinner. He had tears in his eyes when I got to the part where the *Fredag* rose to the surface. After coffee, liqueurs, and cigars we were escorted to a first-class cabin with a Jacuzzi and a "balcony" view over the ocean.

You could hear a pin drop in the large assembly hall at the Norwegian Maritime Museum when I showed the colour-slides from D-day- disaster day.

All the 500 seats were taken by small-ship owners and people with dreams. I noticed my audience squirming in their seats when I described the Big Crunch and our beautiful yacht's descent into Davy Jones' locker. The applause felt good- and so did the profit from the ticket sales and earnings from newspaper interviews.

Despite the lure of a few warm gatherings of friends and family around log fires with pickled herring and aquavit, we made the decision that the land of low temperatures and no midday sun was no place for us. My theory was that homo sapiens were born and evolved in the tropics. If not, we would've been covered in thick fur. As we had no winter clothing, it didn't take us long before we were once more on our way to the tropics.

We were now able pay our way by ferry to Copenhagen. The bartender recognized us from the newspapers and the drinks were on the house. In contrast, the Aeroflot flight attendant from Copenhagen to Colombia via Cuba was not at all service-minded. After we complained about the rotten egg for breakfast, the stewardess gave us a pitiful look and said, *Better luck next time.*

I should have known not to complain when travelling on Aeroflot. Travel is like an endless university. You never stop learning.

The *Fredag* was almost ship-shape again, but there was not enough money left for a new engine. Not to worry. We had signed an agreement with a Norwegian charter company tucked away in some remote place so far north that the inhabitants hadn't seen the sun since it crept over the mountain ridge at midsummer- on the 21st of June! A fax from the manager of Sunshine Tours told us that a group of twelve punters would be waiting for us in Trinidad in ten days.

They would bring pickled herring, lumpfish caviar, brown goat cheese, and 1300 US dollars in cash. It was a two-week charter ending 200 miles further north in Martinique. A new group would be waiting for us there for a two-week long charter in the Grenadines. Life was beautiful again. We set sail for Trinidad as soon as we landed in Caracas.

We once more had a new crew. Three young Danish backpackers materialized as we were preparing to cast off. They wanted to hitch a ride to Trinidad where the annual carnival would be held the following week. Since we were heading to Trinidad, they were more than welcome to come along for the ride. Even though Mariann was as good as three able seamen, it was always reassuring to have extra hands on deck.

The distance along the north coast of Venezuela from the port of Cumana eastwards to the island of Trinidad is about 100 nautical miles. This time of the year there was very little wind, quite an onshore swell, and a strong current against us. The light winds during the day were right on our nose. However, there was a way. According to the British Admiralty's Sailing Directions, dated 1898, if we kept within five pistol shots from the mountainous shoreline, we would, during the months from November to March, most likely encounter a slight east-going counter-current. It was now December, and we were going east towards Trinidad. After a quick search in our Encyclopedia Britannica, we worked out the distance for a pistol-shot to be about 1200 feet, or 0.2 of a nautical mile plus some leverage for dodging protruding rocks and reefs. I discovered that by shining our powerful searchlight on the shore, I could get a rough estimate of a distance of one mile. If we saw nothing, we were too far out. If we saw a seagull off the bow *standing* on something under the surface, rather than *sitting* on the surface, we were too close.

With full throttle on the engine we were able to move along at a steady 4 knots. A slight current aided us along. We should be able to do the 200 miles in 48 hours, giving us sufficient time to get ready for our first charter and then celebrate carnival. As we passed the half-way mark, five recommended pistol-shots off the village of Morro de Puerto Santo, our engine stopped with a loud crunch and a groan. Our propeller had picked up the rope from a fish trap. Fish traps along this coast were normally put out about five pistol shots from the shoreline. You just can't win.

Between the engine's flywheel and the gear box there was a connection called a damper-plate- a steel plate consisting of an intricate system of springs- a miracle of modern engineering. It was supposed to take up shock and protect the engine and gear box if the propeller hit something like a whale or a submerged log- or a length of rope tied to a fish trap.

No problem. We have two weeks to go before our charter guests arrived in Trinidad with long-awaited cash and pickled herring. Plenty of time to tack our way against the prevailing winds and current.

Unfortunately, it's against the laws of aerodynamics to sail directly against the wind. We had to crisscross, or to use a more nautical term, tack at an angle to the wind. A technique that worked well when there was wind, but it still increased the distance and took more time. It was necessary in the good old days when the combustion engine had not yet been invented, the good old days when sailors sailed. No problem, we would sail.

However, there was a problem. It was too risky to tack so close to land without having a working engine. We had to take long tacks out to sea and back to shore, with only a light breeze during the day and complete windless nights. The off-shore current was dead against us. After a week of tacking we managed only sixty miles. We had another forty to go.

We passed Puntas, the three-pointed cape. We set off from the protruding cape at sunrise, headed back from far out at sea at midday and arrived at sunset at the cape only a pitiful hundred yards further on from whence we started. Our Danish crew proved themselves as first class professional sailors, constantly trimming the sails. They kept us moving forward at the closest possible angle to the wind, which was not very close in an old-fashioned gaff-rigged tub like *Fredag*.

A voice from the galley announced that we were running short of provisions, but had enough porridge to last us at least a year. I hated porridge, carnival was underway in Trinidad, the trolls would be arriving tomorrow, we were only half way there, and we had no way of contacting the punters. Our VHF radio had perished in the water off Union Island. There were no telephones ashore. No roads. Only a very steep and high mountain range covered with dense rainforest nearly all the way to our destination.

There was no sign of life on these shores and the area was notorious for piracy. We saw occasional lights at night- most likely fishing boats. We extinguished our navigation lights just in case they were out for other reasons than to catch fish.

Depression set in. We were not going to make it. After a two-week struggle against the elements, our fix indicated we still had another 30 miles to go.

A sail on the horizon. A tiny yacht. We "flashed" them with our bathroom mirror. They changed course and came along-side. They promised to call Port of Spain's harbor master with the message that *Fredag* was a bit delayed, but underway, and not to worry. I hoped that our charter guests were clever enough to make inquiries with the harbor authorities when they couldn't find us.

After sixteen days at sea, covering a distance along the coast of only 170 miles, the wind died completely. We were now moving along in the wrong direction, or more accurately, we were rolling along sideways to the long Atlantic swells in the wrong direction.

More depression set in. We tried towing *Fredag's* 30 tonnes with the rubber dinghy equipped with a two-horsepower outboard engine on its stern. This proved impossible in a swell- it was a daft idea.

I decided to try the last resort and do some high-tech engineering; to repair the engine on a rolling and heaving workshop.

We disconnected, then lifted out the 300 pound gear-box from the engine room and secured it with a network of ropes to various secure points in the galley- not an easy task while pitching and rolling. The broken springs were assembled in plastic sleeves, cannibalized from a fishing rod. All the bits, springs, bolts, nuts and collets were put back in position and covered with a thick layer of epoxy. After 18 hours of work, our make-shift damper plate was mounted on the flywheel, and with the gearbox positioned and connected, I said a prayer to Poseidon- the Greek God of the Sea.

I started the engine and with the engine slowly turning over, I inched the gear lever forward.

We all held our breath. The propeller shaft was turning.

A loud crunch. The engine was running, but the shaft had come to a standstill.

We repeated the whole operation. This time we put our reinforced epoxy "cake" in the oven for it to harden properly.

Success! We were moving along at two knots. I dared not push it. Two knots seemed like moving along at the speed of light.

Before we knew it we were in the *Boca del Dragon,* The Dragon's Mouth, the strait between the northeastern end of Venezuela and the island of Trinidad. The strait was named for its many teethlike, rocky islets and unpredictable strong winds and current, all hazardous to navigation. In the days before steam and diesel engines the strait was one of the world's largest ship cemeteries. However, we had an engine, and it was working. We now had a strong current of more than four knots running with us. We had needed a bit of luck. Had we arrived any later, the strong current in the strait would have been against us.

A big yellow catamaran passed us on its way out of the strait. It seemed as if they were not moving as we thundered along, passing close by. People on deck were waving to us. They were shouting something, but we couldn't hear them due to the rushing water. We politely waved back.

After running up the steps to the harbour master's office in Port of Spain's marina, we discovered that there had been no message from our guests and the office had not received any message from the yacht we'd contacted last week. It turned out the message *had* arrived, but at the harbor master's office for *commercial* shipping, which our guests had not checked out. Couldn't blame them. We were a yacht, not an oil-tanker.

A sailor in the marina informed us that our guests had given up waiting, had chartered a big yellow catamaran and had just left for Martinique.

We immediately set sail for Martinique, hoping to find our punters on the way.

There are about two dozen islands along the Caribbean island chain between Trinidad and Martinique. We wouldn't find them- the trolls, not the islands.

We'd blown it- 999 pounds sterling, five jars of pickled herring, and all the rest of it. Even our high hopes had vanished.

Pierre in Martinique was a diesel mechanic. At least that's what he claimed to be. We discussed the price and he said that it was a very good and special price- complete overhaul, including parts, and finished within two weeks, *garanti mon ami*. Ten thousand francs in advance. There were still four weeks to go before the next guests arrived.

Two weeks passed and I stopped by the workshop. The engine was strewn across the floor in individual parts. A young boy who was repairing a bicycle said that the *mécanicien*, Monsieur Pierre, was visiting his sick mother in France.

The day before the charter guests arrived, Pierre finally appeared. He demanded five thousand more francs; the diesel pump had to be replaced which he had not counted on. A whole day passed with quarrels and language difficulties. We had no more money than what he said it would cost, and that amount was exactly what we would get from our guests. It ended up with him allowing us to pay the rest later, if Mariann gave him her grandmother's pearl necklace as security.

Two taxis arrived with a load of middle-aged and enthusiastic Norwegians. The engine had been assembled, with only a few parts left over, but the bill had to be paid before the Peugeot came on board, and unfortunately, that couldn't happen until tomorrow afternoon, *peut-etre*. I was about to lose it, but somehow I managed to keep my anger under control. It would give my charter guests a bad first impression if we were to behead the Frenchman. One must have such things in mind when chartering. Our entire future depended on a successful completion of this cruise.

I gave Monsieur Pierre a broadside with all the verbal fire-power I could muster. He didn't really understand what French nuclear bomb testing in the Pacific had to with the repair job.

Neither did I, but it helped let off some steam.

A helpful Swedish sailor solved everything by taking my charter-guests on a spin around Martinique, and I threw in a few cases of beer, six bottles of wine, and a bucket of ice-cubes, and regretted everything bad I ever said about our brotherly Swedish neighbours.

There seemed to be a light at the end of the tunnel, but the engine still had problems starting. When it finally decided to run, everything was just as before- almost no power, and it spewed out black exhaust and oil. I was told that Pierre was with his sick mother again. The supportive baker across the street told me that he hated the mechanic and that he was hiding out in a nearby bistro.

I grabbed hold of a policeman on the street, as if that could do me any good. He did not understand a word of English. I was about to go ballistic again- boiling over with anger. A passing-by motorist pushed me onto the pavement with his bumper and screamed something incomprehensible. Since I didn't understand French, I responded with body language, twisted off his side mirror, and recommended a certain Frenchman who could fix it for free when he returned from his sick mother.

It was time to get out of Martinique.

My guests turned out to be a lively lot of merry Vikings. We set sail with fair winds. No more problems, we thought. They were an active gang of punters, especially when it came to raising the glass. They started with aquavit for breakfast and continued throughout the day with beers and petit punches in large quantities. These punches were always accompanied by traditional drinking songs. I finally relaxed and Pierre and Grandmother's pearl necklace soon passed into oblivion. Our guests were happy, the weather was great, and the cooler was full. After a full day's sailing south to the next island, St Lucia, with our garbage full of empty bottles, we approached the north coast of the island of Saint Vincent.

"Look Captain, over there, fireworks coming out of the volcano."

Close to the rocks, below the volcano, a red parachute flare slowly fell into the sea. A beautiful two-masted schooner lay broadside, dangerously close to the angry surf near the shore. We changed course and sailed over to check them out. As we sailed closer they shouted that they were in desperate need of assistance. Their propeller shaft coupling had broken and the shaft has slid back and locked the rudder to port. It was too dangerous to jump overboard to fix it in the choppy seas. They were requesting a tow, and they needed it fast- they were drifting close to the rocks.

Our passengers were not skilled sailors so it would be easier to manoeuvre by engine power. Of course, the engine didn't start.

"Haul in on that rope you are standing on."

"Tie the loose end of the line on your left to that thing by your right foot."

"Grab those big white rubber balls and tie them to the outside of the railing."

"Heads down now, everybody."

All this wasn't very maritime-sounding, but in such circumstances, anything went. It was vitally important to make myself understood.

And the situation was critical. There were children on board the disabled schooner. They were all wearing orange life jackets and the life-raft was already in the sea, tied alongside her starboard beam. We came about and tacked up towards her to do another pass. We had a lifeline ready, attached to our new two-inch hawser. I threw them the long, thin line with a small sandbag on its end, but they were unable to grab it, even though it landed close to where it was supposed to land, as it always had when I was a boy-scout. My past as a scout was notably unsuccessful, with the exception of throwing a life-line to someone who had fallen through the ice.

Our towing hawser was too heavy to throw and it fell into the sea. We shouted that we would pass again, and that they must throw a line to us, with the wind. We made a new, somewhat daring attempt. This was our last chance, and their last chance as well. Under foresail alone we sailed towards them downwind as close to the schooner as possible- so close we could almost lay our hawser on their deck. There was no need for them to throw a line. We had just enough speed to manoeuvre.

"Quick! Tie the hawser to the foot of the foremast, not a cleat, for God's sake."

The yacht was called *Balliceaux*, named after the uninhabited islet east of Bequia. She was a newly built sixty-foot, very heavy schooner, so I was prepared for the worst. Something was bound to break.

I ordered my crew to lie down on deck. Just in time! The crew on the schooner whipped the hawser around the foot of their mast, and it suddenly tightened with water spurting from the strands. The hawser made a cracking sound but held its enormous load. We had caught the biggest fish yet on the end of our line!

Because the schooner's rudder was locked to port, she wished to go only one way- towards the land. But the *Fredag* was a heavy vessel. She was designed and built to tow a large fleet of small fishing-vessels under terrible weather conditions. With all our sails set, we slowly powered the larger *Balliceaux* away from the treacherous rocky shore with a rather unwilling and beautiful lady in tow.

We turned south and were now in the lee of the volcano. A man was hauling himself along our hawser in a small inflatable dinghy. Richard, the owner of the *Balliceoaux,* climbed over our stern. The million-dollar yacht was on her maiden voyage with his family and crew from Taiwan to Australia. He was a happy man. Very happy. He said that they had been calling the coast guard on the radio for over four hours with no result. He'd tried to call us too, but we still had no radio. He wanted to discuss a price for the salvage operation. He made me aware that the boat was newly built, but still uninsured. I remembered what we had promised Uwe on Union Island, the German engineer who'd helped us so much with our own salvage endeavour.

It felt good to be able to say, "Forget it, we were sort of bored, and it was great to have some excitement along the way. A good bottle of wine will do."

I wasn't talking on behalf of my entire crew. Most were unenthusiastic about the rescue, in spite of no one getting hurt, with the exception of an insurance salesman who had a bump on his head- *'cause he didn't follow orders to lie flat*! He deserved to be keel-hauled for not doing what he was told!

We towed *Balliceaux* into a small bay. A case of wine and a bottle of superior Cognac was dumped on our deck before we had dropped the hook. Both vessels were anchored in a calm and idyllic bay with only one small building. *Wallilabou Bay's only and best fish restaurant*, read the sign on the beach. This was pretty obvious as it was the bay's only restaurant. But would it be the best if there were more? Our guests decided to check it out.

Before Mariann and I had all the sails packed, our charter-guests had placed themselves around the restaurant's only table. Scandinavian guests unfortunately do not have the habit of inviting their hosts along when they eat ashore. It was salted porridge on board for me and my mate. Mariann got the knack for making salted porridge after a charter with a Scottish farmer. I hated the stuff, but couldn't do anything about it- she was in charge of the galley and the finances.

Balliceaux's owner/captain noticed the Viking invasion at the restaurant. He called the proprietor over the radio and said, "Let them eat and drink anything they want, and as much as they want. I will pick up the tab in the morning." This, of course, was unbeknownst to us.

"Wow, they're really out on the town tonight," I said to Mariann while I saw through the binoculars that huge plates of lobster and buckets of champagne were being placed on the table. Mariann said nothing while she mashed out lumps in her porridge.

Our guests wanted to visit as many islands as possible. They seemed to believe that the more islands they visited, the more they would get for their money. They were up before dawn, and they knocked back several glasses of old Danish aquavit before the sun was over the horizon, ready to haul in the anchor before I had one leg out of my bunk.

Eventually they had the right tan and had used up all their film. At the end, everyone was happy, and of course they promised to return next year.

And it really had gone well, considering. Occasionally, the engine started, and we could recharge our batteries so that our guests didn't have to sit in the head (toilet) in the dark. The insurance salesman was a bit upset after being hit on the head by a block during the salvage operation, but I assured him that the incident would only add more spice to the story after he arrived home to tell it.

We waved goodbye at the airport and collected on all the empty bottles. I called our agent in Norway to say that the last trip went above all expectations and asked when the next guests were coming. I was told that there would be no more guests, the company had gone bankrupt.

The large book on diesel engines, over six hundred pages, was still intact after being submerged for several days. I took the engine apart and found cracks in the cylinder liners. Mariann made a little doll, looking similar to Monsieur Pierre, and we stuck long needles into it while mumbling voodoo curses and threats. With the engine block in a supermarket trolley, I took the bus to a recommended mechanical workshop.

The industrialized world's throwaway mentality had not yet reached the West Indies. Everything here could be fixed and recycled, said one of the five mechanics who owned a workshop under a tarpaulin between two breadfruit trees. A radio played reassuring music- "Everything's gonna be alright" from Marley's *Three Little Birds*. The oldest and most experienced of the five took a brief look, shook his head, spat something brown onto the sand, and said two words.

"New engine."

The dreaded Peugeot was thus written off and ended up as a permanent mooring for a friendly Vincentian fisherman. We had fresh tuna for two days and graved tuna for the rest of the month. Before the engine was dumped over the bow, I drew a picture of the Frenchman on it- with a knife sticking out of his back.

Back on Bequia, now our "home" base, there were tourists everywhere who craved for a little sailing trip to the other Grenadine islands, but the problem was that nearly every evening they had to arrive at a restaurant or find a telephone to call home, or to have their flight departures confirmed so they wouldn't miss their flight home. It wouldn't be fair to have them stranded on the ocean waves in windless conditions with no motor to watch their flight pass overhead.

The ship's safe contained passports, ship's documents, two silver buttons, one dead cockroach and seventy-five US dollars. I found a bottle of red wine that I'd managed to hide from the thirsty trolls, and we decided to drink it and head north to Florida. I'd heard that Florida was a good place to sell boats. We could then buy a Harley Davidson with a sidecar and head to California to build a new and smaller boat to sail around the world. It seemed to be a good plan- better than selling the boat here for a load of bananas and flying back to Norway. The sea was our home.

Just as I was about to pop the cork on the wine, believe it or not, the *Balliceaux* entered the harbour. They had thought that the entire charter group at the restaurant were their rescuers and had planned to meet us the next morning, but we had already left Wallilabou. They had somehow heard the story of how the owners had been left on board eating salted porridge, and they'd sailed around for weeks trying to find us. They'd also learned about our hopeless financial situation and wanted to help. We stood firm on what we had promised. If their yacht had been insured, it would have been a different matter. But we couldn't refuse the invitation for a night on the town. How about some lobster and champagne?

Early the next morning *Balliceaux* was gone. They had sailed on their long journey to Panama to cross the Pacific. But during the night our new friends had sneaked on board *Fredag* without waking us or our hopeless watchdog. When we eventually awoke around noon, heavily hung over, we found an envelope on the chart-table, an envelope stuffed with hundred-dollar bills, and a brief message reading:

"How can you save us again if necessary if you don't have a proper engine. Get yourselves a new one."

We were told we could find a good second-hand engine at a reasonable price in Venezuela. We set our course south again. We had plenty of time. We made landfall on every island along the way. On one of these, we met a hotel owner who asked if we could ship him wine from Martinique. Another person heard about the wine shipment and inquired about us bringing him a load of IKEA furniture. Great news- our engineless home had been converted into a small freighter in less than two weeks.

The rumour that we were now in the shipping business spread quickly. We drew up a contract to move a complete dive shop to Venezuela and then sail back to the Grenadines with aluminium sheeting and profiles. It wasn't exactly what we'd imagined when we left Oslo, but that didn't matter. Everything was starting to look up again. As long as we didn't hit another reef or commit another major blunder, we would be fine.

11. Big Blunders

The Swedes have this thing about Norwegian sailors goofing and screwing up all the time- "Have you heard the story about the Norwegian who...?"

Coming from Norway, I found these stories a bit unfair. Wasn't it the Norwegian Vikings who discovered America? Hadn't they heard of Thor Heyerdahl, Roald Amundsen, Fritjof Nansen and Peter Roren?

The latter, for those of you who can't remember, was the guy who crossed the Atlantic in eighty-four (that's 1984!) on his maiden voyage without the aid of GPS, refrigeration, night vision binoculars, or other technological gizmos.

Has anyone ever heard of a famous Swedish explorer? The only one I knew was some fellow who took off on an airship, went the wrong way, and got lost. The most famous of all was the guy who invented dynamite, which resulted in a whole lot of people goofing up and losing their fingers. And then there was the guy who designed the *Wasa*, the 172-foot pride of the nation warship. The ship foundered 10 minutes after being launched in Stockholm harbour.

Enough Swede-bashing. We Norsemen enjoy criticising and picking on our brothers across the border. It works both ways.

Big nautical blunders are an international problem and affect us all in different ways regardless of race, religion, or sexual orientation. Anyone can make a mistake or two. It was my screw-up of gigantic proportions that resulted in us being stuck here in paradise, shipwrecked on a treacherous reef. Who was I to laugh at other people's mistakes or to write about them?

In the West Indies we have a regular daily ritual called "Happy Hour." A well-known and much too short hour in a bar where you get two drinks for the price of one. In other words, you get twice as intoxicated for the normal price, and liver failure twice as quickly. In some bars it even lasts 2-3 hours!

Admiralty Bay on the island of Bequia is a favourite anchorage for many cruisers and bare-boaters exploring the Windward Islands, and they tend to arrive in the late afternoon, during our "hour of happiness."

During this hour before sunset we gather to take advantage of this wondrous offer. However, the real attraction is the chance to enjoy some live entertainment- to witness our fellow sailors' blunders and bloopers. The Germans call it "schadenfreude." Here are a few of my favourites.

The "schadenfreude" spectators were propping up the bar, glowing in anticipation. Single-handed Harvey had just dropped his anchor in a most professional manner a few hundred feet off the dinghy dock. No noise. No fuss. He'd obviously done this a few hundred times before.

Only the day before we'd witnessed a bareboat skipper slam his engine in reverse so hard that his dinghy, on a very long line, ended beneath his bow. Unaware, he yelled to his wife to drop the hook. She'd followed orders and the anchor ended up in the dinghy, punching a triangular hole in the forward compartment. That was great entertainment; the verbal abuse that followed, aimed at his wife, was not.

Harvey inflated his battered Avon dinghy in no time with something that looked like a foot-operated accordion. The inflatable was one of the very old models with tubing all the way around and a rubber bottom that gave the passenger the feeling of walking on an unstable floating waterbed. The two-horsepower Seagull outboard was equally antique, hanging on for its dear life on a rusty stern bracket.

In spite of all this obsolete and rickety equipment the old Seagull ran on the first pull, and with a trail of blue fumes bubbling in his wake our friend was happily chugging his way towards the dock- a short distance after a long passage. He was devilishly thirsty and looking forward to his double happy hour reward.

His audience had given up on any excitement when the Seagull developed something like a hiccup and expired, just a few feet from the dock. With the current and wind against him it was obvious he wouldn't make it. There was no one was on the dock to catch his line, and nobody went charging out of the bar to lend a hand. We were all waiting to see what would happen next.

The obvious solution was to restart the engine since Harvey had no oars. Who needed oars when you had a Seagull, right?

Our thirsty friend had somehow lost the starting cord, but, as with most cruising sailors, he would find a practical solution to his problem. His idea was to use the long dinghy towline. All was not lost.

The ingenious cruising rocket scientist wrapped as much of the towline around the exposed flywheel as possible and gave it a mighty pull. Old Faithful spluttered off again on the first go, but the towline got stuck and wrapped itself around the spinning flywheel. As the line got tighter, the bow lifted up and backwards with the result that the inflatable totally enfolded our hero. The engine stalled due to the strain, and the dinghy now resembled a floating hamburger.

In spite of our tremendous applause and laughter we could hear poor Harvey's surprised and frantic calls for help inside the folded tender. As if this were not enough, and before anyone could mount a rescue mission, the strain on the outboard bracket tore it clean off the stern and the outboard flew forwards as the dinghy flattened out again, and both dinghy and outboard crashed into the dock.

The engine's propeller and exhaust pipe had jammed under the steel pipe where visitors normally tied up. The inflatable had returned to its original configuration, exposing the still composed victim.

Admiralty Bay

As if this whole scenario was a daily event and completely normal, he calmly lit a bent cigar. With the air in the dinghy's stern chamber slowly hissing out through where the prop had made a long slash, he nonchalantly stepped ashore. Without casting a glance back towards the expired dinghy that now resembled a floating carpet, he stooped to tie his shoelaces.

He didn't even check out the amazing tie-up solution with the engine jammed under the dock-rail. The issue had been sorted. Totally relaxed, Harvey strolled to the bar and perched on a barstool as if nothing had happened.

"Two Heinekens. Ice-cold please. Anyone around here do dinghy repairs?"

Most of us, like our friend Harvey, have the ability to laugh at our own mistakes and mishaps. Some don't. These halfwits have a tendency to blame others when things don't go as planned.

A fifty-foot Moorings charter boat approached the bay. The punters aboard had already taken in their sails a mile or two out to sea. This in itself was an indication that we could expect something interesting to happen.

As they came steaming in under full power there were two people on deck. The captain sported a US coast guard cap with gold leaf, and he positioned himself strategically behind the gigantic stainless steering wheel and engine controls. A blonde model wearing a skimpy bikini and posing in a very provocative manner was on the foredeck, a drink in one hand and the anchor windlass remote in the other. They were under full power.

The captain had done his homework and believed he knew the principles of anchoring. He most likely had done a fair bit of sailing, but as with many bare-boaters, he probably hadn't had much experience anchoring. Back home many weekenders went from marina to marina, or from marina to mooring buoy, or to some combination of both.

But he seemed to have a plan, as one should when entering a new anchorage. It was obvious that he was determined to drop the hook exactly where *the little anchor mark was positioned on the chart!*

He did precisely this, in spite of two Italian vessels anchored there already, whose owners both had the same ingenious idea. What about the several square miles of opportunity with sufficient room to settle elsewhere? It was an ample bay for hundreds of yachts.

"Give clear and comprehensible orders," says the do-it-yourself-manual.

The happy hour audience had seen and heard a lot, but we had never heard anyone give *themself* an order!

"Plenty of room here! On with the brakes! Full astern! Damn those Italians!"

Black exhaust bellowed from the stern. The rented Beneteau came to an immediate standstill and started reversing. All eyes, except our captain's, were on the towline anticipating a common incident of propeller wrappage with maybe a chewed-up inflatable as the grand finale.

Instead the dinghy continued forward, slowly and determinedly on its long towline. Unnoticed by the roaring commander in chief, it passed gently alongside the yacht until it could reach no further- right under the yacht's bow.

"Anchor away!" yelled the captain, misquoting the phrase *"anchors aweigh,"* which actually means to bring up, or, to be more precise, break loose from whatever junk was on the bottom.

On the foredeck the buxom blonde was having a problem with the remote. The order was repeated loud enough to be heard all the way down to Lower Bay with accompanying vocabulary not fit to print. She was perhaps confused by the nautical terminology "aweigh," but she finally understood. With the right button pushed, the anchor- as you have already guessed- dropped straight into the dinghy. *Déjà vu all over again* our American friends would say.

"Full speed backwards and astern," yelled this master of manoeuvres, and he rammed the gear-shift lever into reverse, resulting in a horrible crunching sound from his screaming gear-box. His crew desperately tried to communicate over the straining roar of the eighty-horsepower diesel.

The anchor was *afloat*, and she was pretty sure it belonged on the bottom with the fishes and not in the dinghy.

He couldn't hear what she was saying, but he could see her lips flapping and the frightened look in her eyes. If he'd looked behind him he'd have seen something that would've given *him* a frightened look.

The Italian boatowners were also yelling. In fact, at this moment the whole harbour was yelling- including the schadenfreuders.

"Put out more chain!" he screamed.

Somewhere in the manual it is written: "The captain always has the last word, and those orders must be followed, even if you are certain he is wrong."

So she did her duty and paid out more chain. The chain dropped in neat coils on top of the anchor making it resemble a *kransekake*- a type of Norwegian wedding cake.

There was quite a lot of damage and paperwork to follow this event and the nasty aftermath went on through the night down below. Our hero ended up having to continue his voyage single-handed with the loss of his deposit to the Moorings Company.

One out of about ten anchoring procedures ended up with a mishap of some kind. Boats and people included. Cussing and swearing. Violence and legal action. Nothing really to laugh about, is it? Quite a few of these incidents were caused by yachts having panic-stricken crew on board with their chain and anchor firmly on the sea-bed. I once saw the captain of a huge gin palace run off towing his anchor as a bottom trawl. He dislodged five small yachts on the way and wondered to himself if there was a hurricane on its way- it looked like the whole flipping fleet had decided to leave in his wake!

I have heard yacht renters demand that new anchors be delivered to them because they'd already *used up* their old ones! Maydays have come from sailors who'd sailed off with their anchor set, convinced that their rudder had failed because they were running around in circles.

I still insist that a well-known seafarer called Christopher something, once and for all established the greatest navigational blunder in world history- the so-called "Discovery of America." I agree enthusiastically with the American humourist Garrison Keillor- of Norwegian descent I may add- who maintained that the US of A should be a Norwegian protectorate.

He states in his book *Lake Wobegon*, "It saddens me that most of the people on this planet are in adoration of this Italian dreamer who made his arrival to The New World so much overdue. And by mistake of all things! He wasn't at all bothered about finding new territory. All that was on his mind was spices, would you believe it? Sailing away in search of peppers and curry? A man on his way to the vegetable market!"

He happened to stumble over the continent that the heroic Vikings had found five centuries before. There were already a bunch of really nice people living there and those buggers had already been there for a thousand or more years before the long ships laden with fierce and horny guys hit the beach.

Ok, ok- maybe they were not the nicest of visitors with all of that burning, rape, and a little pillaging, but at least they knew where the hell they were going, and they didn't enslave the locals to mine for gold. The really bad news was that this Columbus guy was credited for his "discovery" with statues, spaceships, firework displays, blockbuster movies, parades, and name-days. There was even a flaming country named after him, far to the south!

On top of all this they named the new land "America," after Amerigo Vespucci- another Italian who had the nerve to draw incredibly inaccurate maps of the New World. By rights this New World should have been named *Erika* after Erik the Red and his son Leif Erikson, who had done all the hard work five hundred years before.

The United States of Erika. Erika the Beautiful. It has a nice ring to it.

And what about the coining of the name *West Indies*?

Some nameless Spaniard in the wake of this Colombo guy was the cause of my mail often ending up in western India, and not only that, another nameless Spaniard caused the world community to be in a state of shock when they opened their newspapers and read that President Reagan had invaded Spain by launching an attack on Grenada.

12. The Broken Mast

"We have to put a reef in. This is too much for her!"

My mate had to shout over the noise of the wind screaming through the rigging. There was a full gale blowing against the current, whipping up the normally gentle Atlantic swells into steep and aggressive looking pyramids. *Fredag* was heavily laden with aluminium profiles and sheeting, commissioned for a customer on the island of Carriacou. Converted to a freighter, our yacht struggled to make progress through the square seas, coming to a shuddering halt every time we slammed into a new swell.

We were exhausted and fed up after battling the elements for three days. Our crew consisted of two animals, Sara, the ship's dog, and Siri, the ship's cat. They were also exhausted, knocked out by seasickness. I felt sorry for them. They hadn't asked to come along on this nightmarish passage.

We were the only living beings out here. I hadn't seen a ship or a single sail over the last two days, not even a friggin' frigate bird. It was just us, our home, and a roaring tropical storm. The latest hurricane warning put the storm centre 120 miles to our east. The weather system was heading towards us at 15 miles an hour. This left only 8 hours until… it was hard not to think the worst. The barometer needle had passed the bottom of the scale and was pointing at the manufacturer's brand-name.

With only twenty miles to go to the island of Carriacou it looked as if we would just make it. Carriacou had the best hurricane hole in the region. A hurricane hole is a protected lagoon bordered by mangrove trees, tropical vegetation that will protect the boat from other boats dragging anchors.

This was the second time we had broken our rule about sailing during the hurricane season. Unfortunately, we had no other options. We had to do what we could to survive. We should have arrived in port already, but the wind was strong and right on the nose. Everything that contributed to making sailing in this area so superb had suddenly turned against us. There wasn't much we could do to stay out of the hurricane's projected path once we'd left port, and even in port we weren't guaranteed safety.

In between the rain squalls, I glimpsed Carriacou, a grey hilly mound on the horizon. The wind seemed to be strengthening, but I was too exhausted to reef the sails further. In hindsight it was time to put in another reef to save a lot of sewing and stitching upon reaching our safe haven.

Fredag had no autopilot or self-steering device due to the captain being a romantic, conservative, and stubborn traditionalist, so we had to have an able-bodied helmsman. The yacht's bow had to be held into the wind when reducing sail, and for some reason it always blew like stink when we were reefing. In light winds there was no problem, but you never needed reduced canvas in light airs unless you were clairvoyant.

The sail called the flying jib was Mariann's personal baby and no one else was allowed to deal with it. I took the helm while she went forward.

Crawling along the deck on all fours she headed for the foredeck and hooked her safety harness to a metal eye on the anchor windlass.

"Into the wind, cap!" she yelled. The sail flapped, cracking loudly, and the foredeck heaved, so that hauling it in was harder than taking laundry off the line astride a wild horse in a tornado.

Normally a flying jib is not hooked to the forestay, the wire that runs from the top of the mast to the end of the bow sprit. Bringing down this sail can be tricky, even with three gorillas hauling the lines. If you have ever held an umbrella in a gale, imagine what it's like holding onto a loose, flying jib, thirty times the umbrella's size.

There was only one Mariann, and although she was as strong as three men, we had decided to have the traditional jib stayed, which created a problem.

A flying jib could be hastily stuffed down a deck hatch- a stayed jib had to be lashed down on the bowsprit.

I must confess that I admired her as she crawled out onto the 18-foot-long, slippery bowsprit to lash the jib. With one arm to hang on, she had to fasten the sail to the boom with one hand, constantly awash with green water as the bowsprit plunged into the waves.

When she took the helm, it was my turn to deal with the mainsail. Although this sail was much larger and heavier. I could at least stand on deck, and I didn't have get soaked every time we ploughed through a wave.

I didn't have to deal with the topsail- it's a fair-weather sail and is only set when I can light cigarettes with a match without taking cover. The mizzen sail had been ripped to ribbons, so there was no point doing anything with that. The staysail stayed where it was, no matter how much the wind blew, keeping us headed into the wind and not lying broadside to the waves.

I secured my harness to safeguard my life to a metal eye on deck. Normally I cussed and swore at this protrusion every time my big toe smashed into it, but now I was happy it was there.

A sudden strong gust heeled us so far over that the port railing submerged. This had never happened before! Fear gripped me as my yacht continued to heel and there was nothing I could do to stop it.

A deafening crack from above led me to think that we'd been struck by lightning, followed by the worst warning a sailor could get, apart from *abandon ship*:

"Look out! Mast coming down!"

The main mast had broken half way up. The top half, together with the gaff, mainsail, shrouds, stays, navigation lights, running rigging, and blocks all crashed down, in slow motion. A section of the port rail was ripped away by the falling mast.

When *Fredag* righted herself, she was lying broadside, exposed to the massive seas. It took me a minute to get over the shock. Glancing up the mast that had once been a 65-foot tall, majestic spruce, born in a remote

Norwegian valley, I noticed that the fractured and splintered end was exactly where the copper sleeve was nailed.

The copper sheeting was there to protect the mast from chafe caused by the gaff-claw. It had been on my mind for a long time to remove that sleeve and check beneath it. I had postponed doing anything about it since finding a new wooden mast in the Caribbean was as likely as finding a coconut palm in Siberia. If I'd checked it out I would've found rot behind the sleeve and would have been forced to do something about it. I could now have had a mast to sail into port, before the hurricane hit us. A loud thump to the hull brought me out of my repentant thoughts and told me it wasn't over yet. The top of the broken mast was still hanging by the rigging, half submerged and threatening to smash a hole in the hull.

My first thought was to cut the whole mess loose, but there were valuable parts attached. I could say goodbye to the sail and mast, but what about the gaff with the beautiful carved oak claw, all the expensive galvanised rigging wire, and all the hand-made metal fixtures?

I soon realized we had drifted for miles and were now getting very close to the north coast of Grenada. It was too risky to start the engine with so much rope and wire in the water. Getting this mess entangled with the rudder and propeller would be of no help whatsoever. Fortunately, all of this debris was overboard on our lee side, and I pretended not to hear the unbearable clamour of mast and boat crashing together.

With wire and lines cut we had salvaged the most important parts. The mast was too heavy to bring on board, but we needed the metal fixtures.

It was now a race against time. Grenada's north shore was steadily creeping nearer, and *Balliceaux,* the vessel we had saved, was by now in Australia and unable to return the favour.

We secured the broken mast alongside. Every time we rolled to port the seas lifted the mast up. By tightening the slack on the ropes every time this happened, we gradually had the threatening battering ram properly secured. I stuffed a couple of mattresses and pillows between the mast and hull. There was no more rope or wire in our wake, so I started the engine.

We slowly made our way toward Carriacou by engine and a single reduced staysail. My once gallant ship looked like a war-struck frigate that had her rigging shot to pieces by cannonballs.

There was no point feeling sorry for ourselves. We were still afloat and moving along, though rather slowly and handicapped. Apart from the mast and the mainsail we managed to save most of the rigging. We lost the starboard navigation light, a beautiful brass lantern that ran on paraffin. It would be difficult to replace it. But we still had one to port- always look on the bright side!

My friends on Carriacou were not at all surprised when I radioed that we were having problems. I gave them an estimated arrival time and assured them we'd make it before the eye of the storm hit. We had no serious problems at the moment but would appreciate if they would stand by on the distress frequency, just in case.

I repeated that there was no immediate danger. I didn't want to throw any more fuel on the fire. We now had a reputation for being in constant trouble, and I wasn't at all comfortable about it. However, they insisted on having two boats stand by, ready to assist us at a moment's notice.

They also informed us that the hurricane had been downgraded and its movement toward us has slowed, but it was still a tropical storm, heading straight at us. If we reached the hurricane hole within three hours we would be safe. With a speed of two or three knots it was going to be a close call, but we would still make it.

We were in the lee of the active volcanic underwater cone, *Kick em' Jenny*. To our east was an island, more aptly described as a huge rock shaped like an Egyptian pyramid. There was currently an official maritime warning for all shipping to keep a safe seven-mile distance from the area since there was a strong possibility of an eruption.

I couldn't believe it. What had I done wrong? As if a hurricane wasn't enough!

We sailed as close to the lee of the rock as we could to save time. This was when the coffee boiled over that my mate had prepared to settle our nerves.

A sign? An admonition? With no coffee and a ban on alcohol at sea, I started smoking again, after an entire year's abstinence.

Two packs of Lucky Strikes later we struck it lucky and passed through the narrow entrance to the hurricane hole. With our engine on full throttle, we ploughed our way through the mud into the mangroves. All our anchors were set out astern in a spread-out pattern, all sails and deck equipment securely stowed or lashed down, and we were ready to meet the devil himself.

Coffee, eggs, and a large quantity of bacon was consumed as if we hadn't seen food for week- which was very close to the truth.

The lagoon, or hurricane hole as we called it, was chock-a-block with vessels of all sizes. I didn't like the look of the big freighters moored close behind us. All the owners and crew were hunched over their radios, following the storm's progress. A few miles to the east a hurricane-hunter aircraft flew into the eye of the storm and confirmed the downgrade from a force one hurricane to only a tropical storm. We all breathed a sigh of relief. We needed some luck.

On the windward side of the island a taxi driver was screaming for help over the radio. His vehicle had blown off the road. There was nothing we could do to help. We turned off the radio, put Vivaldi on the tape deck and opened a bottle of Chablis.

It's amazing what you can find hidden on a yacht if you're desperate and keep searching. It's also amazing what you can accomplish and get through- if you don't give up.

When we awoke the sun was shining, the sky was blue and the birds in the mangroves were chatting away. The storm had passed. There was no further damage to *Fredag*, but my last pack of Luckys had blown away during the night.

Carriacou has always been one of my favourite Caribbean islands. About the same size as Bequia, it was different in many ways. With the airport, or more appropriately, the *airstrip* now completed, the islanders said that Carriacou would become a new Barbados, but nothing much had changed. The present is as the past was, and the future will most likely be like the present. However, there was a difference between the two islands. Although Bequia was "laid back," Carriacou was even more so, and the citizens of Carriacou

preserved their heritage and traditions more than any other island. This resulted in some amazing events and spectacles.

As on Bequia, the population was mixed. Descendants of African slaves lived on the lee side of the island, and the Scottish and Irish descendants of political prisoners, outlaws, and debtors of the 17th Century- indentured servants once known as *redlegs*- lived to windward in more or less perfect harmony and unity.

During my first visit to Carriacou I took part in carnival celebrations. This annual event encompassed all the ingredients of a traditional West Indian carnival, with one notable exception.

In the centre of the capital, Hillsborough, a basketball court was transformed into an open-air theatre, with a stage and benches for the audience. Two men dressed in outfits resembling pyjamas covered with tiny mirrors entered the stage and started bashing each other on the head with cricket bats made of paper-mâché. They wore helmets that looked like something out of *Ben Hur*.

While they were performing this violent Punch & Judy act, they shouted at each other in a strange language. After ten minutes of shouting and bashing their performance was over. The audience politely applauded, the actors left the stage, and a panel of very serious looking judges in the front row made notes. A new, similar dressed pair entered the stage, and the whole sequence was repeated, with exactly the same dialogue which still made no sense to me.

It was only after watching three rounds of performers that I discovered they were speaking a form of English, stranger than the normal dialect. After another few rounds, what I unearthed was unbelievable. What these pyjama-clad guys were reciting was the last act of Shakespeare's *King Lear*!

I asked an old man sitting on the bench beside me what this was all about.

"Dis an ol' Carriacou tradition," he replied. "De best man win twenty dollah."

"Do you know who wrote the words?" I carefully asked.

"Nobody write dem words, dis just an ol' tradition."

"You ever heard of the name William Shakespeare?" I tried again.

"Who he be?" the old man replied curiously. "A yachtsman in de harbour?"

Nobody has ever been able to give me a plausible explanation of this extraordinary event. It was just an old Carriacou tradition. And William Shakespeare was laughing somewhere in the harbour.

The inhabitants of Carriacou are also strongly rooted to their African origins and traditions.

I was once fortunate to get invited to a *stone setting* party. When people died on this island, they were put in the ground with all the traditions and rituals of an old-fashioned Christian funeral, with one exception. The placement of a tombstone to mark the grave of the deceased was erected between 2 and 3 years after their death, dependent on the funds available and the ability of relatives to travel home for the occasion.

This was usually a grand occasion, celebrated with a fete comparable to a wedding. The memory of the deceased was honoured every year, but once the stone was set, the spirit could rest comfortably. There was a party in memory of the deceased- a celebration of his or her life- filled with fun and dance, goat-water, barbecued chicken, and very strong Jack Iron rum.

This was the best part: several times a year, and sometimes at weddings and stone-setting parties, the people of Carriacou displayed their African origins with a traditional performance called the Big Drum Dance. The drums looked and sounded just like those I encountered while sailing up the Gambia River. Another dance was called the Stick Dance, and it was only performed by men. It was from the Zulu Tribe, and the men sang in Swahili without understanding all the words.

There were more strange and unusual events. During the traditional three-day weddings on Carriacou's windward side, where the MacGregors and the McIntoshes lived, the participants played the pipes and danced on two crossed swords.

Added to all this, the island had a museum- the first and only museum of its kind I had found in the West Indies. It was small but well-organized and full of treasures. It even had its own department covering the US led invasion of the "mainland," Grenada, complete with pieces of downed helicopters and an amazing collection of photos documenting the whole sad event- an incident many Grenadians would rather forget, when a group of local radical Marxists killed their leader, Maurice Bishop, and many of his followers, precipitating the US incursion.

For some reason the people of Carriacou have held on to their national heritage more than on any other island. Although a few very old people on Bequia can recall similar traditions, they say, "Dat all done gone now!"

With one notable exception. In the old days, not too far back in time, when the roads on Bequia were muddy tracks full of potholes, people in Lower Bay were so afraid of the rough ride to the cemetery that they found a way to give the deceased a smoother ride by ferrying them to church across the water. A few years ago, when a prominent and popular man passed away, he was brought to the burial ceremony by boat from Lower Bay to the church in Port Elizabeth. "Mackie" had his last ride in a longboat with eight men on the oars. The oarsmen rowed in a most unusual way- one stroke through the water and the following one through the air. The stroke through the water was for the body, and the stroke through the air was for the soul. I once saw an identical practice take place on a river in Senegal, West Africa.

Everything is on a small scale in Carriacou and moves very slowly, if indeed it moves at all. However, something extraordinary existed here. The planet's most powerful short-wave radio station was located on Carriacou, run and financed by the Mormons from Salt Lake City. Around the clock it broadcasted their message of salvation and damnation to the world. The locals said that if you stood for an hour within 200 feet of the transmitter you will never need to purchase a condom again, and you could have safe sex for the rest of your life. "Safe" in this part of the world meant having no babies, never mind the AIDS epidemic!

I personally appreciated these radio transmissions. They served as a great navigational aid. If you pointed your transistor radio in its direction, you had a course for Carriacou.

Once a day a small, light aircraft landed on the beachside airstrip. Aircraft could land when the air traffic controller closed the gate to the road crossing the tarmac and after he had chased off the sheep and goats.

The cargo and passenger vessel *Alexis* was the only other means of transportation to and from the island. It left early in the morning for Grenada and returned late in the afternoon- that is, if there were enough passengers, and if the engine worked.

If for some reason the engine was down, you had to book a seat on the plane, assuming you were lucky enough to find a working phone. That was the main difference between Bequia and Carriacou. Carriacou had about as much infrastructure as Santa Fe had a hundred and fifty years ago.

The capital Hillsborough was falling apart and was as close as you could get to one of those small towns in a wild west movie, with its dusty, potholed streets and dilapidated facades, mangy dogs dozing in the hot sun, and where there was shade you would usually find some local sound asleep. Nothing moved in town- or anywhere else for that matter- during the heat of the day. Sunset brought the island to life with the aid of music and the slamming of dominoes in countless rum shops.

Carriacou belonged to Grenada, although its inhabitants didn't exactly see it that way. "We don't belong to no one!"

They regarded Grenada as a nuisance and a source of trouble. Traditionally the main business and income for the citizens of Carriacou has been smuggling. Originally it wasn't considered smuggling as there were simply no import duties or taxes. It didn't help relations between the people of Carriacou and the government of Grenada when the latter applied duty and VAT tax on nearly everything imported.

However, the people of Carriacou found a solution. They simply refused to pay, and that was the end of it!

All these points added up to create one of the most interesting islands in the Caribbean. I came across some more fascinating discoveries as I criss-crossed the island searching for a long piece of wood suitable to be used as *Fredag's* new mast.

One of the reasons I chose to build a traditional old-fashioned sailing vessel was that if she were dismasted anywhere in the world I could simply walk into a forest and cut down a tall straight tree. Unfortunately, coconut palms are out of the question as they are too flexible, and cedar trees are anything but straight. To buy and ship an aluminium mast from Europe or the US would be astronomically expensive. It would also be a serious violation of wooden boat tradition.

However, what you *did* find anywhere in the world wherever humans walked and lived were telephone and electric poles! By chance I stumbled over a huge pile of them on the beach. It looked like they'd been there for eons-long and straight as a ruler, made of the best imported Canadian pine, and impregnated with smelly, black creosote. Made to last a lifetime. The only problem was that the longest of the poles was ten feet too short. However, a short mast was better than no mast.

All I needed now was to find someone in charge.

After many hours wandering around the island plus hundreds of mosquito bites I found the assistant to the man in charge for the erection of telephone poles. He was slouching in a rum shop on the windward side of the island. He listened politely to my breath-taking adventure as I bribed him with cold beers and described in great detail our sad story.

He followed up with a lengthy lecture on dry rot in wood and an even longer narrative about "madman Alex" who lost his vessel on the Saba Banks when his mast went overboard. After eight beers between us he ended up with a longer story about his neighbour's attempt to poison another neighbour's dog.

When I finally got around to asking him if he could help me sort out my mast problem he gave me a straight forward *No*.

He sent me on to the "electric city" man.

The man from the power station was just as talkative and had just as much on his mind as the "pole" man. Didn't these guys have anything else to talk about other than the disputes of next-door neighbours? He rambled on for almost an hour about a dispute concerning a right of way and access through his property.

"No wonder nobody gets no work done around here," he concluded.

The same went for the line-inspector, the fire chief, the head of police, and the harbourmaster. What the harbourmaster had to do with telephone poles was beyond me. They didn't get many tourists dropping in to buy telephone poles.

Finally, I was back where I originally started with the assistant chief of poles, who for some reason had a different title the second time around- the Assistant Deputy to the Director of Planning! I asked him if this title would make any difference to my request for the purchase of a pole. He then launched into a long story about an uncle in Canada who had seven vehicles, three mistresses, and eight jobs, and that he wished he could go to Canada, too. In the middle of this highly interesting and intriguing story I pulled a bottle of 170 proof Jack Iron rum from a brown paper bag.

With a big smile he asked me how was I doing and how did I like Carriacou.

The bottle was half empty and I couldn't feel my mosquito bites anymore, my vision was blurred, and I felt I was never going to get anywhere with this man when suddenly he said, "Ah tink me have ah solution, white man. Ah tink you have to meet a pole yerself in yer own way. But don' tell no one, mahn, don't tell no one ah say so!"

I had noticed before that it was quite acceptable on these islands to "help yourself," moderately, but only when in need. When I asked a young man why he had stolen a pack of Luckys from me he said, "Ah ain' tief dem, ah met dem on de table when you was in de restroom."

However, the thought of spending time locked in the dungeon at Fort George for two years living on breadfruit, lentil soup, and fish heads made me think that it was probably not a good idea to help myself, and certainly not to "tell no one who said so."

When the rum was nearly history, the pole man and I were buddies. I was the coolest and weirdest tourist he'd ever met and my new friend Sylvester seemed to understand how desperate I was. As he poured out the last shot of rum he informed me that he would call the best friend of a cousin of the Minister of Works on Grenada, and ask him to put in a word for me. The Minister had the final word concerning everything lying around the island belonging to the Government.

"But best you send she to see de Minister," he said, pointing a long bony finger at Mariann.

As we staggered down the hill, we waved and he waved back shouting, "An' mek she put on a pretty dress, mahn!"

Three weeks passed and we still had no mast. A new tropical storm was brewing off the west coast of Africa. I had a client who wanted me to ship a complete scuba dive shop to Margarita, and now he was getting impatient and had mumbled something about using FedEx.

I had no reply from the Minister of Works in Grenada so I decided to take Sylvester's advice and send down my emissary- in her prettiest dress.

We still had one major problem. Even if Mariann managed to charm the Minister, there is still the freight to Carriacou to worry about. To sail down there by engine was too risky. In addition, I was told that there was no lifting facility in Grenada. It had to be done here. It could take a week to rig the mast which would put us very close to the day when the scuba shop guy planned to call the FedEx agent.

The ferry *Alexis* was on her way back into the bay. I could, in the distance, see Mariann standing at the bow in her red dress, waving both arms. I knew immediately all had gone well. If not, she would've been sitting at the sternpost, staring out to sea. I could see by her posture, a mile away, that she was smiling. Grenada's longest telegraph pole was cast overboard, and before the waves from the splash had reached the beach, I raced out in our dinghy and fastened a line to it.

Five hundred easy come, easy go EC dollars, with no receipt, was what the Minister required for one of his precious poles. It was the longest one to be found, but still not long enough. I had to add a small topmast. This was not as originally designed, but I was pretty sure Mr. Colin Archer would have approved.

There had been numerous problems in Grenada. The main obstacle was the police, who refused to give permission to transport the pole through the capital of St. George's during the day. Only in the night with a police escort, they said. "And that will cost five hundred EC dollars!"

"But the Alexis leaves at 5:00 in the afternoon, and it'll be a whole week before she returns, and there's a hurricane out there and...."

"I says only in the night and oh, I forget, you have to pay *overtime*, too," said the seemingly cooperative Chief of Police.

"Ah cyan' go no furder" said the driver, parking his long transport vehicle on the outskirts of St. George's.

"But I have approval from the police," said Mariann, waving her stamped document under the driver's nose. A police car pulled up. The cops wanted to know what was going on.

With all the confidence and authority she could muster Mariann called out to them, "Hey, you guys! I'm in a goddamn hurry. Escort me and this heavy load down to the careenage immediately. And make it snappy! I've got a ship to catch. If I miss it, this log is gonna block traffic for a whole week."

"Yes Madam," they replied. They had been trained to be helpful to tourists and to follow orders without question. They were used to all kinds of strange situations with visitors, but they'd never seen the likes of this lady.

Tironga, the floating crane

The *Alexis* was about to cast off when the truck transporting the pole arrived at the careenage, escorted by three police cars with flashing blue lights. The big yellow forklift, paid in advance, that should have been waiting on the dock was of course elsewhere, but thirty helpful hands soon had the oily pole on board. The police all got a big hug from my emissary.

The captain gave the order to cast off to the applause of the astonished crowd that had followed the event. Mariann collapsed onto a pile of rope, worn out by the whole procedure, her red dress covered in black creosote. The captain smiled and gave her the V-sign with the only two fingers he had left on his right hand. She responded by making a circle with her thumb and what was left of her index finger.

Mounting a mast on a boat, if you have no crane available, demands a certain amount of inventiveness. One way is to anchor under a bridge, another way is to use the mast from a bigger boat to lift it in place. My friend May, the owner of the hundred-year-old schooner *Tironga*, came to our rescue.

With May and his crew's help, we gently lowered the mast into its hole on *Fredag's* deck. The silver coin under the mast- an ancient tradition- was replaced, the tradition being that the value of the coin would cover the cost of a new mast. As long as the mast was on top of the coin, nobody could steal it.

A tiny Norwegian commemorative jubilee coin would of course not cover the cost of our new mast, plus shipping and bribes. But that wasn't the point. Keeping an old tradition was important, and breaking such traditions might result in bad luck. We'd had enough of that by now.

Stepping a mast without a crane required some ingenuity

The "electric-city" pole was too short and had to be stepped, using part of the old mast, to make a topmast.

Sometimes at night I wondered if it really was a good idea to go sailing around in this fragile shell of a vessel in a dangerous environment. Was I pushing myself and my crew too hard, taking risks above an acceptable limit in order to meet a challenge?

My friend May was gone; only a few weeks after the mast job May was returning back to the *Tironga* from a shore party. He said goodnight and waved goodbye to his friends on the dock as he rowed away in his own tender. That was the last anybody saw of him. Two days later a search aircraft found his tender capsized 40 miles out in the Caribbean Sea. May's body was never recovered.

I quite often think about seafaring friends and acquaintances who have gone to meet their maker at sea.

It is natural that we who live on the sea form many close friendships as we are all in the same boat, so to speak, constantly putting ourselves at risk. Although, come to think of it, speeding along the motorway in fog under icy conditions far exceeds the odds of losing your life in a storm in the Bay of Biscay.

Frequently these new relationships become very close and intense, and normally don't last very long as we are all sailors more or less on the move. That is why it becomes a special occasion when we meet up again after a long passage or circumnavigation.

In many ways it's a small world for the sailing community and we are well aware that when we wave goodbye, we will meet up again somewhere sooner or later. We also aware of the probability that we never will. It's a small world and word travels fast, even when carried by the wind. We will soon find out when disaster strikes and a friend is lost at sea.

The only Chinese sailor I ever met was Lee, another victim of the seven seas. He nearly always sailed his little yacht on his own. He was a single-hander. That was the reason why I gave him my self-steering device. In any case, the complicated contraption couldn't handle my heavy yacht.

He was crossing the Pacific on his way home when the accident occurred. The yacht was steering herself. A young Australian lady who'd never been on board a small boat before was accompanying him on the long passage. It's important to keep a lookout, even on autopilot. With two or more people on board there is always someone who can keep watch.

The young girl woke up one morning with the yacht moving in an unusual way with her sails flapping, making a terrible racket. Up on deck she found to her horror that Lee was gone. She had no idea of how to turn the boat around and do a search.

It was quite amazing that she eventually managed to reach a safe haven and live to tell the story. It didn't take long for the news to reach the Caribbean. Even the most experienced cruising sailor could make that last serious mistake one day.

Peter Tangvald, born in Oslo in 1924, was a Norwegian sailor and adventurer. He was known as an early deep-sea cruising pioneer and as author of his book *Sea Gypsy*. He achieved notoriety after the second of his six wives was lost at sea. His first wife, Lydia, was shot dead on board their yacht by pirates in the South China Sea. His last wife, Ann, fell overboard 20 miles south of Grenada. She was struck by the boom when the yacht accidentally jibed. I met Peter a few days after he'd lost Ann. It was a broken man that sailed into St. Georges in Grenada.

Ann was never found. Peter continued sailing with his two children, Carmen and Thomas. He was so scared that his children might fall overboard that he locked them in the main cabin while he spent three days being interrogated by the local police. The harbour was of course full of gossip and slander. People were whispering, "He has done his wife in, and he doesn't want the kids to tell anyone."

Peter was quite a well-known figure in yachting and explorers' circles. Ironically, he had written several books on the subject of safety at sea, including a best-selling autobiography.

In Grenada journalists poured in from all over the world, hoping to get a scoop with "The Serial Killer of the Seven Seas." When the police eventually found that nothing was amiss and that it was most certainly an accident, the tabloid press went loopy and still wouldn't give up. Nobody involved felt like talking about the tragic incident, so the journalists, who had travelled so far, had to have something to write, and they made up the most outrageous stories. It was all pretty ugly. Peter was marked and maimed for the rest of his life by this cruel episode.

He had been married six times, so people would whisper, "There goes the guy who dumped his six wives overboard."

It has always been my opinion that if I wanted to get rid of my wife, I would simply sail away and leave her on the dock. No mess and not a chance of being charged with murder.

It's a well-known and undisputed fact that people die at sea. The chances of having an accident on a boat are 150 times more possible than in your home. Accidents happen!

I was in Bonaire when Peter and his children approached the island on their way southwards from Puerto Rico. He might have underestimated the strong south-going current and overslept because he hit the reef off the east coast.

This happened in spite of the weather being fair and the lighthouse working.

His wooden yacht broke up immediately. His son, Thomas, managed to jump onto a surfboard and paddle away to safety. At sunrise we discovered the bodies trapped under the reef. Peter was still holding little Carmen in his arms when the divers found them.

Thomas was lucky to escape from the accident, but suffered a similar fate when his own yacht was lost at sea some years later, after he had written the last chapter in his father's autobiography. It was entitled *At Any Cost. Love, Life, and Death at Sea.*

These incidents, and many similar tragedies, have over the years made me take more precautions and fewer risks. I have learned to respect the sea, even when it's not cruel.

I've always had everything ship-shape, ready to leave port in a hurry. I have learned over the years to repair things as soon as they break. When leaving the yacht at anchor I always check that the tender is equipped with water, fuel for the outboard engine, a pair of oars, a bailer, a small anchor, and a very long line. I make sure that there are always emergency provisions on *Fredag*, sufficient fuel and water, spare flashlight batteries, and a first-aid locker that is well stocked.

Out on the empty ocean hundreds of miles from land there are no doctors, mechanics, electricians, plumbers, or sailmakers. We have to solve and fix all problems ourselves, with our abilities and the help of the Do-It-Yourself section of our library. We have to be a jack of all trades and try to master them all.

Mariann and I had built our yacht without outside help, so we had a fairly good idea how to fix things. I had some mechanical and electrical skills from serving in the navy, and we both had gone through 500 hours of paramedic training. I could, if push came to shove, perform an appendectomy at sea, but I'm not sure the poor sod would survive!

We both had backgrounds as child behavioural therapists, a profession that really wasn't very practical in a nautical setting. I had never missed the work- too depressing. It was difficult to be objective and to avoid getting emotionally involved.

However, my mate was feeling otherwise. She was getting a bit fed up and bored running contraband such as coffee, wine, and aluminium up and down the islands. She had a higher moral standard than I. In addition, customs officials were starting to complain that our bribes were too low and were asking too many questions. It was time to try something else.

That was how Mariann persuaded me to consider doing some field work again and "save some kids."

13. The Slave Ship

Put the young bastards to work. Let them feel what hard labour is all about, moving rock and dirt. Force them to build mountain roads. That will sort them out. Send the buggers to sea.

For many, this was the solution for sorting out juvenile delinquents. As an inexperienced and newly educated child welfare officer, years before sailing off to explore the world, I became involved in an experimental project with the long title: "Utilizing the Marine Environment as a Socio-Pedagogical and Behavioural Therapeutic Method for Rehabilitating Juvenile Delinquents." Quite a mouthful, but to simplify it- *Send them to sea so they can grow up!*

Seven boys in their early teens involved in male prostitution and the lethal sniffing of glue were rounded up on the streets of downtown Oslo and "enlisted" as crew members on board a small schooner. Also on board was a shrink, a psychologist, and a psychology student who had conceived the project, plus myself as Captain. The whole idea had the blessing of the Ministry of Education and Social Affairs. The objective was simple and clear enough. Change these young kids' behaviour within a period of three weeks so they will disembark as well-behaved young gentlemen who will follow social rules, be prepared to join the boy scout's movement, and to help little old ladies cross the street. In short, to do what they were told, which would make all social workers, teachers, law enforcement officers, and most of all their parents very happy.

In theory the idea wasn't too bad, with its devious professional and cunning therapeutic techniques. The theory focused less on sanctions for negative behaviour, with an emphasis on ignoring bad behaviour. Instead of beating up these victims of society or throwing them in jail, the whole idea was to reward them if they showed good and acceptable behaviour. In other words, if you're a good boy you'll win in some way or other, like in a game.

How it worked was that if you could function and behave as the captain's "team" wanted you to behave, if you were able to deal with the challenges you met without breaking the rules of the ship and the laws of the land you would be rewarded. This sounded like a good idea, but the problem was that they were in fact rewarded in advance, with a three-week exciting cruise on a sailing ship. The project was doomed from day one, and if there was any progress made to obtain a reward in this great corrective programme, it did not make any difference since there was absolutely no follow-up when the kids were back on the street.

Although the juveniles more or less volunteered to embark on this grandiose scheme, they gradually disappeared from day to day. Not by jumping ship, but by being arrested and incarcerated for committing misdemeanours along the entire coast of southern Norway.

Understandably, as the deterrents and obstacles increased by every nautical mile, they couldn't take it. The only way these youngsters were able to avoid facing difficulty was to get away from the problem- as far away as possible either by climbing to the top of the mast or by swimming ashore.

That was actually what happened when the crew of the *HMS Bounty* couldn't hack any authority, rules, or regulations. They couldn't swim ashore in the middle of the Pacific so they became mutineers, sending their captain away in the tender. Fortunately for me, our crew hadn't been at sea long enough to handle the vessel themselves. They hadn't even figured out which side of the boat to pee over in a strong wind.

The plan was to sail from Oslo to Copenhagen in Denmark, a distance of about a hundred nautical miles, including brief stopovers in various fjords and ports- some voluntary, some not. Copenhagen was the liberal drug capitol of Europe, with various varieties marijuana sold over the counter as if they were exotic spices. It didn't help. They would rather hang out in "hippy village" than go on rides at the Tivoli theme park.

On arriving back in Oslo, I only had one faithful crewmember left on board. The whole project seemed to me to be like a broken pencil- pointless. Except for the lad that had survived "the voyage of his life," including the much-anticipated visit to the Tivoli Fair in Copenhagen, it did not make much sense. The academic team in the project claimed to have made some thought-provoking observations and made some noteworthy calculations in their reports, the enthusiastic project creator got his Master's degree, and I had an interesting sailing experience on a beautiful old classic schooner. For the young boys, it was just a short break and a holiday away from their living hell on the streets.

However, a few positive results took place that made me think twice. I gained some knowledge and understanding on what was going on in the minds of these unfortunate young people. They were full of hate and fear. Hate towards authority and the authorities, and fear of what would happen to them. They were also full of craving- not for drugs, but for a deep longing for love, understanding, and being able to prove themselves worthy. The basic idea and strategy would probably have worked if planned properly. It just needed more time, that was all.

What inspired me most happened a few years after the project. I was doing a stint as a taxi driver to make a few extra bucks to finance the building of my dream. I had a passenger who was an educational therapist, working with kids who had dropped out of school. As we both had similar backgrounds, he mentioned an incident with a young man in one of his classes. The boy was actually being paid by the government to attend school. The rationale was that as long as he was in class he wouldn't get into any mischief and the state would thereby save a lot of money. An easy fix to the problem with nothing pedagogical involved. He told me that the boy in question always sat in the back row of the classroom and never participated or reacted to anything the teachers threw at him. However, during art classes the boy actually seemed interested in something for the first time. To the teacher's surprise, he picked up a length of rope and made a perfect eye-splice on the end of it. His interest in ropework led to the therapist getting him an apprenticeship with a sailmaker.

The story rang a bell for me. I wondered if this could be the boy that at a distance of ten feet always seemed to be keeping an eye on me when I was practicing my knots on board the "failed" schooner project. When I told the therapist his name, he confirmed it was the same boy.

Not long after I had a bunch of lively and drunk teenagers in my taxi. The news on the radio reported on an act of piracy in the Persian Gulf, and the loudest of them exclaimed, "I went to sea once! I was on board a real sailing ship. We sailed through a storm that lasted seven days. It was a nightmare. Can't remember the name of the ship, but the captain's name was Peter something. We called him Captain Asshole, and he was. He was a real asshole, but it was the best experience of my life."

Mariann was in the same business doing the same work so with all this experience between us it made sense to continue our effort, but now in a completely different environment. We were thousands of miles away in the Caribbean where we could be free to design our own project based on the same idea, but with lots more time to effect change. Time to actually achieve something concrete and set these youngsters on a new path in life.

In Kipling's novel *Captains Courageous*, it took Captain Troop a year to transform a spoiled, pampered, and unsociable young Harvey to a responsible, mature, and well-behaved young man. With that in mind, the *Fredag* was transformed into a rehab institution.

There were a lot of young people in Norwegian institutions who fancied themselves as Caribbean pirates, sailing between tropical islands with huge marijuana plantations. However, they were soon told that this would be no pleasure cruise. On the contrary, they were being offered a voluntary position as crewmember on a combined floating work place and learning facility. The number of volunteers diminished, as was to be expected, when they heard the words "work" and "school."

A few of the existing institutions that dealt with juveniles that didn't fit into society were defined as "experimental reform institutions." I was, therefore, not surprised when the authorities sent us their most serious and "untreatable" cases, the ones who had been through a long row of reformatory institutions and foster homes.

I was taken by surprise when our new crew- three boys and a girl- arrived on board. I couldn't help but notice how pale, thin, and timid they all looked, and how quiet and polite they were. These guys were supposed to be a terror to society? I expected them to be more menacing, tough, and strong- intimidating gang leaders with tattooed arms, multiple scars from gunshot wounds- tough street kids.

I decided to try to talk *with* them, instead of talking *to* them. That didn't work. They had nothing to say and asked no questions. They must have had a lot on their minds, but they showed little desire to verbalise their thoughts. They just listened to what I said and occasionally gave a slight nod in return. I rambled on for an hour or so about the fact that what they had volunteered for was not a Caribbean cruise, that the deck they were sitting on was to be their future work place and that down below would be their school for the next nine months. I told them that this was no foster home where they would be pampered and treated like family, that they had simply enlisted onto a sailing vessel commanded by the world's worst and evil master- Captain Bligh the Second!

I went on and on about how great it would be if we could all work together, and if they were prepared to take responsibility and follow the rules, this would work to everybody's satisfaction. Halfway through the long list of rules I noticed that they were not with me anymore. One was looking out to sea and yawning, another was staring down at something on the deck that didn't exist, and the other two were sound asleep due to jetlag.

Then at last I got it. My welcome speech approach just wasn't working. They had heard it all before. I had started to get them institutionalized before we'd even sailed out of port! The experiment was going to be very demanding on the leaders and would test our skills as behavioural therapists.

I soon realized that this wasn't going to go like clockwork. However, we did have one advantage over them. We were well-prepared and they were not. They were startled and nearly jumped out of their skins when I suddenly threw all my notes overboard and shouted, "F*** these stupid rules! Let's row over to the beach over there and grill some f****** sausages. I'm starving and I need a beer. Who's coming with me? Shit. Who's got a cigarette? I'm out."

This turnabout completely broke the ice. Although it was just a hairline crack, things began to look more positive for the future. I now had their attention. A big crack was about to come, and it happened in a very strange way.

One of the conditions they agreed on before they embarked was that they had to work. Real work- learning the ropes and sharing watches, doing maintenance on the boat and participating in daily chores. For their contribution they were to receive a salary. Although not very large, and probably way below the minimum wage for a Philippine crew on a Panama registered freighter before the war, they were to be handed a salary by the end of the month. Incorporated in this salary arrangement was a complicated system of benefits, subsidies, supplements and bonuses. There were also deductions and withheld bonuses. The point underlying this structure was that if they worked hard and followed the rules they would be rewarded. The higher the input, the higher the output.

Nothing was mentioned about what would happen if they didn't follow the rules- no details concerning penalties, deductions, and punishment. Their pay checks at the end of the first three weeks would amount to the ship's minimum wage, barely enough to buy a bag of peanuts. They could take it or leave it. They took it. None of them wanted to fly home. I wondered afterwards how I would have dealt with the situation if they had wanted to leave.

They refused to work in the galley. They refused to cook. Why? They didn't know how! Not one of the them had ever boiled an egg, but a course in culinary arts would be an impossible undertaking at this stage.

Hauling the anchor, shopping ashore, fishing, even scrubbing the decks was acceptable, but cooking? "No way, man! Go jump in the lake." Their refusal to become galley slaves was unanimous and they were in the majority, four against two. Someone at their institutional life had put into their heads this weird democratic concept.

I had to make the point to them that on the good ship *Fredag* democracy didn't exist. The Captain decided. They had the right to speak their minds and come up with suggestions. We would listen and consider, but that was where the road to democracy ended. It was a compromise between democracy and dictatorship, they thought.

I presented them with a list of all the daily chores and responsibilities. We let our crew discuss the list and give each job a value on a scale from one to ten. As a result, cooking got a score of ten, fishing was at the bottom with a score of one, and the rest of the jobs scored somewhere between one and ten, with the not so popular jobs scoring the highest. They had to, by themselves, divide the workload between them, all ending up with the same number of points. They also had the right to decide our workload.

I was not surprized with the result. The first mate and the captain were given all the cooking between them and the rest of the crew did everything else, resulting in each of them having a long list of chores. We signed this agreement by taking a drop of blood from the finger of each crewmember and smearing it on a signed scroll. We put it inside a bottle and mailed it off to King Neptune, emphasizing the point that the King did not take too kindly to those who broke the trust of the *Brotherhood of the Seven Seas*.

This agreement worked, but only for a short time. After nine days, I was summoned to a meeting on the foredeck. The crew wanted to change the system.

"It isn't fair," said the crew's democratically elected spokesperson. "It takes the cook only half an hour or so the rustle up some pancakes, and less than an hour to fry up fish and potatoes, while it takes us all day to get through the washing up, scrubbing the decks, cleaning the waterline, trimming the wicks and refilling kerosene lamps, going shopping, fishing, doing the daily engine check, pumping bilges, while you "officers" are stretched out in your hammocks reading and sipping iced tea. It isn't fair. We never have minute off."

So, what was to be done? They suggested dividing all the work fair and square between each person. The negative side to this solution was that I only now had one good meal a week, the one Mariann cooked.

On the positive side we won the "we will not cook" round in our power game, and they learned from the experience that they could, with a little help, do the impossible- bake a loaf of bread. That meant a lot to them. It meant so much for the girl we had on board that she would not let us eat her first miracle bake. She kept the loaf in her locker until it became a health hazard and had to be thrown overboard.

Many years following the work-list affair, the young lady in the group wrote me a letter saying, "That was a smart trick you pulled on us. I just wanted to let you know that I used the same method on my own kids when they refused to do their chores. Thanks Cap."

This was just one instance of how clever we had to be, careful not to fall into the "institution" trap. We always had to be one step ahead of them.

Occasionally I would snap and in anger threaten a slacker with house arrest, or employ the saltier threat of walking the plank, or being lashed with the cat o' nine tails. I never used the sanction of sending them home, even though it was sometimes very tempting.

On board a vessel there are ways to make solutions much easier to accomplish. If you can't be bothered to pull up the anchor or set the sails you will go nowhere. Simple as that! It's no fun just lying there in the same boring place when there's a vast world out there full of adventure, excitement, and discothèques.

If you couldn't be bothered to take your turn on the helm the frigging captain would just steer around in huge circles for days on end and you would never reach that disco just over the horizon. As time passed, fewer and fewer discouraging and undesirable events occurred, and we gradually became more of a ship's crew, and even to some extent, a happy family. The Captain and Mate were tyrants on the high seas and a bit softer in port or at anchor. Responsibility and accountability started to make sense to them. With their self-esteem gradually rising and reaching a new level their health also improved. They were always hungry with so much sun, salt, and wind, with absolutely no access to fast food, snacks, or sweets.

Creating boundaries wasn't easy when you removed the deterrent of punishment when they were crossed. It was not the most brilliant idea to let the crew decide the level of punishment if they crossed a boundary of what was acceptable behaviour. For some odd reason, they suggested such strict and extreme sanctions that it would be impossible to enforce them. Seventeen lashes for stealing from the provisions?

What normally worked best was for the officers to be a bit unconventional. When the youngest boy asked what would happen if he got drunk or stoned, I replied, "I personally don't care one shit, but at your age you will most likely throw up all over the place, make a fool of yourself, and wake up with a splitting headache, causing you to be late for work the next morning and lose lots of precious stars and points, and it's going to take you ages to get back to where you were!"

Drugs and alcohol were not really a major problem on board, apart from my own addiction to smoking. Maybe it was due to the fact that we were not focused on the issue of drinking. We actually had no restrictions in these areas. We didn't talk about it. Sometimes, on special occasions, I would pour out a glass of watered wine for each of them as if we were one big Italian family. An act that back home would have been utterly impossible to within 10 nautical miles of Norwegian jurisdiction.

Strangely enough, they didn't consume or enjoy any kind of booze. When it came down to it, they preferred Coca Cola to the bitter South American beer. Rum was considered to be the devil's brew and even worse than vodka or mentholated spirit. However, that bottle of sweet cream Spanish liqueur that the captain had under lock and key? Now that was a totally different story.

We were into our third month of sailing around the Caribbean when Ole, standing at the helm, opened up to me for the first time. "You know what, Cap?" he said shyly. "Before, I could never do stuff for a long time, you know. I just noticed I did a four-hour watch, and if it's OK, I'll gladly take another watch if you give me another star." That alone showed that the system worked!

During his next watch I dug out his epi-crisis summary from the safe for the first time. I read that Ole was, among other things, extremely hyperactive, and without medication he was unable to concentrate on any task for more than five minutes. This same Ole could hang out all day, patiently waiting on the edge of the reef with a spear in his hand. He always came back on board without anything to show, shivering and with his teeth chattering. But he was determined not to give in. Someday he'd spear that big blue fish.

One day he came shopping with me on the island of Margarita. I hate shopping, especially when I have to drag someone along with me, but he could help carry the shopping bags. I knew he hated shopping too, so I gave him 10,000 bolivars, which is the equivalent of three dollars, and I told him to wait for me in an amusement arcade.

When I returned an hour and a half later, I found the little undernourished blond Viking manoeuvring his galactic spaceship with such professionalism that the proprietor told me that he had never seen anything like it. A large crowd of admiring Venezuelan teenagers had gathered around him, applauding every time he made a hit against the enemy. His record scores had given him continuous playing time, and he still had 1000 bolivars left in his pocket. I made a mental note to write and tell his shrink up there in the arctic north to get stuffed and get another job!

The technique that seemed to work the best was the "freedom game." I can describe it, in all its logic, in a few words. The more freedom you show you can handle, the more freedom you will get. It worked like this.

To begin with, we were very rigid and strict where shore-leave was concerned- absolutely no going ashore without supervision by an officer. If all went well, shore-leave was granted, to begin with, for only a few hours, and gradually more time was allotted. Basically, if they showed that they could manage to get back on board on time without any problems or a police escort, leave would be extended the next time. In other words, managed responsibility resulted in freedom. Or, as I saw it, freedom gave them responsibility. But if they failed, they were back to square one and had to start all over again. Just like in a video game.

For their own safety we came to an arrangement. If they were not back on board by the agreed time, we would go into *Code Red*. Activating *Code Red* meant that we would alert the local police, harbour-master, hospitals, coast guard, and Salvation Army.

Code Red was only activated once. They arrived back an hour late. They said that there had been a problem with the taxi that was to bring them back from a discotheque high up in the mountains.

The taxi-driver had a different version. When we made them continue their taxi journey to all the organizations that had been put on *Code Red* alert, the kids were obliged to call off the search at their own expense.

This turned out to be quite expensive and a huge embarrassment for them. They were never late again.

At the end of six months they had reached a stage where they could stay out all night as long as they were up and ready for work at six in the morning. This option was never made use of. They found it more enjoyable to sit in the cockpit playing monopoly while gorging themselves on Mariann's chocolate cake, listening to the captain's salty yarns- it didn't matter that they had heard the stories before.

Then there was the issue of education and the dreaded schooling. The only way we could get these kids through any learning process was to take an unconventional approach to teaching.

With this in mind we sent a fax to the Ministry of Church and Education in Norway to place an order for books on the subjects of sharks, marine biology, the history of South America, Simon Bolivar, famous pirates, and the indigenous tribes- anything that had to do with, or that they could associate with, their surroundings. The books never arrived in Venezuela. Two years after our "students" had left I collected a box of books from the tiny post office in Bequia. Books with the following titles:

The History of Christendom in Norway.

The Complete Book of Mathematical Tables.

Henrik Ibsen's A Doll House.

The Complete Works of William Shakespeare.

French for Beginners

and a dozen more with no local interest whatsoever. The books were donated to the Bequia Library. The only one that could have been useful was *Learn*

How to Sail. But they already knew all about that after the first six weeks on board.

I once completed a course developed by a genius Italian educationalist. He based his teaching on what he called *Lizard Pedagogic*. The main objective was to concentrate and connect all tutoring to the student's own environment and situation. The suburbs of Milan were crawling with lizards, so the kids dissected lizards to learn how the critters worked in order to teach biology. When teaching history he told his students to ask their grandfathers what they did during the Great War instead of making them memorize the names of Kings and Queens down through the centuries. He used literature for research and self-discovery. Being unconventional soon had their attention, and he was able to stimulate an interest in any subject. Books on geography? Forget it. We were anchored off the coast of one of the most exciting continents on the planet. A floating classroom with first rate access to biology, science, and geography.

Their thesis was to be called, *A Study of the Culture of Contemporary Ameri-Indian Tribes in The Lost World of Sir Arthur Conan Doyle*.

Sounds quite impressive!

I hired a watchman with a shotgun and machete to guard our home and school. My attempt to hire a Land Rover was futile when the rental company learned of my destination. However, for the neat sum of 500 dollars, I bought a battered jeep from a guy who said he was the owner. The engine and brakes worked, but not the air-conditioner. Best of all, I could sell it back to him when I returned, if I could find him.

To quote the owner of the old heap of rust, he actually said, "If you return."

He said this with a devious smile on his lips as we headed off into the hinterland, loaded with camping gear, maps, provisions, our extensive first-aid kit, cameras with lots of film, a microscope with a cracked optical lens, my antique Remington typewriter, and the 10-volume encyclopaedia from *Fredag's* library.

Our destination was the southern area of Venezuela's Amazonas region. Our objectives were to locate the world's biggest arthropod- the goliath bird-eating spider that lives on the Auyán-tepui near Canaima, to interview an indigenous Indian teenager with the help of sign language, and to explore and survey the Kavanayou river, a short tributary to the Carrao which leads to Angel Falls, the highest waterfall in world.

Our time span was; however long it took.

Crossing the vast tropical grasslands of the Orinoco we passed thousands of working oil wells. The jeep seemed like it was losing as much oil as all those wells produced. The air conditioning turned out to be a dozen or more holes in the floor. What I thought was a bridge on the map turned out to be a ferry. We crossed the Orinoco on a wooden raft with a 500 HP Yamaha outboard, and we continued southwards until the road went no further. After three days and 30 hours of driving, we'd done an average of 15 miles an hour. Added to this, we had three punctures and several breakdowns. The kids were

getting restless. They'd been through all the dirty songs they could think of ten times over and had seen half a million grazing cattle and dozens of road-kill, and that was about it on the zoological side.

At the end of the rainbow you'll find a pot of gold the saying goes. We had come to the end of the road and could go no further on four wheels. A rusty road sign told us that the little dusty town with the long row of two storey wooden buildings was called La Paragua. Derelict buildings on each side of an enormously wide dirt road reminded me of the set of *Gunsmoke*. There was even a saloon with swinging hinged doors.

There was nobody around outdoors. Only a scabby old horse tied to an empty water trough. We entered the saloon, but by now we were really not surprised when we found another "movie set." This time with real "actors." Five men with huge moustaches, all wearing high leather boots and wide hats were leaning against the bar knocking back shots of whiskey. One carried a pistol in a hip holster. They eyed us suspiciously but didn't utter a word as we nervously crossed the floor in a long line.

A giant oriental-looking bartender with a dirty apron slid six Cokes along half the length of the counter top. My young crew seemed fascinated by the scene, and when I nonchalantly leaned against the bar with one hand on my hip, they did exactly the same, looking as if they came here on a regular basis. The oldest, who I had never seen smoking, lit up and flicked the match to the floor with a tough Clint Eastwood squint.

I found it extraordinary funny but managed to control myself.

The bartender asked if we have come looking for gold. La Paragua turned out to be a small mining village, and for 10 dollars a day we could rent 6 pans and 10 meters of river bed. I was a bit concerned though. What if we made a strike? I imagined tomorrow's headline, "SIX GOLD SEEKING TOURISTS SHOT."

Some of those gun-slinging dudes at the bar looked a bit scary to me, but we voted later to go for it! Believe it or not, Ole, the skinny little kid who was never able to spear that big blue reef fish, made a strike the very next day- a tiny gold nugget! Standing knee deep in the river, staring at the treasure in his hand, a 3 mm. diameter nugget, was too much for him. He turned his back to us so we couldn't see his tears.

His gold nugget was the only find between the six of us. Returning to the village we exchanged it for cash with a trader. We found him asleep with his feet up on a chair and his hat over his face. On the table lay his revolver, scales, and a sign in English reading, *We By (sic) Gold.*

Ole desperately wanted to keep the nugget to show to his pals on the street back home. I also wanted for him to keep it, but the deal was that any gold found belonged to us all. The sale barely covered the river rent, pans, and the six-mattress room in the amazing *La Florida Roach Hotel* but it was well worth the excitement and experience.

There was only one phone in town. Ole had a magical way of making calls from phone booths without paying, and they weren't collect calls. We had no idea how he did it. This whiz kid was connected within 10 seconds. I was never able to make a single long-distance call from a phone booth in Venezuela, even by paying. I couldn't help overhearing a bit of the excited conversation. The tiny nugget had suddenly grown to the size of a tennis ball.

I was on good terms with the bartender. When I asked him if he could help us find a guide to take us through the rainforest to the village of Canaima, he stepped back in horror, muttered a prayer to the holy Virgin Mother, and told me I must be "loco" to attempt such a trek through the jungle. When he was finished revealing to me all the dreadful things that could happen on such a dangerous venture he offered to arrange our transportation.

We were taken to a 500-foot-long clearing in the rainforest to a bumpy dirt-surfaced airstrip. A single-engine bush plane awaited us. The pilot was as big as his aircraft was small. He just managed to squeeze into the cockpit, and I wondered if this flying calamity could lift his weight, never mind ours. The aircraft had four seats with a bit of room for cargo behind. The doors were missing and there were no seatbelts.

The cargo was a pair of plastic drums filled with gasoline, tied to the back of the seats, and they both leaked badly. Three of us had to sit in the rear together with all our gear and the leaking drums. The pilot warned us not to smoke. I wouldn't smoke within 200 feet of this flying Molotov cocktail.

The plane shook violently when our pilot revved the spluttering engine before take-off. With the engine on full throttle, the rickety aircraft somewhat calmed itself. The pilot released the brakes and we lurched forward.

We just managed to clear the canopy at the end of the runway, and our pilot kept the plane at a very low level for the rest of the flight, dipping a wing or doing a slight roll to show us something interesting below. A big hole in the exhaust manifold made it impossible to hear what he was yelling. His altitude gauge showed what appeared to be a constant 800 feet. Every time the engine coughed or missed a beat, he touched a little figurine of Our Lady of Guadeloupe hanging from the overhead compass which, I noticed, never moved. It was nearly impossible to read the oil-pressure gauge as it was half-full of black oil.

The former Indian village of Canaima turned out to be a huge construction site. A tourist resort and airport were nearly completed and ready to welcome tourists. The Indian village and resort were situated next to a scenic lake with a small version of Niagara Falls. Somewhere up the river lay the world highest waterfall, nineteen times higher than Niagara- Angel Falls.

We were all pretty shaken up after the *Molotov cocktail* flight. We needed a rest. At the resort we were told they could not give us any prices. The establishment had tried to resemble a cross between a Mayan temple and an Indian village; it was a French-owned all-inclusive, pre-booked by credit-card arrangement with "bargain" prices, and they'd actually never had anyone knock on the door to ask for a room. When I was finally quoted an outrageous price for two rooms, some extra mattresses and a shower, I renamed the place Hotel Exorbitant, told the management to stuff it, and led my troops off into the rainforest.

After a half hour of chopping our way through the dense foliage to try and find a place to raise our tent, I discovered that we had just made a new path parallel to an existing one. Following this path, we eventually came across a suitable spot to set up camp. While my crew was doing their boy scout thing, I stole off into the bush to light a cigarette. I'd told my crew I'd quit again after giving a long lecture about the importance of self-discipline.

To my surprise I discovered the path led to a dwelling of basic design. We had set up camp next door to someone's home. The woman residing in the mud and straw hut was as surprised as I was when I stumbled out of the bush. She told me that this was her home, she had lived here all her life; she had been to Caracas once, and that her husband had died a month ago when he went over the falls on his way home from a drinking spree in the nearby village, bless his soul.

She also told me that I reminded her of Harrison Ford, and in the same breath she asked if I would like to see her bedroom, pointing to the straw hut. I saw that special look in her eyes, so I told her I'm married and that my wife and four children are hiding in the bush right behind her.

She gave me a big toothless grin and invited us all for supper.

The straw covered hut was small, and I guessed it was most likely used as her bedroom. The rest of the "house" consisted of six wooden posts holding up a roof of corroded galvanized sheeting. Between the posts hung two hammocks. The kitchen was an open fireplace made with loose construction blocks. Black sooty aluminium pots and pans hung from hooks on the posts next to a very old General Electric refrigerator. I saw no electric wires running to it. There were no electric wires anywhere. There were magnetic pictures of Jesus Christ and Simon Bolivar attached to the fridge door. A faded photo of her husband, pasted on the side, reminded me of Groucho Marx. A mangy hen sat roosting on its top.

"Cerebro de mono," she said as she served us the main course. It looked a bit weird but had an exquisite taste. My brave crew, who normally wouldn't touch anything with garlic or even look at a bloody or medium rare steak, gazed at the dish in shock and despair but dared not embarrass our hostess by refusing to eat it. They were also very hungry. They chewed, smiled awkwardly, and breathed through their mouths at the same time, not saying a word.

I was extremely proud of my well-behaved young Vikings when they leaned back in their chairs, closed their eyes, swallowed, and muttered politely, "Good stuff, man." I translated to our hostess, and to her guests' horror she dished out more. I never did translate to my crew that "cerebro" and "mono" meant *brain* and *monkey*.

"Be careful on your way back to your camp," said the old woman in a mixture of Spanish and something guttural that came from deep inside her. "Every time I cook, there's always a five-meter-long snake in the vicinity."

With their heels together and giving a slight polite bow, my crew shook hands with our hostess. "*Takk for maten*," thanks for the food, they said in Norwegian.

Our hostess was delighted, she had never seen such enchanting young people, and she told me that I should be a very proud father. I didn't tell her that the bastards were not mine, and they were really the worst of all the juvenile gangsters to be found in the Land of the Midnight Sun.

Our surroundings screamed with the sounds of the rainforest at night as we stuck close together in a line, moving along the path back to our camp. Our flashlight beam flickered nervously around the foliage searching for the five-meter-long anaconda. There was no sign of the snake, but that didn't help us much to feel more at ease. We couldn't sleep. In between the steady racket of tree frogs and crickets, the howler monkeys regularly went into a shrill, ear-splitting frenzy accompanied by screeching parrots. The occasional screams and thuds seemed to get closer and closer. When I started telling ghost stories, I got cussed and bombarded with slices of watermelon.

I had never done any white-water rafting, but I'd seen it on TV. It looked to me like a bunch of crazy people going down raging rapids on inflatable rafts.

For twenty dollars, two flashlight batteries, and set of Phillips screwdrivers, our two Indian guides ran us up the Carrao River in a long dug-out canoe. It was equipped with an eighty-horsepower outboard engine lashed to the stern. We traversed the rapids, dodging rocks as they appeared, and held on for dear life as we raced upstream to where we obviously could go no further, nearly right to the foot of the 3200-foot high Angel Falls.

Angel Falls, the world's tallest waterfall, cascades down from the Auyan Tepui into what is known as the Devil's canyon, 979 meters below. The indigenous people call it *Kerepakupai-merú*, but it is officially named Angel Falls after Jimmy Angel, an American bush pilot and gold-hunting adventurer, who "discovered" it in 1937.

Jimmy crashed his plane on the top of the tepui, a flat-topped mountain. It was a miracle that he survived, especially when you saw the remains of his aircraft, still recognisable but overgrown with vegetation. I was told the local authorities planned to remove the wreck and sell it to a museum in the USA.

Jimmy was very impressed with the falls, but not too happy about having to climb down the waterfall and make the long trek back to civilisation with a broken leg.

After a four-hour journey up the Carrao River, a ride that would top any nail-biting, nerve-wracking theme park roller coaster ride, we were dropped off at the Kavanayou tributary that led to the waterfall. We were asked when we wanted to be picked up for the return. I told them we would walk back. The boat captain shook his head and mumbled something that sounded like *mental locomotive.*

The vegetation was dense and soaking wet. We couldn't see the falls but we could feel the ground vibrate and hear the roar. It should have taken an hour to traverse the river, but it took all day. One of the assignments of the expedition was to survey and map the Kavanayou river. Doing a shoreline survey, our students would observe, map, and record ecological issues, flora and fauna, water conditions, natural resources, and human activity.

I told them that the river had recently been discovered and had never been surveyed, which was a load of BS, but they would learn geometry and trigonometry. There was reputedly gold and diamonds in this area, but we didn't find any. Water conditions were perfect- everything was soaked- and were the only human activity.

We camped at the foot of the falls. The water fell freely over 900 meters and shot back up as a misty spray. Our only problem was sleeping. Even with earplugs we couldn't sleep due to the vibrations in the ground.

I recognized many of the tropical plants my horticultural grandmother used to have in her greenhouse- only these plants, drenched in constant drizzle, were gigantic, at least ten times the size.

The under-brush was alive with all sorts of creepy-crawlies, but no huge spiders. They supposedly lived on top of the tepui. I was told there was a way to get there by climbing the cliff close to the waterfall. After an extensive study of the route, I dropped the idea with the unanimous consent of my crew, particularly from young Kari who suffered from arachnophobia- the fear of spiders.

We camped by the foot of the falls for two days. Communication was difficult due to the continuous thunder of the falls, and we were soaked. To the tune of *Singin' in the Rain* we started our long trek downstream, back to Canaima, following the river-bank. It was hard going but no one had wanted to shoot the rapids down that treacherous river by canoe. A shorter direct compass course would take about two days, but by keeping the river within sight and hearing distance there was less risk of getting lost and having our remains eaten by jungle creatures.

Once safely back in Canaima, we learned we couldn't fly back to La Paragua. I was truly relieved when I heard that the reason was engine problems on the flying Molotov cocktail. However, the price to fly on a commercial carrier was way above our budget. We were by now running low on expedition funds Our best option was to follow a path going east through the rainforest. After 25 miles, if we didn't wander off or get lost, we would end up at an Indian settlement, said our former pilot.

We were told to ask for Shori, the shaman. He made a regular trip down river to El Dorado, a village with bus connection to the outside world. Shori owed a favour to the pilot, who guaranteed that Shori would help us. He also advised us not to stay in El Dorado- *muy peligroso*- too dangerous!

It took us two hot and humid days to reach the Pemon settlement.

It wasn't the first time the children there had seen a white man, but they'd never seen *young* white people, especially kids with long, golden hair. They queued up and take turns touching the heads of our all-blond crew.

The incident reminded me of a story an American cruising couple told me. They had anchored their yacht in a remote bay on the northern coast of Papua New Guinea. They had heard that there was a native tribe in the area that had never met or seen a white man. After months of searching, my friends made contact with the tribe by setting out gifts in a clearing in the jungle. The gifts mysteriously disappeared until one day their gifts were exchanged with a return gift. In another month the couple was accepted as part of the tribe. One of the most interesting aspects of this indigenous tribe was the fact that their facial expressions bore no relation to ours. They smiled when they were sad and frowned when happy.

When the day arrived that my friends had to leave, a smiling tribe held a big farewell party. On the menu was a young man from a neighboring tribe that had been killed that same morning. My friends knew what they were eating, but they felt strongly they had no choice but to go with the flow and join in with the feast.

On their way back to their yacht they met some hunters from the rival tribe. Even though the couple had eaten one of their brothers, they quickly established a friendship with them, but they politely declined their dinner invitation.

The Pemon tribe was not as isolated as those my American friends had encountered, and they didn't eat humans. They were indigenous to areas of southwestern Venezuela. Most lived like average Venezuelans in towns and villages with modern housing, TV, and clothing. However, there were a fairly large number who preferred to preserve their culture and traditions and to live with nature.

We had arrived at one of their many rainforest settlements. Their traditional housing consisted of huts whose walls were made of clay and bark with roofs made from palm leaves. Hammocks hung from the roof beams, and a fire burned in one corner. Arrows, knives, axes, and fishing rods were stacked in the opposite corner. Baskets and carrying sacks hung on the walls.

They were friendly and invited us for dinner. I was pretty sure that we would not be eating one of their neighbours, but I was concerned that monkey-brain might be on the menu. Not to worry, we were served yucca and *aurosa,* both vegetables, together with plantain and piranha fish.

After we had eaten, we were served *cachiri,* a drink made from bitter yucca paste that had been grated, chewed, and mixed with a grated red root. The mixture was then boiled for a whole day. It was mildly intoxicating. We were then obliged to finish off with a puff from a passed-around pipe. Whatever it was we were smoking made us smile. In my report to the Norwegian Child Welfare authorities there was no mention of the latter two items.

After a full day of paddling down the winding river, Shori suddenly became very excited. With the help of sign language and drawings in the mud on the riverbank I got the picture, literally. He wanted to know if we would like to visit a white man.

We discovered Hans living all alone on a tiny island in a large straw and bamboo house on stilts. He didn't seem surprised to see us, so I suspected that the shaman often brought him visitors. The old silver-haired German hermit told me he'd been living here a long time. When I asked him when he arrived, he didn't answer.

He invited us in for tea. The single room contained very little in the way of furniture, but he had the largest collection of books I'd ever seen in a Venezuelan home.

One can always find out a lot by studying a person's library. I was surprised that in this vast collection of serious and interesting classical literature, there was a copy of Hitler's *Mein Kampf*. This didn't necessarily mean the guy was a Nazi- I have a copy of the Holy Bible in my library and I'm an atheist.

After a third cup of tea I asked for the bathroom, which was rather stupid in the middle of a rainforest. He pointed towards the bushes.

I stumbled across a small outhouse. I couldn't resist having a peek inside. On the wall hung a German Wehrmacht uniform. In spite of the warm, sticky, humid air, my blood nearly froze.

My god, I thought, *I've found Joseph Mengele, the Angel of Death*. Then, to make my day, a huge spider dropped from the ceiling and stopped a foot above the floor- a Goliath Spider! It was on our checklist of what we'd come for. But how could I show the kids without Hans finding out that I had seen his uniform?

After careful consideration and since we were miles from a phone, I decided not to call my friend, the editor of Norway's largest newspaper. I decided not to make a big fuss. There was something about the old man that told me that he was not a war criminal. Furthermore, a two-chevron insignia on the uniform- if it was his- put him in the lower ranks of evil *just following my orders* Nazis. What if I opened this can of worms and Hans had only been an innocent guard or a regular soldier? If I were someone who'd committed crimes against humanity, I would never have invited a bunch of tourists in for tea.

I returned to the tea-party and asked Hans if there are any big spiders on the tiny island. He said they normally lived on top of the tepui mountains, but he did have a tame Goliath as a pet.

Would I like to see it? Kari shrieks a definite no. So did the rest of them.

Back on board, safe and sound on the *Fredag*, all the data was sorted and processed. After three weeks of hard work, their thesis, or project report, was completed and mailed to the government, who reluctantly had promised to pick up the one thousand-dollar tab.

As far as I know no one has ever read it. It was probably filed away somewhere together with all my monthly reports. If someone had read the extraordinary piece of work, they would have been very impressed- so impressed that I'm sure they would have called or written to me by now.

We sailed back to the island of Grenada. After nine months the project was running smoothly, but for some reason that I didn't understand why one of the boys was restless, moody, and at times quite aggressive. As he became more and more difficult, and after we'd tried everything to reach the boy, we decided to ask for help.

I put in a request for counselling by a specific behavioural therapist from London, a person I knew well who could stay on board with us. My request was approved by the government, but some department geek must have missed out on some of his geography lessons and was trying to save money. Believing that Grenada was in the south of Spain, they found a psychologist in Gibraltar. When all was resolved, the Norwegian authorities sent down a psychiatrist from New York.

The shrink arrived with his wife, three kids, five suitcases, and very little time on his hands. He only had the weekend, and he was hopping mad that I hadn't booked him a hotel, plus he'd promised to take his kids water-skiing and go scuba diving because he'd arrived at a diving paradise.

We were sitting with the shrink in a bar overlooking the bay. The crew were on board cooking dinner. I spent about an hour giving him the full picture. His listened attentively for a while, then turned away from me, not saying a word. When I asked a specific question, he replied with a question.

Looking out over the horizon, he asked, "So how do *you* feel about it?"

I asked him if he would like me to bring a couch- so I could lie down on it and tell him how I feel. He pretended not to hear me.

His youngest boy was present and constantly interrupted. His father pretended he didn't exist. The kid then threw a tantrum, so the shrink whacked his son across his ear! I could not believe what I was witnessing.

I had some ideas on how to approach the problem, but I wanted my crew to be part of finding a solution, because it concerned us all.

The shrink wanted a different "line of attack" as he phrased it. He wanted a meeting with the kids first, on board, without me and Mariann present. I reluctantly went along with his strategy.

While he was on board *Fredag,* I was baby-sitting his son in the bar. I walked around in circles, fuming, muttering cuss words. I went through three packs of Camels in two hours. The spoiled brat of a son kept pestering me, and now I felt like whacking the little monster!

A young messenger from *Fredag* was sent ashore. I was summoned by the shrink back on board my own ship! Good Grief!

The child refused to leave the bar. He wasn't getting any more ice-cream, so he threw another tantrum. My first mate wanted me to stay with the kid, have another drink, and cool down. She would sort out the shrink. I declined her generous offer and left her to deal with child from hell.

The atmosphere in *Fredag's* saloon was thick with gloom. The kids were huddled in a corner, and the psychiatrist stood as tall as his five-foot, two-inch frame would allow. "Doctor Freud" said he had it all sorted out. He said that we were in the middle of a crisis.

Great work man, we figured out two weeks ago that we had a crisis!

Pointing his finger at my crew, he said, "If you guys can't sort this out, pull yourselves together and behave, there's no other solution than to send you home."

Damn! I'd forgotten to tell Sigmund here that sending them home was akin to capital punishment, that it was no solution at all.

I immediately broke up the meeting. The shrink started to protest. I point my finger at him saying, "Are you aware who is captain of this ship?"

One of my crew started sniggering. Ten seconds later, the shrink was in the dinghy, waiting to be rowed ashore. I let him sit to roast in the hot sun for a while.

Returning to the bar I found that Mariann had capitulated and gone to get an ice-cream for the screaming child. The shrink threatened to lock him in the bathroom if he didn't shut up. All further counselling was cancelled.

Returning back on board to apologize, I found that my crew had vanished. The safe has been broken into, but they'd only taken 200 dollars of the three thousand. I had a desertion on my hands- not a mutiny- the tabloids back in Norway would get it all wrong.

Not much happens in Norway in July and August. These are the two months of the year when nearly everyone takes a long holiday, even criminals. Everybody except the press. A journalist on holiday in Grenada heard about my crew's desertion, and within 12 hours the story made the front page of every newspaper in the country.

These are some of the headlines:

SAILING DOES NOT CURE CRIMINALS

MUTINY ON THE FREDAG

SPOILED THEIR CHANCE OF A LIFETIME

TAXPAYER'S MONEY WASTED

SOCIAL WELFARE ON THE ROCKS

DREAM CRUISE ENDS IN DISASTER

In one report there was a photo of my daughter and myself. It showed her "punk" hair style. The picture was taken while I was building *Fredag* and it gave the reader the impression that she was one of the juvenile delinquents.

One story went like this, including horrendous mistakes, bad grammar, and punctuation:

MUTINY HALTS PIONEERING DRUG REHAB PROJECT

Unhappy with the treatment and conditions on the sailing ship and drug rehab project FREDAG, run by the two psychiatrists Petter Rore (44) and Mary Anne Palborg (38), the entire crew jumped ship in the marijuana capital of the world, the Caribbean island of Granada. They are hiding out somewhere in the jungle and in an exclusive interview the children tell a story of horror and desperation, locked up on a vessel resembling "a slave ship from hell," deprived of the bare necessities in life. Projects like these, focusing on the losers and the delinquents in society, are costing the taxpayers millions every year, while good honest hard-working kids have to pay for their own luxury cruises, that is if they can afford it. Most young people today can't even afford to go on a bicycle trip across the border to Sweden. The project leaders have gone into hiding and refuse to comment.

The only thing the journalist had right was my age. Several of the journalists who flew to Grenada couldn't get much information out of anyone, and they had to come home with some kind of story.

Grenada in the Lesser Antilles is a small island with a population of around 90,000. They are about 90% black. Four white and blond teenagers would have to stand out.

We found out where they were hiding, but what was more important, I discovered what the problem was and why they'd run away.

They were afraid of going home soon! Back to where they were before- back to the streets or to some miserable institution. They simply didn't want to go home! They wanted more travelling and for us to continue to believe in them. It was all quite logical.

I'd been thinking about what was going to happen to them when they returned home. Every time the thought popped up I'd try to think of something else. Such thoughts had been on the kids' minds since day one, and it was now getting hard to think about anything else.

I had to inform the authorities in Norway and Grenada that they were missing. The Grenada police were very helpful. They knew that the kids were hiding out with some law-abiding Rastafari in the mountains, but the police needed my consent to arrest them. After a long discussion with the chief of police, he understood perfectly what was going on, and he arranged for an undercover Rasta officer to infiltrate and keep an eye on them for a few days. I wanted to nominate this chief of police for a medal when this was over. The Rasta officer was a smart man, and the chief assured me that the officer would persuade the kids to come down on their own.

I always believed that something good could come out of anything bad.

The kids didn't know that the Rasta-man was an undercover cop. They befriended him and asked if he could discreetly pass on a message to their Captain and his mate.

"Tell them that we are OK, have not spent the money and will be home soon."

Wow, they now called it "home!" We both had tears in our eyes when we read their note.

With the Rasta cop as a safety link between us, I rested and tried to make the most of it our time alone, but I had to admit that I missed them quite a bit, and I was pretty sure they were soon going to miss life on board and, not to forget, Mariann's chocolate cake.

The Ministry of Church, Education, and Social Affairs decided that our clients, as they called them, had to fly back to Norway immediately. The press and the opposition in Parliament were blowing things out of proportion. Two social workers would fly down to escort them back. I tried to protest, saying that my crew didn't need to be taken home in chains- they were perfectly capable of traveling on their own.

When the "escort" arrived, it felt as if the child welfare-people had come to take our children away from us.

However, the two social workers were not to blame; they were just doing their job. I managed to convince them to postpone their departure for a week "due to unforeseen difficulties and acts of God."

We went sailing again, and the two welfare officers were impressed when our crew dished up a three-course meal in heavy seas. My crew were doing their best, hoping they would be allowed to stay, even though we were all aware of the fact that the project had been planned to last a maximum of 9 months.

Of course, the officers had not read my monthly reports. They had the impression that things were out of control on board. They'd heard that the kids could do more or less what they wanted- they could stay out all night if they wished, and that we had smoked pot together in the rainforest because it wasn't illegal there, and that we had encouraged drinking and immoral sexual acts letting boys and girls share bedrooms.

Bedrooms? Sex? First of all, sex was extremely difficult in the four narrow bulkhead bunks in the saloon- bunks so narrow that you had to squeeze in head first. And how do you stop two teenagers from creeping behind a bush on a desert island for a bit of hanky-panky if they are so inclined?

I found it more meaningful and educational to *talk* about sex than to worry about them *having* it- to talk about sex in a spontaneous and natural way, and I don't mean about the birds and bees. I was trying to put it into perspective- how hard it was to walk around for months with a belly the size of a watermelon, how painful giving birth was, how an unwanted child could wreck your life and eat up your paycheck, how awful baby poop smelled, and how easy it was to die of AIDS if you didn't use a condom. This worked better than putting them in different "bedrooms."

Drugs? We never discussed the subject. Drugs were not a problem and there had been no interest. Alcohol? No interest. The only minor problem was when they once took a fancy to my Kahlua coffee liqueur and watered it down, hoping I wouldn't notice. They lost five points each on that one, and it never happened again.

If you are invited by an Indian chief to take a puff from his five-foot long peace pipe, even if it contained some really heavy stuff, you just don't say no. You have a puff, just like you eat monkey-brain or even a neighbor from the valley beyond.

I never asked the kids what took place in those mountains in Grenada. By the look in their eyes and by the way they proudly held their heads when they returned on board, I knew it had been something special.

Just like their time on board *the slave ship from Hell*.

After nearly a year of working around the clock as therapists, teachers, jailors, and substitute parents, with very little support and salary, I thought we'd done enough to save the world. Mariann wanted the government to ship us a new crew. I disagreed and argued that after our crew's "mutiny" the idea would be dead in the water. Furthermore, within a week after the kids left, we received a fax with bad news. There had been no follow-up or evaluation and they were all sent back to their original institutions and foster-homes. The police were looking for one who had done a runner from his foster-parents, and the others had locked themselves in their respective rooms, waiting for a response to their request to embark on *Fredag* for another year, refusing to discuss any other option. Mariann strongly felt we had accomplished something significant, and that there was good reason to build on what we had achieved.

I strongly disagreed. Marianne floated the idea that we should legally adopt Ole and the others. This was not what I had signed up for. I already had children. Our discussions on the subject turned into hefty arguments. *Fredag* became an unhappy place to be.

We concluded that we needed space and time for ourselves to think things over. I needed to jump ship for a spell and find a peaceful, land-based resort where I could figure out my next move. Mariann was quite happy to remain on board, safely moored in the marina, so there was no need to cut her into little pieces and feed her to the sharks, though at times we'd both felt like doing that to each other.

14. The Last Resort

The resort manager, Poco, picked me up in his wooden peñero on time and we sped across the bay to Punta Camaron with the aid of his powerful 100 horse Yamaha outboard. "Cape Shrimp" is really not a cape, but rather two curved peninsulas which form a horseshoe-shaped little inlet, topped by low hills covered with cacti and tamarind trees. The transparent water alternates from green to turquoise blue in deeper parts of the bay.

A white sandy beach with a couple of deck-chairs had a massive sign saying "500 Bs for rent." It wasn't clear if this offer was for the chairs or a room! A new wooden dock with gas lamp posts led to a stone pathway and connected the four completed buildings: a beach bar and restaurant, staff quarters, a cottage for me, and a separate bathroom. All the buildings were circular, constructed of bamboo and whitewashed adobe with thatched palm-leaf roofs.

This was Poco's dream, conceived as he watched the film *South Pacific* in a drunken stupor after celebrating a lucrative business deal. The place did have a Polynesian feel, especially its soothing tranquillity in marked contrast to the distant noisy "mainland" of Venezuela. The only sounds were the cheerful chirps of mockingbirds, the rustling of lizards in the bushes, and the gentle murmur of the waves under the dock.

A friendly old mongrel dog was the only sign of life ashore. He greeted us with an eager wagging tail and a big smile- as only dogs can smile. Welcome to Punta Cameron!

After a quick inspection of my cosy little cottage, built high on teak stilts to keep out snakes or whatever else might be crawling around, I headed straight for the bar. Poco prepared a welcome rum punch with a heavy kick while lecturing two workers in rapid Spanish for sleeping on the job, all with great pathos.

The two young employees, Jesus and Leandro, took turns at being cooks, bartenders, bouncers, room-maids, gardeners, caretakers, and construction workers, but they only seemed to work when Poco was around. No wonder it had taken five years to get this far in the construction of his dream resort.

The young men were instructed to cater to my every need- to get anything I wanted if they had it- to wash the bathroom every time I used it, to turn off the salsa music when I was in the bar, and to run the generator when I needed it to charge my lap-top or listen to my tapes.

The boys just couldn't do enough for me. It was really weird calling for "Jesus" every time I needed something. I got a special kick out of calling for Leandro to bring me a beer. He was not trusted with such a difficult task and inevitably answered, "Jesus is coming, Jesus is coming!"

It was all very nice and tranquillo- just what the doctor ordered.

Poco spent most of his time sleeping or sleeping it off! When he wasn't sleeping, he consumed gallons of beer and Scotch whisky and talked endlessly about his lost love.

Poco was three years into an affair with a beautiful young Venezuelan when she sailed away two weeks after meeting a gringo sailor, a good friend of his. He discovered soon afterwards that she'd helped herself to a couple of million bolivars from his account; they hadn't been heard from since!

I tried my best to lighten his misery, telling him that at the ripe age of 48 he was still a young man, good looking, and that the world was full of gorgeous women. I told him how by chance I'd met an attractive woman, just as everything was looking very gloomy indeed. I showed him a photo of Mariann and he started crying, saying that he missed his lost love, and he opened another bottle of whisky. By the time the bottle was empty he'd given me advice on every aspect of keeping women under lock and key.

He conjured up yet another bottle of whisky, but halfway through it he fell asleep. In the morning he was gone- probably off hunting for a new sweetheart.

Jesus and Leandro shook their heads at this, saying "Poco is loco," and "It's not the first time. He never learns. He's a magnet for malo women." They told me that many times he had woken up looking for his wallet.

The boys desperately wanted to "Espeakey Ingliish." They wanted to be prepared for the big day in the distant future when the resort officially opened. Until now they only had Sunday picnickers, Venezuelans visiting for the day. I'd rather have brushed up on my Spanish, but I resigned myself to help them. They were nice young men with a future- probably more than I had. They didn't seem to worry much about women, as Poco and I did.

When I hinted how "perfecto" everything would be if only I could have a "good smoke" they brought me something that tasted like manure but did the job. After that, I thought of how great it was to be alive, here and now.

On Friday Poco returned and the three of them went fishing for the day. I was instructed to either go fishing with them or to stay and look after the place. I was never particularly good at fishing, so I chose to stay put. I recalled fishing with my Norwegian uncle who would catch great halibut and cod, while I never hauled up anything. Uncle Hans retired after forty years of dentistry and had time to ply the waters where the rebellious cod lay in wait. "Open wide," he would say. "This may hurt a little bit. Okay. Now bite down, thank you." My uncle had a way with them!

So now I was the resort manager for a day. I inspected the premises, escorted by the dog, who obediently followed my every step.

Here was where I would put the pool and tennis court. We'd throw in a slide for kids in the pool and show Wimbledon matches on video by the bar.

Over there was a perfect spot for open air roulette, we could line the bar with one-armed bandits, and this was where Marianne could sit in the reception and count all the money coming in…

"I'm so sorry," she would say. "We're fully booked until 2007. The manager? I'm sorry. He's busy finishing his fifth novel and can't be disturbed."

Over here we could set up a huge stage and present famous opera, and on the grounds we could put on magnificent fireworks displays.

I'm ripped from my reverie by loud barking. A small sailing boat was approaching- my first *real* chance to act as a manager!

As the boat entered the bay, I noticed she flew the Norwegian flag. They anchored, pumped up their little dinghy and paddled towards the beach where I stood, looking as much like the boss as I could, legs apart, arms crossed, and old faithful by my side.

Twenty feet from the water's edge one of the three called out, asking if I could speak English. I cupped my hand behind my ear and pretended I couldn't hear, but beckoned them to come ashore. They looked warily at the dog and mumbled something in Norwegian that sounded like: "Ae trruer fahn imeh dreetsecken eh stock dhoev!" (The muddah%#^* idiot is f*%#in deaf!") which I recognised as a local Finnmark dialect, not spoken by many Norwegians, and certainly not spoken in such a vulgar manner to strangers, but then *this* hombre wouldn't understand, *would he?*

They waded ashore, still looking around suspiciously, like Columbus entering the New World. Again the question, though not the same one Christopher asked as *he* waded ashore.

"Do you speaking English?"

"Si Senores!" I answered in my best Margariteño accent

The most educated-looking one started an obviously well-prepared speech, slowly and painstakingly stuttering in broken English.

"Ja, and good day, and have you cold beer, and can we lunch have, and where is the town and do you have telephone jack- thank you, please?"

It was like a language from another planet!

I looked them over closely and then gazed from them to their dinghy, then to the boat, and then let my eyes rest on the horizon for a good half a minute, thinking, considering.

Finally, in the best Norwegian West-Finnmark dialect I could come up with I replied, "Kah farschken truer dokkar detta eh foh nocka dah, ett nonnehkloastr?" ("What the f%*# do you think this is- a bloody monastery?")

Their jaws fell open and they resembled choirboys ready to accept Holy Communion. They looked at each other, dumbfounded, and couldn't seem to decide whether the situation was hilarious or if they ought to be hopping mad.

I resolved the impasse by swinging my arm towards the bar, saying, "The joke and the beers are on me," and we all started laughing. They were still laughing as they unsteadily and in full song (all Norwegians sing too much when they're drunk) made their way back to their boat to record the incident at Cape Shrimp in their logbook.

Later, Poco told me I overcharged them. No matter. They were from Finnmark, and they'd tipped me as well!

15. Ensenada Pargo and Jungle Exploring

Returning back to my yacht and mate, there was another fax from Norway with more bad news. Ole, who'd run away, had died from an overdose. We were shocked and saddened by the news. The issue of doing another therapy-cruise with kids was laid to rest. Ole had become more than a crewmember or "patient;" Mariann had even contemplated adoption. The best way to deal with emotional distress was to set sail and find a nice peaceful harbour to heal our sorrows.

Ensenada Pargo, my favourite hideaway, was located on the north-eastern tip of Venezuela. On first impression I thought I'd been transformed into a double-page spread from *National Geographic*. A pristine bay half a mile wide was surrounded by high cloud-topped mountains.

During the summer when the winds were east to south-east the bay would be a perfect anchorage. The rest of the year with wind from the north it would be a good idea to hold on to your coffee cup when anchored there.

I preferred quiet anchorages; I had to accept some rolling around at sea, but in port I wanted to be comfortable. In Ensenada Pargo I took the bad with the good since the overall ambiance was so special.

The cruising guide had only a few lines about Ensenada Pargo, saying that the bay was "a fairly good place to stop for lunch," and that it had impressive natural surroundings, a small, friendly community, and that fresh water was abundant.

The first time I visited I was in awe of its sheer beauty. With *Fredag* tied to a palm tree and an anchor over the stern I could sit for hours, spellbound, and gaze at the towering mountains covered in rainforest. Ensenada Pargo was a gigantic fertile botanical garden reaching into the clouds, where a short burst of heavy tropical rain fell almost every hour.

Pargo Village, *Fredag* in the bottom left corner.

Due to the nutrient-rich current which swept up from the mouth of the Orinoco River, the bay teemed with life. I never tired of watching the struggle for survival- it was better than back-to-back episodes of David Attenborough's nature documentaries. The fish that didn't end up in a larger fish's mouth would sooner or later be gobbled into a pelican's bottomless maw. These ancient, bizarre looking birds appeared to be out of *Jurassic Park* and were constantly in a feeding frenzy. From a height of ten stories they'd fold their wings and swoop down like an arrow, disappear underwater for a few seconds, and always resurface with a catch. They never seemed to miss.

The fish that survived these prehistoric dive bombers only managed to do so because they were present in such great numbers. The terns, boobies, and frigate birds were not nearly as good hunters even though they were much better fliers and aerodynamically streamlined. They were also part of the food chain, victims to the eagles and falcons that occasionally swept from the mountain tops. For some reason, none of these birds of prey wanted to eat a pelican. After hours of bird-watching I was hungry. I too had the hunting instinct.

"I'm going shopping. What shall we have for dinner today?" I asked Mariann. "Lobster or dorado?"

"Grilled barracuda. And don't forget to pick up some mussels on your way back," she replied as I dove into the pellucid sea.

Shooting fish with a spear gun was not exactly "fair play." The fish here were inquisitive and they came up to investigate. Before they knew what hit them, they were speared. On the other hand, using a line or a net you caught all sorts of weird-looking creatures that looked so ugly you lost your appetite. You could also catch something so stunningly exotic and beautiful that you ended up with a guilty conscience that lingered long past your meal.

My thoughtlessness once led me to spear a black and yellow French angelfish, the most beautiful of all tropical reef fish. The inquisitive French angelfish came so close that I had to back up to make room for my spear. Although they were known to taste good, I must confess I had a bad taste in my mouth for days afterwards.

The worst part was that these fish lived in pairs their entire life. After the "assassination" I felt like a murderer every time I came across another angelfish. The black and yellow has a drawn face with sad human features. The next one I encountered looked heartbroken and even gloomier than I had felt when I'd roasted her handsome husband on the barbecue. Years later I still feel a twinge of guilt.

The constant erosion by the waves had undermined the rocky shoreline and created incredible submerged formations- caves that were great natural hiding places for marine life. The fish were so tame I could choose from an extensive menu. However, these fish soon learned to be wary of intruders. To outwit these sensitive creatures, I frequently changed my hunting grounds.

My favourite was barracuda, grilled on the beach over an open fire of smoking coconut husks and drenched with fresh lime juice.

The barracuda was an intimidating sight as it came close to my diving mask. He threw me a threatening gaze and showed off a long snout with protruding razor-sharp teeth. "Barry" has a bad reputation, just like the elusive shark. This is only because Barry *looks* so ruthless. Generally, it is only hazardous when thrashing in the dinghy biting wildly at anything within reach. I have never heard of a single incident where a barracuda has attacked a human being in the sea, but people are warned not to wear silver jewellery when snorkelling, as it might attract these undiscerning creatures.

I occasionally forgot about dinner as I became more and more dazzled by the flourishing underwater life.

My friend Jerry

I paid a visit to my friend "Jerry." Jerry the jewfish was a giant grouper. He had over many years grown to the size of a mature pig, and he hid in a submerged cave. I never found the opening so I viewed this solemn and strange-looking giant though a narrow crack in the rock. Maybe it swam in through the crack when it was small and stayed there until it became too big to get out. There was something very gloomy about the enormous face with its sad eyes and down-turned mouth. I suppose I would've had the same expression if I 'd been locked in an underwater jail for the rest of my life!

I was attacked by a tiny fish. It was a brave little damsel-fish. Flat and about the size of a penny, it dashed around tirelessly in a vertical position, protecting its territory. I could feel it nip me on the elbow. Fortunately, it wasn't much of a bite. The little damsel is the only fish that will attack a human unprovoked, at least in these waters.

All the stories about attacks by sharks, killer whales, barracudas, and moray eels are certainly greatly exaggerated or simply false. These yarns belong in Hollywood. I felt much safer in Pargo Bay than off the beach near my home town in Norway, swimming among hordes of stinging jellyfish and speeding water craft.

I have seen statistics from Australia showing that out of one thousand fatalities among swimmers and divers, only one a year is due to shark attacks, one hundred are caused by jellyfish, five hundred by pleasure craft, and the rest by excessive drinking, drugs, suicide, and by diving into shallow water.

A study of fatalities caused by sharks in the Caribbean show that not one single person, from Trinidad up to The Virgin Islands, has been admitted to the hospital after encounters with sharks, although there are many rumours of people being eaten alive by these so-called menacing creatures. I am not counting the Italian thrill-seeker from Mustique who stuck his arm in a shark's mouth while being filmed for a documentary. Stupid is as stupid does, and this man was lucky to still have an arm when the shark wiggled its head.

The most dangerous entity in the Caribbean is the blazing sun, which can cause serious burns to pale white tourists' backs in record time as they snorkel over the reef. Coming in second is the red and orange fire-coral which can cause terrible pain and suffering to those who don't listen to advice to avoid touching it. In addition, you have a variety of fish with poisonous spikes and defence mechanisms that can send you off to bed with intense pain for days.

If you follow the rules it shouldn't be a problem. The most important rule being, *Look and don't touch*. Don't touch anything at all.

If you are foolish enough to put your hand into a crevice where a moray eel resides you must expect it to protect its territory and take a healthy bite.

Although most divers and snorkelers are well aware of this risk, an amazing number are walking around with missing or badly damaged fingertips. It is like the well-known fact that some people just have to touch that newly painted bench with a sign saying, *Wet Paint- Do not touch!*

There is a strange-looking exoskeletoned creature called a trunk fish or cowfish. It actually looks like a suitcase or a trunk with a triangular-shaped head and a tiny tail. Its face has cow-like features and behind its human-like lips is a beak similar to that of a parrot. This tiny fish is not the fastest of all marine life and is as tame as a kitten. It can be very tempting to tickle their lips only to discover that one of your fingertips is missing. They taste extremely good and are easy to prepare. I throw the whole fish onto the fire. After 10 minutes, I poke it out, let it cool down, and crack the black, burned shell open in order to scoop out the boneless fillets with a fork.

A four-foot long barracuda looks more like five or six feet underwater, but in spite of this I decided I would have one for dinner. Though well aware that I shouldn't spear anything over half the size of myself, my hunting instinct was stronger that my common sense. I unlocked the safety catch, aimed, and pulled the trigger.

As I shot the spear, Barry made a sudden move and the spear penetrated his body rather than his head, and off he went with me hanging onto the line.

The Bequia whalers call it a Nantucket sleighride when a humpback whale swims off with the whaling boat in tow. I desperately tried to put on the brakes with my flippers, but Barry was too powerful. I was water-skiing underwater. I forgot to bring my knife to cut the line, and I didn't want to let go and lose my precious spear gun.

Barry dove deeper. I could either let go or hang on into Davy Jones' locker. I preferred the first. I had learned another lesson in life, recalling the incident of the poor goose that became headline news after it was spotted flying with an arrow through its neck. This wouldn't make a similar headline, but I felt as bad as if I'd shot that goose.

We had mussels steamed in white wine and red snapper flambé for dinner instead of barracuda. Red snapper translates to *Pargo* in Spanish.

The most amazing feature about *Snapper Bay* was that every time I visited it I'd make new discoveries. While trolling a fishing line across the entrance of the bay I discovered an opening in the cliff at sea level. I hardly noticed it at first due to overhanging vegetation. The cave inside was just large enough to anchor the dinghy. I found another, smaller opening leading further in, which was only visible when the swells were at their lowest.

After ducking through the narrow crevice, a much larger cavern opened up. There was a small ledge to crawl onto. After my eyes adjusted to the dark there was enough green daylight coming in through the underwater opening to reveal a stunning stalagmite cavern. The only thing missing was a pirate skeleton and an open treasure chest filled with gold and jewels.

During my travels around the world I had seen many caves. These were normally grottoes where you had to queue up to buy a ticket to enter. You shuffled along a floodlit path with a crowd of tourists and a guide that told you in seven languages what you already could see, and we'd gape at the hanging stalagmites bathed in artificial coloured lights- natural wonders that had been given names in accordance to what they resembled, leaving little to the imagination. This often took place to the accompaniment of muted classical music flowing from hidden speakers.

This was a different story. I felt like Alexander Humboldt, the great German explorer who unveiled so many wonders in the New World. I'd found a magical cavern, unknown to the outside world. The locals living in the village later warned me to keep out- it was full of the souls of drowned fishermen. It took more than ghosts to keep me out.

The half-submerged tunnel led on though the mountain. The walls were polished smooth by erosion over thousands of years. Could this once have been a river bed? I was just able to touch the bottom with my chin above the water. Could it also mean that the tunnel had an exit into the next bay, Ensenada San Francisco? The groaning sound was eerie, but not enough to put me off. But my batteries were getting low, so I had to turn back.

I would have to try later, bringing Mariann with me and spare batteries. That's if she dared to venture further in than thirty meters. It probably wasn't going to happen. Rule number two was- *Don't go anywhere without a buddy.*

Mariann was very good at diving from the top of the mast, but diving below the surface was not for her. And I could forget bringing along a fisherman, for obvious reasons.

Quite near the beach where we normally anchored there was another natural wonder. An open crevice led from the sea to a little pebble beach just wide enough to haul our dinghy. Fresh water dropped over a smooth rock surface, but with the help of hanging lianas a fifty-year old Tarzan could easily ascend the slippery slope, following the flow of water. The stream led me up and into a small cave where the water cascaded through a chimney-looking funnel, narrow enough to find foot and hand holds on either side. After a twenty-foot vertical climb I found myself in yet another cave with a circular pool. Daylight from a hole above streamed through the many ferns and huge tropical plants, giving the place a green shimmer. The cascading waterfall kept the pool filled with cool, clean, fresh water- my own personal, secret jacuzzi. It was heavenly.

The village in Ensenada Pargo consisted of about fifteen small structures built of bamboo, mud, and galvanized sheeting, with a population of about fifty. They survived on fruit, fish, and some strange looking potatoes called *camote*. Their ultimate feast, however, was grilled howler-monkey. The method used to catch these primates was quite resourceful. The villagers made a mixture of various fruits in a calabash bowl and topped this fruit cocktail with very strong rum. The brew was strategically positioned on a steep mountainside overlooking the sea. The monkeys devoured the contents and fell into the sea in drunken semi-consciousness. That's all it took; the fishermen, waiting below in their wooden pinéros, scooped up the little fellows and had them for dinner.

People there saw me as undernourished. I've always been lean and a bit thin, and I was constantly getting dinner invitations. I must admit I had a problem taking part in this culinary delight of grilled monkey. Their tiny hands with humanlike fingers and nails were too close to homo sapiens to my liking. But when in Rome…

The inhabitants looked very much like Peruvian Indians and their language was close to Spanish, sounding like a mixture of Spanish and Arabic with a few guttural African clicks thrown in. They were polite, helpful, and hospitable. They made it very clear to me that the river that ran through the village was for me to use in any way I wish.

"Mi casa es su casa." My only warning was not to catch the crayfish, another delicacy that lived under rocks in the river.

It transpired that in exchange for fresh water crayfish they loved our Norwegian stainless-steel fishing hooks. This commodity worked extremely well for bartering wherever we went- forget the traditional marbles, beads, and bibles!

Fredag had a reputation on this coast of being a ship mastered by people with magical powers. It all started when locals brought us their children with straightforward ordinary infections, which were successfully treated with antibiotic cream. Then they brought patients with strange skin ailments, and I tried in vain to convince them that there was a big difference between a paramedic and a fully qualified doctor.

I did a little test with cortisone cream on a baby and it worked like magic. The village chief decided that I had saved the child's life. We didn't have to worry about fruit and vegetables for the next month. I prayed that they wouldn't bring me a case of appendicitis.

We had three more cases of the mysterious skin disease before we ran out of cortisone cream. The chief held a meeting, and it was decided that they wanted us to be a part of their community. We were presented with a small plot of land the size of a tennis court on a ledge overlooking the bay, complete with a tiny waterfall and several fruit-trees.

I got carried away. Wasn't this what we were looking for? Hadn't we sailed away to find Shangri-La? Mariann was not with me on this one. In any case, if the rest of the planet became uninhabitable it was nice to know we had a piece of real-estate in paradise.

The rainforest was luxuriant, bountiful, and inviting to anyone who wanted to do some exploring. I never understood why people were attracted to exploring mountains covered in snow and ice. Besides the freezing cold, the mountains were boring with no vegetation and not much more wildlife than a few mangy mountain lions. I guess such lovers of nature, on the other hand, wouldn't understand what was so special about a hot, steamy, mosquito-infested jungle, with 200-pound pumas hiding in the underbrush.

The path up the mountainside was steep and nearly impenetrable. The best way for me get through the dense vegetation was to follow the river. With good footwear, a camera, lots of mosquito spray, rope, and a grapple hook to scale the many waterfalls, I came close to mounting a genuine rainforest expedition without getting lost.

When the path forward looked hazardous and I'd had enough bites, I reversed course and followed the stream back down to the bay. Moving quietly, I could observe a variety of exotic birds, lizards, and small wildlife; fortunately, the chief had informed me that the puma only came out at night.

The tall trees met in a canopy of entwined branches and leaves. Thick brown lianas and dark green vines intertwined and climbed towards the sun. Bromeliads, orchids, and mosses covered the tree branches, and smaller broad-leaved plants and lacy forest-floor palms grew in their shade.

There was an incessant whirring, buzzing, and clicking from a multitude of insect species. Now and again troops of red howler monkeys would crash through the treetops. The squirrel monkeys followed every step I took and enjoyed throwing fruit at me.

Screaming male birds called *pihas* let their female counterparts far and wide know that they were desperate to mate; their sharp, piercing cries lasted all day long. Green parrots, blending in with the foliage, imitated the shrieking *pihas* to perfection.

The most amazing discovery I made on my Pargo safari was not a puma but a butterfly. Not an ordinary back-garden variety, but the king of lepidoptera, the male blue morpho. It was the world's largest butterfly- the size of a fully-grown sparrow, light blue in colour underneath and cobalt blue on top.

In the late afternoon the blue morpho gave a magical show of sparkling light and dark blue flashes as it fluttered a few feet over the stream.

The South American continent has over 90% of all the planet's species of butterflies and moths, and the blue morpho is one of the rarest.

In Bequia I was later fortunate to meet a collector of moths and butterflies. When I told him that I had sighted dozens of blue morpho on a river in Venezuela, he went ballistic and chartered my yacht for a butterfly hunting expedition along the entire coast of the country as well as into the interior.

The inhabitants of Pargo Bay village couldn't believe their eyes when they saw him running in ecstasy up the riverbed with a huge net on the end of a pole. "Loco, loco," they cried, making the international gesture of madness by circling their index finger close to their temple. "Surely there's not much food in those fluttering insects?"

The sale of one perfect specimen at an auction in London brought in enough money to pay for the entire charter. Before his departure, my guest gave me a nearly perfect specimen as a present. It had been carefully prepared and conserved in a wooden box.

A few years later, having nearly forgotten about my treasure, I met another enthusiastic collector. "Wait till you see what I have hidden in the bilge of my yacht." I said. When I opened the box, all I found were the remains of a spiny skeleton. My blue beauty had been consumed by roaches!

Traversing the little river in Ensenada Pargo, climbing the waterfalls, and spending a night high in the rainforest was the inspiration that triggered another river exploration- this time on a really big one.

The 1330-mile Orinoco River originates in south-eastern Venezuela on the border of Brazil, slices across central Venezuela, and crosses highlands, rain forests, and tropical grasslands. It eventually flows into the Atlantic Ocean close to Trinidad.

We decided to motor our yacht all the way up to the harbourmaster's office in Puerto Ayacucho on the border with Colombia, a distance of more than six hundred miles. It was a tedious journey, and after 3 weeks we were not even half-way, so we threw in the towel. We were continuously getting stuck on the many shifting sandbanks, despite having experienced pilots on board. We had to change pilots often and the journey was costing us a small fortune. On top of that we had to change the strainers for the engine cooling-water every 6 hours due to so much muck and debris in the river.

I would have to take a rain-check, as the Americans might say. I'd be back. Eventually I was, years later, and not with *Fredag*.

With a special permit from the Department of Indian Affairs in Caracas, I was granted permission to travel into Venezuela's southernmost state of the Amazonas territory. The dense rainforest area here is the size of the United Kingdom and home to the *fierce people*- the Yanomami Indians.

On the western edge of Yanomami territory, the Orinoco is connected to the Rio Negro, a tributary of the Amazon River. It is joined by a 200-mile-long channel called the Casiquiare, linking the two great waterways together. It was therefore possible to travel from the delta of the Orinoco all the way up through Venezuela and Brazil, passing through the city of Manaus and ending at the mouth of the Amazon.

On my first insane attempt to visit the renowned Brazilian opera house in Manaus by way of the Orinoco I fell violently ill with fever. I had gone as far as the Casiquiare channel when I was forced to turn back. I'd survived and outwitted caimans, anacondas, pumas, and all the nasty, biting, creepy crawly creatures, but I was forced quit because of a mosquito bite. On my second try the rainforest was on fire. Further progress was impossible due to choking smoke. Although it would make more sense to take a taxi to the opera, the Grand River Expedition is still on my bucket list, though I have no illusions of being a Stanley or Livingstone. I seem to have better luck with the sea than across jungle, and I would rather explore coast-lines and tiny islands in spite of the navigational difficulties.

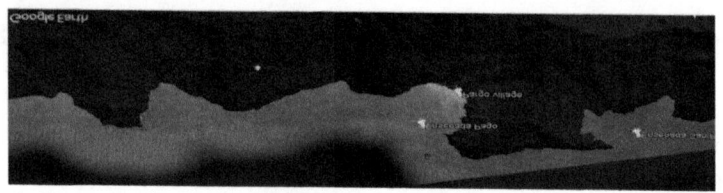

Ensenada Pargo on the Peninsular de Paria, in case you want to visit. You will not find it on any map, it's location is at $10^0\,42$' N, $62^0\,03$' W.

16. The Revolution

Venezuela was culturally closer to my liking than the Grenadines. I found the latter tedious at times with monotonous steel band music, ridiculous beauty pageants, and non-stop soca. I missed going to the movies, theatre, and opera. I yearned to wander through art galleries and to travel far and wide for a change of scenery. Life isn't just a beach!

In Venezuela, a country of diversity and low prices, having pockets stuffed with US dollars I could enjoy a life of exploring and entertainment. I'd run out of funds sooner or later, but the budget lasted longer here.

In contrast to my lavish lifestyle as a tourist, the people suffered. Their weekly pay check barely covered basic necessities. Widespread corruption and the privatisation of the oil industry under President Peres had brought the country to the brink of bankruptcy. For some Venezuelans the only solution was to break the law. But compared to today, Venezuela was still a relatively safe country.

Due to *Fredag's* unwavering tradition of running into trouble and encountering dramatic situations, I was not surprised when we were there during a good old-fashioned Latin American revolution.

We had an agent in London who regularly sent us groups of young people who were seeking adventure, and we were enjoying being back in the charter business again.

Our "Adventure cruising on a shoestring" was not your traditional charter business. The punters had to pay a few dollars a day for "enlisting" on a sailing vessel where they had to provision, cook, wash up, scrub the decks, hoist anchor, and take the helm. Gone were the days when you were paid for this kind of work.

The crew made democratic decisions on where to go and when, and I would do as little as possible except to teach them some basic navigation and give what I believed was good advice. My first mate showed them how to bake bread in a pressure cooker, gut and clean a slimy octopus, and how to tie important knots.

My first mate and I had a small cabin in the bow, and it suited us perfectly to be at the captain's table every evening for dinner. The rest of the yacht belonged to our guests- we only ate and sailed together. It was a great arrangement except for having to listen to *Abba* morning, noon, and night, and nearly everyone was happy.

I say nearly. Sometimes we had crew who'd been sent out by their travel agents to do something exciting and adventurous, but their Caribbean cruise on a shoestring wasn't quite what they'd expected.

Ray was a dentist and a very orderly man. He was obsessed with cleanliness and good hygiene. On his first encounter with my stowaway roaches he freaked out. The best way to combat these pests was to whack them with whatever was at hand. With a dozen crew-members on board we had a crusade against roaches. On a notice board was a list of names. Every time someone squashed a *Blattaria Germanica*, the German Brown Cockroach, they marked it down. The person with highest tally at the end of the month was awarded a bottle of Black Label. They all found this quite amusing.

Our friend the dentist was not amused. Neither did he have a sense of humour. He wrote a letter of complaint to my agent in London, threatening to sue; he wanted a complete refund. We kept a framed copy of this hilarious document hanging in the head.

The rest of my crew were thrilled with the competition; their faces lit up every time they dispatched another loathsome critter. After six months of this, we had nearly eradicated the little beasts.

Apart from our dentist the majority of our guests- or more appropriately, our crew- were delighted with our concept of a cruising vacation.

Charlotte, a young lady in her mid-twenties, had worked in a post office for many years before applying for a position on our adventure cruise. At the end of a three-month stint on board she told me that the most daring thing she'd done before was to jump onto the platform of a London double-decker bus while it was in motion.

She had never seen the sun rise. Fish were rectangular sticks and came frozen in a cardboard box. During her time with us she'd scuba-dived a sunken wreck fifty feet deep surrounded by hammerhead sharks. She'd survived a storm at sea on a sailing ship, jumped off a mountaintop with a hang-glider strapped to her back, swum into a submerged cave full of the souls of dead fishermen, spent a night in a tree in the rainforest full of nasty beasts, and seen a glorious sunrise out of the sea at the Tobago Cays.

She signed on for another three months. She didn't want to work in the post office anymore. Charlotte started her own business- a travel agency specializing in rafting, mountaineering, bungy-jumping, and scuba-diving!

The highlight of our cruise was when I dumped my crew with minimal clothing on a deserted island the size of a football field, then sailed away for a week, leaving them with a radio transmitter, a spear gun, tents, flour, salt, a knife, and a lighter. It was voluntary, of course.

What wasn't voluntary was getting involved in a Latin American revolution.

On February 4th 1992, we were in the marina at Puerto Cabello, the base for the Venezuelan Navy. We were at the end of one of our adventure cruises and in the middle of a farewell party for our departing crew. During dessert- a blazing banana flambé- bombs began falling from the sky!

The local military garrison was only a few miles from our restaurant, and the air force had started bombing their own navy. The entire naval fleet put out to sea, and there was total chaos over the whole republic. The TV announcers were just as bewildered as the waiters in our restaurant.

It had finally happened. The long-held rumour about unrest in the army was now a reality. What should never happen in a modern democratic republic had come about- a revolution.

It was an attempted coup by a group of low-ranking army officers. Colonel Hugo Rafael Chavez was *El Comandante* of the rebellion, and we were smack in the middle of it- where else would we be? It soon became evident that the revolutionary comrades were on the losing side- the rebellion gradually turned into a soap opera. Colonel Chavez and his gang had not done their homework.

Chavez, a charismatic admirer of Fidel Castro, had conspired to oust the government together with military leaders from all of Venezuela's 22 dependencies. He'd united the generals who weren't happy with their pay checks with President Perez at the helm. Colonel Chavez had also prepared a patriotic propaganda video that he planned to show on national television- a video telling the people that the Great Liberator Chavez was now in charge, with the blessing of the military and all those who believed in a new and prosperous Venezuela, adding that even God himself had blessed him.

The video promised that the new republic would be a better place for all. He promised higher salaries for the military and lower gasoline and food prices for the poor. His plan was to take control of the national TV station in Caracas, and he had decided to play the video in prime time, to secure the maximum numbers of viewers. But there was one hitch.

When the revolutionaries stormed into the control room, armed with grenades, bazookas, and the notorious video, they found to their horror that the cassette wouldn't fit into the big professional VCR machine, because they'd brought a standard VHS tape like those purchased at Radio Shack for $1.99.

As this disaster was taking place, the President was enjoying a sun-downer in the Ayacucho room of the Miraflora Presidential palace. He'd had the foresight to have a tunnel built from the basement of the palace to the TV station, which was located across the street.

As the rebels exited the front door of the TV station to find a company that could transfer the mutinous recording onto a suitable cassette, the President was seen running up the steps to Studio One. He was on the air before he could catch his breath.

All the networks in Venezuela picked up the transmission. The entire population of the country, including the crew of the good ship *Fredag*, watched the drama unfold on TV. Still panting from having run up seven flights of stairs, the President of Venezuela delivered a reassuring message to the people.

He was one smart cookie, our Mr. Perez. He made a very clever psychological move. He had received an intelligence report of the entire plot with all the details. He knew which generals were waiting on the side-lines to back the coup. He then contacted the collaborating military leaders, live on TV, and they were all taken by surprise- they hadn't expected to see their old President on live TV, still in charge.

He asked them, one by one, for a vote of confidence, starting with the most loyal general, and the others had no choice but to promise to defend the constitution and stand behind their democratically elected President. They did so with the President live on camera, presumably with one hand over their heart and the other hugging the Venezuelan flag.

At the end of the "confirmation hearing" they played the national anthem, and from that moment on it was obvious that the attempted coup was doomed.

The diners and personnel in our restaurant had been gathered around the TV set. They exploded with applause while the bombs were still exploding over the garrison.

The interrupted soap continued on TV and the mutinous army officers decided that their show must go on too. In Puerto Cabello and in Caracas, the fighting went on for three days, leaving the streets strewn with dead soldiers, burnt out cars, and looted shops.

The authorities were anxious that we'd be get caught in the crossfire so my crew and I were put under house arrest in a five-star hotel, with the government picking up the tab.

My replacement crew had just got off the plane and were stepping onto the tarmac at Caracas International airport when they heard the first shots. They had come here to sail, not to be war correspondents, and they were not happy about being arrested and incarcerated in a five-star, all-inclusive hotel even if there was a bar and a jacuzzi in their rooms and the city's best discothèque in the basement.

I was having a hard time convincing them over the phone from our hotel that a genuine Latin American revolution was a pretty rare event, not a daily occurrence, and it should be thus seen as an added bonus to their holiday- truly something to write home about.

"Dear Mum and Dad. Yesterday we had a revolution. I'm OK and safe, but all the shops have been looted and are empty. I forgot to buy sun tan lotion before I left. The streets are full of burning tires and the morgues are overflowing with dead soldiers. I am under house-arrest at the Hilton, but the government is paying for it. My eyes hurt because of the tear gas. Hope all is nice and peaceful back home."

After three days, all was calm. The supermarkets were guarded by armed soldiers, though most items on the shelves had been looted. I went shopping and discovered later that I'd mistakenly put a piece of Swiss cheese in my pocket without paying for it. I remember thinking how embarrassing it would have been had I had been checked at the exit, and I envisaged being left on the floor with as many bullet holes in my body as there were in that cheese.

The coup leader, Colonel Chavez, was captured and imprisoned by troops loyal to the president, but he still declared that his Revolutionary Movement represented the majority of his fellow officers.

Surprisingly, the officers involved in the coup were not lined up and shot. The grand traitor himself, Chavez, got off with house arrest. In an interview with CNN he declared he would soon emerge and enter the political arena through fair elections- which of course, he would one day go on to win.

I'd possibly been a witness to the last revolution in South America. Our new crew arrived on board after being let out of "prison." They were all ready to go sailing. That's what they'd come for after all. The weather forecast was not the best for an 80-mile-long passage to the Los Roques atoll. I decided to postpone our departure another day.

We were outside the "hurricane path." The coast of Venezuela was a safe cruising area during the hurricane season, from July to October, and it was February. However, there was something about the forecast which was unusual, so I decided to wait another day and see what happened.

On the fax machine information from the met office gave us reason to be concerned. An unexpected storm for this time of the year had developed in the Caribbean. Coinciding with a full moon, an upper level trough, and a southbound current, the met office in Caracas sent out a marine advisory predicting extremely high ocean swells.

Our new crew had just stepped on board when the first swells arrived from the north. Normally the full moon, combined with atmospheric conditions and currents, caused a high ground swell, but with the additional storm up north, these "normal" occurrences were intensified.

In no time the conditions at the tiny marina where we were moored deteriorated. Our new arrivals were already seasick, and we had not even gone to sea! Feeling sorry for them, and to be on the safe side, I sent my new crew to a nearby hotel.

The swells got bigger and bigger and were washing over the breakwater. There were at least fifty large Venezuelan cabin-cruisers in the marina; I called them gin-palaces- their owners called them mega-yachts. They were anxiously trying to secure their precious glass-fibre dreams, and to do their utmost to prevent them from being reduced to pulp.

When I saw a huge wave wash over the lighthouse at the end of the breakwater, I decided to run out to sea as quickly as possible. All hell was breaking loose in the overcrowded marina. The entrance was nearly blocked with sunken cabin cruisers. Only their fly-bridges, antennas, and long fishing rods remained above the water.

I was just about to let go of our last mooring line when a floating dock trailing lots of loose rope bore down on us. A line tangled our prop and the engine stopped as the dock and my yacht were a collision course.

When such an incident occurs and it's a matter of saving lives and property, one often reacts without judgment and common sense. I dove in with a bread-knife in my teeth. I cut away the rope from the propeller and just managed haul myself back onto the floating dock a split second before the dock and *Fredag* collided.

There was no time to put fenders between them, and I'm not very suitable as a fender- I'm too skinny. I shouted, "full ahead, it's now or never," and as the engine started, I forgot that I had still one last line attached to the dock. The docking line was a strong 1.5-inch nylon rope, but the heavy oak cleat, on which the rope was fastened, ripped out of the deck and flew towards me. It smashed into my leg.

As the seas washed over the breakwater, I just managed to squeeze *Fredag* out through the marina opening, avoiding the sunken wrecks. Several other boat-owners noticed our desperate breakout and made an effort to leave the marina, but by now the entrance was completely blocked.

When we were safely in the open water, the pain in my leg set in.

My leg was broken, but *Fredag* was safely at sea. We dropped anchor a good distance from the end of the breakwater. The depth sounder showed alternatively three and twelve meters as we rose and fell on the huge swells, but the anchor held us well.

I heard on the radio that we were encountering the highest waves that had hit this coast in over a hundred years. The hotels along the beach had been evacuated. The streets were underwater, and what little that had been in the supermarkets after the attempted coup had been looted.

I was confined to a local hospital bed with my leg in a cast and had no idea what was going on in the harbour. The anchor chain eventually parted, and our second and third anchors were too light to keep the heavy yacht secured. Mariann was alone on board and had no other option than to put out to sea under engine. A helpful French sailor followed her out and came to her rescue with a new heavy anchor.

On arriving back at the marina with my leg in a cast I found my yacht and first mate back at anchor again, as if nothing had happened. By the time I was back on board the cast has been completely dissolved by salt water.

The good news was that the swell was settling down, including the swelling of my leg. When the new crew arrived, I discovered that they had all been recruited from a medical school- two doctors, five students, and two nurses. A new cast was immediately set and I received doctor's orders to stay in my hammock for the next month and do as little as possible.

This suited me fine. The only problem was that nobody took orders very seriously from a bedridden captain.

The sea was still lumpy and my fresh crew had all turned green again as we battled our way on the 80-mile-long passage to the Los Roques atoll.

The bowsprit snapped, a running backstay broke and ripped a large gash in the mainsail, we lost a chest full of fruit and vegetables to King Neptune, the galley stove caught fire, and our dog fell overboard and had to be saved- all in one night! With the bowsprit spliced by the doctors and with my own spliced leg in a plastic sack, Mariann put out the fire, sewed the sail, and hauled a miserable wet dog out of the sea. The rest of the crew were hunkered down below deck, only emerging to empty their buckets of vomit. The victims of this nightmare passage could not understand why Mariann and I were still smiling while trying to convince them that this was normal and merely another challenge- part of the joy and pleasure of sailing.

Naturally they couldn't see the pleasure of constantly throwing up and couldn't understand why we were smiling and laughing when it felt like the end of the world was at hand. To be quite honest, we didn't normally smile when we were alone and in deep shit. The smile that we put on for our crew was the same smile that the crew of an airliner wore when something was seriously wrong with the plane.

By now we were both hardened. Nothing would put us off balance any more, not even the highest seas. We could take almost anything. We were survivors, just like the cockroaches.

At sunrise we slipped through the gap in the barrier reef of Los Roques- into the beautiful and tranquil calm of the great 30-mile-long lagoon. Our crew's fear vanished and was replaced with joy and amazement.

In this archipelago of delight, with calm clear water, where you could see the bottom at a depth of fifty feet, zigzagging among a maze of several hundred tiny uninhabited islands, it seemed as if nothing could go wrong. But it inevitably did.

Our new medic crew

Harry, one of our crew, had gone fishing in the inflatable dinghy and not returned. We were anchored off one of the last islands in the archipelago and there was no land downwind before Nicaragua, a distance of more than a thousand miles, so we were worried. He was alone, and it would be dark in a few hours.

Harry was a city person and had only been to sea once, on a pedal boat in Hyde Park. He had extremely pale skin- almost blueish white- red hair, and he suffered eczema from the sun.

Without fresh water under a scorching tropical sun, I gave him three days to survive. Like the others on board, he had attended a crash-course on safety and security. When using the inflatable dinghy or the wooden tender to go somewhere out of sight of the yacht, a long list of items had to be on board. He'd been instructed to inform someone where he planned to go and when he planned to return.

He hadn't told anybody about his escapade, and the equipment he should've taken with him was still on board the yacht. He was last seen motoring towards the beach.

A quick search on the island revealed nothing. Harry had vanished, drifted off to sea. We all feared that Harry had gone to his maker.

Darkness comes quickly in the tropics. There was no way we could take *Fredag* out at night to do a search. The uncharted area was infested with dangerous reefs. I had done this before and we knew how that had ended.

The nearest coast-guard station was out of radio range. All I could do was put out a request for all shipping in the area to keep an eye out for a very white man in a tiny inflatable rubber dinghy the same colour as the sea. We couldn't put to sea before sunrise. By then Harry would be miles away and it would be like looking for a needle in a haystack.

The spare two horsepower outboard engine was attached to the wooden sailing dinghy. I took one of the doctors with me, and we set off in the dark night carrying flashlights, spare batteries, fuel, flares, and a mobile radio. I strongly felt that we'd lost Harry, but good fortune had followed me so far, so it was well worth trying to do a search.

His only chance was that he might drift onto the tiny island of Carenero, but that was unlikely since the wind would take him past the island and out towards the open sea. If he didn't reach Carenero he could be torn to pieces on the barrier reef surrounding the island. This was the last island in the atoll and the waves grew massive over a 30-mile fetch.

"Doc" and I tacked in a criss-cross pattern downwind, making longer tacks as we proceeded, stopping the engine every five minutes to call his name. There was no reply. All we could hear were the breaking waves, and all we could see were a million stars.

Searching for a person in a tiny grey dinghy in two-meter-high waves was like looking for that legendary needle. Even with his orange hair in daylight he would be extremely hard to spot. It was akin to searching for a snowball on a glacier at night wearing sunglasses!

Harry had run out of petrol and was drifting out to sea. Nobody on board *Fredag* could hear his screams for help. We couldn't hear him because *Abba* had been on full volume.

All he was wearing was a pair of shocking green shorts, and his only equipment was a pair of pink flippers. He soon gave up a frantic attempt to paddle back using the flippers, and he'd started to get cold when the sun set.

Shivering, after being sunburned after a long day of spear-fishing, he suddenly remembered Captain Bligh's lecture on safety and security. But it was too late. Harry was not a person of faith. His religion was primarily football and then gambling. But he started praying anyway. He lay on the floorboards in a fetal position and prayed.

He hadn't noticed that his prayers had been answered when a big wave gently lifted him over the jagged reef and dumped him inside a small lagoon.

Harry was extremely lucky. The wind had not pushed him on the course I estimated would take him *past* the island of Carenero. A strong current, unnoticed by us, had swept him on a more southerly course, and by some incredible luck had swept him safe and unhurt into the island's lagoon.

When Harry noticed that all was quiet, he looked up and discovered that he was not in heaven. Tall palm trees partly blocked out the stars and through the mangroves he heard Latin American salsa music.

He secured the inflatable with all the five knots that the first mate had taught him and started climbing through the mangroves in the direction of the music. The rough branches hurt his feet so he put on his flippers. The mangrove forest was nearly impenetrable, and he didn't make much progress. He kept getting his feet stuck, and he cut himself badly trying to free himself. The music was getting louder, though, and he eventually saw a light in the distance.

Juan Gomes de Castro and his brother Frederico were fishermen camping out on the beach that night. Juan had turned up the volume on his transistor radio to quell the sound of his brother's voice as he read out loud from a Stephen King horror story. Juan didn't like horror stories, and he nearly had a heart attack when he heard a voice call out from the mangroves, "Help me. Please help me."

He picked up his flashlight and pointed it towards the disembodied voice. "Jesus Maria Magdalena, Mother of Christ!" he cried.

He would never forget that night in the mangroves. Hovering a few meters above the ground was a pale and ghostly creature with flaming red hair, pink torso, florescent green shorts, and pink webbed feet. The monster had a fearsome expression on its face and was bleeding all over.

Harry was blinded by the powerful light and heard someone scream. The light went out and the music stopped suddenly, then an outboard engine revved to life. As he frantically tried to free himself from the mangroves, the sound of the engine grew weaker until all was quiet again. He found himself on a deserted beach beside a smouldering fire. A burned tuna was attached to a stick over the embers. Beside the fire lay a half-empty bottle of rum and an open Stephen King novel with its pages flapping in the light breeze. There was not a soul to be seen. Out by the reef he spotted an anchor light.

Harry, the fisherman.

An American cruising sailor reported over the radio that he had found a terrified tourist from London on the beach at Carenero. The shipwrecked young man was safely on board his schooner. He mentioned that the victim was in a state of shock and torn up, but very much alive.

From that day on, whenever any of my adventurous crew went off on a little expedition they were equipped as if they were going on a circumnavigation. Anything can happen to you out there- even if you're on a large vessel. Even a rogue wave might occur.

17. The Rogue Wave

Other than the horrible news about Ole's overdose we have had no news regarding our rehabilitation project since the kids left for Norway. Nor had we been contacted by the Norwegian authorities. They failed to respond to my letter informing them that we were willing to continue under the condition that we were better funded and considered an institution, not temporary foster-parents. We were professionals and felt that we should receive funds appropriate to our training.

We were frustrated that there was no follow-up in Norway. The responsible bureaucrats obviously found our methods too unconventional. They most likely believed more in what the press fabricated than my factual reports. I had reason to believe that my monthly, detailed reports had not been read. No one confirmed they'd been received, and there were never any comments or questions.

The good news was that *we* felt we'd done well. We'd given the kids something important so that they might make positive changes in their lives. Other than the "mutiny," we hadn't had a single accident or disaster. We even had enough cash to buy Christmas presents for each other.

We were in the middle of hurricane season so we decided to hang out in the Laguna Grande in Venezuela, south of the path of hurricanes. Once a week we hauled anchor and sailed ten miles to Cumana to restock ice, steaks, and video-cassettes. Anchored in this tranquil and isolated area we thought about the past and started planning for the future. We decided to sail north to Bequia to find work chartering.

Fredag in Laguna Grande

The same stretch of Venezuelan coastline that had once taken us 16 days under sail now took us only two days with the help of the engine, helped by strong gusts coming off the mountainside. Then the mainsail split, and we had to seek refuge in a little bay on the north-eastern side of the Paria peninsula.

We were upset we weren't going to reach Bequia in time for their Old Year's Night celebrations. But three incidents made me feel optimistic. The big mirror in the head (bathroom) fell but didn't break into pieces. A white albatross had followed us for more than eighty miles. I found this strange because I'd heard these magnificent birds didn't venture into the northern hemisphere. When we anchored in our favourite Ensenada Pargo we discovered that a 20-pound tuna had jumped into our dinghy. Lucky us, we were getting low on fresh provisions. I'm not superstitious, but three signs of good fortune in one day?

While pondering on this, a large catamaran joined us at anchor. I recognized the two on board as charter operators based in the Grenadines. After dropping anchor the captain shouted, "My guests cancelled their charter and we're loaded with steak, lobster, caviar, and champagne. Care to join us for dinner?" Now I was sure that King Neptune had forgiven me for all my nautical wrongdoings and was on my side again.

With the exception of that one notorious passage, I always enjoyed sailing along the Paria Peninsular. Five thousand-foot high peaks covered in rainforest reached to the clouds and dropped abruptly into the sea. Occasionally I caught a glimpse of a tiny village crouched at the foot of the mountains behind raging white surf. A few fishing boats bobbed at anchor off the beach. Scrutinizing the mountainside with my binoculars I discovered small huts and open spaces where someone was growing something stronger to smoke than tobacco. The law needed two long arms and strong legs to reach the farmers up there.

The swell coming from the north had eased a bit, and so had the hangover from last night's party on the catamaran. We had reached the end of the peninsula and were taking advantage of the swift current that swept out through the *Dragons Mouth*. We changed course for Bequia. The pilot manual warned me to show caution in this area because of unpredictable gusts.

There was little we could do other than hope that our old rotting sails would hold up. We had a sewing machine on board, but sailmaker Mariann wasn't keen on stitching tough canvas. She lived in fear of that tearing sound so much that every time I opened my foul-weather jacket, I had to shout, *It's only velcro!*

The mainsail ripped again, but this time the old sail was too far gone. It had to be downgraded to a tarpaulin. We managed to stay on course under staysail and mizzen. The jib was packed and lashed to the bowsprit- it was in the same state as the main.

We still had half of the tuna that had jumped into the dinghy. I let the cat have some and gave the rest to the sharks, an act of generosity I would regret later.

The safety line was stretched over the entire length of the yacht and all our thermos flasks were filled up with coffee. It was slow going and promised to be a long night's sail. My watch was nearly over. The moon had set and the clouds blocked any starlight. I woke my first mate and said her watch was going be long and bumpy. Then a sudden squall tore the staysail. We had no more working canvas other than the mizzen.

To make any progress we had to start the engine. On a final check on our surroundings I noticed, to my surprise, a white line dead ahead on the horizon. Although we had a strong current behind us, my hasty calculation showed that it couldn't be Grenada fifteen miles ahead.

The white line was getting wider.

"It's a wave!" I shouted. "A huge goddamned wave!"

A giant wall of breaking water was rolling towards us. For the surfer on a beach in Hawaii this was great, but that was not the case for us. We were helpless as the huge wave smashed *Fredag* on her quarter, lifted her up, and turned us broadside to the wind. The ocean poured into the cockpit, down the companionway, and into the saloon. We held on as best we could. The masts were more or less parallel to the sea, and as the yacht rose to an upright position the mizzen sail was filled with water. This was too much for the mast and it snapped like a matchstick.

"Oh no! Not again!" I cried in despair.

Apathy took over. I let go of the helm and collapsed onto the cockpit floor, feeling sorry for myself. I daydreamed of a little white cottage behind a picket fence somewhere on the south coast of Norway, a cottage with a rose garden and a horse- one that didn't need much maintenance, just a handful of oats now and then. The house was securely fixed to granite and unsinkable. In a tranquil little bay was my sailing dinghy that I loaded with a case of cold beer, and I'd tack back and forth in the bay until I was ready to drop the hook and take a walk ashore to pick wild strawberries.

I was brought back to reality with my first mate hitting me on the head with a life-preserver, shouting, "Pull yourself together, man. Don't give up now. I need you!"

If I didn't do something, here and now, I'd never be able to make that dream of the little cottage and rose garden come true. I switched off the engine to prevent debris hanging over the side from being dragged into the propeller. The mizzen mast had broken a foot above the cockpit floor. The upper part was jammed under the metal traveller bar that crossed the cockpit.

As the mast fell it smashed the tiller. Half the rail in the stern was missing. We were unhurt- quite amazing as we were directly beneath the falling mast. Things were not as bad as with the last dismasting. We were lucky to be still on board; Mariann had been secured in her harness and I'd become tangled with some loose rope when the sea tried to grab us.

We had the mast and rigging back on board by sunrise. I could see Grenada ahead, a beautiful green smudge on the horizon. My little white cottage was history. Our unreliable engine was running as it should, pushing us along at a steady two knots. Grenada gradually rose ahead of us. Grenada Radio reported that there had been underwater volcanic activity near the isle of *Kick 'em Jenny,* just north of Grenada. This had possibly caused a rogue wave that had damaged several villages on Grenada's north and west coasts. There were no other vessels in the immediate area in the early morning of New Year's Day. The ill-fated sailing vessel *Fredag* had been there of course. We were extremely fortunate in spite of losing another mast. We were talking about how lucky we were to survive when there was a loud bang in the engine room. The engine had quit.

It was bad news- a broken crankshaft. After an Indian war dance on the engine room hatch, I cooled down a bit but cursed the guy who sold me the engine, including Mr. Perkins who built the damn machine and even Herr Diesel, the inventor. These gentlemen were fortunate not to have been standing on deck- I would've flogged and keel-hauled 'em on the spot!

When my rage subsided, I called a crew meeting. The two animals didn't have much to say as usual, but my first mate agreed- we had to call for help. We were dead in the water, drifting wherever the wind and current took us. If we did nothing we'd end up somewhere in Central America a thousand miles away.

It was very hard for me to call for help on the radio. How often had I laughed at tourists calling *Mayday* when they couldn't start the engine, though all their sails were up? Most of the time they'd forgotten to push in the kill-switch after pulling it out to stop the engine!

We were adrift in the Caribbean Sea- a serious situation, but not serious enough to call in a *Mayday*. We weren't in a life-threatening situation.

We had ample fresh water, a sack of porridge oats, enough flour and dried milk to make a thousand pancakes, and the ocean was full of fish. We weren't hungry, though a cold beer would've gone down easily. We weren't sinking and I could receive the BBC on short wave radio. Best of all we were only ten miles from the south coast of Grenada.

As our lives were not in danger, I transmitted the international call for assistance. "*PAN PAN, this is sailing yacht Fredag.*"

Several hours passed before the coast guard responded. They had a problem understanding me. There was some misunderstanding as they weren't familiar with standard radio procedure- they thought I was calling Yacht Panpan! They asked were we had come from and our destination.

"We are out of Venezuela, via the *Dragon's Mouth* and are on our way Bequia."

"Please contact the coast guard in Trinidad; they cover the area by the *Dragon's Mouth*."

I shouted into the microphone so loud that they may have heard me without the radio. "Man, I can see the tower of the airport on Grenada!"

"Roger, but we have no aircraft available."

It seemed obvious that they were trying to find an excuse not to put to sea. It was rough out and blowing like stink. I felt sure they understood quite well what I was trying to tell them because they responded, "Call the coast guard station on Saint Vincent. They will be able to give you a tow to Bequia."

They knew very well I wasn't requesting a tow all the way to Bequia, only a short ten-mile tow to Grenada. The seemed determined not to be helpful; anger surged up inside me. I mustered all my energy to be as calm as possible and asked the radio-operator's name, rank, and the name of his supervisor.

By now I was sure that he knew there were a lot of people listening, so he had to be careful what he said to me.

He didn't answer my question, but he thought hard before replying, "Roger, Roger. We are coming to your assistance, sir. Give me your position. How many people on board, sir?"

I gave him our bearing and distance to the airport tower and the following crew list: Peter, Mariann, Sara, and Siri. I didn't clarify that Sara was a dog and Siri our cat.

It was late afternoon and the coast guard was nowhere to be seen. In fact, we hadn't seen a single vessel all day. Grenada was getting smaller and smaller on the horizon and it would be soon dark. I called the coast guard again.

They responded immediately, "We have been searching, but cannot find you, sir. You must have given us the wrong position. You must be further away than you think you are."

I told him I could see the lights at the international airport. He responded that they were most likely the lights from the airport on Carriacou! I asked him when had they started landing Boeing 747's on the shortest airstrip in the region, and furthermore, if we were as far north as he suggested, I wouldn't be able to contact him by VHF radio.

"*Fredag,* you are breaking up. I cannot read you. Over." He didn't sound very convincing.

I switched to the BBC on shortwave. This didn't help, but the announcer's voice had a calming effect on me. He was reporting a massive fire on a ferry off the coast of Sweden that had taken many lives. We stopped feeling sorry for ourselves, lashed the helm, hung a paraffin lamp on the forestay and went below for a game of scrabble. An empty bottle rolled back and forth over the saloon floor. I couldn't be bothered to pick it up.

At sunrise Grenada was gone. We made an unsuccessful attempt to rig a makeshift sail. Dark heavy clouds indicated more squalls and thunderstorms. I managed to get a noon sight on the sun, but my position wasn't very accurate due to the pitching and rolling. It was difficult to balance on a heaving deck while trying to operate a sextant with both hands. With our broadside to the seas, we rolled so far that the gimballed cooker couldn't cope. We had to stand by the cooker, holding the kettle. On top of this, I was seasick. Just to do a simple subtraction was a nightmare.

I had to calculate an exact position if a tug was going to find us out here in between the squalls and the high seas. I did the equations over and over, with Mariann checking the math, and I pencilled in a dead reckoning cross on the chart.

Christ almighty! Twenty miles west of Grenada! That was about the range of the VHF radio! I tried to call up stations all though the island chain, but only got static in return. We had a long-range shortwave radio, but it was only a receiver. We could not transmit.

I no longer bothered putting on my foul weather gear each time I went on deck to do a scan of the horizon. I nearly leapt out of my skin when a voice boomed over the VHF radio, "Fredag Fredag. This is Charlie Alfa Bravo. Can you hear me?"

Chris Gomez was a ham radio operator on Grenada. He told me that he'd been listening in and had followed our conversation with the coast guard. He also told me that the coast guard vessel was in Florida for repairs and that they only had a small inflatable available. If indeed they'd ventured out in a dinghy, they wouldn't have gone very far. No wonder they hadn't found us.

He promised to relay our call for assistance to the coast guard in Saint Vincent. I gave him my warmest thanks and our most recent position. Chris was stationed on one of the highest mountains in Grenada and he had a signal booster on his transmitter. We would be able to keep in touch with him up to a distance of eighty miles.

"Don't give up," he said. "See if you can repair the engine. If we should lose contact, listen in on the shortwave."

He gave me some frequency numbers and continued, "As I said, don't give up. Keep a light on deck and look out for other traffic that might confirm your position. I'll call you every four hours to let you know what's happening here."

I thanked Mr. Gomez and told him that he should apply for the job as Commander of the Grenada Coast Guard.

It was going to be another long night, but Chris had me fired with optimism, and for the umpteenth time I listened to Bob Marley's *Three Little Birds*, believing once more that *every little thing's gonna be alright*. As the sun set I received the message that the Vincentian Coast Guard would be with us at sunrise. With a perfect fix on a star, combined with a bearing on the landing lights of an airliner approaching to land in Grenada, I believed I had a reliable position.

We scanned the horizon for hours at first light. Nothing. Not even a friggin' frigate bird. The radio was dead and we hadn't heard from Charlie Alfa Bravo for over 20 hours. Without an engine I couldn't charge the batteries, and I didn't want to drain them by transmitting too often on the radio.

The day passed, and another night. There was no sign of the Vincentian Coast Guard. In the morning, after five days adrift, I somehow managed to get a good position again, showing that we were drifting more to the northwest than I had expected. If this continued, we might reach Jamaica in three to four weeks. We'd never been there, but without battery power for the radio, we'd most likely end up on the rocks instead of in a marina.

For some strange reason the fish would not bite. Maybe that was because of the many sharks that gathered in larger numbers as the days passed. This was the worst part of our misfortune. The sharks were like vultures, ready to make a kill. I decided to try and establish contact with Chris again. As I held the microphone Chris's voice boomed out to us. "There you are!" he shouted. Thank God! How are you? And speak English please!"

After we'd previously been in touch with Chris, I'd been so excited that I'd inadvertently jammed the mike between the sextant and some astronomical tables, locking the button in the transmit position. From that minute on, the *Fredag* had been a drifting radio transmitter sending out hours of personal conversation between Mariann and me. Good thing we hadn't had an argument! In spite of this mishap the batteries were still up and running.

Chris and his wife had been up all night listening in and were unable to contact us. They hadn't understood a word of what we were saying in

Norwegian and they couldn't understand how we had managed to stay so calm. They periodically understood that Mariann was talking to the animals, and guessed that we were having eggs for breakfast. They also guessed that something was terribly wrong when they heard her shouting, "Hai, hai!"

Chris' wife called her Swedish friend, and when she learned that "hai" was Norwegian for *shark*, she had burst into tears. They both felt they were in some way on board with us.

Chris had some bad news. The Vincentians had changed their minds. They were willing to come pick us up, including the two animals, but they would not take us in tow. Chris told us that fishermen often run out of fuel and demand that the coast guard tow them home. I told Chris to tell them that we were not prepared to leave our home and that they could go stuff themselves.

The Saint Vincent coast guard recommended for us to call the US Coast Guard in Puerto Rico, a thousand miles away. We were foreigners, after all, right? He was trying to say that it might be more appropriate for the Americans to save us. Why not just as well call Oslo Coast Guard? "Hey you guys up there in the Land of the Midnight Sun. How's the weather? Listen, we've got a bit of a situation here. Could you just take some time off and nip down here to the Caribbean. We are drifting northwest of Grenada. You can't miss us. We're hungry too, so bring some Norwegian goat's cheese and make sure it's well packed- it's hot down here. Don't take too long now!"

Our friend Chris came up with a plan. His father was prepared to come to our assistance in his 35 ft catamaran. I managed to convince Chris that this wouldn't work. Towing a 40-tonne ketch with a tiny catamaran powered by an outboard engine in 15 foot swells with the wind on your nose was not a good idea. "All right" said Chris with relief. "I just wanted Dad to hear you confirm this! Oh, by the way, isn't Thor Heyerdahl a fellow countryman of yours?"

"Yes, he is. He drifted across the Pacific on a balsa raft, wrote a book about it and made a fortune. I'm afraid I don't have a similar motivation. I'm not drifting towards Jamaica to prove that it is possible that some Vikings did it thousands of years ago."

I then added that I would rather set fire to my ship, just like Heyerdahl did with the *Ra*. I would rather burn her in protest at the coast guard's incompetence, instead of leaving her to her own fate. Our only other option was to order a commercial tug whatever it cost. Chris said he would look around and try to arrange something.

After six days adrift, Chris called to inform us he had found a commercial tug. Our batteries were coming to an end. It was just in time.

"I have a guy who is prepared to come on the conditions you have given. The captain is not present at the moment but his son will sort you out. He is not very well qualified in navigation, but he has one of those new Global Positional gadgets. Please give me your latest position and…"

His transmission started to break up. We were obviously getting out of range. I gave him our position and closed down the radio, praying that my calculations were accurate.

The tug would arrive at sunrise if all went well.

During the dogwatch I saw a ship. This was the first time since leaving Venezuela over a week ago that we had seen any sign of life. It was a comforting sight, and I didn't feel so alone any more.

She was a Greek cruise ship out of Miami heading for Bogotá. They asked if they could be of any help. They probably had heard our radio transmissions. I told them I would be very grateful if they could confirm our position.

They gave me the coordinates and said something that sounded Greek to me, but it didn't matter. I had a big red cross on my chart, only a couple of miles from my own estimated position.

The sharks had vanished and suddenly life was good again.

Our Angel of Salvation came steaming out of the morning mist. Before we had his towing hawser on board his entire port rail had been ripped off by our bowsprit. It wasn't only navigation that the young man was not expert at. It didn't matter. Even though it would be a long haul, we were going home. Back home to Bequia.

After being in tow for a couple of hours, a huge C130 aircraft appeared with U.S. COAST GUARD written on the fuselage. It buzzed our mast top. The plane circled around again and I heard a powerful voice with a Texas drawl calling us on the maritime calling frequency.

"*Free dog, free dog.* This is the US Coast Guard out of Puerto Rico. Can we be of any assistance?"

They informed me that they had a rescue vessel ready to come to our aid 400 miles away. They wanted to confirm our situation before sending the ship to us. They could see that we already had assistance, but wanted to ask us anyway.

I thanked them from the bottom of my heart and told them I was sorry they came all this way for no reason. Their reply was, "No problem. It's not far for us, and besides, we need as much training as we can get. Do you need any medical help? What about provisions?"

This was just amazing!

I replied that we were OK and had all we needed and suddenly regretted it. I wondered what they would have dropped if I'd said we were starving? Kentucky fried, or maybe a Big Mac?

Throughout the night I kept having to crawl onto the bowsprit to disengage the hawser that kept getting tangled on the bowsprit stays. The hawser could snap it and I didn't want any more breakages. A big wave tore away the lashing on the jib and large pieces of white sail flew by, ending in our wake. The rain whipped down on us and the visibility was very bad. With the batteries almost dead, we kept radio communication with the tug to a minimum.

The captain of the tug had never been to Bequia and asked if we could act as a pilot to guide him in. His fancy satellite navigating gadget told him he was only a couple of miles off West Key, a treacherous group of rocks jutting out from the entrance to Admiralty Bay. I couldn't see much due to the rain and the tug's bright stern light. I told him to keep a good look out for the light on the last islet. I made a call to the coast guard on Saint Vincent, seven miles further north, and asked them if the light on West Key was working.

"Roger affirmative Roger. We can see the light from here. Have a good trip! Over and out." I told the signal station operator thanks but that I didn't have anyone on board named Roger.

The tug captain told me that he couldn't see any flashing light on West Key, but he could see a little blue light to port. I asked him to switch off his stern light and picked up my binoculars. I found the blue light. It read *BARCLAYS BANK*. "It's the big neon sign on the friggin' bank for God's sake! Come hard to port immediately! Head straight for the blue light!"

Another minute and he would've been on the rocks, with us in tow.

I was trembling with anger when I called the signal station and enquired what they were doing, that due to their incompetence lives had been jeopardized. My first mate put her hand over the microphone and shook her head. A few minutes later a pleasant voice came over the speaker, "*Fredag* this is ZQS Saint Vincent Signal Station. How are you? Thanks for your information about the light on West Key and have a pleasant voyage."

It took me some time to get over the nerve-wrecking incident.

I felt much better after I'd organized a campaign to tweak the signal station- I asked all my friends to call and enquire if the light was working every time they passed West Cay at night. We couldn't help laughing when one night the signal station answered, "We ain' sure mahn, but call up the sailing yacht *Fredag*, they will know."

It was great to be back in Bequia. Word had spread. Everyone knew about our latest mishap before the anchor was down and were happy that we'd survived once more. Judy, the Pizza Queen of the Caribbean, invited us over for breakfast at *Mac's Pizzeria*. It was the best breakfast we'd ever eaten.

The little white cottage, the rose garden, and the maintenance-free horse was once again history. It was time to look forward, to find a new crankshaft and put *Fredag* into the charter business so we could make enough money to pay for the salvage.

18. The Crankshaft

Bequia had become our base port. The tiny village of Port Elizabeth had four yacht chandleries, but none of them stocked crankshafts. I was told that one of them might be able to help. The owner of the *Bosun's Locker* had no idea what a crankshaft was, but he had an interesting variety of floating key-rings and Welsh flags in all sizes. If I purchased a flag, he would send a fax to his contact in London. The fax cost 15 dollars- and the reply would be another 10.

The clattering fax machine brought bad and good news. The bad news was that our Perkins engine went out of production in 1958; the good news was that they had an efficient network to find second-hand spare parts. If I was not in a rush they'd get back to me. I faxed back that I would hang on. In this part of the world time means little, and I was used to waiting.

After many hours, forking out more dollars for faxes, the Perkins dealer in the UK found a demolished and reduced engine in a scrapyard near Birmingham. He could have the crankshaft "smartened up" and sent tomorrow to the West Indies by express overnight delivery for a total of two hundred fifty pounds sterling.

I liked the express overnight delivery part of the fax. It meant we could be back in business in a week or two. I was smiling again as I left the *Bosun's Locker*, having located a replacement crankshaft for the cost of fifty EC dollars and a Welsh flag.

However, we needed funding for the new crankshaft. It didn't matter how we did the financing, as long as it was legal. There were many ways to make a dollar in the Caribbean, especially if you owned a vessel. It had to be legal, though, or it might result in a lengthy locked-door accommodation behind barred windows with breadfruit and water thrown in once a day.

Our new venture was appropriately named *Sunset Pirate Cruises*. The plan was to fill our ship with as many tourists as possible and take our holidaymakers for an afternoon sail with free rum-punch. For the insignificant amount of only 10 U.S. Dollars they had the pleasure of hoisting our heaviest 400 lb anchor, with a risk of disembarking with an inguinal hernia, muscle rupture or, if they were lucky, just a few blisters.

Flogging the captain for a price

Those who survived hoisting the anchor got to hoist our sails. There were risks here as well. Ropes under tension and wooden blocks and pulleys out of control might send them to the hospital. They could also badly burn their hands if they didn't let go of the ropes when Mariann shouted "Let go!" Maybe they wouldn't let go because they didn't understand her as she often spoke in a strange mixture of English, Norwegian, and Swedish.

Added to this mayhem was a taste of 17th century swearing inspired by my imitation of Captain Bligh. All this pandemonium was accompanied by the last movement of Tchaikovsky's *1812 Overture*. The cannon blasts and church bells were so loud that our ghetto blaster vibrated and took a walk across the deck. Those of my voluntary landlubbers who didn't comply or who hesitated were threatened with keel-hauling or the cat o' nine tails. The fake flogging took place with the victim tied to the main boom. The bloody abuse, with ketchup substituted for real blood, was recorded on instant-developed film and sold to the victim upon disembarking for an astronomical price. If the victim wished, the roles could be reversed, with the punter flogging the captain- for a higher price of course!

My Bequia crew, functioning mostly as bartenders, were dressed as pirates to suit the occasion. I wore baggy pants with my lower leg tied upwards and a wooden peg leg attached to my knee, a stuffed imitation parrot glued to my shoulder, and the obvious patch over my eye. Mariann only wore her strumpet outfit if there were no children on board.

We started off our "Disney World" cruise by sailing downwind out of the bay. When the waves started picking up and we noticed that some of the passengers were turning a bit green, we turned back and served a free rum punch every time we tacked on our way home. The wind was normally light, causing us to perform many tacks. For some of the passengers there was one tack too many.

When the sun dips under the horizon the last refracted rays give off a green flash- a natural tropical phenomenon which has to be seen to be believed. It was best observed from the deck of *Fredag*. Those who didn't see it could come back tomorrow. The spectacle literally took place in the blink of an eye. Blink and you've missed it, and if you've done too much tacking you might be headed for an early bunk back at the hotel.

The whole ridiculous charade was over as anchor and sails were dropped in front of the bar at the *Frangipani Hotel*.

The captain shouted, "Have we had a good time?" and the holidaymakers mumbled their approval. "One more time," I'd yell. "Have we had a good time?"

This time there was a load response in unison, "Yes!"

Many of the people enjoying happy hour at the hotel's bar would watch our tacking between the anchored yachts. Often many of them booked their passage for the following day.

I wasn't all that happy about putting on such a silly act, but it only lasted for three hours, and it was helping us get back on our feet financially. Quite often we were invited for drinks and dinner by our passengers. It was a win-win situation, and we made many new friends. They wanted to hear our story. I'd give them the short version. For the long one, they'd have to buy the book- if it ever got published.

There was a fax from the Perkins dealer. A four-week payment deadline was out of the question. The shipment had to be paid in full before it was dispatched. Not a problem. We had affiliated our business with the hotel and a short-term loan was secured; a new, second hand crankshaft was on its way!

Aeroflot may have had a bad reputation, but LIAT, short for **Leeward Islands Air Transport**, had to be the most incompetent airline in the western hemisphere. The company was a collaboration between several Caribbean governments. The fact was these tiny republics had major collaborative problems at all levels, never mind trying to operate something as complex as an airline. Over many years they had only lost one plane. Passengers, on the other hand, were always losing their luggage and temper. It was therefore with some anxiety that I contacted LIAT in Barbados to find out if my crankshaft had arrived.

FedEx had done their job flying it across the Atlantic, but LIAT was in charge of flying it to St. Vincent. The freight documents had arrived at the customs office, but a heavy box addressed to yacht *Fredag* was missing. A week later, after a lot of phone calls and faxes, we had an explanation. LIAT had shipped our crankshaft back to England due to a misunderstanding. Nobody could tell me exactly why.

On the second try I had a new FedEx arrival time in Barbados, and I called LIAT immediately after the plane had landed. I was told there was no box addressed to us. I declared this absolute bullshit because I had a confirmation from FedEx that the shipment had been loaded onto the plane at Heathrow. If it hadn't fallen out in the middle of the Atlantic, then LIAT must locate my shipment, I shouted.

LIAT's freight manager did not appreciate my tone. He said that the shipment wasn't on the plane because there were no shipping documents. Eventually, the manager in charge of the lost freight understood that I had the shipping documents because they arrived a week ago when the shipment came the first time. They would check it out immediately and get back to me.

Another day passed before I found someone in the department for lost freight who had checked for it. I was told that the shipment *may* have flown out of Barbados to the wrong island. This happened once in a while. Really? They were going to send out a search warrant. I told them that a search warrant was what the police needed when they knocked on your door looking for contraband. I no longer had any confidence in them, and I got a list of all the outbound planes from Barbados on that specific day. I called Suriname, Trinidad, Venezuela, and Martinique, without result. Another week went by and our phone bill reached an astronomical level. This was becoming an expensive crankshaft. I suspected it might be in St. Vincent because I had exhausted all other options. I took the ferry to the airport on the "mainland," as we call the largest island in the Grenadines.

I recalled that when my daughter came to visit me her suitcase had disappeared. We had filled out a lost-luggage form in triplicate and called LIAT every day for three weeks. When her return journey took place, I journeyed to the airport to wave goodbye. The departure of the LIAT plane was of course delayed, and while strolling around I passed an open door with a sign saying, *Unauthorized Access Prohibited*. The room was full of luggage and I immediately recognized my daughter's suitcase. It had been there all the time! The problem now was that I didn't have a copy of the lost luggage form with me, so they refused to hand it over, despite the fact that the suitcase had her name tag, she had an ID on her, and she could describe the contents in detail. The customs officer in charge wouldn't hand over any luggage out without the form. I said I would write out a new form. He demanded the original.

What always helps in such situations is to bring up a notepad and ask for the name of the employee. This almost always leads to a positive outcome and is much easier than howling and screaming and threatening to call the police, your lawyer, or the news-media. The officer went no further. Without another word, he handed my daughter her suitcase.

It had been costly for my daughter to arrive without clothes and the things needed when on holiday. She wanted compensation. The airport manager shook his head. By now the limit of my patience has been reached. I threatened to take legal action. He said that there was no point in taking LIAT to court. The proceedings would take many years, and he pointed to a large pile of documents that were similar complaints. It was then I understood why the popular acronym for LIAT was "Luggage In Another Terminal."

Eventually I got a call from Barbados. A box had been sent to St. Vincent as passenger cargo. I could hardly believe it.

"Oh, it's you again," said LIAT's freight manager. "No, it didn't come with the morning flight." I contacted LIAT's cargo office in Barbados again. I was told that the boss was home with a headache. His assistant asked me who had called from his office. I said I also had a headache and had no idea who called. I was simply told that my shipment has been flown to Saint Vincent. Saint Vincent said it had not arrived. Either someone was lying or the plane had vanished!

"Wait a minute," was his reply. Five minutes later, "We have no indication that an aircraft has crashed, but we shall check closer. Call us back in a while." The undefined "while" lasted three hours.

"Mister Roren, sorry for the inconvenience. What happened is that the box left the shed on a fork lift. The pilot thought the cargo was over the weight limit allowed. The engine part, even without its box, was far too heavy to go as passenger cargo. It's now in shed number nine and will be shipped out as soon as possible."

It was best to let Mariann take over. I thought I'd go fishing.

19. The Island of Bequia

There had been problems smashing a bottle of champagne over the bow during our launching in Oslo ten years ago. It was not something you wanted to happen if you were the least bit superstitious. After all the hair-raising issues that had taken place, I often wondered if it really had been a good idea to sail away on Friday the thirteenth!

My knowledge of the West Indies when I was "sofa-sailing" around the world was that Ronald Reagan had just invaded Grenada and that some years earlier, a guy called Columbus had missed the Grenadine islands and settled in Santo Domingo, today's Haiti and the Dominican Republic. He stubbornly insisted to his death that he'd discovered the western off-shores islands of India.

Sitting in front of the fireplace studying my World Atlas, I had failed to notice the little island with the peculiar name- Bequia- a tiny speck on a page showing the western hemisphere; an island that would become so important in my life.

This is my island in the sun, Where my people have toiled since time begun, by Harry Belafonte was a popular hit. Little did I know then that an island in the sun was where I would soon be toiling for thirty-odd years.

Petroglyphs and remnants of settlements have been found from before the time of Christ, as waves of "Indians" paddled from South America and settled on most of the islands. The Arawaks were vegetarians and were killed and occasionally ritually eaten by the warlike Caribs who came centuries later. They took the Arawak women as wives, which caused a bit of a communication problem since the women perpetuated their original language.

The Brits and the French followed and planted sugarcane. After breaking numerous peace-treaties the colonizers systematically exterminated their foes. In Grenada, the Caribs committed mass-suicide by jumping off a cliff rather than surrender. In St. Vincent, after a protracted war in the late 18th Century, the Caribs and a separate tribe who had intermarried with escaped slaves to make "Black Caribs" were deported to Balliceaux, a tiny uninhabited island east of Bequia. Over half of them perished while waiting to be deported to Roatan, off the coast of Belize, due to a lack of water and food.

Apart from a few indigenous Mayans, their new home was an uninhabited piece of real estate where there was neither gold nor spices, just mangroves and a lot of mosquitoes. The king named it British Honduras. The country has since been renamed Belize, and many Belizeans today are descendants of Black African slaves and the deported Caribs of St. Vincent. They call themselves Garifuna, and they are teachers, shop-keepers, and middle-class consumers.

The Spaniards were not at all interested in Bequia because it had no gold or silver. France and England were constantly at war over which king should sit on the throne and own the islands that Spain didn't claim, so the island of

Bequia was constantly changing hands. The great protected harbour, Admiralty Bay, was a perfect anchorage for more than a hundred ships. Admiral Nelson's West Indies fleet had been repaired in the bay after the French shot holes in their topsides and made a mess of their rigging. *Fredag's* trustworthy mooring was- believe it or not- the remains of one of Nelson's old stock-anchors. However, through my research, there was no evidence that the one-eyed Admiral ever set a foot ashore, preferring what is now *Nelson's Dockyard* in Antigua.

At that time, Bequia was awash with wells and spring water. But the groundwater eventually ran low, and the navy needed building materials and tried to cut down the entire cedar forest. Soon the settlers would bring slaves to plant and harvest sugar cane for making rum.

While the English and French battled for superiority and the flag at the forts changed often, the mixed immigrant population lived in peace and harmony. These immigrants consisted mainly of farmers from Ireland, Scotland, and Brittany, as well as freed slaves from Trinidad, and a Norwegian whaler from Sandefjord. They were all of the opinion that they themselves, and no one else, were the rightful owners of the island, and they couldn't care less about which flag was raised over the forts, or who sat on the throne on the other side of the world.

These days, with the exception of New Year's Eve, or Old Years Night as it is more commonly known in the Caribbean, all is peaceful and quiet and the cannons have become rusty photo objects for the tourists. The 32 islands and rocks that make up the independent country called St. Vincent and the Grenadines are one of the world's smallest states, and all is well.

At the eastern entrance of the bay there lies a submerged rock appropriately named *The Devil's Table*. Between the rock and shore was a discarded fishing boat; on its topsides it read, "Belongs to Haakon." Haakon Mitchell was a man who had too dark a skin to be called Haakon– but he had blue eyes. He insisted that his first name was a one hundred percent Bequia name. His father and grandfather were also named Haakon. He said that the name was pronounced *Haycon*. He didn't believe me when I told him that the previous Norwegian king was also named Haakon and that I had the same middle name, with double a's, and that both my father and my son were also named Haakon. To convince him, I had to show him my passport. I asked if he knew anything about the origin of his first name. He had no idea. He couldn't believe that a white foreigner could be called Haakon! He and his ancestors were one hundred per cent genuinely black men and women– and the name Haakon went back to the days when dinosaurs roamed the island, which according to Father Adams, took place 3000 years ago!

Most Bequians lived in the present and had very little interest in the past, but since I was so interested in history and had picked up the tab for three bottles of Guinness, he promised to investigate the origin of his name. He said "us," so now it had become a joint project.

Haakon's ninety-two-year-old Aunt Julianne could tell him that his great-great-grandfather came to Bequia a long time ago to buy some lime, mangoes, and paw paw because his teeth were falling out. He arrived on a big sailing ship. He had been hanging out a very long time down near the South Pole catching whales and the crew had become ill. The ship had originally come from a country far up north somewhere, and the man had had enough of life at sea. He jumped ship in Bequia and fell in love with a local. He was the original Haakon. The surname had long gone into oblivion- most likely too difficult to pronounce. When this man was asked where he came from, he always answered "nowhere." It sounded like Norway to me!

Another peculiarity, which may be related to the man from "nowhere," was that there was also a guy here called Sandeford. Sandefjord is a whaling town in southern Norway. In this case I had to throw in the towel. For some reason, Sandeford Williams wouldn't talk to me about dead relatives.

Bequia, the gem of the Caribbean, is about seven miles long and two miles wide. On the map it has the shape of a big S with the bay and "capital," Port Elizabeth, tucked into the centre. The rest of the island consists of green-clad hills and peaks, steep cliffs, and magnificent sandy beaches. The sea according to its depth changes colour in all shades of green, turquoise, and blue. In short, a very special and beautiful island.

The block-buster movie *Pirates of the Caribbean* was shot in St. Vincent, and I volunteered as an extra. I became a red-coated British soldier despite my previous short-lived career as a conscious objector. In the opening scene in the first film, when a cannon ball smashed the pier and a dozen soldiers were thrown into the sea, you might have had a short glimpse of my right foot.

Some of the cast. I am behind the white post.

A year later, I meet a very sweet Norwegian journalist who wanted to write an article about me and Bequia in her local newspaper. I was honestly not very keen on such PR, but she was very sweet and I always get enthusiastic and cooperative when approached by beautiful women. And what was wrong with a little free marketing to bring in more tourists.? I mentioned the movie and had to name-drop that I'd met Johnny Depp.

The sweet journalist kindly sent me a newspaper clipping of her interview with the shipwrecked sailor. The headline, in bold across the front-page read: *Norwegian Sailor with a Foot in Hollywood.*

You probably will not find Bequia in a regular Norwegian travel catalogue, and there is most likely nobody employed at a travel agency there who has heard about the tiny island. In spite of this, I've met five tourists from the Land of the Midnight Sun, who due to that article, decided to visit. Two of them invited me out for dinner, as if I were some kind of celebrity, which I suppose I was in some obscure way.

Bequia is pronounced *Beck'wee* or even *Beck'way*. There are very few visitors who can pronounce the name correctly. Among long-distance sailors from Europe and the US it is well-known and very popular, especially for Scandinavians at Christmas when most make landfall in the Caribbean after crossing the Atlantic. They usually arrange a Christmas Day pig-roast party on the beach, but because pigs are harder to find, a skinny goat may be used as a substitute. They bring along a plastic decorated Christmas tree, soggy outdated pickled herring, and of course the required lukewarm Aquavit. The main Bequia attraction for these post-war Vikings was for many years our traditional Gløgg (mulled hot wine) gathering on Christmas Eve. *Gløgg* consisted of "bring your own" cheap wine, and Mariann would throw in some raisons, almonds, and cheap Polish vodka.

The annual Gløgg party originated aboard *Fredag* but had become such a popular event that we had to move it ashore. The record number of guests was 120, and we nearly sank when the sea came rushing in over the edge of the toilet bowl- our home was floating dangerously deep in the water.

Three small hotels and half a dozen guest-houses accommodated the few tourists who found their way to the island. It wasn't easy to find Bequia at the travel-agency, but it was even harder to get here, unless you came over your own keel and had GPS. Travelling by air from Europe or the US you had to change planes in Barbados, Grenada, or St. Lucia. From there a small LIAT turboprop took you to St. Vincent, and if you were blessed to find your luggage, it was a nerve-wrecking 15 minute taxi-ride to the ferry-dock, often to discover that the last ferry for the day had left. You spent the night at a noisy hotel in Kingstown. And the next day you usually motored across rolling Atlantic swells in a flat-bottomed car ferry. One could choose from three ferries: *The Admiral, The Bequia Express,* or *The Friendship Rose,* popularly called *"The Rose,"* which was a 70' locally-built schooner equipped with an engine.

Now, you might find this hard to believe. In fact, I could hardly believe it myself when I discovered that that *Admiral* had been a part of my past. When I was 12 years old she sailed between the Norwegian villages of Kinsarvik and Granvin on the Hardanger Fjord. Twice a day I would make the trip to and from school. Twice a day she now ferried schoolchildren to "mainland" St. Vincent and back to Bequia. How's that for an unbelievable coincidence?

The *Admiral* was designed and built for the tranquil and protected fjords. It had never been intended for her to be tossed around on huge Atlantic swells.

When the tidal current between the islands clashed with the North Atlantic current, the swells often rose to a height up to four meters- and even more if there was a strong trailing gale or Christmas winds.

Once a truck loaded with cement blocks did a slide from one side of the car-deck to the other. It smashed through the railing, toppled over the side, and disappeared into the deep! Thereafter, all heavy vehicles were chained down for the hour-long crossing. The passengers also had to secure themselves while vomiting over the rail, promising themselves this would be the last time ever. The old sea-dogs gathered in the bar for a few shots of strong rum. That bar had once been a cafeteria where the restrained, temperate inhabitants of Western Norway drank strong coffee. The cafeteria was gone, but the sign on the bulkhead was still there, written in a local and strange west-coast dialect.

Translated to English it read: NO ALCHOLOLIC BEVERAGES ARE ALLOWED OR TO BE BROUGHT ON BOARD OR CONSUMED ON BOARD THIS SHIP. PASSENGERS ARE REQUIRED TO REPORT TO THE CAPTAIN ANYONE SEEN BREAKING THIS LAW.

PLEASE HELP TO KEEP ORDER AND HAVE GOOD BEHAVIOUR AND DO NOT SPIT ON THE DECK.

Under the sign sat a stoned Rasta man staring into space with a happy grin on his face. I recognised him as "I-Man," chairman of The Marijuana Grower's Association. Yes, there actually was such an organisation.

The captain's name was Elvis Presley- Elvis Presley Gooding, that is. His mother must have been a great admirer of the King. Elvis helped sail the ferry from Norway to Bequia across the Atlantic. If I was to tell my old Principal in Norway that I'd sailed with Elvis in the Caribbean, on board my old school-ferry from the Hardanger Fjord, he would probably have me admitted to a psychiatric institution for further observation.

The other way to cross the strait between the two islands was with the old schooner, the *Friendship Rose*. She did the run once a day with passengers and their varied cargo- everything from chicken, goats, and turtles to Land Rovers. She carried mostly cement home and empty bottles back to St. Vincent. The brewery found it a too risky to ship cases of beer with the *Rose* and sent them on the *Admiral* instead.

The Friendship Rose

Captain Lewis was the Master of the *Friendship Rose*. He was a Seventh-day Adventist. Therefore, there was no sailing on Saturdays, but over the last forty years he had not missed a single daily passage, and his vessel departed and arrived on time. Before the engine was installed, however, the ship was once becalmed and took 17 days to get to Kingstown! After Hurricane Lenny passed north of Bequia, the seas were so large that the ferry had to lie a-hull and anchor in the bay overnight before they could get their exhausted passengers ashore.

There were rumours that *the Rose* would soon set sail for the last time with passengers and cargo and become a day-charter vessel for tourists. A new, fifth-hand Norwegian ferry was on its way; I wished all the best to the unfortunate crew and all who would roll with her across the Atlantic.

For some illogical reason, all three ferries always departed at 6:30 am, and it often happened that the sailing vessel arrived first. This occurred when the channel became too violent and there was a possibility that the motor ferries would become submarines. When Elvis Presley on the *Admiral* was forced to slacken speed, Captain Lewis on the *Rose* smiled, and keeping an eye on the massive swells, would give the order to bring in a bit more on the mainsail.

There weren't many holiday destinations on this planet where you arrived on a schooner with cotton sails, hemp rope, and where you might get tar on your luggage and salt in your hair.

Sometimes the passage turned to be out quite dramatic. I was on the *Rose* when a heavy squall heeled the schooner over so far that a load of cement-blocks shifted. To prevent the vessel from capsizing the captain had to reduce sail. The sky had turned steel-grey, the wind was howling in the rigging and horizontal rain lashed the terrified passengers on deck. Only a few children managed to squeeze into the little wheelhouse on the stern.

Fortunately, Father Adams happened to be on board. While the pastor clung to the mast as seas were crashing over the gunwale, he led his congregation in singing <u>God Is Our Refuge and Our Strength</u> until the crew got everything under control, and the *Rose* rounded Devil's Table and slipped into the calm of Admiralty Bay. There is a painting in the National Gallery in London with the same dramatic portrayal. I can't remember who painted it, but I will never forget the incident with Father Adams and his terrified congregation huddled around the mast.

With its historic connection to the sea, it's understandable that Bequia has a maritime influenced population. Until quite recently, as soon as young men had finished primary school they fished or were off to sea. Many worked on merchant ships. As soon as they had saved enough money they came home to settle down for good, find a wife, build a house and a fishing boat, or buy a car and start a taxi service. Bequia must have the world's highest number of taxis per capita. They were only busy when a cruise ship arrived and the tourists got an eight-mile tour of the island.

Old Mr. Tannis was one of the elders who started his career in the merchant navy on board a Norwegian freighter. He therefore spoke a little Norwegian with a local West Coast dialect and could recite the first verse of *See Norway's Flowering Valley*. In 1969, he signed off the freighter in New York and worked there for ten years as a crane operator and made waffles every Sunday at the *Seamen's Church*. Now he was the proud owner of the *New York Bar* on Bequia. He also drove a taxi when he came home, but there were problems combining taxi driving and running the bar. The remains of his taxi lay at a depth of 5 fathoms just off the ferry-dock. Nobody knew how it got there.

There were an abundance of taxis to choose from. You never had to queue up to wait. You could find them all in the shade under a huge almond tree in Port Elizabeth, which one taxi-driver claimed Admiral Nelson had planted. Throughout the day they all sat in the shade and discussed politics and who should win the next Miss Bequia pageant competition. Their taxis had amusing names like *Jump in Taxi, Just in Time, Man Just Arriving* and *Fat Man*. The owner of *Fat Man Taxi* was the tallest and skinniest of them all.

There were many taxis but not many miles of roads. It took a long time getting anywhere due to all the potholes on the very steep and narrow roads. However, things were gradually getting better as the main roads were paved with concrete. On one stretch of road you might exceed the 30 mph speed limit, but anywhere else you'd be putting your life at risk or "mashing up" your car's shock-absorbers and suspension. Speed bumps called *sleeping policemen* were built to tame the speeders, so that even with the new concrete surface it took nearly as long to get from one place to another, and cars fell apart as quickly as before. I was fortunate to own a 1943 Citroen 2CV, the only one on the island. It arrived on the banana boat from Southampton.

The ideal island car

The Taxi-drivers were envious- due to the special suspension system on the 2CV, I could fly over the speed-bumps at full speed. It was a great island car. On a sandy beach, you could remove the seats in a jiffy and use them as deck-chairs; you could roll back the roof to let in the trade-winds, and you could fly over potholes and speedbumps. The locals loved it and I had countless offers from interested buyers- even from the Chief of Police, in spite of it having been spray-painted with marijuana leaves.

It also didn't help you to get to your destination on time when other drivers with time on their hands kept stopping in the middle of the road for a chat. Nobody is ever in a hurry here. It could take 40 minutes to drive seven miles from Port Elizabeth to the village of Paget Farm on the south side of the island. Time is a relative and somewhat uncertain term on Bequia. There's a general opinion here that "the time you enjoy wasting is not wasted time."

Times are changing. It has now become difficult to find work on merchant ships, resulting in high unemployment. In order to start any kind of business, an investment is required. Continuing education beyond elementary school is not done by the poor if they fail their Common Entrance Exams at age 11. There is nothing much for young people to do other than hang around and hope to make a dollar during the short tourist season. Fishing was much too hard and dangerous work and required a boat.

One was lucky to get a government job cleaning the road gutters for a salary barely sufficient to feed a cat. While the girls worked and struggled with unwanted children, the men sometimes acted as if it wasn't their problem. One of my local crew members proudly boasted that he had twelve children, of whom he knew the names of four and had contact with one. He might possibly have had some kids in Sweden as well, but they didn't count, because it was only a *possibility*. Having brought so many children into the world was a clear and present proof of his manhood.

It's not so easy for us northerners to grasp this cultural divide. We often misunderstand and see their values in a negative context. Here's an example. A North-American businessman was sent to Bequia for convalescence by his doctor. Over a period of two weeks he'd been studying a young, muscular West-Indian man who spent most of his day under a palm tree with a spliff, chatting up the white girls who passed by. Hopefully a rich white woman would one day supply him with money to purchase a second-hand taxi or a small fishing-boat. He had friends who had hit the jack-pot in this manner. Occasionally, the young man would summersault into the surf or go for a short spin around the bay on his windsurfer. The following conversation took place when he returned.

The businessman asked, "Don't you have a job?"

"No man. Why work?"

"Well, there are many reasons why one should work. Most of all to financially secure your future. If you work hard now, you will be able to relax and live the good life without any worries when you get old."

"Right mahn," he replied," But that's exactly what I'm doing now. Relaxing and living the good life with no worries."

Based on our values and how we live our lives, it isn't easy to comprehend such a devil-may-care attitude. However, the more time I spent here, the better I understood West Indian culture and mentality. It seemed contagious.

I've become "West Indianized" by just being here, whether I wanted to or not. For example, I walk much slower now. I've even adopted a bit of the undulating stride. I'm starting to consider that the handsome Adonis under the palm tree does have a point where seizing the day comes to mind. It's also pretty obvious that much of this culture came across the pond with the African slaves, who in their homeland were mostly hunters, gatherers, and people who lived in the present.

Consider, for example, the stable climatic conditions that make it unnecessary to plan or stock up to survive the long, cold winter. There is summer, sunshine, and frequent rainfall more or less throughout the year. Coconuts, yams, and breadfruit are abundant and the sea is teeming with fish. You don't even have to climb the breadfruit-tree to gather the Caribbean alternative to potato. You only need a long stick with a hook on the end. Why struggle with the cultivation of potatoes, cabbage, and tomatoes when a breadfruit tree can provide food for a hundred years? A tree like the one Captain William Bligh of the *Bounty* planted here over two hundred years ago still stands in the *Botanical Garden* of Kingstown. And it still bears breadfruit.

You just needed some sheets of corrugated iron over your head to keep the rain out, and you built your home as straightforward and low-cost as possible. Sooner or later, a hurricane would sweep it out to sea or scatter it over the mountainside. Winter insulation, double glazing, and a steep roof angle? Forget it. No point in planning or worrying about what *might* happen. All was well yesterday, all is well today, and everything will most likely be fine tomorrow.

Of course, West Indians do not live in mud-huts with thatched roofs of banana-leaves any longer. But their ancient and inherited ways and outlook on life still persist. A culture so different than ours can lead to a number of unusual and interesting situations. Unusual for us so-called "civilized" people who claim we know so much better.

I had an old Swedish wood-burning stove on board. This wonderful device saved my life when *Fredag* was trapped in the ice at the bottom of the Oslo Fjord. The children here were wondering what this strange looking round metal box was all about.

I explained, "When it is cold outdoors, cold like it is inside a refrigerator, we can make a fire inside this round metal box and it keeps us warm." I also told them that it could be so cold outdoors that the sea froze to ice and I couldn't use my dinghy to go ashore. I walked on top of the ice to get ashore and the sun didn't shine for many months. I needed a flashlight in the middle of the day to avoid getting lost.

The kids found that really hard to comprehend. Ice was something tourists had in their drinks- and only Jesus could walk on water.

Conversely, tourists and newcomers had problems understanding Caribbean ways. An example was service within the tourism sector, or more correctly, the lack of service. Many viewed this as locals having a chip on their shoulders. I saw them as a friendly and caring people who would go out of their way if you were in need. However, when it came to some friendliness and service in a restaurant or bar, there could be a total lack of it. There seemed to be a certain unwillingness to serve and assist, as if doing so you lowered yourself to a submissive position, that of a servant or even a slave. Could this be a result of recent history and traditions where slaves were brutally mistreated by their owners? It certainly had little to do with racism. They often treated their own the same way. I also thought that having a 10% service charge included in the price of your meal did little to motivate those serving you. Whether you liked it or not, here you are charged 10% for service.

I also discovered that I was treated far better as a customer if I didn't behave like a bad-tempered, impatient asshole.

Here's an extreme example- our favourite eatery on Bequia was a little bar that served rotis, a low budget meal in wrap. A roti is a combination of soft flatbread, curried meat or fish, and potatoes. The service here was so bad that the establishment was seen as a curiosity by some, and for those with a sense of humour, a tourist attraction.

Mariann and I were the only guests and it was our first visit to the place. In spite of there being no one there it took ages before the waitress came shuffling and stood at the end of the table, without a word. No "hello" or "good afternoon." With her arms folded, she gazed out at the horizon.

We ordered two chicken roti and two beers. Without a word she shuffled back to the kitchen. After fifteen minutes she slammed two beers on the table. There were no glasses, but we have learned that this is normal in the Caribbean. I asked her to bring me a glass. I don't like drinking from a bottle. I once had a front tooth knocked out once during a bar-brawl. After another fifteen minutes she returned. She had three words for us.

"No chicken roti."

"Then we'll have two beef roti."

"No beef."

"How about conch? And we would like two more beers, please."

She raised hand, a gesture that here can mean *don't push me!* And then she disappeared back into the kitchen. We started asking each other- did she hear what we ordered? Did the gesture mean she was going to check if they had conch? Would it take another 15 minutes? It had become humorous to us. We had all time in the world. It was great just sitting there and watching life pass by in the harbour. We took side bets on the outcome.

An hour after we arrived, our roti were on the table. They were cold.

"My dear," I said politely, "how do you heat up food here? Do you have a microwave?"

"Oven," was her short answer.

"My dear," I continued in the same manner, "Our roti are cold. We don't like cold roti. Could you heat them in the oven for us?"

She looked down at the roti as if they were something that had crawled out of the sewer. Another short answer: "No."

"Why not?"

For the first time she looked us straight in the face, first at me, then down at the roti and then at Mariann. She folded her arms and looked out to sea again, sighed and replied, "I'm so tired."

We ate our cold roti, paid the bill, and at a safe distance we dropped down on the sand roaring with laughter. I now had two hilarious restaurant experiences to write about.

The previous incident concerned a restaurant that served really good fish meals. Due to the exquisite creole sauce, it became our favourite eating place. We sailed away for a while and when we came back, we aimed right for our favourite dinner.

"Sorry," said the owner, "We have fish but no creole sauce."

"Why not?" we asked.

"Too many people wanted it."

Bequian humour is quite special, with a certain amount of irony. The ten best jokes I'd ever heard, though quite funny to me, might cause no reaction whatsoever. However, if I said something spontaneous without trying to be funny, the locals often fell over howling with laughter. One day I took the dinghy to the dock to fill my water containers. I tossed all the jugs on the pier. Then I carried them over to the water tap and started filling them with the hose. The dockmaster looked at me with a curious expression.

"White man, why don't you keep dem jugs in de boat? You can fill dem wit' de water hose. You been too long in de West Indies!"

The three most important events after Christmas celebrations are the annual Carnival, Easter Regatta, and partying as often as possible. Bequians use every opportunity and excuse to party. There need be no special reason, just enough music, food, and drink. Alcohol consumption is the most important ingredient when partying where I come from, but here it's all about dancing to reggae and calypso, and one also gets thirsty dancing in the heat.

A "Jump up" is such an event. Quite descriptive, because it is all about jumping, swaying, or swinging with the music. You can move like you're wading in syrup, but remember to slowly swing your hips and backside. After a couple drinks it all feels natural. No three steps forward and two to the side in this part of the world, and for the ladies to have to wait for an invitation to dance is unknown. You can dance by yourself or with a partner regardless of gender or colour. Basically, if there's music in the air you move to it. I have seen a policeman directing traffic while dancing with earplugs and a cassette player attached to his belt. It seems that everyone must have music while they work, from the air traffic controllers to the crane operators. Imagine a jigging crane driver with ten tons of cargo swinging to and fro!

A steel-band is an orchestra with musicians who beat out music on a lot of empty oil-drums. They literary hammer it out. The origin of this musical success is actually of recent date. When the US Navy abandoned Trinidad after World War II, they left a lot of empty oil-drums behind. In good old African tradition, the drums were turned into musical instruments by the locals hammering out concave indentures on one end of the drum. The inventive Trinis discovered that when they hit their mallets on the various size indentures, it gave off different notes, depending on the size and shape of the indenture. A good steel band has rhythm, melody, and harmony.

However, some bands were simply torment to your ears. The repertoire of a trio playing at one of the Bequia hotels was limited to twenty-five verses of *Yellow Bird* and just as many of *Island in the Sun*. But the tourists find it fun and exotic. In Trinidad there are huge orchestras with over 100 musicians. I witnessed such an orchestra playing a Bach fugue in the *Holy Trinity Cathedral* in Trinidad- quite an experience!

And then there's Carnival, the very meaning of life- the highlight of the year for young people and participants of all ages. It's a popular two week long party that requires great effort and enormous resources from the authorities and organizers, culminating in a Queen Contest on Saturday night, The Calypso King contest on Sunday night, J'ouvert Morning on Monday, and Mardi Gras on Tuesday. On J'ouvert ("I open") the revellers "chip" through the streets of Kingstown behind trucks playing the year's soca hits. On Mardi Gras Tuesday the many costumed "bands," many featuring six or seven sections under a single theme march though Kingstown to blaring soca. Some of the women wear next to nothing but a few feathers, and there are band sections with just children, or young women, or older fat women, or just men, each wearing costumes that complement the others in their "band."

The song that is played most on the trucks gets the coveted "Road March" award. It doesn't have to be great, just the most danceable, often with double-entendre lyrics that are politically scathing or overtly sexual.

Bequia also has its annual carnival- as do all the other islands. They take place on different times of the year so you can actually travel from carnival to carnival. I prefer only one a year. That's enough for me. I'm getting too old. Bequia's tiny Carnival is several weeks before the main one in Kingstown, St. Vincent. The revellers dance behind a single music truck, back and forth through Port Elizabeth until the hot sun fries their brains and more alcohol is required. I may join the fun, but not without ear-protection. Yeah, I'm actually getting old.

Carnival ("farewell to the flesh") had its origin in Trinidad in the 1780's. It was started by French planters, freed blacks, and eventually their slaves to celebrate the days before the beginning of Lent. People would party and gorge themselves ("Gross Tuesday" is the translation of Mardi Gras) before their 40 days of sobriety. With the abolition of slavery masquerading was the thing, seasoned with pageantry competitions featuring beautiful women.

According to VS Naipaul, a British-Trinidadian writer and historian, the respected English governor of Port of Spain was fed-up of seeing black people being abused and owned. He took the matter into his own hands and released the slaves and imported labourers from India. The King of England wasn't happy about this and sent a replacement governor with a letter of dismissal to the rebellious one, but the replacement never arrived. The noncompliant governor ordered a false lighthouse to be set up at the narrow strait of the *Dragon's Mouth*. The ship slammed into the dragon's teeth and the replacement governor became crab fodder.

Each island has its own carnival, but Trinidad carnival is known as the greatest street party on earth. You have probably heard of the carnivals in Rio, and Mardi Gras in New Orleans. Caribbean carnivals can be just as spectacular, with displays of colour and imaginative costumes. Engineers and artists work for up to a whole year in advance creating imaginative themes, so spectacular and complicated that they require hydraulics and engine power to make them work. Although the daring visiting tourists do their best to impress, dressing up as Arab sheikhs in borrowed hotel-sheets,

Arab headwear, and drooping moustaches, they cannot compete with the amazing kaleidoscope of the locals' imaginations. Traditional local costumes are Sailors (from WWII days) and American Indians, but may also include Vikings or even Martians.

I'm not quite sure how the Trinidadians got the impression of what Vikings looked like, but to me these Trini-Vikings resembled a cross between a Roman gladiator and Miss Afghanistan in a leopard bikini. One of the most hilarious segments I've ever seen was a two-hundred foot caterpillar condom bearing the text, "YES TO AID, NO TO AIDS."

A vital part of the parade is the music. Sometimes it is fifty musicians with their steel drums on wheels, or a music truck loaded with loudspeakers as big as phone booths, blasting out deafening soca. Derived from "soul calypso," soca's fast beats and provocative lyrics provide the soundtrack for Carnival. I prefer the Calypso. Originating in Trinidad and Tobago, calypso music is characterized by social or political commentary or satirical lyrics sung to ballad rhythms, quite often with a sexual content.

My favourite was a masterful masturbatory revelry called, "I Love Miss Palmer," by Trinidadian calypsonian *Explainer*, and arranged by St. Vincent's own Frankie McIntosh:

I love Miss Palmer/ We stick on together/ I love Miss Palmer/ I love she forever/ I don't wanna fear any AIDS or her-pees'/ Or any kind of sexually transmitted disease/ Neither no heartache/ Neither no heartbreak...

(Chorus) I love Miss Palmer/ Like birds of a feather/ I love Miss Palmer/ We al-ways' come together/ I don't have to worry about pregnancy....

Bequia's most well-known and popular event is Easter Regatta, where local boat owners and sailors from the region and across the globe come to race and party for five days. What made this regatta unique was its simplicity. In the early years there were a few simple rules and the purpose was to have fun, not necessarily to win. Nowadays, however, the competition is fierce for the CSA handicapped yachts and the seven classes of local double-enders. Anything that floats or moves with the wind can participate, from large antique 100-foot schooners to small model boats in a separate competition for young boy swimmers. If you are a visiting tourist and would like to take part as crew in the regatta, you can choose from a variety of yachts.

The regatta is divided into four main groups: racers, cruisers, and J 24s race with the yachts, and traditional double-enders race separately in six or seven classes, according to length.

The first day of the event starts at five pm with registration of the boats and the skipper's briefing. After this meeting there's free rum punch for all participants until sunset. From then on to midnight there is steel band music, dancing in the sand, and refilling of rum. It's amazing that so many sailors are able to arrive at the starting line the next morning.

I usually shanghai a crew among tourists at the bar during the party. To shanghai someone is to kidnap or trick them into working for you. The traditional way to shanghai a crew was to drug them and put them on a ship. When they awoke they found themselves at sea. We don't actually shanghai them that way, but close enough, and you can imagine the result.

We lure the victims on board with waffles and free rum. Normally they are mostly inexperienced landlubbers. *Fredag* weighs thirty tonnes and is designed for dealing with gale-force winds, not light trade winds, so we are nearly always the last yacht to cross the finish line.

The good news was that we always received a consolation prize, and it often was a very nice, sentimental keepsake. This was possibly due to the fact that Marianne and I were both on the prize-committee. We won our class just once. This happened because the only vessel in our class (Classical Gaffers) besides us thought they had won. They were a quarter of a mile ahead, opened the champagne too early, and forgot to cross the finish line, resulting in disqualification. We received a consolation prize in addition to the first prize, because we had had a very bad year with our masts breaking and lots of misery.

Crazy preparations

On the last day of the regatta, the prizes were handed out by the Prime Minister. The school choir sang the national anthem and there were thank-you speeches to everyone who'd participated in organizing the event and those who'd donated money and prizes. And finally, a thank you to the yachties who'd travelled a great distance to be here. There were lots of prizes- prizes for the most interesting Miss Wet T-shirt, the guy with the ugliest face, the slippery pole and sand castle competition, wind-surfing, and for kids who swam with their model and coconut boats. The double-ended fishing boats received cash and a trophy. And then we must not forget the class that brought the most spectators: The Crazy Craft Race.

This event, for both children and adults, was all about building your own craft. The construction work should take place within 24 hours before start, but that rule was never enforced. The course ran along a mile-long beach where half way across there was a raft with Mariann on board. Dressed as a witch, she handed out ice cream to the kids and rum for the adults; refreshments for those who so far along the way had not sunk or lost their mast. The craft must be built of scraps or driftwood and must only be driven by the power of the wind, and the crew must stay on board at all times.

Many of the local homeowners on Bequia have 18-30 foot open sailing boats in their yard or stored on the beach. Every Easter they haul them out from under a tarp or a cover of palm branches. They get a new coat of paint before the race starts and repairs are made. Each boat has a minimum crew of three, but the largest classes have up to seven, with a boy or young man designated as bailer.

The starting line is on the beach. The crew make adjustments to the sprit-sail rigs, and sandbags are loaded as ballast, then the boats take off with the smaller classes going first, accompanied by spectators' cheering and jeering, while the sailors shout and cuss. Off they go to circumnavigate the island- downwind across the bay with more shouting and cussing, zigzagging between all the anchored yachts in the harbour.

Once out of the protected bay, the open craft are exposed to the elements, and power boats are on hand to pick up capsized crew and tow in their boats. Often the crew manage to right their ship, bail, and are on their way. Capsizing is generally due to carrying too much sail or consuming too much rum underway. So far, there have been no serious accidents, and it's really a miracle, as lifejackets are nowhere to be seen, and rules of the road are virtually non-existent.

The more relaxed and elderly whalers also participate with the last of the two surviving whaling boats under sail. In this case the competitors show better seamanship, but the competition is just as fierce for the biggest trophy of all.

Hunting endangered whales around Bequia is a controversial undertaking. St. Vincent belongs to a group of small nations that have permission, due to an agreement by the International Whaling Commission, which allows them to catch four humpback whales each year under certain conditions. These conditions are that they hunt and kill the whale in a traditional manner, using only sails and oars for propulsion and tossing hand-held harpoons, like the 19th Century Yankee whalers.

When I first arrived on the island, I found it intriguing and acceptable, and I couldn't quite agree with the environmentalists who believed it was wrong to "murder" whales. Pigs were smart, sheep pretty, and we ate them. I had probably eaten an entire whale during my childhood in Norway where whale-meat was on the menu every day except Sundays and Christmas Eve. However, after logging many miles at sea, experiencing these magnificent creatures in close proximity and lying in the bilge with my ear against the hull listening to them sing to each other, I had second thoughts.

The island people were no longer dependent on whale meat and the precious oil. Also, it was bad for much needed tourism, which the island depended on. I agreed that cultural traditions are very important, but when the whalers were not following the rules or cheated after the kill, having power boats tow back the whale, I tended to fall in line with the anti-whaling camp.

I tried to keep a low profile and not get involved in the pro or anti debate about whaling. Maybe that's why I was lucky to be invited for a spin in a real whaling boat. It was all because I mentioned to one of the whalers that a distant relative of mine had killed over a thousand whales off Antarctica.

The Atlantic swells rolled into Bequia's north coast. The whaling-boat was hard on the wind with a course set towards the neighbouring island of Mustique. The open wooden boat rose and descended on the waves, sending a continuous spray of water over me and the six-man crew. The boat was twenty-eight feet long and rigged with a sprit-sail main and jib. The helmsman sat on the stern deck, and the harpooneer, skipper, and owner-

Athneal Ollivierre- stood near the bow with his back against the jib to keep his balance. He was looking for humpback whales.

Athneal was over seventy years old, a tall and handsome man with weather-beaten face and grey-green eyes. His eyes and skin colour clearly showed that he was a descendant of Brittany fisherman who came to Bequia in the late 18th century. This unusual man was Bequia's hero and among the world's last whalers- a man who battled against the planet's largest mammals equipped only with a hand-held harpoon, a long-lance, and a surplus of courage. His skill and boldness were comparable to Herman Melville's harpooners in *Moby Dick*.

In Spain there is a similar controversy around bullfighting. The difference between the bullfighter and the whaler is that the latter is not dressed in gold and velvet, prancing around an arena full of cheering spectators. Athneal's arena is the endless open sea and the spectators are only a few frigate birds and an aging crew that would rather sit in the shade of a mango tree playing dominoes.

When he was not at sea Athneal was a quiet and modest person who did not stand out. He didn't not drink, smoke, swear, or hunt on Saturday; he was a Seventh-day Adventist.

Athneal on the hunt in his whale boat, *Why Ask?*

Throughout the day we had been tacking between the islands without seeing anything other than flying fish and dolphins. Back on shore he smiled for the first time since we'd set out. I thanked him for the ride, and he told me that this was his last hunt. According to those who knew him well, he has threatened to quit many times over the last ten years.

He said it was sad there was no one to take over. He claimed the cause was not a lack of courage from younger men, but that there was little to gain from whaling nowadays. There were less dangerous ways to make a living.

However, only a week later the phone rang and he was informed that whales had been spotted. Athneal was unable to sit idle after hearing this and the whale boat "Why Ask" was quickly launched.

Here's what happened, according to one of the oarsmen I met after the hunt. Over a few Guinnesses, he gave me a detailed narrative.

One of the crew shouted, "There she blows, a little to port."

Fifty meters ahead, the black glistening back of a huge whale broke the surface. A geyser of mist and bad breath erupted from the whale's blowhole with a loud hissing sound.

"Oars out and bring in the sail," whispered Athneal, so as not to disturb the whale after its long and lazy journey south to raise her young. The splash of an oar would scare the beast and make it dive. The sails were brought in and the oars laid out. With quiet and powerful strokes, the distance between whale and hunters was reduced. It was important to make a surprise approach from behind, in the whale's blind spot. Athneal picked up the heavy harpoon. A sixty-yard long line was spliced onto the end. The strong nylon line was coiled and evenly distributed in three oak barrels.

A final, powerful stroke sent the boat alongside the whale as the oars were brought in. The harpooner stood in the bow and braced his leg against the thigh-board, weapon in hand, poised for action. When the boat was within a few feet of their prey, he plunged his barbed weapon into the whale's back. At this dangerous moment, the crew backed the boat away as the whale sounded (dove) in pain. The tail of the 50-ton behemoth had once smashed their boat and sent the crew tumbling into the water.

The whale dove with its embedded harpoon. The crew allowed the line to run out to prevent the boat from being dragged under. When the whale eventually surfaced to breathe it towed the whaleboat at speeds over twenty miles per hour, showering the crew with spray.

The whale tired and the crew hauled in the line to draw the boat close for the kill. *Momento de verdad*- the moment of truth. In the same way as the Toreador gave the final death-blow in the bull-fight arena, Athneal, carrying a lance, jumped onto the back of the whale and plunged it into its heart. The whale lurched forward, thrashing its tail and spouting blood through its blowhole. Athneal fell into the sea.

As the whaleboat backed off again with Athneal climbing over the stern, the crew observed the awesome spectacle of the whale's death. The end came when it beat the water with its tail, shuddered, and turned "fin out," a whaling term meaning that the whale has expired and turned over on its side. A crew member would sometimes have to sew the whale's mouth shut to keep it from swallowing so much water it would sink.

While the animal was being towed to the whaling station, the news of the catch spread like wildfire. Using a rusty winch, fifty men hauled the carcass ashore, with half its 25 tonnes in the water and the other half on the beach. The cutting up commenced. The islanders arrived with buckets to pick up whale-meat, blubber oil, and to party. A few tourists had also arrived, eager to film the butchering and possibly a shark feeding on bits of meat and blubber.

With the job done it was party time with tough and chewy whale steaks from the grill, strong rum from the mainland, and reggae from the ghetto-blasters. Catching a whale always creates an atmosphere like Carnival on "Whale Cay" where the butchering takes place, as well as across the entire island.

20. The Move Ashore

Some days I had the feeling I was back on the treadmill of the rat race. Being based in Bequia would then feel like being stuck somewhere, though constantly on the move working on various freight assignments and in the day charter business.

Work? Business? Wasn't that something of the past? Was I starting to have second thoughts? I was starting to wonder if I really had chosen the right path, and if the great change in my life to be a sea gypsy was still happening.

I had sailed over the horizon to leave behind a materialistic world filled with stress and worry. Perhaps the blood in my veins I inherited from my restless and adventurous ancestors was coagulating, and the dream of finding an old grandfather along with a treasure-chest was nothing more than childhood imagination. I had dreamt to find a hidden Shangri-La, a tropical island paradise, and to live in a bamboo hut, growing food and spear-fishing on the reef without money worries or responsibility.

A tourist once said to me, "You don't need to go anywhere for a holiday. Here you are free to sail around when you feel like it and enjoy living in paradise!" But I was forced to find work to pay for food and boat maintenance. The charter business only lasted here from Christmas to Easter, the four winter months, and *Fredag's* freight business had become unprofitable due to the customs officials on various islands actually doing their job.

I did a very short stint as a teacher, but the headmaster didn't approve of my teaching methods. I would not follow the curriculum. History was the memorization of on English kings and queens, cricket heroes of the past, and stories of colonialism and slavery. Charles Darwin was the devil himself, there was no such event as The Big Bang, and dinosaurs walked the earth a few thousand years ago.

It was the first time in my life I'd been fired. Sad. Not for me but for those kids who needed to be told the truth about what was important. They needed the truth to be told and to get a higher education.

Maintenance work seemed to never end. I started at the bow, sanding, painting, varnishing, and replacing rotting wood, and when I finally reached the stern after four months, it was back to the bow again.

Admiralty Bay could be a noisy place to drop anchor, especially if you stayed for a while. The noisy steel band, or dustbin-men as I called them, were not always a melodious delight hammering out endless verses of the same tune. Mass gatherings of street-dogs held hourly board meetings throughout the night and the roosters crowed as soon as the dogs shut up. I was told that since the "electric city" came to Bequia the roosters had become disoriented and bewildered.

Something had changed. Negative thoughts were starting to dominate my outlook on life. Thinking about all the hardships we had endured, with probably more to come, the depressing feeling of being stuck sent me into an emotional place I didn't want to be.

Weighing anchor and sailing away from it all was out of the question. I had to admit that my yacht was too big for only two people to handle, both physically and financially. It was time to throw in the towel. Time for a new chapter by selling our home and finding a new one ashore. Mariann and I did not agree at all. She wanted to continue sailing. I had had enough.

At the start of the *Fredag* project we had an agreement that if one of us wanted out of sailing ship or relationship, we would sell and split the proceedings. There was a lot of arguing but no compromise. Our relationship felt like it was on the rocks. We finally agreed to sell.

It took only a few days to sell her. A tiny newspaper ad in Norway did the trick; we sold the boat to the Norwegian government for the treatment of juvenile delinquents.

Just like that, I was no longer a boat-owner! It felt like a load off my shoulders.

Mariann had no other option. She reluctantly moved in with me in our new rental home. Our dream had been replaced with a house, securely fastened to a concrete foundation.

To complete the move from sea to land, I acquired a new nick-name. Nearly everyone on the island had a nick-name. Generally, the name was irreverent. Sometimes reverent with a reason. *Pickup* was the name given to a young boy put in a basket when he was a baby and left in the middle of the road. An old lady picked him up and took care of him until he was old enough to manage by himself.

I was originally nicknamed *Whiteman*, not because of the colour of my skin, but because, being a charter captain, I was always dressed in white. Some called me *Mister Freedog*. When Mariann became popular due to her charity work, I became *Mariann-man*. I was not too happy about that one. Now everyone calls me *Fixman* because I fixed things for people in my own workshop, known as *Fixworld*.

A new identity and a new environment helped me over my depression. I no longer needed to worry about my life and belongings dependent on a long, rusty chain.

Problems keep surfacing in our relationship. We were both exceptional and unusual and not always easy to deal with. During the 25 years we'd been together, our relationship had often been quite stormy, but we stuck it out. It was not only because we had the same interests like sailing and exploring, but we also had a common goal. Our cohesion was at its strongest when we were both exposed to threats such as storms, disasters, and money shortages. We'd always been good at solving almost anything that would hit us.

But now nothing worked between us. We split up, each in our own little house on top of a hill. We were once more neighbours and good friends, as we were when we first met and started building our floating future.

Had I made the right choice? I was starting to doubt. The house I built of plywood and bamboo was being eaten by termites. The basement continuously flooded during heavy downpours and muddy water had to be pumped out. Shutters, awnings, furniture, fruit-trees, livestock, and a million other items needed to be lashed and secured when there was a warning that a threatening storm was on its way. It was almost like being back on board again.

However, there were some advantages of living on land. If there was a passing shower, I didn't have to panic and run off from the bar in the middle of happy hour to close our hatches. I had windows that could be left open. I didn't get my breakfast in my lap when the ferry thundered past at full speed. And since I had loads of fruit in my garden, I don't have intrusive vendors banging on my home's topside wanting to sell me rock-hard limes.

Most importantly, if there was a storm approaching, I didn't need to panic and sail 40 miles to the nearest hurricane hole. My new A-frame home was well-secured and would not drag anchor or sink, and it was cheap to rebuild since it was mostly made of bamboo and plywood.

Many years ago, bamboo was widely used for house construction. Today there are no bamboo houses to be found. They are seen as a poor man's dwelling. The Prime Minister once said, as he looked up from the aft deck of the ferry at my house on the hill, "That disgusting looking house up there shouldn't have been built."

It probably didn't have much to do with the fact that it was built with bamboo and had roof tiles made of stone. It was probably the architectural design I chose. The A-frame design belonged more on a mountain slope in Switzerland than on a tropical island, where most houses were built with cement blocks. They had nearly flat galvanized-sheeted roofs, glass-paned windows with aluminium frames, and shutters- solid termite-proof buildings built on concrete slabs and surrounded by concrete gothic-looking balustrades with gate-pillars topped by concrete lion heads. I hate concrete- I'm a wood man.

My neighbours were wondering why on earth I built a house with bamboo shutters, doors that can't be locked, and nothing to keep out mosquitoes and jumbies. Jumbies are Caribbean ghosts or spirits; I had never seen one, but I had a local friend whose friend had seen one.

It was only the members of the Rastafarian religious movement that appreciated my unconventional and, in my opinion, environmentally friendly and down-to-earth construction. My neighbours, on the other hand, did not. Mr. Ollivierre next door was afraid that the value of his property would drop, and Mrs. King envisioned hordes of whites taking over the neighbourhood. There seemed to be anxiety and concern on the both sides of my boundaries. Maybe it was because I was different in so many ways. I had seen this before.

It reminded me of when I saw a black person for the first time. I was only 12, living in a small coastal village as far north as you could get in Norway- a place where most people had little knowledge of the world outside. One day a telegram arrived addressed to the local newspaper saying that a man with very black skin was on his way on board the coastal mail boat.

When the ship docked a huge crowd eagerly awaited, hoping to get their first glimpse of a black man. Aside from a few old salts most of the villagers were present. The moment of embarkation was characterized by silence and wonder. The black man walked somewhat uncertainly down the gang plank. When he stepped onto the dock the silence was broken by a gasp from the spectators as if an extra-terrestrial had stepped from a flying saucer.

Most of us youngsters had seen black people on film. Pastor Ananiassen would show flickering 8-mm documentaries that missionaries had shot in

Africa. We only attended the events so we could glimpse the topless women. I was once told off for having a Playboy Magazine under my mattress, but seeing black boobs on holy ground was no problem. I never understood why.

The man from the mail boat had come to stay. He was nicknamed *Blacky*. He told the Pastor that he'd had a dream where God commanded him to travel as far north as possible to preach the gospel to the pagans, settle down, and make the place his home.

He didn't feel much at home, even though he was well prepared. He had actually learned to speak the language. He could not find a single bible at the library; Pastor Ananiassen had removed them all, believing he had the exclusive right to teach the gospel.

People avoided *Blacky* like the plague. He built a small house of cement blocks with a flat roof of galvanized sheeting, and he painted the house vibrant orange and green. The neighbours complained to the local council claiming that his house didn't conform with theirs of wood, painted white. It didn't help that some of the local women believed the rumours that black men were rapists, and that their proximity could give you malaria, sleeping sickness, and leprosy. The local fishermen were afraid of losing their women when they went to sea because they'd heard that black men had larger penises, and they were sure their women had heard it, too.

This black man, who had come with good intentions, found out that this was not the place for him. He had no interest in fighting village ignorance and racism. He packed his suitcase and headed to Oslo, where people were more educated and liberal and had read *Uncle Tom's Cabin*. There was nobody on the dock to see him off. He had nearly lost all faith in humanity, and he lost his faith in God and became an atheist.

Blacky and I had a lot in common- we didn't conform with the local culture or beliefs. I wondered how long would I last. Would it be better to join up with the white foreigners living on the eastern part of the island? But then, I had this handed-down genetic urge to explore my surroundings and challenge any difficulties that might arise.

The alternative to settling down on the ex-pat's Beverly Hills Estate, as referred to by the locals, did not seem very fulfilling. Could I be happy living in a stately villa with local servants and a Rasta gardener? Did I need a marble castle with a chlorine-filled swimming-pool, surrounded by a 6-foot wall topped with barbed wire and burglar alarm, patrolled by aggressive rottweilers? An orderly garden with a flagpole where I could hoist the red, white, and blue Norwegian flag on Independence Day and the King's birthday? Or celebrate the birthdays, fourth of July, Saint Patrick's Day, Bastille Day, Calgary Stampede Day, and Guy Fawkes Day with my rich neighbours? (I never had a problem celebrating the anarchist Guy Fawkes, which they actually did on Bequia by lighting bamboo cannons filled with kerosene on top of Mount Pleasant.) Anyway, such a lifestyle was out of the question. What was left of half of the boat sale proceeds would not even cover the construction of the water tank. And where was the challenge?

A local rumshop

I decided that living in the village with open doors was the right decision. I had no walls with barbed wire, but a flag-pole where I could hoist the yellow, blue, and green Saint Vincent flag on Independence Day. I would be brave and meet all obstacles with my head held high, as my sister and mentor had taught me.

The first major obstacle occurred when I stopped by Mama Browne's rum shop a little further up the road. On my way there I was wading through garbage. The streets of Port Elizabeth were the village's garbage dump, except for Front Street where the tourists passed through on their way to the restaurants and bars.

Mariann had this theory that the amount of garbage in a village was proportional to the inhabitants' friendliness and hospitality- the more garbage, the more friendliness. I'd been living on this street for a while so it was time I showed up at the local rum shop. I might even find out if Mariann was right.

It was Friday afternoon- pay day- and the bar was full of local men. They sent me a suspicious glance when I stepped into a room smelling of herb, cigarettes, and strong local rum. The noise level was high, typical of such establishments. Dominoes were being slammed on a table in the corner, accompanied by swearing and belly laughing, and reggae music screeched from a boom-box through an overloaded speaker. In other words, it was a regular Friday evening in an ordinary Bequia rum shop.

After buying a round or two I felt that I was beginning to be accepted. I joined in on the debate, mostly complaining about government. But then I made the mistake of not thinking before I opened my mouth. I declared that our street was a blemish on this beautiful island- a street so full of garbage and decaying food that one would think that there were pigs and not people living here. We should do something about it because the government did nothing, and we should all stand shoulder to shoulder and together clean up our environment.

I had only told one person my opinion, a person I knew well, but it seemed that everyone in the room had extremely good selective hearing despite all the noise. It was as if someone had switched off the rum shop sound. If it wasn't for raspy Bob Marley's voice, you could've heard a pin drop. Chief Harry, the local community's person of importance, started talking. He seemed to be speaking to somebody outside the door when he turned slowly towards me. He spoke slowly and quietly to begin with, but gradually got louder as he pointed a finger directly at me.

"Who de hell are you to come here to tell we how to behave and what to do wid our garbage? You go back where you come from and deal with de garbage problem there 'cause it ten times worse. I seen so on CNN."

He continued with louder and more explicit language. I had to wonder what garbage had to do with sexual intercourse and with even his mother's most intimate body part. When his monolog ended, all hell broke loose and I headed for the door. I could hear them quarrelling as I kicked at the garbage on my short way home. I hadn't solved anything, but at least I'd started a discussion.

The following day I nailed a poster outside of Mama Browne's rum shop.

ON SUNDAY AFTERNOON I PERSONALLY INTEND TO CLEAR THE GARBAGE OFF THIS STREET. ANYBODY WHO WANTS TO HELP ME IS MORE THAN WELCOME. BRING A SHOVEL, RAKE, AND PLASTIC BAGS.

WHEN THE STREET IS CLEARED I WILL SUPPLY RUM, BEER, SHARK & BAKE, BREADFRUIT, AND MUSIC SIGNED MISTER FIXMAN.

Lo and behold, we had a huge turnout. Three strong men, thirteen big ladies, and a few kids came equipped with shovels, rakes, and garbage bags. When the street and gutters were cleared the party began. Everyone in the neighbourhood joined in on the bash though most of them hadn't been involved in the clean-up. When the street party was over plastic plates, cutlery, and left-overs were bagged and ended up in the heap at the end of the street, ready to be dispatched to the garbage dump. As people were leaving a kid threw a plastic bottle into the gutter. Mama Browne slapped him behind the ear and ordered him to put it where it belonged. Everyone seemed happy with themselves, Mister Fixman was now OK, and Mariann was proven right about the relationship between garbage and friendliness.

Shortly after what I thought was Bequia's first voluntary community endeavour, street and beach clean-ups became regular events. But then people started to complain. Was this really their job? Before long the government shipped a large green garbage truck to Bequia. Once a week, it passed every homeowner and picked up what was put neatly outside their gate if the dogs hadn't ripped it apart, and it was dumped in a land fill, unfortunately situated a mile to windward of Port Elizabeth.

By getting involved I eventually became an accepted part of the community. Integration takes time, but a little provocation really helped to speed things up.

As a former child welfare officer, I have sworn a professional oath to protect all children from any kind of abuse, psychological or physical. I therefore had a problem when I witnessed my neighbour beating his little boy with a piece of 2 x 4. Without thinking, I intervened. I vaulted his fence, grabbed the wood, and hurled it behind me without thinking. It went right through his window. The window was closed and I felt righteous when the glass shattered. I told him that next time it would not only be a broken window, but a police report as well.

In return I received a lecture on human rights. It was his human right to beat his own son as much as he wanted. Corporal punishment was not a criminal offense in his country, and he rested his argument by telling me to go back to where I belonged or somewhere that was much hotter than here.

A week later, during another visit to Mama Browne's enchanting establishment, I found the regular customers split into two groups when I entered. They were discussing the "violent interlude" down the road. I soon discovered that one faction was on my side, and a smaller faction was not- they held onto their solidarity with the assailant.

As with the garbage incident, I had started a discussion and engaged in local politics without intending to do so. This time it was about child abuse. I chose to keep a low profile and I headed for the door, complaining it was too hot inside. When I got home an old lady sat outside my house. She'd been waiting for me. She had come to tell me that the man who had abused the boy was not the boy's father, not even a relative. She encouraged me to get going on that police report. I choose not to, hoping that it wouldn't happen again. It didn't.

There was a big mango tree on my property. Before I built my little house, the property was a "no man's land." There were some ancient fruit trees, and people had helped themselves to their fruit for generations. But now a white man had come along and said stop, you cannot thief my fruit- it's illegal and it even said so in the Ten Commandments- Thou shalt not steal. Did Fixman believe he could come here to do what he wanted? Oh no, man. Dem mangos belong to all ah we!

This conflict wasn't going to be easy to solve. I knew that they knew I couldn't possibly consume two hundred pounds of mango during the short ripening period. But I had to make them respect my property and regard me as a human being on equal footing with them, even if I was a white foreigner and that my umbilical cord wasn't buried on the island. You could have a passport and citizenship, but you were not really a true Bequian if your umbilical cord wasn't buried here.

Mariann suggested that I give my neighbours the option that if they asked for permission, then they could help themselves as long as they gave me some and didn't break any branches. I tried this method a couple of times, adding that white people weren't very good at climbing trees, which made them laugh their heads off.

This was a better idea than taking the advice given by Mama Browne. When I asked her how to deal with the situation, she studied her toes for a while, then at the mango-tree, shook her head and said, "Stupidity, stupidity." There was a long pause, then she then looked me straight in the eye, gave a big toothless grin and said, "When dey come to t'ief, cuss dem out, and if dat don't wuk, t'row a big rock at dem!"

One of my neighbours, Mr Lewis, sent his youngest boy up the mango tree, my mango tree. Mariann's method did not work. I followed Mama Browne's advice and yelled to his father so the whole neighbourhood could hear- he must get his offspring out of my tree immediately. I threatened to throw a rock at the child. When that didn't get a response, I cussed the father with the worst language I could muster. That didn't work either. However, when I threatened to castrate his kid with the Norwegian cheese slicer I held in my hand, he called the boy down from the tree. I felt like putting the cheese slicer on display at Mama Browne's rum-shop as a warning to all fruit thieves.

After that everyone asked very nicely for permission to pick mangos. Mrs. Quashie helped herself to my cashew nuts, roasted them over a fire and always gave me half of what she harvested. Mr Lewis kept asking me how the Norwegian cheese slicer really worked.

They found it strange that I didn't close my windows or lock my door, and that I didn't have air conditioning. All whites had air conditioning! And they thought it strange I didn't worship and that I never went to church, that I didn't believe in jumbies, I didn't bake myself for hours in the sun to get a darker skin, I didn't want to talk about whaling, and I played loud Italian opera every Sunday morning. But what they thought was the strangest about me was that I lived alone.

Maybe the man was gay? No woman, parents, grandparents, or children, and just a single dog that rarely barked. He also had a weird rooster that croaked like a frog. They didn't know why. The story behind the croaking rooster was that I gave it cooked rice with too much hot sauce. The label on the sauce bottle read, "Rectum Fire. Made on Bequia."

The rumour that I was gay or lonely, or a lonely gay, may have been the reason why an unknown person made an appearance one night through the always open entrance. The intruder climbed up the spiral staircase to my bedside, stroked my hair and whispered into my ear, "Are you lonesome tonight, Mister Fixman?" Was I dreaming of someone stroking my hair? I woke with goose bumps all over my body. I opened my eyes but saw nothing in the dark other than a big smile of pearl-white teeth, like that of the Cheshire cat in Alice in Wonderland. The smile hung right above my face; when I recovered from the shock, I screamed for the intruder to get the hell out of my house.

After the uninvited intruder fled down the stairs in panic, there was a slight scent of perfume, which made me come to the conclusion that it must have been a woman, and I regretted freaking out. The Lady of the Night would never come back, and I had no idea who she was. Judging by the beautiful teeth, I was sure she was *not* Mama Browne!

It wasn't always easy living as a minority in a small island village. But it was very rewarding. There were many difficult challenges and a few well-deserved victories. I was glad I didn't give up. Other than the colour of our skin we are all the same. And Mama Browne's motherly relationship with me? It started the day I helped repair her roof after a hurricane had torn it off.

Although there have been many tropical storms, over sixty years have passed since Bequia experienced a direct hit from a hurricane. There are few people around to tell of that story, but a large stone cross is on the waterfront for those lost at sea in Hurricane Janet. However, I can tell you the story of one that came dangerously close.

The people of the Caribbean are used to the regular warnings of approaching cyclonic storms during the hurricane season, which lasts from June to November. The islanders are well aware of the consequences of the unbelievable forces of Mother Nature. There is ample TV footage of the damage and suffering caused by these natural disasters. Naturally we try to be well prepared and stock up on batteries, water, and plywood.

On many occasions these hurricane warnings have sent people scuttling to the shops to purchase supplies and Port Elizabeth resembles Piccadilly Circus at rush hour. But over the past six decades nothing serious has ever happened. The hurricanes have usually turned north. Most storms pass far enough away to cause no damage other than a sleepless night.

This time was different. It was the morning of September 7th, 2004. It had been an eerie night. I woke up hours before sunrise to complete and unusual silence. It was as if all the dogs, roosters, tree-frogs, and crickets had vanished from the face of the planet and the world was coming to an end. I couldn't sleep. It was too quiet and scary. All the ferries had left port and the harbour was empty except for three yachts. An average of about forty yachts would normally lie at anchor in Admiralty Bay at this time of year. They were all gone- Admiralty Bay is open to the west and no hurricane hole.

A couple a hundred of miles out in the Atlantic hurricane Ivan was heading straight for Bequia. This massive storm had been on a straight and steady course for several days and there was no reason for Ivan to change direction. With sustained winds of 150 miles an hour, it was already a category four hurricane and the strongest on record moving along on such a low latitude.

I had boarded up my house and stored away my computer, music, and precious belongings, and now I had to make a decision on where to go. The nearest local hurricane shelter was the Anglican School.

I reckoned the safest place to survive a hurricane of such magnitude would be the Old Fort Hotel on Mount Pleasant. However, I felt I should be with my neighbours in the shelter at the school. This could be a major disaster and those near the harbour might need all the help they could get. A generator repairman and qualified first aid provider might come in handy.

Upon finding the school building empty I reckoned the people of Bequia put more trust and faith in their own homes. One look at the huge, rusty galvanized roof and termite ridden rafters confirmed my reckoning. I was ready to leave for The Old Fort. I couldn't find my cat Lulu. Cats have premonitions of natural phenomena.

At the last moment, when it seemed that doomsday was approaching, all the church leaders along the Windward Islands got together and organized a prayer to persuade the Lord to make the threatening monster turn away from their islands, either go north to the French islands or south to Trinidad and Venezuela. Whatever happened to Christian empathy and Love Thy Neighbour?

A miracle took place, at least for us. Ivan the Terrible stayed on the 12th parallel North, never turning more northward. Bequia sits on the 13th parallel. Someone speculated on the radio that reason for this was that the people of Grenada weren't taking part in the prayer. The meteorological experts in Miami thought otherwise and said that it was due to an upper level shear in the intertropical conversion zone. My knowledge on meteorology was limited, but I understood this was good news for us on Bequia, but disaster for the citizens of Grenada.

Within the sturdy and several foot-wide walls of the wine cellar at the Old Fort Hotel, you could probably survive a nuclear blast. The dungeon-like room was packed with the owner's friends and family, including me, my dog Zooty, and crates of wine. The mood was good and improved in accordance with the number of Chardonnays we opened.

The radio announcer informed us that we will only be affected by the outer wind-bands, meaning gusts of "only" 80 miles an hour. Bad enough. Two frightened donkeys outside stuck their heads through the narrow window opening, one above the other. They wanted in, but there was no room for them.

It was difficult to describe the screaming winds and the sound of objects flying through the air and crashing into the fort's walls. On several occasions I heard an elongated moooooooo. The only thing that came to mind was a flying cow. Anything was possible. The wind was howling at nearly a hundred miles an hour.

There was a short lull in the storm. I left the cellar and climbed up the steps to the tower at the top of the hotel, and peered out through the window to see what was going on. The view down into Ravine Bay was the most frightening. It had been transformed into a turbulent inferno of white foam and spray. I noticed two hummingbirds hovering over a flower that looked like it might blow away any minute. It was incredible that these tiny creatures weren't hunkered down somewhere.

My cell-phone rang. The person calling had dialled the wrong number. She said she was sorry and asked where I was and if I was all right. It was a long time since I'd heard anyone say sorry to have dialled the wrong number. For some strange reason my heart went out her, and I asked her the same question. We talked together for nearly an hour, about wind and weather, about the meaning of life and so on. We agreed to meet up after the storm, but then her credit ran out before we could specify where and when. Furthermore, I'd neglected to ask for the name or address of my new acquaintance. The display on my cell-phone said *Unknown Number*. It showed how an outside threat could bring people together, and how technology could spoil it all.

I was impressed by the government of St. Vincent and the Grenadines, specifically those in charge of disaster management. The Government's radio station on St. Vincent showed commendable professionalism. The Prime Minister came on the air at five minutes to every hour to calm and reassure his people that everyone would be safe if they just stayed indoors.

Then, after every recorded reassuring announcement, the radio-station played Bob Marley's *Three Little Birds*.

Throughout the night the nation's leader went around to the shelters comforting people and making silly jokes. He would most likely get a lot of votes due to this in the next election, approval for the courageous way he acted during the crisis, so different from how the Prime Minister of Grenada had behaved. He has been flown by helicopter to a British warship outside the hurricane's path.

I had expected things to deteriorate further, thinking that we were not through the worst of the hurricane, when the wind started to subside. By sunrise all was quiet and peaceful. I could hear the tree frogs, crickets, and birds again. The only sound reminding me of what had taken place was the thundering surf down below me. The sky was as clear as I had ever seen it. I could see the mountains of Grenada, seventy miles away. The isle of spice looked so tranquil and serene from my viewpoint. Far from it.

The TV was up and running again after two days of screen static. The footage from Grenada showed devastation on a horrendous scale- 20 people killed and 90 per cent of the island's buildings had lost their roofs or been totally destroyed.

I did not complain about losing my mango-tree to Ivan the Terrible. I didn't complain when I found my car has been turned over on its side. It was a light-weight Citroen 2CV, so I was amazed it was still around. My Swiss chalet was still standing but about twenty roof tiles had been torn off. The good news was that nobody had been killed or injured, and Miss Knights' hardware and grocery store made a fortune selling food, plywood, and batteries.

Sadly, there was a lot of damage to the ramshackle houses on the mainland, mostly due to flooding. The government promised to rebuild them. I doubted it.

Mama Browne had lost her roof, so rebuilding her roof became another voluntary community effort. She wouldn't get any government aid because she was known to vote for the opposition party.

21. The Fixman

Today's breakfast consisted of fried eggs, mangoes, and passion fruit from my garden and strong Colombian coffee. The eggs were generously supplied by my faithful chickens. The mild trade winds were on the move after a quiet tropical night and are already providing relief. The rooster, who lived in the breadfruit tree, thankfully had given up his usual racket.

People in the village below were also on the move. The pilot was slowly on his way to the harbour in his battered Land Rover, driving slalom between sleeping dogs. Like most Bequia residents he had plenty of time. He was on his way to board the cargo ship that was waiting to depart. Miss Knight had opened the doors and shutters of her grocery store. Captain Gooding lowered the car ramp on his ferry and was ready for the first trip to the "mainland."

The mechanic Sandeford was having an argument with the police chief, most likely about an unpaid bill. It was the same people every morning on their way to their daily chores. I knew them all now. The start of the day was the same every morning.

Watching this morning activity unfold reminded me of Captain Cat, the main character in the Welsh poet Dylan Thomas' poem *Under Milk Wood*. The poem began with him sitting by his window when the village awakened, watching the villagers starting to go about their daily business.

While I poured myself another cup of coffee, a hummingbird hovered above the passion fruit vine. It hung silently in front of me with its wings beating so fast they couldn't be seen. As I looked past the bird over the bay a huge manta ray leapt completely out of the water, twisted around, and landed on its back with a big splash. There was no need to subscribe to *Animal Planet* where I lived.

Eighteen years had passed since July 1984. I had swum ashore after having been wrecked on the reef at Union Island, but I was still here. Stuck forever. There was nothing wrong with that. But I often warned visiting yachties and tourists, telling them not to stay here more than a couple of weeks. If you stayed longer you could get stuck like I did.

Among the expectations I'd had concerning my dream voyage there was always in the back of my mind a foreshadowing of becoming shipwrecked, stranded like Robinson Crusoe for the rest of my life. Sometimes the vision turned into a nightmare, but more often it was like the rendering below.

While not exactly like this fantasy, my life was certainly no nightmare. I was not alone. I was living among great people who would not cook me in a pot. Some were even descended from other shipwrecked sailors. I had fit well into this environment and was very happy about it. I had made the right choice.

I hadn't found buried gold, and I couldn't survive on coconuts, bananas, and spearfishing on the reef. It wasn't always easy in such a different culture. I'd made mistakes along the way, though a few turned out well in the end, like the garbage event and the child molester incident. Occasionally, when things turned against me, I imagined being a Caribbean sailor shipwrecked on an island in northern Norway- an island populated by narrow-minded farmers and fishermen. Then I had to admit that I actually had it pretty good.

When I was a boat-owner I sailed to Kingstown on the mainland to buy water. A young man on the dock took my mooring line and lay it neatly over the bollard. "That will be twenty dollars, thank you," he said. I decided to have a word with him. I asked how much was the minimum wage for unskilled labour.

"Twenty EC dollars a day. Fifteen for women." I did the math and found that it amounted to about 3 dollars an hour. The work he performed for me had taken about 10 seconds. Therefore, I figured that I owed him about half a dollar.

"It's like this," he said. "Yachts seldom come here, and I have to get paid for the time I wait for arrivals." Rather than tell him that he should pick bananas instead of waiting for a yacht to come along, I came up with a ridiculous premise.

"If you, young man, had arrived with your yacht in my home town in Norway, I would have greeted you with a hearty welcome and taken your mooring line for free." Thinking of the absurdity of what I'd just said, I was at a loss. So was he until he looked me straight in the eye and said, "If so, I will pay you back your twenty dollars."

I shook his hand. "OK, we have a deal, and here's an extra ten towards your passage to Norway."

Breakfast-time was over. It was time for me to go to work. There was no hurry even though it took a while to drive the five hundred meters down to my workshop. I had to repeatedly stop and talk to people- it was considered rude not to greet and have a chat. And it was important to remember names. I used the association method, but it was not easy with names like Jesshaia, Lucintha, Vercille, and Keisha.

I was the proud owner and chief executive officer of *Fixman Marine Engineering*, also known as *Fixworld*. The proceeds from the sale of my yacht went to build a modest building, a dock for a small dinghies and the purchase and import of various Chinese machines and tools.

Naturally, I had the nickname *Fixman*. The white captain's uniform was replaced by blue coveralls. *Fredag's* wooden tender had been replaced by an old Land Rover with a crane mounted on the back. I called myself an engineer, with a hidden crutch- my much-needed DIY engine repair manual.

The Fixmobile

The engineering title wasn't protected in the West Indies. Because I had a drill press, battery charger, lathe, milling machine, and lots of special tools, my customers believed that the man behind the enterprise was a genuine engineer.

My principle was "No fix, no pay." If what I tried to repair didn't work, my customers owed me nothing. It worked. They had nothing to lose.

The start-up was a learning process. I learned something new every day. With the help of the DIY manual, I got by. With my naval background I could deal with engines and electrical stuff, but refrigeration, electronics, and welding were not my cup of tea. Why not bring in some apprentices? *Fixworld Technical College* became a fact. I sent a couple young men abroad to attend courses with travel and accommodation paid by Volvo Foreign Aid. Soon I had a small staff of experts- a welder, a cooling technician, an electronic wizard, and a secretary to carry the daily income to the bank.

My electronic wizard had this great idea to import and set up satellite dishes on people's roofs so that they could watch international TV. The dishes and receivers sold like hot cakes until, after only a month of operation, the transmitting satellite crashed into the sea off Honduras, nearly bankrupting Fixworld.

There were other problems. The island's unemployment rate was ridiculously high, especially among young people. Most of the youths coming from high school had no skills to find work, and menial labour jobs generally went to stronger adults unless one had a family connection.

There was a queue of youngsters outside my workshop waiting to be interviewed. However, when they were told how little they'd get paid to begin with- that the first year was really an apprenticeship where they would learn a trade- they'd vanish.

I had never met so many young people with such high self-confidence as on this island. They assured me that they could do absolutely anything. There was nothing in this world that was impossible. I never once heard a young Bequian say: *I can't. Sorry, I don't know how to do this. I have no idea.*

It was great to have self-confidence, but it could lead to trouble. I was often impressed how my apprentices managed to recover without losing face.

Sometimes I felt bad rejecting those who politely knocked on my door to ask for a job. Sometimes they were not very polite. Sometimes the applicant became aggressive when told that there was no job available if they were unskilled. For some, the word *unskilled* is the same as *useless*. I found a solution on how to deal with such situations. This is how a job interview might go at Fixworld.

"Gimme a job, nuh, Fix-mahn."

"What can you do, young man?"

"Anyt'ing, boss. I can do anyt'ing."

"Can you weld?"

"Yes, mahn. Best welder in the Caribbean."

"OK. Take these two bits of flat steel into the workshop and weld them together at a 90-degree angle."

"Yes boss. Eh, just going out to buy a cigarette. I be back in a while."

Everything on Bequia happens in a while. The *in a while* in these cases lasted forever. They never came back. I might meet them later somewhere. They would smile and chat, but never mention the job interview.

My first customers were the islanders. My first job was to straighten out a dent in a kettle belonging to an old lady, who was probably as old as the kettle. The next high-tech job was a toaster that didn't pop up the bread, then there was the police chief's revolver that had jammed. It took about two weeks before anything more challenging came to Fixworld, like washing machines, refrigerators, or outboard engines. Many of my customers were "a bit short," not in stature but in cash. However, after the fishermen had their outboard engines working again they often paid me with lobster. I had so much lobster in my freezer I was getting fed up with having to eat it!

I had the same problem with the authorities. They were always a bit short. Government departments were responsible for most of our outstanding invoices. There were five unpaid bills for repairing the fire truck at the airport, three for fixing the toilet in the hospital, and one for repairing the harbourmaster's wife's hair dryer.

After persistently studying my bible- the engine repair manual- high season was knocking on my door, and so were the cruising yachtsmen. Boat owners and charterers who came to my workshop could continue on their journey after a visit to Fixworld. If I failed to help them, at least there was no charge. I always gave my customers a one-year warranty on my work.

Some unconventional advertising with cartoons in the local newspapers brought us some business. Some people would come in just to meet the Fixman. I was flattered to be shown as a Viking or intergalactic saviour coming to people's rescue in the following illustrations done by yachtsman/artist Dudley Campling.

Once I received a complaint from a Swede who had struggled for 200 miles to return to Bequia, battling strong headwinds and current. It had taken him a whole week. It took me five minutes to mount the part I had forgotten to replace on his generator. Obviously, the guy was furious, screaming at me and sort of blaming me for Norway starting a war with Sweden in 1814. I hit back with the subject on Swedish "war heroes" during World War II, and the grand Swedish blunder that took place when their flagship *Wasa* capsized and sank in 1628, only half an hour after launch. It was starting to get ugly when my assistant defused the situation. It helped when I presented the Swede with a bottle of Sainte Claire Chablis 1989 and filled his now working freezer with 15 lobsters. (The wine had been a present from a happy French sailor after I'd fixed his high-tech corkscrew.) For some strange reason he returned my gesture the day after with a bottle of Aquavit. By the time it was empty, we were like brothers. Which we were in a cultural and geographical sense. So wherever he is in the world, I once more send my apologies to the Swede.

What really had the business going was the reputation that I was a magician and genius when it came to fixing diesel engines. This capability was due to something that had happened to me when I was thirteen.

22. The Reverse Combustion Engine

My DIY engine repair manual stated the following: *The Diesel engine, named after Dr. Rudolph Diesel, is an internal-combustion engine in which air is compressed to a sufficiently high temperature to ignite diesel fuel injected into the cylinder.*

The 1930 Wichmann single cylinder diesel engine

My Great Uncle Hans had a 1930 Wichmann single cylinder semi-diesel internal combustion engine in his 27-foot dory fishing boat. According to him this ingenious contraption was the best miracle in modern engineering since the invention of the wheel. Even in 1956 he still looked upon his Wichmann as modern. He would talk to it as if it was a human being, just like some people talk to plants. I was soon to understand why.

He had named his dearly loved engine *Big Bertha*, after his not so dearly loved third wife.

Big Bertha (the engine) stood five feet tall and weighed as much as the dory itself- his wife wasn't far off in comparison. Just like his wife, Big Bertha's behavior was unpredictable. If she wasn't treated with the utmost passion and care she might fly into a wild runaway mode, causing havoc and destruction to everything around her.

My first encounter with Big Bertha took place the day Uncle Hans invited me on one of his numerous fishing trips. Being a passionate and patient fisherman, he would make great hauls, and though I used identical equipment, I never caught anything but seaweed. Uncle Hans had a way with cod. He also had a way with Big Bertha.

The engine room on the *Cavity II* was inconveniently located beneath the wheelhouse and took up nearly half the volume of the hull. There was no companionway through the narrow opening in the wheelhouse floor. You had to slide into that unpredictable cavity holding on to various oily pipes, levers, and wheels. It was dark down there- very dark. I could hear my uncle's vigorous cussing, ranting about something I didn't understand, something about his mother's private parts.

I could see blue smoke emerge through the opening. The wheelhouse was filled with the sweet, nauseating smell of diesel oil mixed with a whiff of burnt gunpowder.

"Come on down, boy!" shouted my uncle. "Enter the underworld through the gateway to hell. And bring some matches with you."

Hesitating a bit, I entered the black hole with a quick glance up towards the event horizon.

"Good thing you came, we really need to have two people down here to get old Bertha up and running."

A tiny oil-smeared light bulb gave off just enough light to unveil a monstrous mechanical contraption, unlike anything I'd ever seen. Except for the enormous flywheel it resembled my Grandfather's clandestine vodka still. It was a Rube Goldberg array of pipes, levers, and wheels, all covered with rust, oil, and streaks of crusted salt.

"Let's put some life into Big Bertha, Peter boy. She needs some exercise and the cod can't wait to leap into the pan!"

Thus followed my first tutorial on how to give life to a 1930 model Wichmann single-cylinder diesel.

"First we turn the flywheel to air out the cylinder on this miracle of modern engineering." He kept repeating the phrase, "We don't want any fuel in her lungs or she'll go on a rampage, rip herself off her mounts, and crash through the hull, making a big hole. The sea will pour in like Niagara Falls and that'll be the end of it!"

I looked nervously towards the opening to the wheelhouse, wondering how I might be able to scramble past a wildly jumping piece of machinery with the freezing ocean filling the engine room behind me.

Turning the massive 200-pound flywheel was arduous. The single-cylinder had some compression with a piston the size of a 3 gallon bucket. It was more a matter of rocking it back and forth than turning it.

On each movement, Bertha gave a deep wheezing sigh, as if saying, *Oh no, not again. Let me rest. Let me rest!* This was the moment I started to feel a personal connection to Big Bertha.

"First of all, we give her some electric battery juice."

Sparks crackled and rained down on us as Uncle Hans connected a nearby hanging copper wire to something on the engine head that looked like an ordinary sparkplug. He then counted to ten.

A faint sizzling sound came from somewhere within Bertha. The scene reminded me of a movie I'd seen where a prisoner on death row got fried after the wardens connected a high voltage wire onto his metal skull-cap.

"Now, while her head is heating up, we give her a taste of modern technology through this hole," he said, while screwing out a polished brass fitting next to the electric heater-plug. Apart from a highly polished brass lever, the fitting was the only shiny part on the entire rusty piece of his miracle of modern engineering.

"Get the matches, boy," my uncle ordered as he stuck something looking like a stick of dynamite onto the brass fitting. "Now! Light the firework, quick!" The blinding blue and white flaming stick was quickly screwed into the head, leaving behind darkness and a cloud of rancid smoke.

"Now comes the moment of truth," he wheezed, coughing due to the smoke-filled engine-room. As our eyes adjusted to the darkness he found the spring-loaded handle on the side of the flywheel, pulled it out, and started rocking the heavy wheel back and forth. "When I say *now,* pull down the injection pump control," he said, nodding towards the brass lever.

"NOW!*"* It was when the enormous flywheel was on its third rocking cycle, exactly at the point when it was as far as it would go to starboard, that I pulled hard down on the fuel pump lever.

This action caused a single shot of diesel fuel to be squirted into the cylinder. Uncle Hans let go of the flywheel handle as if it were a red-hot poker, and the heavy wheel shot back with considerable force. When it reached as far as the compression would let it travel on its return journey, Uncle Hans shouted *NOW* again!

A loud and heavy thump came from within Bertha's bowels, causing the *Cavity II* to shudder violently. My heart was racing and I felt terror creeping up my spine. The flywheel flew back again with gathered speed, fast enough for it to barely turn over a full revolution. As if for some magical and advanced technical reason, the brass fuel pump handle now moved up and down by itself on each revolution.

Big Bertha was running again, happy to be alive, and slowly laboring away at a steady sixty revolutions a minute. Thump. Thump. Thump…

"Not more than two pumps on the handle, boy. If you give her more, she'll run wild," he shouted with a wide Cheshire cat smile. "If you're too late or too early on the fuel pump, she'll run backwards. Running backwards is bad news, really bad news."

The smile left his face and he gave me a serious look.

"The bad news is that the oil-pump will not work as it should and Bertha will seize up and that will be the end of everything." It was as if he was describing the end of the universe.

My feeling of terror left me as I sat in wonder staring at the automatic brass pump-handle moving up and down on its own. My heart's rhythm slowly adjusted to Big Bertha's steady, hollow thump.

Uncle Hans made his usual big catch that day. I hooked nothing but seaweed, but it didn't matter. I was quite content to lie on top of the wheelhouse watching Big Bertha blow perfect white smoke rings out her tall pipe funnel, enjoying the slow rhythmic metallic thumping from her bowls.

All this happened a long time ago, and since then every time I turned the ignition switch on a modern diesel engine I remembered my first encounter with Big Bertha. On the other hand, I had completely forgotten about Bertha having the ability to go backwards. Right up to the day when the whole world seemed to run in reverse.

It was the day I received a frantic call from one of the islands three dive-shops. Their electrically driven compressor for filling up dive tanks wasn't working. Being the island's sole mechanic, I was used to all sorts of requests for everything from engines to electric fans.

There was no oil pressure to lubricate all of the compressor's moving parts. Eager customers were lining up outside the dive shop to go scuba diving.

The desperate owner and I had the compressor totally apart. The oil pressure pump had been assembled and re-assembled a dozen times without us fin anything wrong. After a whole day of troubleshooting we were just give up when the owner of the dive shop next door called in to b tanks from his competitor.

There was also a problem with his compressor. No oil p

What a coincidence! My first thought was what did these two compressors have in common? Air and electricity. The air was the same for both, and there couldn't be anything wrong with that. It *had* to be something to do with the electricity.

A quick call to the local "electric-city" headquarters confirmed that their workers had been doing repairs on the three-phase power line. They had been distracted due to the West Indies cricket match and mixed up the wiring. Both compressors were running backwards.

It was the day most of the island's three-phase electrical appliances ran the wrong way. I cursed myself on forgetting that when Big Berta ran the wrong way, the oil pump would blow air *into* the oil reservoir instead of sucking it *up* to lubricate the works.

By another strange coincidence, only a week after the compressor incident, I got a call for help from the owner of a Danish yacht. His little single cylinder Bukh diesel had no oil pressure. I took a quick look at the tiny red wonder and asked the owner which way the engine turned.

"Clockwise when looking aft, clockwise towards Denmark," he answered, thinking I was having him on.

"Start her up," I said with an air of confidence.

Lo and behold! She ran backwards, counter-clockwise, towards Venezuela!

It was due to a faulty adjustment on the timing regulator, performed by a French mechanic up island who'd replaced a broken timing-wheel after having had too many *petit punches*.

The owner was baffled and very impressed with my amazing skills and engineering knowledge. It took only a few minutes to adjust the engine's timing. I left him with the impression that I was somewhat of a genius. I 'idn't mention that he should thank Big Bertha and my Uncle Hans.

23. The Butterfly Effect

"A butterfly can flutter its wings over a flower in China and cause a hurricane in the Caribbean."

The butterfly effect has become a metaphor for the existence of seemingly insignificant moments that alter history and shape destinies.

A cockroach in the coffee cup of the *Titanic's* helmsman irritated him so much that he sideswiped an iceberg, tragically ending the lives of 1517 souls.

A wasp led to an insignificant little pin causing a tiny hole on board the *Island Time*, blissfully initiating a love story that led to the life of Julie Bequia Garner.

The Island Time was not an entirely happy vessel. There was a substantial difference in opinion among her Chicago crew. They could not agree on how to make use of the two weeks of bareboat chartering down the island chain.

John and Jimmy were two middle-aged sailors who felt that each minute on board was costing them an arm and a leg. They were constantly monitoring their progress according to a schedule they had mapped out. They would both check their watches with the same worried expression that passengers had in a taxi while constantly checking the meter.

John and Jimmy were there to do some serious sailing- to challenge the elements, beat that damned French yacht to the next island, and hook a marlin while downing as many cold beers as possible. It was the women's job to hand them beers on cue.

Their patient wives Joan and Jenny were on board because they had no other choice, although there *was* the possibility of getting a good tan. They longed for a beach of course, certainly not while being tossed around on those awful ocean waves. The damned sails would often blot out the sun, and Joan and Jenny would constantly be ordered to move if they ventured on deck. The safest refuge for them was down below, occasionally passing up cold beers and snacks. They had also been told by some expert that when below, close to the centre of gravity, there was less chance of becoming seasick.

The women longed for their world to stop bouncing and leaning to one side. They wondered if the next island's souvenir shop would have the same collection of bikinis as they had last year. The ladies were hoping that they wouldn't have to haul anchor at sunrise the next morning and every following morning after that. They were hoping that they didn't have to gut and cook the smelly fish their husbands caught. They were dreaming of not being anywhere near a kitchen, sitting at a candle-lit table with proper porcelain plates and wineglasses made of glass, not plastic. They longed to sit at a table that didn't roll- a stable, wide table full of exotic food, gastronomic delights cooked and presented by somebody else. And finally, to have someone else to do the dishes.

And then there was young Irene. Eighteen years old and provocatively good looking with deep green eyes, she had not been trusted by her parents to be home alone while they were on holiday. Her favourite hangout was sitting on the stern pulpit with heavy metal booming from her earphones to drown out Jimmy Buffet blasting from the cockpit speakers. Irene was dreaming of returning home to her loving dog and much missed friends. This was not her idea of the holiday of a lifetime.

She glanced at the date on her watch- another ghastly nine days to kill.

Irene felt much better as she lay in the shade of a tamarind tree. Her mother and Jenny had won last night's battle. They were to spend an entire day on Bequia. Her mum and Jenny shopped for bikinis, while her dad and Jimmy went looking for more line and tackle, more charts, and a case of beer.

She was half asleep when an angry wasp swept down and stung her on the stomach. Her scream brought a young, local man crashing out of the bushes behind her. As soon as he understood what happened he disappeared, but soon returned with some green, slimy stuff in the palm of his hand.

"Let me put this on, it will ease the pain." he said. Not waiting for an answer, he smeared the slimy substance all over her bare midriff and a few other places in case she was stung elsewhere.

"*Fixman, Fixman.* This is the *Island Time* calling. Do you read me?" There was a note of desperation in the voice over the VHF. "We have a problem with our engine, and we need to be on our way!"

Being the island's only mechanic, I would get an average of six calls a day concerning cranky engines. Two-thirds of these were caused by the manual engine shut-off button being left in the "off" position. However, this was not the problem- it wasn't so easy to diagnose. After several hours of checking I discovered there was air leaking into the fuel line.

"Aha!" I exclaimed as I discovered a tiny pin hole in the rubber fuel line. With the problem fixed and the bill paid, I left *Island Time* wondering how it had developed in a brand-new fuel line.

"*Fixman, Fixman.* This is the *Island Time* calling. Our engine won't start again for some damn reason. Can you please come back?"

How I hated those hot, cramped and smelly conditions when trying to troubleshoot and do repairs with one hand through a tiny opening in a bulkhead. Every time a tool dropped into the oily bilge, I cursed the designers who had given more thought to the crew's headroom than the mechanic to have easy access and to work with both hands.

Irene was all that time looking over my shoulder, and she seemed to be very interested in what I was doing but said nothing. When I discovered the loose fuel-injector I immediately suspected foul play. Sabotage!

It could be nothing else. The anxious look on Irene's face confirmed who the perpetrator might be, but I kept it to myself. Not saying anything about my suspicions, I simply tightened up the fuel injector and wished them a bon voyage.

On the third time around with engine trouble on the same boat, I found the same injector to be damaged in such a way that it could not be repaired. I told them it would take at least three days to get new parts shipped in. John and Jimmy were not happy. In fact, they were absolutely furious. They thought they could speed things up by inviting me on board for drinks. Joan and Jenny were all smiles. Irene was very quiet and avoided eye-contact with me, but she seemed smugly self-satisfied.

"It's Thursday," Jimmy exclaimed, "And we have five more islands to reach. The fan in the aft cabin doesn't work either, and there's a weather-window for perfect sailing conditions approaching. This is no damn good! I'll sue the company! How the hell could this have happened to that stupid injector anyway?"

"I really don't know. It is odd. It must have been a defect from the factory," I replied, glancing at Irene who was studying some distant point on the horizon. There was no doubt in my mind. She had to be the culprit.

During the next three days, I decided not to air my suspicions to anyone. My job was to fix engines, not human relations.

Six years later, Irene and a handsome local man suddenly appeared in front of my office desk. "Do you remember me?" she asked. I recognized her immediately, and the young man looked very familiar to me as well.

"How could I forget you and the unusual occurrence on board *Island Time?*" I replied.

"I just came by to say thank you. And to tell you that you're partly responsible for the existence of this lovely little girl." I leaned across the counter and looked down into the deep, green eyes of a beautiful little brown-skinned girl. "May I introduce Miss Julie Bequia Garner."

"But how did you know how to do that to the engine?"

Irene hugged her husband and gave him a big smile. "I didn't. Rocky here knows all there is to know about diesel engines, because he used to work for you. He told me how to do it. Which makes you even more responsible!"

24. The Long River

The Orinoco is South America's second longest river. Over 1300 miles long, it's the main means of transportation in Venezuela. Its source is far south in the Amazonas territory near the border of Brazil. It flows north along the border of Colombia and continues eastwards towards its estuary near Trinidad.

About two hundred and fifty years ago a Jesuit priest by the name of Manuel Roman was paddling up the upper part of the Orinoco when he came across some Portuguese slave-traders who had travelled up the Rio Negro, a tributary of the Amazon. Manuel joined the slave traders on their way back to their settlement by the Rio Negro. The route they took was a long, narrow river that connected the Orinoco with the Rio Negro. Many years later, the great explorer Alex von Humboldt travelled 1,500 miles to the source of the Orinoco, where he made the first of many major geographic discoveries. The Orinoco and the Amazon, South America's two mightiest rivers, were connected. He called it the Casiquiare Canal.

Today's surveyors can confirm that this previously concealed river actually exists. With the help of satellite imaging that can penetrate the rainforest canopy, we now have an accurate position and map of the canal.

After reading a book about Humboldt's legacy in Venezuela I decided that I had to explore this connection. My quest was to travel from the Orinoco estuary near Trinidad all the way by river to the Manaus Opera House on the Amazon, as I have briefly mentioned earlier.

I made my first attempt in my deep-keeled *Fredag* in 1987. The plan was to sail her up the Orinoco to Puerto Ayacucho, near the Colombian border, leave her there, and hopefully hitch a ride onwards as far as possible- at least as far as to the Casiquiare Canal. I didn't get very far on the first leg, due to our continuously clogged filters for engine cooling and exorbitant river pilot fees. After 150 nautical miles, one third of the way to Ayacucho, we threw in the towel at Ciudad Bolivar.

Even after I had sold my yacht, the dream was still present. On my second attempt I reached Ayacucho by bus only to find that many thousands of acres of rainforest were on fire and further travel on the Orinoco was prohibited.

On my third attempt, I flew with *Aeropostal* to Ayacucho. I rented a half-rotten *pinero*, 10 jerry cans of fuel, a pile of camping gear, and I paid a small fortune for various permits. All set to go, I once again had to abort my plan; the *pinero* was stolen property, most of jerry cans had leaks and there was a war going on along the border of Venezuela and Colombia, exactly where I had hoped to make my way south.

I was waiting for my flight to get back to Bequia. Broke, discouraged, and a bit depressed. I met Fritz over a double whisky in the airport bar. He had just arrived. He was on his way to Angel Falls, but after hearing my story he got all excited and managed to persuade me to change my plans and make a fourth attempt, accompanied by him.

He had a little money, some camping gear, a map of the Casiquiare, and most important, a lot of optimism- enough to make a many thousand-mile journey in order to experience an opera in a rainforest. His plan was to hitch a ride, most likely hundreds of rides, the whole way. He claimed that this was guaranteed to work as there were people living along the river almost all the way. Where people live there is commerce, and with very few roads they must go by boat. No problem at all, said my new optimistic Dutch friend.

We decided to start the expedition at Ciudad Bolivar, near the Orinoco estuary and find a ship going up river. I spotted a Vincentian flag on the stern of a freighter. She wasn't not ballasted, so it was obvious she was headed up-river to take on cargo.

There was not a single Vincentian on board. The entire crew was from the Philippines. The good news was that the captain hailed from my home town in Norway.

We were offered a ride all the way to Puerto Ayacucho, where they were to take on Bauxite. There was a slight snag- we had to paint the deck in return for our free passage. It was a huge deck, but we had five days to do the job.

It was slow going with the current against us and we had to take on board a new pilot every day. Why we needed a pilot was beyond me. The river was buoyed all the way and it certainly didn't coincide with my vision of the Orinoco being bordered by tropical rainforest with alligators, small picturesque villages, with waving friendly Indians in front of their thatched mud huts. It was day after day of desolate grass plains dotted by occasional oil rigs and pipelines. Not a soul was in sight except for the frequent visit of river pilots and two freighters loaded with bauxite travelling in the opposite direction. So much for Fritz' theory of people living along the banks of the Rio Orinoco.

So far it was not a journey full of exciting discoveries. I discovered that painting 1500 square meters of deck in tropical heat was really not for me.

We were about half way when something interesting happened. We were boarded by armed soldiers who wanted to find if there was anything on board that shouldn't be onboard. With the entire crew lined up on deck, except the pilot and helmsman, the soldiers inspected the cargo holds, they checked the crew list, and did a body-count. There were two individuals on board who weren't on the crew list. Carrying stowaways was a criminal offence. Our captain, who spoke as little Spanish as I did, tried to explain to the soldier with most stripes that we were not stowaways but paying passengers and that passengers did not have to be on the crew list.

The sergeant uttered a word which I translated as "bullshit." Everyone had to be on the list, or they must go ashore, *inmediatamenta*!

Our clever captain said that is no problem, and he took a ball pen out of his pocket to add us onto the list. *No es possible*, unless you *pagar una multa*. The fine was not astronomical, but neither was our budget. Of course, the fine didn't include a receipt. Our captain said he'll pay the fine. We declined the kind offer saying he had been more than helpful already. We would manage on our own the rest of our journey.

The soldiers ferried us ashore. The sergeant asked us where we were going and why were we here. I answered, "up the river," and that we were tourists, without going into details, mostly due to a lack of Spanish.

"Aha, turistico, muy interessante." He rambled on and it seemed he wanted to show us something of interest. We were slightly worried when the soldier's rubber tender continued speeding up a small tributary, but we kept our mouths shut. Three hours later we were dumped ashore by a small village.

"Hotel. Muy Bueno," said the sergeant pointing to a ramshackle building.

Hotel *Apure de Extravagante* lay on the bank of the Apure tributary, and we were told that tonight we would experience a once in a lifetime event.

The hotel with the extravagant name certainly didn't appear extravagant. It looked as if it might collapse any minute, but every room was booked. No problem, the hotel manager simply "re-booked" some Colombian pilgrims somewhere else. He knew a Norwegian lady by the name of Bergen- who I believed had a different name, but may have come from there. He laughed at our protest about him evicting his guests.

As the sun set, we noticed a lot of people passing by, walking in the same direction. We joined them to find out what was so *muy intressante*. After a twenty-minute walk, passing countless stalls selling plastic religious artefacts, we ended up by a tall waterfall. Hundreds of pilgrims had assembled at the foot carrying a lit candle. We were told that The Virgin Mary would soon appear in the cascading water.

As the full moon appeared over the forest canopy, we heard a loud gasp from the crowd. I didn't see anything that looked like a virgin in a waterfall. However, in the reflection of all the candles, I did see something that appeared be a very tired Golda Meir. Maybe you saw what you wanted to see- or expected to see. Fritz said he was sure he saw Queen Julianne on her deathbed. Nothing made sense to me; I really didn't want to see Golda Meir and I can't imagine why Fritz would want to see a Dutch Queen taking her last breath.

Anyway, after the Virgin Mary revelation, the crowd moved on and we followed the flow until we arrived at the foot of a high wooden crucifix with a half-naked man nailed to it, looking sorrowfully down on us. The man was thankfully not real, so it was a bit strange that after an hour of waiting the nailed man started to bleed from his palms. To call it strange was an understatement, it was a bloody miracle, in the right sense of the word.

Many of the spectators were in wheelchairs. Amazed at what they had seen they tried to stand up- and fell over. Many threw away their crutches and also fell over. Hysteria broke out and people were fainting all over the place. This kind of made sense as most of them were most likely exhausted after travelling by bus for days, or after having walked hundreds of miles to get to witness these so-called miracles.

It was time to get back to the hotel. Taking a short cut behind the crucifix I noticed a transparent plastic tube running through the grass and into the foundation of the wooden cross. The tube contained a red fluid.

Two miracles in one night was enough. Our friendly and helpful hotel manager was leaving on a fishing boat for Ayacucho in the morning and we were invited along for a ride.

Now *that's* what I would call a miracle!

I was convinced that few or most likely none of the sick were "cured" after the night's happenings. However, my craving for cigarettes had strangely diminished. Fritz on the other hand had become very ill, very ill indeed.

Puerto Ayacucho is the capital and largest city of the Amazonas State and is located across the Orinoco River from the Colombian village of Casuarito.

The city was founded to facilitate the transport of rubber and other goods past the Atures rapids on the Orinoco River in the late 19th century. The Venezuelan army and navy were based here, conducting their continuous war against drug-runners from nearby Colombia. The climate was equatorial, and the surrounding rainforests are some of the world's least explored and most untouched.

We found accommodation in a very reasonable but derelict guest house. In contrast with the *Extravagante* this one had no guests. We were the only ones there apart from a few thousand cockroaches.

Fritz was trying to shrug off a very high fever. *Dengue*, said the doctor. However, he would survive. If he was going to die it would most likely be from nicotine poisoning, he said as he looked down on Fritz' yellow stained fingers and teeth. Poor Fritz had a red rash over his entire body. His body ached; he had pain behind his eyes, and he was vomiting continuously. There wasn't much more to do than to keep him away from cigarettes and rum and force him to stay in bed as long as it took- drinking a lot of water and swallowing Tylenol pills. When he felt better, he should eat as many oranges as possible, said the doctor.

I was not looking forward to hanging around nursing my friend. I hid has stash of cigarettes. He was too weak to go out to buy rum or beer. He wanted to go home. In a dramatic and theatrical manner he begged me to continue the expedition in his name and to mail him a copy of my adventures.

There was no point discussing his melodramatic decision, especially when he gave me the rest of the exploration funds of five hundred dollars. One hundred dollars were to go toward a load of Tylenol and salary for an alternative nurse.

What struck me at the time was the coincidental similarity to when Stanley said goodbye to Livingstone, who was dying of malaria, and went off alone to find the source of the river Nile.

Nurse Maria was so beautiful that Fritz recovered substantially after only three days.

The day I was ready to continue my journey I met our helpful captain. The freighter was dockside not very far from our guest house, ready to leave for Trinidad loaded with bauxite. The captain was willing to take Fritz to get proper treatment in a hospital.

I rushed back to the guest house to give Fritz the good news and found him in bed with Maria. Fritz had converted into a devoted catholic, and within an hour Frits and Maria were on their way down the Orinoco and I was on my way up. Fritz did not see La Virgin Maria in the waterfall, but I was pretty sure he'd be seeing her in the future, for some time to come and certainly not as a virgin.

I couldn't find the map. Fritz had taken it with him. In spite of Puerto Ayacucho lying nearly a thousand nautical miles inland, it was a port of entry for ships. The harbourmaster became extremely suspicious when I explained to him my intention to continue up the river. Eventually he agreed to let me carry on with my journey and tried to sell me a map. He informed me that I also needed permission from The Minister of the Interior and from the Department for Protection of Indigenous People. The Minister and the Department was situated in Caracas. It was an eighteen-hour drive by bus to the capitol. I also need two medical clearances including five different injections. I would also need to leave a deposit with the harbourmaster. I asked him if the deposit was earmarked for a rescue mission. He didn't answer.

I told him that I didn't have all the time in the world and that I was a professor of entomology on a five-week long research expedition for *National Geographic*. I passed him my examination document on Behavioural Therapy from Oslo University, which I had used many times when being confronted with foreign bureaucracy. The folded document had a pretty impressive stamp and included two twenty US dollar bills.

It worked once again. The bills magically vanished into thin air and my document was handed back to me with a big smile.

The harbourmaster meticulously inspected the contents of my backpack to see if it contained any bibles or drugs. His smile widened when he found the stuff Fritz left me: A portable typewriter, camera equipment, a book titled *Insects of the Amazonas*, and a worn-out *National Geographic*, which Fritz for some strange reason had wanted me to carry. He'd hoped to find a special, rare beetle- a beetle that apparently gave off endorphins that women found irresistible. My knowledge about him told me that he personally had no need for such endorphins.

There was one more problem, said the harbourmaster, looking very serious. From here the Orinoco had series of dangerous rapids for fifteen miles- the

Aturés- used by crazy gringo rafters going downriver, and it was extremely dangerous to follow the riverbank by foot. The border of Venezuela and Colombia ran along the middle of it and the area was controlled by a cocaine cartel.

There was a narrow dirt road running fifty miles along the Venezuelan side of the border, nearly all the way to a village named San Vicente. What a coincidence! I had come from the Caribbean country of Saint Vincent, had sailed here on a ship registered in Saint Vincent, and now I was going to a remote village somewhere in the rainforest named San Vicente.

Unfortunately, there was no public transport along this road. No problem- for a small fee, military transportation with a bodyguard could be arranged all the way to San Vicente. The harbourmaster's cousin lived there, and his cousin owned a boat. His "cusina" might be able to help me get further upstream. But this would cost me a "few" bolivars.

How much? Special price for you, amigo. Only nineteen thousand bolivars, about half the price of a taxi and it included protection.

A rough calculation of nineteen thousand Bolivars came to about nineteen dollars. Quite acceptable, especially when protection was included.

I didn't get a receipt. The word "receipt" did not exist in this part of the world. My pocket Spanish dictionary had the word for invoice and bill, but nothing for receipt.

The information about no existing public transport was of course incorrect. Along the narrow fifty-mile-long road we overtook two former military trucks, artfully transformed into colourful buses. The harbourmaster obviously had knowledge of river transportation, but when it came to roads it was another matter- either that or he was a bit of a trickster. I knew from experience that the standard price for a bus ticket in Venezuela without air-conditioning and adjustable seats was about one dollar for every fifty miles. I just had write-off my nineteen dollars as foreign aid. There had been quite a bit of foreign aid handed out so far.

It took a four-wheel drive vehicle to get anywhere along the dirt road. The vehicle was a 1960 model Land Rover Series III just like the one I had in

Bequia. Like mine, this one had seen better days. So had my driver and protector. He was only about 30 years old but looked as worn out as the Land Rover. The insignia on his arm ranked him as a corporal, and he had a loaded automatic rifle on his lap. I thought it was loaded because he kept looking sideways into the bushes. Whenever he did he took one hand off the wheel and he fingered the trigger. He never stopped talking about his family- his brothers and sisters and eight children.

"They are a blessing," he said, looking at me for the first time. "Sometimes," he added, touching the crucifix hanging from the cracked rear-view mirror. I was not quite certain why he added the qualifier.

I had become a bit worried when the harbourmaster said he'd arrange transportation *nearly* all the way to San Vicente, but that was where the road ended. "Food and sleep here," my protector said, pointing toward some mud huts with straw-covered roofs.

"San Vicente that way", he said, pointing into the rainforest. "Follow path- only five kilometres," he added, holding up ten fingers, and he started laughing. I could still hear his laughter as he turned and headed back to Puerto Ayacucho.

All the huts were empty except one. The one inhabitant would not tell me his name. I had been told that the Indian population here believed that giving away their name to a stranger brought bad luck.

The man, only 5 feet tall, was wearing a penis-sheave and a dirty blue T-shirt with the words I LOVE SWEDEN written in yellow. He had a bowl-shaped haircut and a stick through his nose, cheeks, and upper chin.

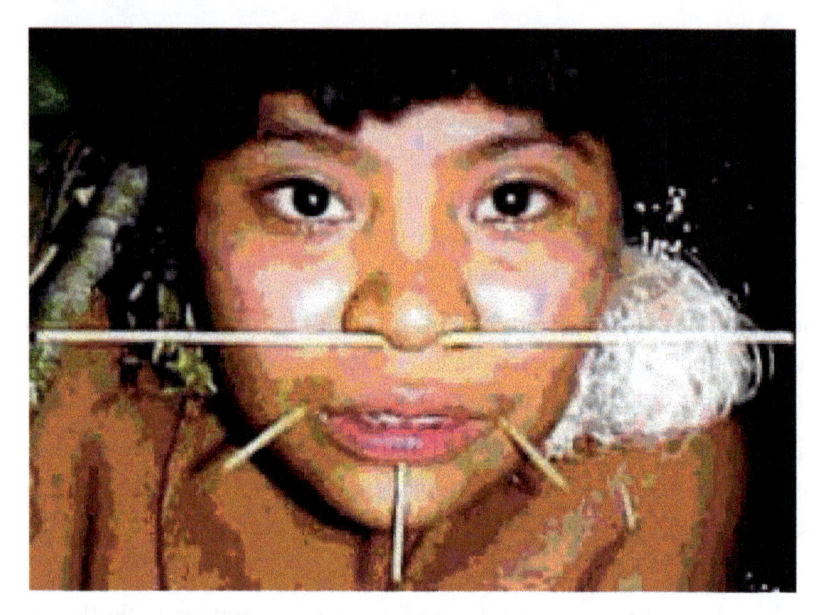

He could speak a little Spanish and told me- with the help of sign language, drawing in the sand, that his father was a Yanomami and his mother a Portuguese deep-sea diver. It was possible that her profession was lost in translation.

It could be that she'd drowned in the river.

I named him Yano.

He invited me to spend the night and share his supper. I was not too comfy about it. If there had been more of these fellows, it might have been different. I knew absolutely nothing about these people. All I knew was based on a two-page article in *National Geographic*- the one in my backpack. The article mentioned the following traditions which were acceptable within their culture: Rape, and to treat women as domestic animals; to make fun of other people's appearances; to throw deformed new-born children to the caiman reptiles, and to eat the ashes of their deceased family. One was not allowed to take revenge by killing someone within their own tribe, and one must never climb into their hammock without first wiping your feet.

It started to rain. That solved everything. I decided to scrap my plan of camping in my tiny tent and consume a tin of cold ravioli. I accepted Yano's invitation.

I was expecting the worst where supper was concerned. It was bound to be something exotic and weird- like roasted termites or grilled snake or something equally alien to a Norwegian/English/Vincyman. I let out a sigh of relief when Yano opened a can of Swedish meatballs. I wondered what the Swedish connection was.

My new friend didn't talk much. It was understandable since we were both very limited linguistically in each other's languages. This suited me fine. I was dead beat and drained. I climbed into my hammock after meticulously wiping my feet first.

I woke to the smell of fried plantain and Swedish meatballs. When I was ready to go, I handed Yano a $10 bill. He shook his head and pointed at my backpack, indicating that I must open it. It was obvious that he wanted something inside. I empty the contents onto the ground, hoping he didn't like the camera. He went for the lip balm, which Fritz insisted be included in our bribing collection.

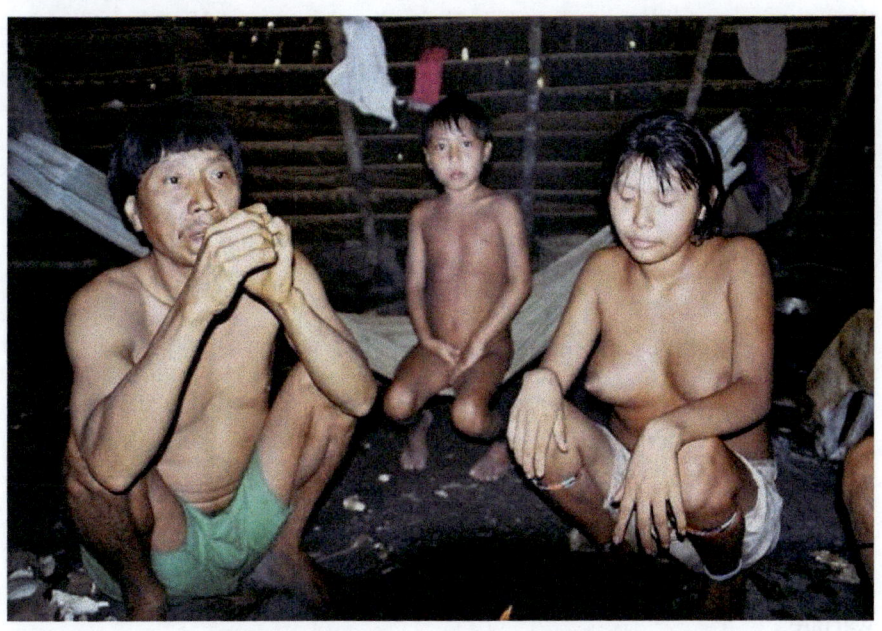

He wasn't finished with me yet. He wanted me to come with him and visit his brother, wife, and their little boy.

As we thrashed through the underbrush, he made a wide arc with his arm. I guessed that meant that our destination was just over the next hill. As the day passed, I understood that the arc symbolized the passage of the sun overhead. It was nearly dark when we arrived at his brother's family's hut.

More meatballs and plantain were served. I asked if the seeming unlimited number of cans had fallen off a lorry. He didn't get it. I enjoyed their company, although communication was often bizarre. I discovered that if for some reason I made a face, they laughed their heads off. I followed up doing the same when they made a face. We spent the evening eating, making faces, and laughing.

However, Yano was able to give me some background. There were three more Yanomami huts in the vicinity. They had come from further south, near the border with Brazil. If I understood him correctly, they had been "imported" by a Swedish entrepreneur to work as a tourist attraction and to help with a rafting project. Aha, that explained the meatballs. Apparently, the government did not approve, and the small group of Yanomamis were more or less stranded.

My worn-out *National Geographic* told me that although most Yanomami lived in peace, many were fierce warriors. Sometimes their warring was to capture women so the best warriors maximized their reproductive success.

The warring villages were usually several days' journey from each other, whereas the tranquil ones were less than a day away. Villages would usually split up when the population reached 100 to 150, but in times of warfare they wouldn't split before they reached a population of around 300.

Villages would go to war for a number of reasons, and warfare made up a large part of Yanomami life. About 40% of adult males had killed another person and about 25% of adult males died from some form of violence. Violence varied from chest-pounding, in which opponents from the same tribe took turns hitting each other on the chest, to club fights, to raids which involved killing other tribesmen and abduction of their women, to all out warfare.

However, there seemed no reason for me to worry. It was all smiles and laughter, and they weren't very big either.

The Yanomami people's traditions were shaped by the belief that the natural and spiritual world are a unified force; nature created everything, and was sacred. They believed that their fate, and the fate of all people, was inescapably linked to the fate of the environment. With its destruction, humanity was committing suicide. The men, when feeling peaceful, were known to smoke a hallucinogenic mixture of plants, and they would even blow smoke up each other's noses for good measure, then lie back and dream. This "peace pipe" would often mark the end of hostilities between two tribes, but it could also be a ruse- in times of war a well-known trick was to disarm their opponents with the peace pipe and then set about slaughtering them with fresh troops hiding in the jungle.

Since outsiders had mostly invaded the Amazon via the large rivers, the Yanomami had been able to live in isolation until very recently. Because of this they had been able to retain their culture and their identity which many Amer-Indians of the Amazon have lost.

They had very little contact with the outside world until the 1980's. Since 1987, 10% of their entire population- over 2,000 people- had perished due to massacres and diseases brought by gold miners and loggers.

Nearly all the Brazilian tribes had now moved north, over the border into Venezuela. With no concept of national boundaries, they understood that they were better protected here.

The Venezuelan government did not want a repeat of the disasters in Brazil in their country. To confirm what Yano told me, the government didn't want Swedes bringing in rafters, spreading bibles and disease.

I was finally on my way without the slightest idea of what to expect. All I knew was that I had over two hundred miles of river to navigate before reaching the Casiquiare canal. I made the decision that the expedition must end at the canal. Further down the Rio Negro and the Amazon all the way to Belem was totally unrealistic.

I didn't have a boat, hardly any cash, there were no banks on my route, and I was not really prepared for the rainforest. I fell asleep thinking of Captain Scott. He wasn't prepared for his journey to the South Pole and look what happened. My hero Roald Amundsen was prepared. He ate all his dogs on his journey and won the race.

I had no dogs; I had lost my Dutch companion, and I had to carry all the weight myself. There was really not much to carry, forlornly little considering how far I still had to go. My belongings consisted of my backpack, a half rotten tent full of holes and no bottom, a cooking apparatus with a quart of fuel, three cans of Rizzo's Ravioli, a Swiss Army knife, a hammock, a book on insects with two hundred and eighty dollars tucked in between the pages, an old rusty Remington portable typewriter with the ribbon full of holes, two dozen sheets of writing paper, 12 malaria prophylaxis tablets, a small packet of band aids, a tiny watertight jug of matches, a green plastic poncho with a hood, a torch with no spare batteries, a map of the Orinoco, a compass, five cans of mosquito spray made in China, and a can of Swedish meatballs.

That was it.

In comparison, Stanley and Livingstone each had 800 pounds of stuff and 50 strong guys to carry it.

I was out of cigarettes- I'd given Yano my last pack. My provisions consisted of three cans of Ravioli and one with meatballs. The canned food had to last for the next two hundred miles where I'd been told there was some kind of a supermarket, which I would believe when, or if, I reached there.

This was shear madness. I was stuck in no-man's land. There was no traffic. I didn't know how far it was to the river to catch a ride back, but with the hope that there might be a restaurant and a cigarette vending machine in San Vicente I trudged on with my head held high.

Fritz had mentioned the rainforest was forty degrees Celsius, but this was incorrect. It was humid but surprisingly cool, like being in a damp cave. It had stopped raining, but it didn't make much difference since it was so clammy. Maybe if it were still raining there wouldn't be so many mosquitoes attacking my flesh.

The path was narrow and winding. I crossed a stream with my shoes tied around my neck and I discovered to my horror that three nasty leeches had attached themselves to my ankles. As if this weren't enough to freak me out, I couldn't find a path on the other side.

A rainforest with no path or stream to follow was unknown territory for me. It was uncomfortably quiet, and I nearly leapt from of my skin when I roused a pair of Macaw parrots.

How far had I walked? How far to go? At least at sea I could trail a log and estimate my distance travelled, point my sextant at the sun and try to calculate my position. The sun here was hidden above the canopy. I had heard that there were plans to send up satellites, and with the help of these and a little portable battery driven unit in your hand you would know exactly how far it was to the nearest village or cigarette machine.

I had my trusted compass. On the first part of the path, before the stream, my course had been more or less towards the south. So I tramped on southwards. It was getting dark quickly. The canopy would not let in any star or moonlight and my torch was on its last legs- and so was I. I had no choice but to camp out in the bush. The rainforest, so quiet and tranquil during the day, was now alive with all sorts of strange, scary noises- a deafening cacophony of thousands of cicadas and frogs punctuated by the occasional scream of God knew what.

There was plenty of water all around despite the leeches; I reckoned it was safe to drink. I was hungry, but not hungry enough to devour anything creeping and crawling around me. I settled for cold Ravioli and a safe-to-eat banana which I had found conveniently lying on the path.

I tried typing down the day's report in my dairy. The light from my torch turned dull and pale. The paper was so wet that it was torn by the typewriter's roller. I was convinced that this madness must end; I decided to follow my tracks back to Yano as soon as I could see where I was going.

A loud guttural howl woke me up- a howler monkey. I'd heard this howl before in Trinidad. Or could it be something else? I tried to recall all I'd read about dangerous wildlife in South America, and I tried to light a fire. A fire would keep dangerous animals at bay. It was like lighting a soaked newspaper in the pouring rain. It was impossible. I found it difficult to fall asleep. It felt like a near death experience. All I could do was to try to keep calm and wait for sunrise, holding my knife at the ready should anything with fangs smell my fear.

At some point I must have fallen asleep. The sun's rays through the canopy were vertical, indicating that the sun was high. I must have slept for more than eight hours.

To my amazement I discovered that I had camped in the middle of a banana plantation. I could hear voices. My fear of been lost vanished when I found I had spent the night 200 yards from the village of San Vicente.

The harbourmaster's cousin turned out not be his cousin after all. He introduced me to Cusina, a beautiful Cuban woman who spoke fluent English. She worked for UNESCO, travelling up and down the river to report on how the indigenous population was doing. She was just about to leave for La Esmaralda, a small town very near to my original destination.

Just my luck! I was invited to join her on her passage further up the river.

My retreat to Bequia was put on ice. It was just the way my life worked. At one moment deep despair and darkness, and then a light always appeared at the end of the tunnel. Best of all, I didn't have to spend anymore scary nights in Fritz's joke of a tent not knowing what would happen next. All I had to do was enjoy the ride up-river and keep talking so Cusina could improve her English.

I was now teaching English to a beautiful Cuban scientist on board a riverboat heading for the source of the Orinoco, stretched out in the bow smoking local cigars. Behind a load of equipment and provisions, lovely Cusina sat at the stern, handling the outboard engine while I kept a lookout for sandbanks and rocks.

Gone were all my worries. The river was gradually narrowing, indicating we were near our destination. The passage so far with Cusina had been an exciting adventure, camping on the banks and learning about the rainforest. She was an expert on the fauna and flora of the Amazonas territory. I told her about my adventures in the Norwegian mountains and a salty yarn or two about my life as a sea gypsy.

I was fascinated when she talked about the Yanomami and their unique culture. She told me their traditions were based on the idea that the real and the spiritual world were one unified force, and everything in nature was sacred. The Venezuelan government did not want the Indians to be forced off their territory and had set up the Ministry for Indian Affairs to protect their indigenous tribes.

Anyone from the outside who had no legitimate business here must stay away from their settlements, and those that had a good reason to travel into the interior must be free of any diseases- including the common cold- and have documentation to prove it.

I suddenly felt very guilty about bribing the harbourmaster. And what about Yano? Could I possibly have infected him and his brother's family? I personally felt great, but I wouldn't want to be known as the guy for who had wiped out the last of the Yanomami.

Cusina told me that the Christian missionaries had been around for the past forty years. To be honest, she said, they'd done some good work and had good intentions, but in spite of this they had not been very welcome.

Over the last decade people had become more sceptical about the missionaries' motives. Chavez accused them of spying for the CIA, for foreign mining, companies, and for pharmaceutical companies who wanted to test their products on the indigenous people.

The Casiquiare branching off from the Orinoco

I was finally at my second leg destination. This was where the Casiquiare flowed into the Orinoco.

It was the waterway that linked South America's two greatest river systems, the Amazon and the Orinoco via the Rio Negro, a tributary of the Amazon.

Actually, the Casiquiare flowed in both directions on each side of the watershed. The river was not particularly wide, around 30 meters, but the current was quite strong, despite the fact that the watershed was only 120 meters above sea level. Cusina said that the current was very strong for the entire 150 km-long length during the rainy season. There was hardly any traffic on the river and thus little chance of hitching a ride. In August and September, when the river was its deepest, I was told that I might be able to join a two week long ECO-tour with tourists, but it cost a small fortune. I wouldn't be allowed to wander off anywhere or connect with the local population. It most likely would have been like the experience I had crossing Soviet Russia on the Trans-Siberian railroad. We had to stay on the train and pull down the blinds every time we passed something of interest.

If I wished to journey on my own I would have to go by canoe and carry proper camping equipment, preferably not without a guide or company. I thought it best to follow Cusina's advice and find another friend like my Dutch companion.

Seven miles up the Orinoco from where the Casiquiare emerged lay the village of La Esmaralda. I was surprised to discover that it was not a mud hut settlement, but a small village with a supermarket and a cigarette vending machine, a dozen modern houses surrounding an airstrip in the middle of nowhere, but with no connecting roads whatsoever. The name of the town was The Emerald. I didn't actually associate the place with emeralds or find the place attractive or hospitable.

I found lodgings where I would be able to build a canoe. There was an airstrip around the corner where I would be able to fly in equipment and there was a phone booth down the road where I could connect to the outside world. I needed to make some calls in order to be able to finance my future exploration and adventures.

The guy from Manchester who said he was interested in buying and running my workshop had chickened out, and my bank manager in Bequia informed me that there were barely enough funds in my account to pay my monthly checking fee.

He went quiet for a few seconds when I inquired about an overdraft. "An overdraft to finance a river expedition in the Amazon rainforest? You must be joking." He was still laughing when I hung up.

I found a friend in La Esmeralda. Davi owned a 12 foot fiberglass tender. He said he would ferry me up the Casiquiare at sunrise and return when the sun was right above his head. He said there would be no camping out and mumbled something about evil spirits and something scary that lived underwater.

Davi told me that there was a hidden treasure somewhere along the river. According to him the myth of El Hombre Dorado (The Golden Man), who in an initiation rite covered himself with gold dust and dove into a lake, took place somewhere along the Casiquiare. My obsession with hidden treasure was still within me. Maybe here lay the legendary El Dorado- maybe this was it! Maybe the bank manager would see things in a different light when I returned home with looted gold dust.

About halfway along the Casiquiare lay Roca Culimacare, a fifteen-foot high boulder of granite. According to Cusina, the famous explorer Alexander Humboldt used to make his astronomical calculations from the top of this boulder. In his notes there are references to several petroglyphs- images carved into boulders. One of these petroglyphs had been found a few hundred meters up the river. The image showed a man with rings above his head, a sort of saint. Strangely, the man was standing on his head. The boulder weighed several tons, so it was unlikely that it had been positioned upside-down after the petroglyph had been carved.

It was this inverted position that led me to think that there might be a connection to El Hombre Dorado. According to legend an Indian-chief covered with gold dust dove into a lake during a consecration ritual. Later the incident was associated with the legend of the "Lost City of Gold," a legend that fascinated many, but though the Spanish conquistadors ravaged the country, it had never been found.

In 1546, in pursuit of the legend, Francisco de Orellana and Gonzalo Pizarro went on an expedition up the Amazon. Orellana had previously been the first European to sail down the Amazon River, all the way from its source in the Andes. They found no City of Gold.

Following a description of this expedition, Juan Rodriguez Freyle undertook a new expedition where he headed up the tributary Rio Negro to a place where the Casiquiare channel ran out. According to Freyle the natives told him about a Muiscaene king or high priest of the Muiscaene tribe who had periodically performed the ritual of diving into a lake with his body covered in gold dust. In 1638 Freyle personally witnessed such a ritual, and he wrote the following report, addressed to the governor of Guatavita:

The ceremony took place during the appointment of a new chief. Before the ceremony could commence, the chief-to-be had to spend a long period in a cave, without women and the prohibitions to eat salt. After hanging out in the cave, he was carried to a small lake where sacrifices to a demonic god would take place. The village population had, while he was in the cave, built rafts of reeds which were decorated with some of their most valuable possessions. The rafts were equipped with burning torches and beakers full of incense. All the villagers, men and women wearing beautiful costumes decorated with of feathers and gold, were gathered on the bank of the lake. When incense and torches aboard the rafts were lit, the same was performed on shore. The man who was to be appointed chief was placed naked aboard a raft where he was covered with mud and strewn with gold dust. At his feet were placed large quantities of gold and gems. When the raft was in the middle of the lake, a signal for silence was given and the "Golden Man" dropped all the gold and all the jewels overboard, accompanied by singing, dancing and drumming of those standing ashore. After he had off-loaded all his "cargo" he paddled ashore, climbed up on a cliff and dived head first into the lake. A new chief and ruler was inserted.

According to Freyle, he witnessed this with his own eyes. Such a ritual took place regularly. Freyle insisted that the lake therefore contained a small fortune in gold and emeralds. But there was no obvious lake in the area, only branches of a very long river, with a thousand lakes.

There would be no continuation of the expedition. Funding was non-existent, and I had an oncoming fever and terrible headache. The bush-doctor diagnosed me with dengue fever. It was time to go home. But I'd be back some time in the future with a kit to build a canoe.

25. The Hidden Treasure

Safe and sound back on Bequia after my Amazonas expedition, I slowly recovered from dengue fever. The dream of finding hidden treasure continued. By chance I discovered I didn't need to go to the South American rainforest to find it. It could be right outside my door. Only two nautical miles south of Bequia was a small, uninhabited island named Isle de Quatre, locally called as *Oily Cat*. The little island was off the beaten track since the entrance to the lagoon was considered tricky. I had to check it out.

The island is about two miles long with an average width of three hundred yards. A longitudinal ridge extends the entire length of the island, with the highest point approximately one hundred meters above sea level. The distance from the highest point to the opening on the reef is approximately one cannon shot- to the beach, one pistol shot.

This was important information. The ridge was overgrown with cedar trees, frangipani and cacti. The beach in the lagoon was lined with coconut palms. I was here to explore, not to lie on the beach for a tan.

It was a tough climb. I had to chop my way through cacti and tropical undergrowth. Twenty feet below the summit I discovered a shack where the roof had fallen in. Most of the timber was in fairly good shape. Close by, mostly hidden beneath creeping vines, I found the foundations of what was once a colonial structure. There were large cut stones of different sizes scattered around and inside the foundation. Some of the stone blocks that formed the foundations had square four by four-inch holes, about and eight inches deep. Obviously for holding standing timbers.

The ridge extended upwards another twenty feet. I hacked my way to the summit where I was rewarded with a 360-degree view. I found more square stones. The area was too small for a building, but the perfect place for a lookout tower.

From the ruins down to a lagoon on the island's north side I found remains of stone steps. To my surprise, I discovered similar stone steps on the opposite side leading to the leeward side.

Despite my research, I had a hard time finding anything or anyone who could shed some light on what these ruins may have been or how old they were. The only reliable information I had was from the historic archives in Saint Vincent. Isle de Quatre was named by French occupiers. The original Carib name was Quate-quate. The *Nautical Magazine and Naval Chronicle* of 1863 mentioned a population of 63, and various local self-proclaimed historians said it was a sea island cotton estate. However, according to *The History of the Windwards*, the island had never been inhabited due to a lack of arable land.

Based on a few facts, rumours, and my vivid imagination, I had come to the following conclusion. The stone blocks weren't the ruins of a fort. The island had no strategic significance. The largest settlement on Bequia during the wars between France and England was at Admiralty Bay. The village could not be protected from the top of Isle de Quatre, seven miles away.

Some pundits suggested it had been a sugar plantation. Not possible- hardly any arable land, no groundwater, and no sign of wells. The same went for cotton, in my opinion. It was purchased by Prime Minister Mitchell's grandfather in 1906 to be used for harvesting the abundant cedar trees. Their curved branches were ideal for shipbuilding, but my personal theory of the island's previous habitation by buccaneers remained.

Pirates or buccaneers ravaged and looted ships all over the Caribbean in the 1600-1700s. There was evidence that two of the most notorious of these pirates, Henry Morgan and William Kydd (whose surnames abound in Bequia today) used St. Vincent and Bequia for water and supplies. Many of these high-sea robbers occasionally needed a break and built themselves well-hidden settlements. These hiding places had to be a safe haven and be uninhabited. Over time these pirates looted small fortunes. Despite legends of buried treasures all over the Caribbean, most pirates had to carry their wealth with them when they were at "work," or they blew it in the first port on rum, gambling, and women. I felt that perhaps Kydd had been different.

Self-portrait, Sir Peter Kydd

It was told through the ages that Captain Kydd was one of the few who had hid his wealth ashore, and that some of his treasure was buried on one of the many small uninhabited islands between St. Vincent and Grenada.

The Kydd family on Bequia claimed they were descendants of this infamous pirate, and that any treasure discovered belonged to them, although this Anglo-Scottish surname was quite common among sea-farers at the time.

The ships of the buccaneers and pirates were small and therefore easy to camouflage. They were much faster and easier to manoeuvre than their heavy naval pursuers. If the pirates had a secrete hideaway on Isle de Quatre and kept a watch from their lookout tower, they would have had plenty of time to escape any intruding vessels. By the time soldiers had arrived to the top of the ridge the pirates would have disappeared over the horizon, with or without their "inventory." If they didn't have time to load it on board, and for some reason they didn't return, my wishful thinking told me it might still be there, buried where X marked the spot.

There were different opinions about who actually owned "my" treasure island. One was that Isle de Quatre belonged to the former Prime Minister, Sir James Mitchell. A story went that he leased the island to an Arab prince who had planned to build a huge luxury resort. Then we heard that the sale went down the drain due to a disagreement over property rights. Another version was that a certain Bonnet family in Barbados demanded the right to half the island.

An English gentleman named Stede Bonnet (1688-1718) was the predecessor of the family claiming to have inherited Isle de Quatre up to the present day. Mr. Bonnet had once owned a sugar plantation on Barbados. There were documents showing that Stede Bonnet bought half the island in 1702 when he got fed up with sugar production on Barbados and shifted his profession to piracy. He became a privateer, a fancy name for a pirate licensed by the English King to hijack enemy ships and keep most of the loot for himself.

Was there a connection here? It didn't hurt to fantasize. You never knew, the day might come when I stumbled over something valuable. Think of what I could do with all that money. I could give it all to island charities- well, at least some of it!

I therefore took all legends and speculations very seriously. I hadn't given up trying to explore the ruins of Isle de Quatre. I kept on investigating and re-visiting the island, only to find the site more and more overgrown and covered by wasps known locally as *jack spaniards*. (Had their names derived from Captain Jack Sparrow?) After many visits, I had only found a gold wedding ring engraved with *Eternal Love 1987*, and I thought, what an unusual place to end eternal love.

26. The Memories

Fixworld now had a new owner, a Scottish former race-car driver and mechanic. Robin Smith exited the fast lane of racing Formula One cars around the world to enjoy the much slower pace of the Caribbean. This modest and humble Scot had no need to brag about his merits, although there were indications that his past had indeed been fast and furious. If speed limits were in existence on Bequia Robin would have held the record for breaking them. He also took over the nickname of Fixman. Once you have a nickname, it stayed with you for life. To tell us apart, I was *Fixman One*, Robin *Fixman Two*.

It was time for a change- a new chapter in life. I was done with being a sea-gypsy and tired of being a contortionist mechanic- twisting and bending my body into strange, unnatural positions in hot and filthy engine-rooms.

What could I do? It had to be something creative. What did I have from the past that could be a key to the future?

Memories. No matter how much suffering I went through, I never wanted to let go of those memories. The thing about memories was you couldn't forget them, especially if you wrote them down.

When I was seven years old my sister asked me what I wanted to be when I was an adult. I remember telling her that I wanted to be an explorer, to sail around the world, and to write a book about my strange and exciting experiences.

I never made it around the world, but I had all the ingredients for a book- my ship's logbook and a suitcase full of notes, memos, and letters. My older sister's advice was that writing was a piece of cake- it was just a matter of getting the right word in the right place.

I wanted to write a book about all my wonderful experiences at sea.

A lot of strange phenomena happen at sea, especially at night. Heavenly bodies and cloud formations, combined with poor visibility, my late-night state of mind and double vision in one eye had been the explanation for many strange occurrences.

It was a very cloudy, dark night as *Fredag* struggled against the current on her way east along the coast of Venezuela. I noticed a little yellow light straight ahead on the horizon. Africa was thousands of miles away, so it had to be a ship. No, it couldn't be a ship because the light was gradually taking the shape of a growing pyramid. It was not uncommon for sailors on small yachts to direct a searchlight towards their sail to alert other vessels of their position, but this light seemed to be at the end of the world. An illuminated sail could not explain this phenomenon, because the pyramid was growing too fast. To make it even more incomprehensible, a new growing pyramid appeared, right next to it. I started on a long elimination process. A floodlit sail was out. Searchlights from a helicopter also. Could it be a UFO- an unidentified flying object? The only flying saucers I had ever seen had been caused by a passing Exxon oil tanker while I was eating breakfast in the galley.

Then the tips of each pyramid stretched for miles into the sky and joined together by what looked like a floodlit, sandy beach. With the beach growing and rising from the sea, the mystery was solved: a new moon, lying on its side, had made its nightly entrance. Because I had spent all my life at northern latitudes where the crescent moon was more or less straight up and down or slightly at an angle and did not lie flat like a hammock, it hadn't occurred to me that an ascending, hammock-looking moon could be the explanation.

As a rule, nearly all such mysterious phenomena often have a simple and straightforward explanation.

We were on our way to Grenada on a moonless night. An orange light appeared dead ahead, just above to horizon. It varied in strength and suddenly shot up vertically followed by a trail of lesser bright lights. A few minutes passed and the mysterious light was back again. Regardless of whether I changed course the light seemed to be dead ahead. Though it seemed far away, I was starting to become a bit anxious, mostly because I had no explanation for the phenomenon. It was scary when something unrecognizable revealed itself through the darkness at sea. It was best to wake my first mate. Maybe she could shed some light on the phenomena. But Mariann was not in her cabin. She wasn't below deck at all. Had she been abducted?

"The only outcome of that investigation was a piece of an Adriane rocket and a Mars Bar paper wrapper."

She was sitting on the bowsprit, chain smoking! After each cigarette had finished, she had flicked the glowing butt into the sea. And here I was, sitting in the cockpit, on the verge of becoming convinced that the phenomenon was a UFO.

The Tobago Cays Marine Park is a popular group of five low, sandy islands protected by a barrier reef, located thirty miles south of Bequia. With unimpeded trade winds coming from Africa, it was great place to fly a kite. Some kids decided to fly theirs from the deck of their boat. It wasn't launched till after sunset. There was no point in flying a kite in the dark so the kids equipped it with an electric light. You can probably imagine the result. There were quite a few visiting yachts in the wide anchorage gorging themselves on lobster and champagne when the phenomenon revealed itself in the night sky- a discus-shaped object that appeared over several hundred meters long, frequently changing colour and brightness and swinging back and forth as if it was trying to find somewhere to land. There was chaos on the marine radio with people reporting this UFO over the reef.

With the exception of a particular area in the United States, there isn't a place on earth that has as many UFO sightings as the West Indies. Just north of Grenada there is a narrow channel between two small islands, often used by sailors as a shortcut. One of these is a five hundred-foot-high pointed rock that the Atlantic swells are constantly trying to tear apart. The French called it "Caye qu'n gene," which can be translated as "the shelf that pulls together." After the French were ousted by the British, the name was anglicized by the locals to *Kick 'em Jenny*.

I have anchored off *Kick 'em Jenny* several times, camping out to keep watch for anything coming or going other than frigate birds and pelicans. I have scrutinized every square inch of the rock looking for proof that might indicate that something or someone from outside our world had paid a visit. I actually found something that came from above- a piece of an Ariadne rocket launched from Guyana which had washed ashore. I also found the wrapper of a *Mars* chocolate bar.

Many UFO believers on Canouan- an island about forty miles to the north- were convinced that *Kick 'em Jenny* was an extra-terrestrial base since there were constant arrivals with a frequency comparable to Gatwick Airport. What they were seeing was aircraft approaching Grenada's Point Saline International Airport, further south, which opened in 1984.

The main reason for all this nonsense of inter-galactic speculation lay at the doorstep of Sir Eric Gairy, the first Prime Minister of Grenada. In 1977 Gairy gave a speech to the UN in which he stated that the United Nations should set up a commission to conduct research on UFOs! Believe it or not, this bizarre speech led to *UN- Resolution 33/426, Resolution on Extra-terrestrial Life.*

Shortly after Prime Minister Gairy asked the UN for financial support to build a defence-facility to ward off an invasion from outer space, Grenada was actually invaded, not by little green men but by the combined military forces of the United States. It was given the green light by President Ronald Reagan, who apparently also believed in UFOs, horoscopes, and Holy Ghosts.

I find it impossible to believe that life should exist solely on planet earth. There are many so-called UFO sightings that have yet to be explained, but I don't think these encounters have anything to do with aliens. I need to see proof, not doctored photos.

This applies to anything supernatural- show me the scientific evidence. If Jesus Christ (who I do believe was a peaceful revolutionary) suddenly flew down to earth (without a parachute), walked across the waves, boarded my yacht, and turned the day's catch of one little flying fish into ten salmons I would say, *Well, well. Look at that. I was wrong.*

I haven't sailed all the seven seas, but I've logged well over thirty thousand nautical miles, of which one third was at night, and to date I've never seen anything that might have come from another world other than tens of thousands of shooting stars. The only beings that could come close to green men have been some of my own seasick crew, hanging over the gunwale feeding the fish. Strange lights from up above were either a plane where the pilot had forgotten to turn off his landing lights, or a Caribbean weather balloon in the jet-stream, catching the last rays of the sun.

It's always dark when you observe mysterious and spooky sightings. Most of these happen beneath the keel. When the sea surface is calm and without a ripple you can see the contours of creatures of the deep, illuminated by phosphorescence. Large schools of small fish near the surface can give the impression of shallow water or a reef just ahead, or even a submarine with its searchlight beamed upwards. These phenomena always occur right on the bow without giving you a second to avoid disaster. Bracing yourself for an unavoidable crash, the shoal of illuminated fish then moves away.

Through history, there have been countless reports from sailors who have witnessed strange events at sea. They've seen it all- from monsters to mermaids. It is quite understandable that during long periods with fatigue, hunger, or stress (or too much rum) one can become susceptible to hallucinations. I would argue that such illusions are often based on what is known as conditioned response. The witnesses are often passengers or inexperienced crew, accustomed to life ashore. It's understandable that when the brain goes into overdrive, when visibility is reduced and vision is weary after hours of combing the horizon searching for land, a riptide over a half-submerged tree-trunk could easily be mistaken for a sea-monster.

For some reason nobody has as many strange experiences as single-handed sailors. For me to spend months at sea in solitude would be impossible, especially without female company. But if I did, I am sure I would be seeing something resembling a mermaid during every spell of loneliness.

In bars and pubs you hear the most incredible yarns, especially those told by single-handers. But to be fair, there also have been incredible events that reliable and sober sailors have experienced- experiences that can be confirmed by witnesses.

One such story was the rescue of the crew of a French yacht by a dolphin. I heard the narrative from the captain himself, and it was authenticated by photos and five crew-members. Cruising along the north coast of Trinidad, they came across a lonely dolphin with a plastic ring around its elongated snout. The animal couldn't eat and would have soon starved to death. The captain jumped overboard and swam over to the dolphin. It made no attempt to swim away and let its saviour cut the ring lose.

It then swam close to the side of the yacht for three days and nights. It was the same dolphin because they could recognize the scars on its back. Upon their approach to the island of Martinique the crew failed to spot a dangerous reef dead ahead. The yacht was 60 feet from disaster when the dolphin swam ahead of the boat and leapt twice from the water, spinning and splashing magnificently, which caught the captain's attention, averting a grounding.

A similar story was told about Brother King from Bequia. He was the skipper of an 80-foot schooner on his way to Martinique with cargo and a crew of three. Twenty nautical miles from their destination, west of St. Lucia, they were hit by a white squall. A white squall, or microburst, is a sudden and violent windstorm. The schooner heeled over, the cargo shifted, and she sank within a few minutes. The crew perished, but Brother King was a good swimmer and also very determined. He was on the verge of giving up, but he had the island of Martinique in sight. Then sharks came out of nowhere- many of them- enough for him to accept that he would never make it.

But it wasn't over for Brother King. A pod of dolphins arrived at the scene. They attacked the sharks and chased them away. A fisherman spotted a large shape near the horizon at dawn, and thinking it was a turtle, he saved Brother King. For many hours later in his hospital bed, he continued doing the side stroke, not realizing he had reached shore. After a short stay in hospital, he was off to sea again, but in deference to turtles, Brother King started the Grenadines' first and only turtle sanctuary on Bequia which is probably responsible for the great increase in numbers of these endangered gentle giants in the last 30 years.

He says his motive for doing so is to give something back to the sea. Some say that there's no evidence to back up his story of being saved by dolphins, some say there is. I personally have seen no proof, but there have been many similar accounts of dolphins helping people in distress.

My dream has always been to swim with wild dolphins- theme parks be damned. Once, close to Isla Caracas off Venezuela, we came across a playful and inquisitive pod. I was quick to dive in, but when I broke the surface they'd disappeared. I don't know why they all retreated so suddenly. I was very embarrassed- it felt like I'd entered a room with many friends and they all decided to leave the room at the same time.

To be honest, I don't really need UFOs, sea monsters, or mermaids to make exploring more interesting. There is more than enough amazing natural phenomena to observe. When the atmosphere is full of dust blown over the Atlantic due to sandstorms in the Sahara, one delights in the most dramatic sunsets. Sometimes it may make you think you're on an alien planet.

I can lie on deck under a clear tropical night sky, distant from the glare of lights on shore, and look up at the starry heavens and sense the infinite greatness of the universe. Sometimes it feels as if the gravity of the Milky Way has an opposite pull (which it actually has), and I can float freely up into space among the stars where we all originally came from. And when the ocean is quiet and calm, I might crawl down into the bilge and put my ear against the hull to listen to a whale singing his love song to a prospective partner thousands of miles away.

No Spielberg special effects could ever come close to the beautiful spectacle of a leaping dolphin, luminously outlined by phosphorescence, leaving an explosion of stars in its wake. Or the emotional event when a whale gives birth and the dolphins swim in a circle around the new-born calf to protect it from sharks. Imagine an octopus that can instantly change its colour and shape so it can imitate any invader to threaten its territory.

We mustn't forget the myriad strange creatures that live deep down in the depths, some equipped with a built-in flashlight and fishing rod with bait. I often lay in the net under the bowsprit, looking down, hoping to catch a glimpse of one. Of course, they belonged to the deep, so it never happened, but it was enough for me to just imagine, because I had seen the evidence on film. I knew they were real. Unlike UFOs.

I am content with my memories and my new home overlooking the harbour. I see the white sails on the horizon, heading towards the bay. I wonder what stories these sailors have to tell. Time to take a walk down to the village to meet with the newcomers and regulars at the *New York Bar*, my favourite watering hole.

27. Tribute to a Mate

After everything on the island had been taken apart, fixed, and put together again, I developed a new fixation- to stop what I was doing and find more time to write. To finish those frigging novels that nobody wanted to publish or look for hidden treasure on another "undiscovered" island.

Cedar Retreat, my geodesic dome house on Mount Pleasant

The urge to continue exploring and battling the elements diminished fast, however. Mariann wanted to pick up where we'd left off, to build a new smaller vessel, and to resume our once common dream. I did not agree. Our life style had changed and with it also our relationship. Looking back, it seemed as if we were the closest when misfortune or disaster threatened our lives. Now we were back to a comfortable job, house, and garden existence which I had once rebelled against, but now it made sense to me. We split up and went our separate ways. I sold *Fixworld* and built a wooden dome house overlooking the Atlantic where I could sit in solitude, write my memoirs, and maybe receive the Nobel Prize in Literature.

I am now a house and garden person. Yet again, my neighbours did not approve of my architectural preferences. The called my new geodesic dome house *the pressure-cooker*. As with my Swiss Chalet, it didn't conform, but on the other hand, I believe it is aerodynamically hurricane proof.

Mariann devoted her new life to charity work and lived in a house nearby. We lived as neighbours and friends in separate homes on top of Mount Pleasant, as far from the sea as possible. She had come to terms with settling down, but was always on the look-out for the right yacht to go to sea again; she just couldn't find the right captain. I took this as a *huge* compliment.

Sadly, my soul mate and ship's mate for many years died of cancer after a short spell of illness, on the 5th January 2009. She was 67 years old.

Mariann "Why Knot" Palmborg was born in Sweden on September 11th, 1941. At age twenty she moved to Norway, became a Norwegian citizen, married, and gave birth to two boys. Mariann was educated in social work and child care. She ran a youth club in Oslo for many years, keeping young people off the streets and away from drugs. I first met my first mate in Oslo when we were both working on a boat-related kids' rehabilitation project.

Mariann was a country girl, her nautical experiences limited to rowing a seven-foot pram on a tiny, tranquil lake. When I told her of my dreams to someday sail around the world, she responded by telling me that small boats and sailing were not for her. Her husband at the time owned a 45 foot ketch along with three other couples, and on the few occasions she'd gone cruising, she'd hated every minute.

Mariann was a tough and active woman, always on the lookout for new challenges. She was very unconventional when it came to a woman's role and position in society. She didn't at all enjoy being banished to the galley or to look after the kids down below. She didn't want to "stay out of the way." She wanted to navigate, haul up the anchor and the halyards- all the physical work that the men did. She told me she had grown to hate sailing. In spite of this she accepted my invitation to go for a short afternoon sail on the Oslo Fjord.

A strong northerly breeze sent us and the tiny 18-foot day sailor flying down the fjord and out to sea on what was supposed to be a short trip in secluded waters. It ended up as a 160-mile voyage to Denmark and back, only because a restaurant in Skagen served the best pickled herring breakfast in the world. On the way home, encountering big seas, her captain became violently seasick and was confined- perhaps to die- in the tiny forecastle cabin. On her first voyage in open water Mariann had to navigate and sail the 20-hour passage home single-handed. When proudly tying the lines onto the dock, she exclaimed, "I want to go with you around the world! Let's get that boat built! Maybe we'll find paradise- or your hidden treasure!"

The fifty-foot Colin Archer ketch *Fredag* had a lot of rope and standing rigging. As it was impossible to find a traditional rigger who could do a one-inch 17-strand Liverpool wire splice; she bought a book on the subject and did it herself. She soon handled power tools and did woodwork like a professional. Within three years she had become a skilled shipwright, rigger, and sailmaker.

Mariann's first entry in *Fredag's* log reads, "Friday the 13th. Leaving to find Paradise and a new life. Course once again set for Skagen, Denmark."

Mariann was always trying to move boundaries- all her life she'd been longing for adventure and challenges, even after being shipwrecked in the Caribbean after twelve months on our maiden voyage. Her dream and her home with all her belongings went to the bottom of the sea, seventeen fathoms deep. She shed no tears nor showed any grief. Her first words after watching the top of our mast disappear beneath the surface had been, "Wow, this is surely something to write home about."

After swimming ashore I sat on the beach staring out to sea in a state of shock and disbelief, not capable of functioning, until she yelled at me, "Come on Skip, snap out of it! Let's get her up and going again!"

Misfortunes and challenges abounded. Bliss was tarnished by hurricanes, rogue waves, Caribbean bureaucracy, dengue fever, financial difficulties, and a South American revolution. When drifting towards Central America with all sails blown out and a broken crankshaft, I was on the verge of giving up and throwing in the towel. She had to kick me back into action. Mariann would not have her captain giving up, although a little house and garden with a picket fence and a horse didn't seem a bad idea at the time.

There was no paradise, no sunken treasure to be found. But Mariann had found something more important. She had built up immunity to hardship, and had developed a strong will to survive, thrive, and give back to others. She discovered that paradise was something you had inside you, it didn't really matter where you were- in slums of Calcutta or sailing around Cape Horn- you kept a bit of it within you at all times, whether you realized it or not.

Bequia became Mariann's paradise- as close as she could get. It was good enough to move ashore. She made her home where she could indulge in her many charities and projects: The Easter Regatta, The Christmas gløgg-party for Scandinavian sailors, Women's Day Celebrations, The Sunshine School for children with special needs, the Mozart Under the Cocoanut Tree concerts, and her most recent animal welfare project *Happy Puppies*.

She gave with all her might, doing her best to give back to a community that had shown her so much acceptance and later so much approval. She was known as the *Why Knot lady* because of her small business selling examples of her marlinspike seamanship, such as her cleverly interwoven rope floor mats, monkey-fist key rings, macramé wall hangings and other curiosities from the back of her beat up Land Rover under the sign *Why Knot?*

Mariann had just received her Norwegian pension, and she had big plans for the future. Sadly, a short period of illness cut short those dreams. Her fighting spirit, immunity to hardship, and determination to get well was no match for the ravenous cancer. Up until her final hours she showed incredible strength and did her best to make her many visitors laugh. She would spend several hours on the phone connected to her island. "I'll be back," she would tell her Bequia friends. "Maybe not in body, but for sure in spirit." She died in Norway with her two boys by her bedside and a lot of people on Bequia praying for her recovery.

Closely connected to the sea as she had been, she wished her cremated remains to be scattered off the stern of the schooner *Friendship Rose* in Admiralty Bay. She wanted the ceremony to be joyful- no tears, sad tedious sermons, or weeping, but a final party with friends from land and sea- a ceremony to give thanks for a great life, thanks to an island and its people who had given so much and made her twenty-five years on Bequia her finest and most meaningful.

The people on the island found the *Why-Knot lady* with the big smile a remarkable and somewhat unusual ex-pat settler, a caring and generous woman working hard to integrate into the community.

Verna Mariann Palmborg (1940 – 2009)

To the many young women who crewed on *Fredag* she was an inspiration and a significant role model. And then, of course, there were dozens of dogs that were rescued, given good homes and loving care.

Mariann was a true sailor, a great companion, and the best and bravest first mate a captain could ever wish for.

Just before Christmas we said our final goodbye to each other in Barbados. She knew then that her time would soon be up. Her final words to me were, "Thanks. Thanks for finding the way to Bequia, my captain. Now you go home to Bequia and say thanks and goodbye to all our wonderful friends who have given me so much and take my ashes and the whole bunch out to sea on my final passage."

Which we did. Three visiting Swedish musicians, one ex-pat guitarist, and Socony, our local bard, all brought guitars onto the *Friendship Rose* on February 9th, 2009 to sing and celebrate Mariann's life. They sang *Bridge Over Troubled Water* as her ashes were committed to the deep, and it was such a beautiful moment on a gorgeous day that despite her admonitions quite a few tears were shed at that moment.

A yacht dips below our horizon on her journey and we
can no longer see or contact her, we are deeply saddened.
At the same time the yacht appears on somebody else's
Horizon, and people rejoice at her arrival on different shores.

28. Tribute to a Ship

Was it depressing to sell the *Fredag* and see her sailed back to Norway by her new owner? In was, to be honest, a little sad. However, the fact that she would to continue sailing with young people made it easier to say goodbye, and to look forward to a new chapter as a landlubber. Maybe we would meet again. The new owner said that there was a possibility that he would make a passage to the Caribbean in the near future. And if I should happen to be in Norway we could go sailing.

After so many years in exile and after only a short nine-hour flight across the Atlantic, it was strange returning to Oslo again. The city had changed over the past twenty-five years. I got lost in my own home town. I felt like Crocodile Dundee did in New York. The sea-front now had a Manhattan skyline. There was hardly any traffic in the city centre. It was all redirected underground.

I was hungry for some urban culture. The new and magnificent opera-house had been completed, but there was a 6-month waiting list for tickets.

Instead of waiting that long, I decided go for a festival of blues and jazz at Skånevik, a small town up a fjord on the west coast. Sitting on the Skånevik dock, daydreaming and enjoying a bag of cooked fresh shrimp, I noticed a yacht making its way up the fjord. As it got closer, I could see that she was a Colin Archer designed ketch. There wasn't much wind, so she wasn't exactly racing along, but when she was only a mile away, my pulse leapt. I jumped up and dropped my shrimp back to where they came from when I saw her name and the dove of peace painted on her bow.

It was my *Fredag*. It seemed they were also coming for the music until they suddenly changed course to go further up the fjord. I jumped onto a cabin-cruiser moored by the dock and asked if I could use their radio.

"*Fredag*, this is boatbuilder Peter from Bequia, over."

"Fixman, this is *Fredag*. What the hell are you doing here?"

"Looking for a boat to go sailing."

They changed course and headed straight towards me, dropping anchor just off the dock.

"Permission to come on board, captain?"

"Permission granted. Welcome!"

It was hard to explain how I felt, being back on board again after so many years. Weird in some way. I was extremely happy that the new owner had kept her as originally built. Her name, the peace-dove on her bow, the old-fashioned wooden dead-eyes, the baggywrinkles on her rigging and the unmistakable smell of sheep-fat on the gaff claw remained. The only change was a barrel- a crow's nest- on top of the mainmast.

There were many changes below- a new interior with several tiny cabins, electric lighting, and a brand-new powerful caterpillar 150 horsepower engine. I was daydreaming under the stars, lying in the net under the bowsprit. Memories came flowing back and I became very emotional when I overheard a phone conversation between a teenager and her mother.

"Mum, I'm not coming home tonight. I'm on board a beautiful sailing-ship and having a supercool time."

This brought back memories of my young crew who'd spent nine months having a fabulous time. There was a lot of reminiscence through the night and forgotten events appeared. I noticed a deep notch on the bulkhead. That was where the frying pan bounced when Mariann got angry and threw it at me. She said it wasn't meant to hit me, it just slipped out of her hand. One of the blocks for the mainsail boom, the one that was partly responsible for being shipwrecked, was engraved with the words "Love you." The block had been a birthday present Mariann bought for me in Colombia. The memory of her gift nicely contrasted with the frying pan episode. I could still see the imperfections in the hull from where we did the repairs after being holed, and there was still an everlasting smell of hemp rope and tar.

To make it all complete, there was also a short sailing trip on the Hardangerfjord without any storms, mishaps, or breakdowns. The young crew did well- I gave them a perfect score of ten out of ten.

Goodbye *Fredag*. See you hopefully next time in the Caribbean.

I had the sudden desire to stay for a while in Norway and do what I like best, mess around with old boats. I found an interesting job at a west coast nautical museum restoring an old Hardanger sloop.

The winter was cold and dark and the Israeli bananas from the supermarket tasted really awful. I had great difficulty breathing in the cold air and my feet were always ice cold, even in bed with a hot-water bottle. I started longing for the tropics, the natural place to be. In comparison with the freezing arctic and its somewhat outlandish and relaxed withdrawn inhabitants, I realized that my Shangri-La was down south, on Bequia with its laid-back and easy-going inhabitants. My island in the sun.

The new owner asked me if I would like to sail *Fredag* to the Caribbean again with a crew of teenagers. It was tempting, but I felt that chapter of my life was definitely over. So my journey continued south on three different airlines. When the heat and the reggae hit me at the airport on St. Vincent, I was convinced once more I had made the right choice.

My next quest in life was to find that elusive hidden treasure, and if that failed, to write about trying!

29. Thanks

My late big sister Giselle, who taught me to stand proudly on my own two feet, brimming with self-confidence to unleash my imagination and face up to challenges.

The American sailor and author Joshua Slocum, the main inspiration for me to cast off from the establishment to sail around the world. He taught me the trick of spreading thumb tacks on my deck at night to protect me from thieves and pirates.

The Danish sailor Troels Klövedal, who wrote an unusually inspiring and personal narrative about his voyage with the "North Cape," and who wrote about a plethora of topics other than sunsets and sail-changes.

My impatient neighbours in Oslo who survived the construction period and dropped all charges so they could get rid of me.

The German engineer Uwe Gertsmann on Union Island who was the genius behind the raising of *Fredag-* a wise man who taught me to give without expecting anything in return.

Swedish Gitta Legler on Carriacou island, who donated her portable Remington typewriter after my old one disappeared somewhere on the seabed after *Fredag* wrecked.

Dutchman Fritz van der Heteren, who due to illness couldn't join me, but still sponsored my expedition into the inhospitable Amazonas region to find a mysterious river.

Lovely Britt Hamre from Bergen who provided warmth and comfort so I could survive two arctic winters while restoring an old schooner outdoors and finish off my memoirs.

The renowned Norwegian author and my best friend Gert Nygårdshaug, who gave me a lot of good advice on how to put the correct word after the previous correct one in the Norwegian edition.

Bob Berlinghof, my editor, who hammered my Norwegian translated English into a readable document.

Dudley Campling for his hilarious drawings and cartoons.

The native population of Bequia who inspired me to be able to find my inner peace, and who accepted and respected a foreign "whitey" who had chosen to live among them.

And most of all to Mariann Palmborg from Sweden, who endured being cohabitant with an often complex and problematic guy for twenty years- a skipper who would often be compared to the despicable captain Bligh of the *Bounty*. She rebelled in her own way but was no mutineer. She believed in me and supported me as long as she lived. Without her there would most likely have been no chapters at all.

And to you, dear reader. So long, and- oh yeah- thanks for all the fish!

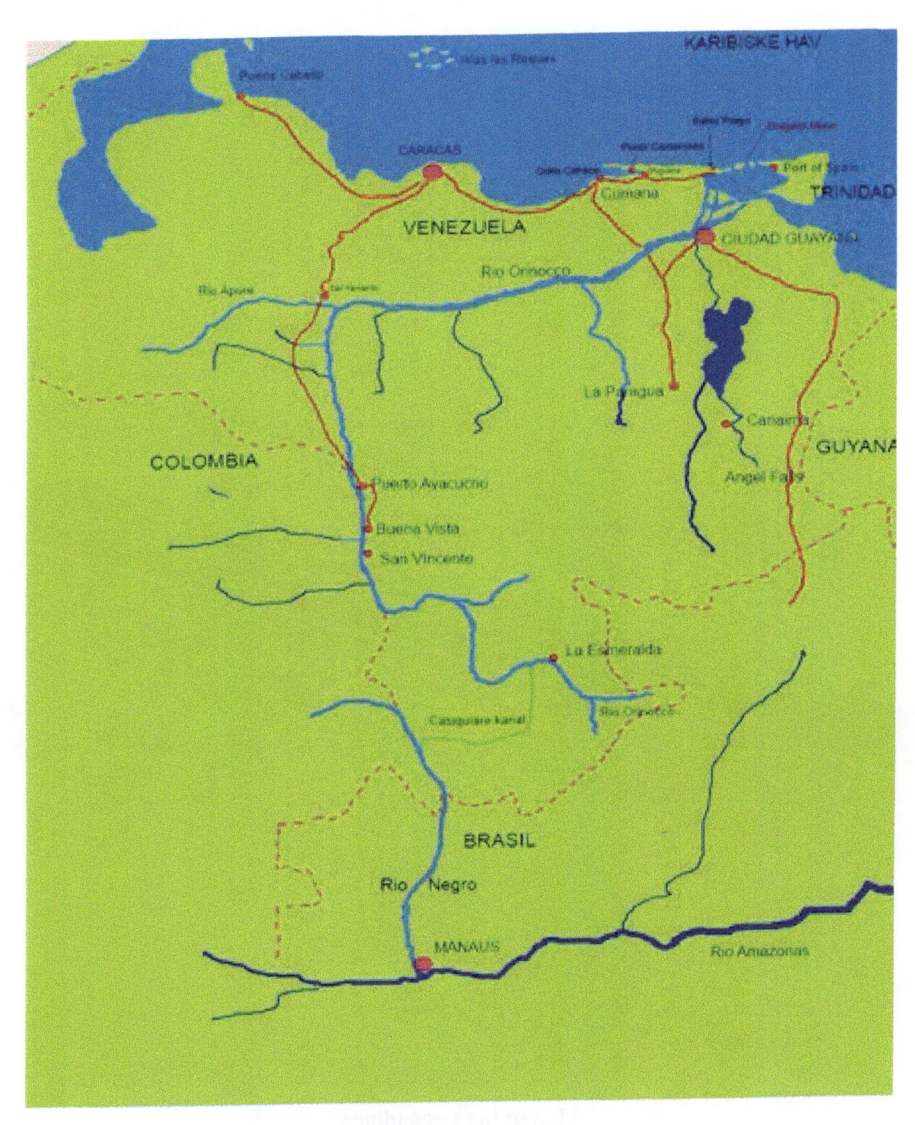

Map of Venezuela

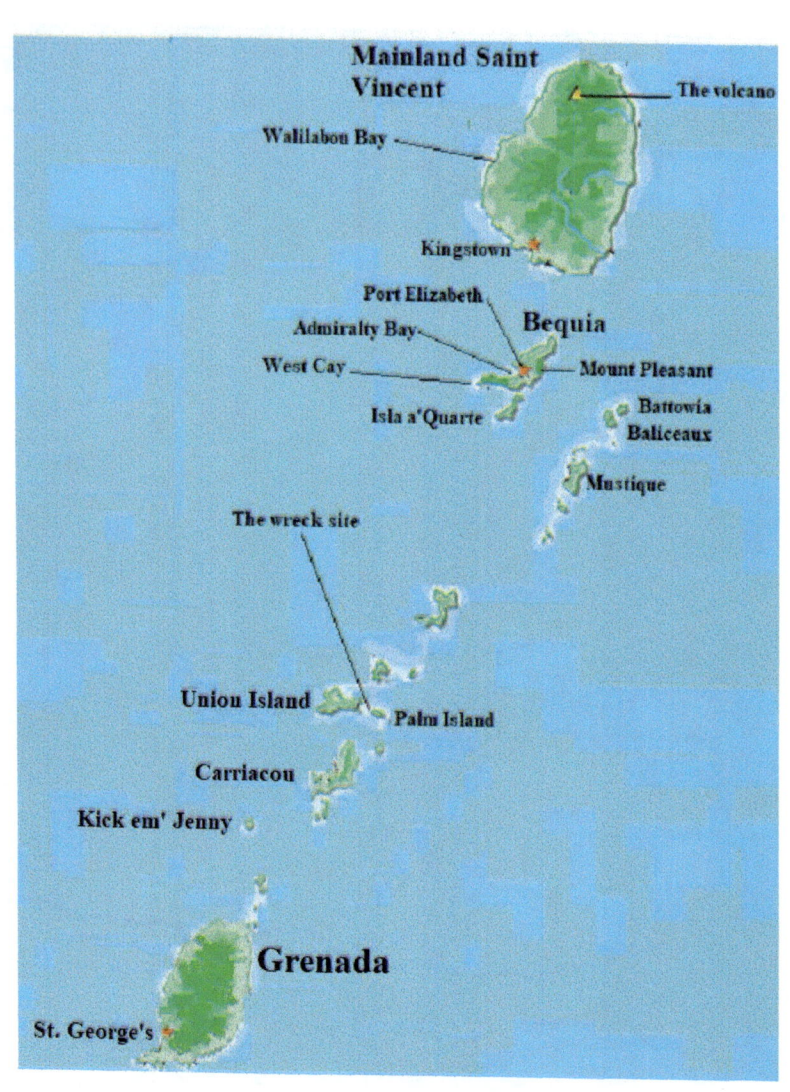

Map of the Grenadines